Miriam Coles Harris

Missy

A Novel

Miriam Coles Harris

Missy
A Novel

ISBN/EAN: 9783337000851

Printed in Europe, USA, Canada, Australia, Japan

Cover: Foto ©Andreas Hilbeck / pixelio.de

More available books at **www.hansebooks.com**

MISSY.

A Novel.

BY

THE AUTHOR OF "RUTLEDGE;"

"THE SUTHERLANDS ;" "LOUIE'S LAST TERM AT ST. MARY'S;"
"FRANK WARRINGTON ;" "RICHARD VANDERMARCK ;"
"ST. PHILIP'S ;" "A PERFECT ADONIS ;"
ETC., ETC., ETC.

NEW YORK:

G. W. Carleton & Co., Publishers.

LONDON: S. LOW, SON & CO.

MDCCCLXXX.

SAMUEL STODDER,
STEREOTYPER,
90 ANN STREET, N. Y.

TROW
PRINTING AND BOOK-BINDING CO.,
N. Y.

CONTENTS.

[vii]

CONTENTS.

MISSY.

CHAPTER I.

YELLOWCOATS.

 FELT sure the train would be late," said Missy, sitting down on the ottoman beside the fire. "It is so disagreeable to have to wait for what you dread."

"But I think you have begun to be impatient too soon," said her mother, glancing up. "That clock is several minutes fast, and Peters always drives slower after dusk. Besides, you know he has the heavy carriage. I think it would be foolish to begin to look for them for twenty minutes yet."

"I believe you are right," said the daughter, with a sigh. "I wish it were over."

"That is natural, but we can't hurry it. We shall have twenty minutes of quiet. Come and sit down, I have hardly seen you to-day."

For the truth was, Missy had been very busy all day, getting ready for a most unwelcome guest. The pale invalid mother, to whom the guest was as unwelcome, had been obliged to lie on her sofa, without the solace of occupation.

"I hope she will like it," said Missy, irrelevantly, getting up and pushing her ottoman over to her mother's sofa, then, before sitting down, going to the table and putting a leaf of geranium in a different attitude, then stepping back and looking at it. An India bowl was filled with scarlet geranium, and the light of a low lamp fell upon it and made a beautiful patch of color.

"I might as well light the candles," she said, "and then I will sit down quietly and wait." She took a lighter, and stooping to the fire, set it ablaze, and went to some candles on the low book shelves and lighted them. "I begrudge my pretty candles," she said, turning her head to look at the effect.

"Why do you light them then?" said her mother, with a faint sigh. "Come and sit down."

"In a moment," answered Missy. "I wonder if the hall is light enough." She had looked at the hall lamps half a dozen times, but in fact she was too restless to sit down. She pulled the bell impatiently, and a tidy maid in spotless cap and apron came. She had perceived an imperfection in the adjustment of a rug, and like a wise housekeeper, she did not readjust it herself. Then she scanned the maid's costume, all with the eyes of the unwelcome guest.

"I thought that you understood me that I did not want those aprons worn again. Put on one of the new set that I gave you."

Mrs. Varian sighed; she could never at any period of life have dared to do the like, but Missy was a little dragon, and kept the servants in good order, aprons and all. The servant retired to correct her costume, and Missy began to look about for something else to correct. But the room was all in perfect order, glowing with warmth and color, delicious with the scent of flowers, there was nothing for her to do. She walked up and down before the fire, with the air of a person who objects to sitting down and having a quiet talk, at least so her mother thought.

Missy was small; her figure was perfect in its proportions; her hands and feet quite worth noticing for their beauty. She was not plump, rather slight than plump, and yet well rounded. Her head was well set on her shoulders, and she moved it deliberately, not rapidly, and while all her movements showed energy, she was not bustling. She was so *petite* she was not severe : that was all that saved her. Her face was not pretty, her complexion was colorless, her eyes very light, her nose *retroussé*. Her hair was soft and fine and waving, and of a pretty color, though not light enough to be flaxen, and not bright enough to be golden. It had the fortunate attribute of looking picturesque and pleasant, whether arranged or disarranged. Missy had her own way of dressing herself, of course. Such an energetic young woman could not be indifferent to a subject of such moment. She dressed in the best and latest fashion, with her own modification as to color and style. Her dresses were almost always gray, or white, or black, and as little trimmed as possible, and she never wore ornaments. Whether this were matter of principle or taste, she had not yet announced. Certainly if the former, virtue was its own reward ; for no ornaments could have brought color to her face, or added any grace to its irregular outline, and her arms and hands would have been spoiled by rings and bracelets: every link would have hid a beauty. To-night she wore a soft gray silk, with crêpe lisse ruffles at the throat and elbows, and grey silk stockings and pretty low shoes with high heels. Putting one hand on the mantel above her, she stretched out her foot to the blaze, and resting her toe on the andiron, looked down at it attentively, though probably absently.

"I hope she will like it," she repeated.

"What, your gray stocking or your new shoe? They are both lovely," said Mrs. Varian, trying to be gay.

"No," said Missy, indignantly, withdrawing the pretty foot. "No—but it—all—the house—the place. Oh, mamma," and she went across to the sofa and threw herself in a low chair by it, "it *is* a trial, isn't it?"

"Yes, my child," said Mrs. Varian, with a gentle caress of the hand put out to her. "But if you do not want to alienate your brother, do not let him guess it." Missy gave an impatient movement.

"Must I try to enter into his fool's paradise? I can't be sympathetic, I'm afraid, even to retain my present modest place in his affections."

"But be reasonable, Missy. You knew he would sometime marry."

"Sometime, yes, mamma. But I cannot think of such a boy as going to be married. It really is not decorous."

"O my dear Missy. Think again. St. John is nearly twenty. It only seems absurd to us my dear, because—because—"

"Because we are so old, mamma. I know it.

Yes; don't mind speaking of it. I know it very well. I am—twenty-seven." And Missy looked into the fire with a sort of dreamy wonder; but her voice showed the fact had no sting for her. Her life had been such that she did not mind it that she was no longer young. She had never been like other girls, nor had their ambitions. She had known she was not pretty ; she had not expected to marry. Her life had been very full of occupation and of duty, and of things that gave her pleasure. She also had had an important position, owing to her mother's invalid condition. She was lady of the house, she was an important person; a good deal of money passed through her hands, a good many persons looked up to her. As for her heart, it was not hungry. She had a passionate love for her mother, who, since the death of her stepfather, had depended much upon her ; and towards her young stepbrother, now on this October night, bringing home an unwelcome fiancée. she had felt a sort of tigerish mother love. There were seven years between them. She had always felt she owned him—and though bitterly jealous of the fond and blind devotion of her mother to him (as she saw it), she felt as if her life were inseparable from his. How *could* he live and love and have an existence in what she had no part ? But it was even so. The boy had outgrown her, and had no longer any need of her. She had, indeed, need of all her strength and courage to-night, and the mother saw it, putting aside her own needs, which were not likely to be less. For this boy, St. John, and this daughter were all she had left her of a past not always very bright, even to remember. But with patient sweetness she sought to comfort Missy, smarting with the

first knowledge that she was not necessary to some one
whom she loved.

"You know we should have been prepared for it,"
she said. "It really is not strange—twenty is not
young."

"I suppose not. But that is the very least of it.
Mamma, you know this is throwing himself away.
You know this is a bitter disappointment to you. You
know she is the last person you would have chosen for
him. You know you feel as I do, now confess it."
Missy had a way of speaking vehemently, and her
words tripped over each other in this speech.

"Well," said Mrs. Varian, with calm motherly justice, upholding the cause of the absent offender, while
she soothed the wrath of the present offended, "I will
confess, I am sorry. I am even disappointed in St.
John—but that may be my fault, and not his failure.
Perhaps I was unreasonable to expect more of him
than of others."

"More of him? Why pray, do theological students,
as a rule, engage themselves to actresses before they
are half through their studies?"

"My dear Missy, I must beg of you—this is unwarrantable. You have no right to call her an actress.
Not the smallest right."

"Excuse me, mamma, I think I have a right. A
person who gives readings, a person whose one ambition is to be before the public, who is only detained
from the stage by want of ability to be successful
on it, who is an adventuress, neither more nor less, who
has neither social position nor private principle, who
has beauty and who means to use it—may be called an

actress, without any injustice to herself, but only to the class to which she does no credit."

The words tripped over each other vehemently now.

"You are very wrong, very unwise to speak and feel so, Missy. I must beg you to control yourself, even in speaking to me. It simply is not right."

"You do not like the truth, mamma, you do not like the English language. I have spoken the truth, I have used plain language. What have I said wrong? I cannot make things according to your wishes by being silent. I can only keep them out of your sight. Is it not true that she has given readings? Not in absolute public, but as near it as she could get. Do we not know that she has made more than one effort to get on the stage? Are not she and her mother poor, and living on their wits? Is she not beautiful, and is not that all we know to her advantage? I think I have spoken the truth after all, if you will please review it."

"Very bitter truth, and not much mixture of love in it. And I think, considering that we have not seen her yet, we might suspend judgment a little, and hope the best of her."

"Perhaps share in St. John's infatuation. Oh!" and Missy laughed scornfully, while her mother's face quivered with pain as she turned it away.

"I do not think there is much danger of your seeing her with St. John's eyes, but I do think there is danger of you driving him from you, and losing all influence over him."

"I do not want any influence over him," said Missy hotly. "I never will stand between him and her. I have given him up to her; he has made his choice.

Mamma, mamma, why did we get talking this way? And they may be here any minute. I made up my mind not to speak another word to you about it, and here I have got myself worked up, and my cheeks burn so."

She pressed the back of her hand against her cheek, and getting up walked two or three times across the room.

"You will be worn out before they come," she said with late compunction, noticing the tremor of her mother's hand, "and all the excitement after, and what a dreadful night you'll have. I suppose you will not sleep at all. Dear, dear, I am so sorry. And here comes Aunt Harriet. I had forgotten she asked me to call her when you were ready to come down. I suppose she will scold, and make everything wretched," and Missy moved across to open the parlor door, as if she thought life a very trying complication of worries and worse. To her relief, however, Miss Varian's rather shrill voice had more question than reproach in it as she entered the room, led by a servant.

"Do tell me if it is not time for the train?" she said. "I have been listening for the whistle for the last ten minutes. Goneril has let my clock run down, and as it is the only one in the house that can be depended on, we are in a bad way."

"That is a favorite fiction of yours, I know," said Missy, arranging a seat for her, into which Goneril backed her. "But as my watch has only varied two minutes since last July, I feel you may be reassured about the time. I can't pretend to hear a whistle four miles off, but I do think I can be trusted to tell what o'clock it is—within two minutes."

"My footstool, Goneril," said Miss Varian sharply, "and you've dropped my handkerchief."

Goneril, a good-looking woman of about forty, a superior American servant who resented her position always, and went as far as she dared to go in endangering it, stooped and picked up the handkerchief and shook it out with suppressed vehemence, and thrust it into her mistress' hand. "Is that all?" she asked, with a sort of sniff, going towards the door.

"Yes, *all*," said Miss Varian, in a tone that spoke volumes. Goneril indulged in another sniff, and went.

"That insufferable woman," muttered her employer, below her breath.

Missy smiled calmly, but said nothing. It always calmed her to see her step-aunt in a temper with Goneril : it gave her a feeling of superiority. She never would have endured the woman for a day, but she was quite willing her elder should, if she chose. The poor lady's blindness would have given every one a feeling of tenderness, if she had not been too sharp and petulant to permit any one to feel tender long. The position of her attendant was not one to be envied. Goneril was an American farmer's daughter, who had made a bad marriage (and the man who married her had not made altogether a good one). She had had high ambitions, as became an American farmer's daughter, and she had come down to living out at service, and what more cruel statement could be made? No worse fate could have overtaken her she was sure, and she made no secret of her estimate of domestic service for American farmer's daughters. She quarrelled incessantly with the servants of humbler nationality in the house, who did not mind it

much, and who laughed a little at her proud parentage.
They did not see the difference themselves. She was
industrious, and capable, and vigorous, and was indis-
pensable to Miss Varian, out of whom she wrung ever-
increasing wages. Her father, the American farmer,
had done handsomely by her in the matter of a name ;
he had called her Regan Goneril. She had grown up
in the sanctity of home as Regan, but now that she
was cast out into the battle of life, she preferred to be
called Goneril. She also hoped to be shielded by this
thin disguise from the pursuit of the discarded husband. The belief in the Varian kitchen was, that
there was no danger of any such pursuit : in fact, that
the husband would go very fast in the opposite
direction. But she liked to talk about it, and about
her goodness in putting up with Miss Varian's temper ;
she placed her service rather in the light of missionary
work. If she did not feel it to be her duty to stay
with the poor blind woman, she said, no money would
induce her to remain. (It took more and more money
every year, however, to stiffen and hold up her sense
of duty.)

Missy took the brawls between Miss Varian and
her maid, very calmly. " It gives an interest to her
life," she said from a height. On this evening, occupied as she was by her own matters, she heard the
story of her aunt's wrongs more indifferently than
ever. And even Miss Varian soon forgot that there
was anything more absorbing than the waited-for
arrival.

" It may be nine o'clock before they get here," she
said ; "that shows the impropriety of letting a girl go
off on journeys with a lover. Such things weren't

done in my time. I shouldn't have thought of doing such a thing."

"You don't know; you might have thought of it, if you had ever been engaged," said Missy, with malice.

"Well, my dear, we have neither of us been tempted," retorted her aunt, urbanely. "Let us be charitable. I have no doubt we should, both of us, have been able to take care of ourselves; but it may be different with your sister elect. These very handsome women, you know, are not always wise."

"That is true," said Missy, tapping her foot impatiently as she stood before the fire. "Mamma, you don't think you'd like a cup of tea? You may have to wait a good while."

"No, thank you," said Mrs. Varian meekly.

She always wore a pained expression when her sister-in-law was present; but as the sister-in-law could not see it, it did no harm. She always dreaded the next word. They had always been uncongenial; but it is one thing to have an uncongenial sister-in-law that you can get away from, or go to see only when you are braced up to the business, and another to have her under your own roof, a prisoner, by reason of her misfortune and your sense of duty—able to prey upon you whether you are well or ill; as familiar and every-day as your dressing-gown and slippers; having no respect for your engagements or your indigestions. When this blindness threw Harriet Varian upon her hands, she felt as if her home were invaded, desecrated, spoiled, but she had not a moment's hesitation as to her duty. A frivolous youth and a worldly, pleasure-seeking maturity, had ill pre-

pared the poor woman for her dreary doom. She
had fitted herself to it with a bitter philosophy ;
for do we not all fit ourselves to our lot, in one way or
another. "*L'homme est en délire s'il ose murmurer,*"
but it is to be hoped Heaven is not always critical in
the matter of resignation. Harriet Varian had submitted, but she was in the primer of Christian principle, as it were ; attaining with difficulty in middle age
the lesson that would have been easy to her, if she
had begun in childhood. When you have spent thirty-
four years in having your own way, and consulting
your own pleasure quite exclusively, it comes a trifle
hard to do exactly as you do not wish to do, and to
find that pleasure is a term unknown in your vocabu-
lary : when you are old that another should gird you
and lead you whither you would not.

But the healthy and Christian surroundings of the
home to which she came were not without their influence. Mrs. Varian's sweet endurance of her life-long
suffering, St. John's healthy goodness, and Missy's
vigorous duty-doing, helped her, against her will. St.
John was her great object of interest in life. All her
money was to go to him, and she actually felt com-
pensated for her dull and restricted existence, sometimes, when she reflected that it swelled, by so many
thousand a year, the fortune that would be his. She
had not lost her interest in the world, since she had
him to connect her with it, and to give her an excuse
for the indulgence of ambition. Of course she had
been bitterly set against all the system upon which
he had been educated, and would have thwarted it if
she had had the power. His entering the church had
been a great trial to her, but she openly said it was

his mother's plan, and no wish of his, and before he was ordained he would be old enough to see the folly of it, and to get clear of it. Then came his engagement, and at this she was wroth indeed, but as it furnished her with liberal weapons against his disappointed mother, she found her own comfort in it. Now she hoped Dorla would see the folly of her course ; now she could understand what other people had known all along : simply that she was keeping him in a false and unhealthy state of religious feeling, that she had forced upon him duties and aspirations all her own and none of his ; that there had come a reaction, that there was a flat failure when he came to see even a corner of the world from which she had debarred him. Here he was, carried away by his infatuation for a woman whom he would have been too wise to choose if his mother had not tried to make a monk of him, and to keep him as guileless and ignorant as a girl. Here he was bound to a woman who would ruin his career, spoil his life for him, spend his money, disgrace his name ; and it was " all the work of his mother." These were some of the amenities of the family life at Yellowcoats. These were the certain truths that were spoken of and to Mrs. Varian by her candid and unprejudiced sister-in-law.

And there was too much fact in them to be borne as Harriet's criticisms were generally borne by Mrs. Varian. Perhaps it was all true, she said to herself in the morning watches, as the stars grew pale ; but of all the failures of her life this was the bitterest. How many hopes, and how high, were centered in her boy ! She had dreamed for him, she had schemed for him, she had seen her life retrieved in him. A career, in which earthly ambition had no part, she had planned for him, and into its beginning she had led him. He had been so easily guided, he was so good, he loved her so ; had it all been a mistake ? could it be all delusion ? If he had been headstrong, a willful, rebellious boy, it never could have been. But to have bound him with his own lovingness, to have slain him with his own sweetness, this was a cruel thought. Why had no voice called to her from heaven to warn her of it ; why was she left to think she was doing the very best for him, when she was truly acting as the enemy who sought his life ? She had led him up such a steep and giddy path, that the first glance downward of his young, untutored eyes, sent him reeling to the bottom. Why had God suffered this ? God, who loved him and her. She had thought that she had, long ago, accepted God's will in all and for all, and owned it sweetest and best. But this opened her eyes sadly to her self-deception. She could not abandon herself to a will that seemed to have put a sword into her hand, by which she had wounded her child unwittingly, thinking that she did God service. She could have borne mistake and misconception for herself, but that her boy should bear the penalty seemed, even to her humbled will, a bitter punishment. The future was all too plain, even without her sister-in-law's interpretation. Yes, St. John's career was spoiled. If he entered the church at all, having made such a connection, it would be but to lead a half-way, feeble life, and to bring discredit on his faith. If he gave it up, there was nothing before him but a life of ease with a large fortune and a natural tendency to indolence. It was not in him to think of another profession and to make

an interest and an aim to himself other than the one
that he had had from childhood : his mother knew him
too well to believe that possible. Humanly speaking,
St. John Varian had lost his best chance of distinction
when he gave his fate into the keeping of this beautiful adventuress. He might have been what he was
brought up to be ; he would never be anything else.

"Think of it," said Miss Varian, tapping her fan
sharply on the arm of her chair, as she talked, "think
of it. I suppose that woman isn't coming with her
daughter, because she hasn't clothes to come in. I suppose every cent has been expended on the girl, and
the summer's campaign has run them deep in debt.
No doubt that poor boy will have to pay for the pow-
der and balls that shot him, by and bye. Not post-
obit, but post-matrimonium. Ha, ha! I don't know
which is worse. To think of his being such a fool.
Why, at his age his father was a man of the world.
He could have been trusted not to be caught by the
first woman that angled for him. But then, mamma
was always resolute with him and made him understand
something of life, and rely upon himself. He was
never coddled. I don't think I ever remember Felix
when he couldn't take care of himself."

Missy had not loved her stepfather, and this comparison enraged her (though not by its novelty).
Naturally, she could not look for sympathy to her
mother, who had been devoted to her husband. So
she had to bite her lips and keep time with her foot
upon the tiles, to Mrs. Varian's fan upon the arm chair.

"There ! " exclaimed the latter at this exasperating
juncture. "There, I hear the whistle." No one else
heard it of course, but no one ventured to dispute

the correctness of the blind woman's wonderful hearing.

"Half an hour at least to wait," exclaimed Missy, almost crying as she flung herself into a chair. "And Peters will drive his slowest, and the tea will all be ruined. What can have kept the train so late." Mrs. Varian pressed her hand before her eyes. It seemed to her that another half hour of this fret and suspense would be worse than a calamity. But she had gone further in her matter than the vehement souls who bemoaned themselves beside her—she could be silent.

"I shall go and walk up and down on the piazza," said Missy, starting up, "I long for the fresh air."

Mrs. Varian looked appealing towards her, but she did not see it; and throwing a cloak over her shoulders, she went out on the piazza. It was a cool, clear October night; there was no moon, but there were hosts of stars, which she could dimly see through the great trees not yet bare of foliage, though the lawn was strewn with leaves. The air cooled and rested her; but her thoughts were still a trifle bloodthirsty.

"Poor mamma," she said to herself, glancing through the window, as she walked quickly to and fro, "poor mamma. If she could only come out and walk, and feel the fresh air on her face, and get away from Aunt Harriet. I believe I was contemptible to come away and leave her. I can see Aunt Harriet is saying something dreadful, from mamma's expression. I wish I could kill her." Missy allowed herself to think in highly colored language. She had so often said to herself that she would like to strangle Aunt Harriet, to drown her with her own hands, to hang her, that she

had omitted to perceive that it wasn't altogether right.
She stood at the window looking in, holding her cloak
together with one hand, and with the other holding up
her dress from the floor of the piazza, which was wet
with dew. So she had no hand left to clench as she
looked at her; but she set her teeth together vindic-
tively and knit her brow.

"If ever there was a wicked woman!" she exclaimed
below her breath. She certainly wasn't a handsome
woman, as Missy looked at her, sitting in rather a stiff
chair by the fire-place, with her feet on a stool. She
was heavily built, and her clothes were put on awkwardly, as if they did not belong to her, or had not
been put on by her. She was nodding her head in a
peremptory way as she said the thing that Missy was
sure was distressing her mother. Then Missy watched
while her mother, with a look of more open suffering
than was usual with her, leaned her head back upon
the pillows, and pressed her hands silently together.
"How pretty she is, poor mamma," she thought.
"Every one admires her, though she is so faded and
suffering. Beauty is a great gift," and then she began
slowly to walk up and down, gazing in at the windows
as she passed them, and looking at the picture framed
by the hangings within. The light of the fire and the
light of the lamp both fell on the reclining figure of
her mother. Her face had resumed its ordinary quiet,
and her graceful white hands were lying unclasped on
the rich shawl spread over her. Her face was still
beautiful in outline; her hair was brown and soft;
there was something pathetic in her eyes. She was
graceful, refined and elegant, the sort of woman that men
always serve with alacrity and a shade of chivalry, even

2

when she is faded and no longer young. She was dependent and not particularly practical ; but there were always plenty to take care of her, and to do the part of life for which she was unfitted. If a woman can't take care of herself, there are general'; enough ready to do it for her.

———◆◆———

CHAPTER II.

ST. JOHN.

 "HERE is the carriage ! " exclaimed Missy, as she caught the sound of wheels in the distance. She darted into the house, her heart beating with violence. "Mamma, I believe they are coming," she said with forced calmness, as she went into the parlor, shaking out the fringe of the shawl across her mother's lap, and straightening the foot-stool. "Aunt Harriet, do let me move your chair a little back. Goneril's one idea seems to be to put it always as much in the way as possible."

"Don't scold," said Miss Varian, tartly. " Your new sister may take a prejudice against you."

Missy disdained to answer, but occupied herself with putting on the fire some choice pine knots which she had been reserving for this moment. They blazed up with effusion ; the room was beautiful. The carriage wheels drew nearer ; they were before the house. Missy threw open the parlor door and advanced into the hall, with a very firm step, but with a very weak heart. She knew her hands were cold and that they trembled. How could she keep this from the knowledge of her guest; it was all very well to walk forward under the crystal lamps, as if she were a queen. But queens arrange to keep their hands from shaking, and to command their voices.

The maid had already gone out to the steps to bring in the shawls and bags. Everything seemed to swim before Missy as she stood in the hall door. The light went out in a flood across the piazza, but there seemed to be darkness beyond, about the carriage. There was no murmur of voices. Missy in bewilderment saw her brother, and then the maid coming up the steps after him and carrying nothing. In her agitation she hardly looked at him, as, at the door, he stooped down and kissed her, passing on. But the touch of his hand was light and cold.

"You have no wraps, or bags, or anything," she said confusedly, following him.

"No," he said, in a forced voice, throwing his hat on a table as he passed it, and going towards the stairs. " Is mamma in her room ?"

"No, in the parlor waiting for you."

A contraction passed across his face as he turned toward the open parlor door, from which such a light came. He went in, however, quickly, and hurried to his mother's sofa. She had half raised herself from it, and with an agitated face looked up at him.

"You are—alone—St. John ?"

"I am alone, mamma," he said in a strained, unnatural voice, stooping to embrace her.

Miss Varian had caught the scent of trouble and was standing up beside her chair.

"Aunt Harriet," he said, as if he had forgotten her,
going over to her and kissing her.

"You are late," she said, as he turned away.

"Am I ?" he said, looking at his watch, but very
much as if he did not see it. "Yes, I suppose so.
There was an accident or something on the road. The
days are growing short. I am afraid I have kept you
waiting."

Then he walked restlessly up and down the room,
and took up and laid down a book upon the table, and
spoke to a dog that came whisking about his feet, but
in a way that showed that the book and the dog had
not either entered into his mind.

"I will go and see about tea," said Missy, faintly,
glad to get away. St. John's face frightened her. He
looked ten years older. He was pallid. There was a
most affecting look of suffering about his mouth. His
eyes were strange to her ; they were absolutely unlike
her brother's eyes. What could it all mean ? What
had befallen him ? She felt as if they were all in a
dream. She hurried into the dining-room, where the
waitress was whispering with gesticulation to the cook
and laundress, whose faces appeared in the further
door full of curiosity. Her presence put them to
flight ; the waitress, much humbled, bestirred herself
to obey Missy's orders and remove the unneeded plate
and chair, and to make the table look as if it were not
intended for more than would sit down to it. How
large it looked ; Missy was so sorry that extra leaf had
been put in. And all the best china, and the silver
that was not used every day. What a glare and glit-
ter they made ; she hated the sight of them ; she knew
they would give St. John a stab. She would have

taken some off the table, but that she felt the demure waitress would make a note of it. She had patiently to see her lighting the candles in the sconces. Poor St. John's eyes would ache at so much light. But there was no help for it now.

"Put tea upon the table at once," said Missy, sharply. There was no relief for her but scolding the innocent maid, and no one could have the heart to deny her that, if it would do her any good.

In a few moments the tea was served, and Missy went to announce it herself. Things were not altered in the parlor. St. John and his aunt were trying to talk in a way that would not convict the one of a broken heart, and the other of a consuming curiosity. Mrs. Varian, very pale, was leaning her head back on the pillows, and not speaking or looking at them.

"Mamma, tea is ready," said Missy, coming in. "St. John, take Aunt Harriet. Mamma will come with me."

"I think you may send me in a cup of tea," said Mrs. Varian. "I am almost too tired to go into the dining-room."

"Very well ; that will be best. I will send Anne to wait upon you."

So the party of three went into the brilliantly-lighted dining-room, and sat down at the table that had been laid for five. Perhaps St. John didn't see anything but the light ; that hurt his eyes, for he put his hand up once or twice to shield them. It was a ghastly feast. Aunt Harriet talked fast and much. St. John could not follow her enough to answer her with any show of sense. Missy blundered about the sugar in the two cups of tea she made, and tried to speak in her ordinary tone, but in vain. St. John sent oysters twice to his aunt, and not at all to Missy, and when the servant brought him her plate he said, what? and put it down before himself, and went on pouring cream into his tea, though he had done it twice before.

"No matter," said Missy sharply, to the girl, who could not make him understand, and who looked inclined to titter. She did not want the oysters, but she longed to see the poor fellow eat something himself, and she watched him furtively from behind the urn. He took everything upon his plate that was brought to him, but the physical effort of eating seemed impossible to him. He could not even drink the tea, which Missy had quietly renewed since the deluge of cream.

The excitement had even affected Miss Varian's appetite ; she found fault with the rolls. This was a comfort to Missy, and restored to her the feeling that the world was on its time-honored route, notwithstanding her brother's troubles. At last it was impossible to watch it any longer. He was sitting unevenly at the head of the table, with his profile almost turned to her—as if he were ready to go away, ah, too ready !— if he could get away. His untouched plate was pushed back.

"St. John," said Missy, "do you want to take this cup of tea in to mamma, or shall Rosa go with it ?"

"I will take it," he said, with an eager movement, getting up. The tears rushed into Missy's eyes as she watched him going out of the door with the cup of tea in his unsteady hand. Then she heard the parlor

door shut, as Anne came out and left the mother and
son together. Missy could fancy the eager, tender
words, the outburst of wretchedness. Her own heart
ached unutterably. "As one whom his mother com-
forteth." Oh, that he might be comforted, even though
she was shut out, and could not help him, and her help
was not thought of. It was her first approach to great
trouble since she had been old enough to feel it intel-
ligibly. How happy we have been, she thought, as
people always think ; how smooth and sweet our life
has flowed ; and now it is turned all out of its course,
and will never be the same again. It was a life-and-
death matter, even though no one wore a shroud, and
no sod was broken ; the smooth, happy boy's face was
gone. She would never look on it again, and she
had loved it so. She thought of him as he had been,
only two months ago, when he went away, easy, frank,
happy, good. Everybody loved him. It was the
fashion to be fond of him, and it did not seem to hurt
him. Missy thought of his beauty, his fine proportions,
his look of perfect health. " Like as a moth fretting
a garment," this trouble had already begun. His
harassed features, his sallow tint—why, it was like a
dream. Poor St. John ! the only thing his sister had
had to reproach him with had been his boyishness, and
that was over and done. He had not the regularity
of feature that had made his father remarkable for
beauty, but he had the same warm coloring, the deep
blue eye, the fair yellow hair. He was larger, too,
than his father—a broad-shouldered, six-foot fellow,
who had been grown on the sunny side of the wall.
About his brain power there was a difference of

opinion, as there will be about undeveloped resources. His mother's judgment did not count; his aunt thought him unusually clever for his age. Missy looked upon him as doubtfully average. His masters loved him, and thought there might be a good deal in him, if it could be waked up (but it hadn't been); his comrades thought him a good fellow, but were sure he wouldn't set the sea on fire. The men about the village, oyster men and stable boys, sailors of sloops and tillers of soil, were all ready, to a man, to bet upon him, whatever he might undertake. And here he was, not twenty yet, a boy whom fortune had seemed to agree should be left to ripen to utmost slow perfection, suddenly shaken with a blast of ice and fire, and called upon to show cause why more time should be given him to develop the powers within him, and to meet the inherent cruelty of life. It was precipitate and cruel; and the sister's heart cried out against it.

What was the mother's heart crying out? Missy yearned to know. But here was, no one knew how much time to pass before she could see her mother. Her duty now was to keep Aunt Harriet away from them, and to hold her in check. And this was not easy. Freed from the restraint of St. John's presence, Miss Varian's anxiety showed itself in irritability. She found fault with everything, and soon brought her tea to an end. Then she called for Goneril to take her to the parlor. While Rosa went for Goneril, Missy said, firmly:

"Wait a few minutes, Aunt Harriet. I am sure St. John wants to see mamma alone a little while."

Then Miss Varian gave way to a very bad fit of temper, only stopped by the re-entrance of the servant. It was gall to her to think that his mother could only comfort him, and that she had no place. But she respected the decencies of life enough not to betray herself before the servants. So while Missy busied herself in putting away the cake, and locking up the tea caddy, she sat silent, listening eagerly for any sound or movement in the parlor.

"If I had the evening paper, I would read it to you," said Missy, having come to the end of her invented business. "Rosa, go and look in the hall for it."

"It is on the parlor table, miss."

"Well, no matter then ; tell the cook to come here. I want to read her a receipt for soup to-morrow."

The receipt book was the only bit of literature in the dining-room, so the cook came, and Missy read her the receipt for the new soup, and then another receipt that had fallen into desuetude, and might be revived with benefit to the ménage. And then she gave her orders for breakfast, and charged the cook with a message for the clam man and the scallop man, and the man who brought fish. For at Yellowcoats every man brings the captive of his own bow and spear (or drag and net), and the man who wooes oysters never vends fish ; and the man who digs clams, digs clams and never potatoes ; and scallops are a distinct calling.

All this time Missy was listening, with intent ear, for some movement in the parlor, Miss Varian listening no less intently. The tea-table was cleared—the

2*

cook could be detained no longer with any show of
reason ; the waitress waited to know if there was anything she could bring Miss Rothermel. It was so
very unusual for any one to sit in the dining-room
after tea ; there were no books in it, nor any easy
chairs, nor anything to do. The waitress, being a
creature of habit, was quite disturbed to see them
stay, but she knew very well what it meant.

At last ! There was a movement across the hall—
the parlor door opened, and they heard St. John and
his mother come out and go slowly up the stairs.
When they were on the first landing, Miss Varian
said, sharply,

"Well, I suppose we can be released now."

"Yes, I think it will be as pleasant in the parlor,"
said Missy, giving her arm to Miss Varian, and going
forward with a firm step. She installed her companion
in an easy chair, seated herself, and read aloud the
evening paper. Politics, fashions, marriages, and
deaths, what a senseless jumble they made in her mind.
She was often called sharply to account for betraying
the jumble in her tone, for Miss Varian had recovered
herself enough to feel an interest in the paper, while
she felt sure she should have no tidings of St. John's
trouble that night. It was easy to see nothing would
be told her till it was officially discussed, with Missy
in council, and till it was decided how much and what
she was to hear. So she resolved to revenge herself
by keeping Missy out of it as long as she could. The
paper, to the last personal, had to be read. And then
she found it necessary to have two or three notes
written. Goneril was no scribe, so Missy was always

expected to write her notes for her, which she always did, filled with a proud consciousness of being pretty good to do it, for somebody who wasn't her aunt, and who was her enemy. Aunt Harriet had always a good many notes to write; she never could get over the habit of wanting things her own way, and to have your own way, even about the covering of a footstool, requires sometimes the writing of a good many little notes; the looking up of a good many addresses, the putting on of a good many stamps, the sending a good many times to the post-office. All these things Missy generally did with outward precision and perfection. But to-night her hand shook, her mind wandered, she made mighty errors, and blotted and crossed out and misdirected like an ordinary mortal in a state of agitation. It was not lost upon Miss Varian, who heard the pen scratching through a dozen words at a time.

"Anything but an erasure in writing to such a person as Mrs. Olor, and particularly about a matter such as this If you can't put your mind on it to-night, I'd rather you'd leave it till to-morrow."

"I haven't found any difficulty in putting my mind on it," said Missy. "If you could give me a lucid sentence, I think I could write it out. I believe I have done it before." So she tore up the letter, her cheeks burning, and began a fresh one.

All this time she listened for the sounds overhead. Sometimes it would be silent, of course they could not hear the sound of voices—sometimes for five minutes together there would be the sound of St. John's tread as he walked backward and forward the length of the room. Eleven o'clock came.

"I am going to bed," said Missy, pushing away the writing things. "I will finish your business in the morning. Shall I ring for Goneril?"

While Goneril was coming, Missy put out the lamp, and gathered up her books. When she had gone up and shut herself into her room, she began to cry. The two hours' strain upon her nerves, in keeping up before Miss Varian, had been great; then the suspense and pity for St. John; and not least, the feeling that she was forgotten and outside of all he suffered, and her mother knew. Mamma could have called me, even if St. John had not remembered, she thought bitterly. By and bye she heard her mother's door open and her brother's step cross the hall, and stealing out she looked after him down the stairs. He walked once or twice up and down the lower hall, then taking up his hat, went out, and she heard his step on the gravel walk that led down to the beach gate. Then she felt a great longing to go into her mother's room, and hear all. But an obstinate jealous pride kept her back. She lingered near the open door of her room till Anne the maid went into her mother's room, and after a few moments came out.

"Did mamma ask for me?" she said, as the woman passed her door.

"No, miss. She told me she did not want anything, that I was to leave the light, and that all were to go to bed."

Then Missy shut her door, and dried her tears, or rather they dried away before the hot fire of her hurt feelings. St. John's trouble, whatever it was, began to grow less to her. At least he had his mother, if he had lost his love ; and mother to her had always been more than any love. And then, he had had the fulness of life, he had had an experience ; he had lived more than she had, though he was but twenty, and she was twenty-seven. She was angry, humbled, wounded. Poor Missy ; and then she hated herself for it, and knew that she ought to be crying for St. John, instead of envying him his mother's heart. It is detestable to find yourself falling below the occasion, and Missy knew that was just what she was doing. She was thinking about herself and her own wounds and wants, and she should have been filled with the sorrow of her brother. Well, so she would have been if he had asked her. She was sure she would have given him her whole heart, if he had wanted it. This was destined to be a night of suspenses. Missy undressed herself, and put on a wrapper, and said her very tumultuous and fragmentary evening prayers, and read a chapter in one or two good books, without the least understanding, and then put her light behind a screen in the corner, and went to the window, and began to wonder why St. John did not come back. The night was clear and starlight, but there was no moon, and it looked dark as she gazed out. She could see a light or two twinkling out on the bay, at the mast of some sloop or yacht. An hour passed. She walked about her room, in growing uneasiness, and opened her door softly, wondering if her mother shared her watch, and with what feelings. Another half hour, and it truly seemed to her, unused to such excitements, that she could bear it no longer. Where could he be, what could it mean ? All the jealousy was over before this time, and she would have gone quickly enough to her mother, but that the silence in her room, made her fear to disturb her, and to give her a sleepless night. At last, just as the hands of her little watch reached two, she heard a movement of the latch of the beach gate, and her brother's step coming up the path. She flew down to the door of the summer parlor and opened it for him. There was only a faint light coming from the hall. He did not speak, and she followed him across the parlor, into the hall. "Where have you been?" she said humbly, "I have been so worried."

But when she got into the hall under the light, she uttered a little scream, "St. John! You are all wet, look at your feet."

The polished floor was marked with every step.

"It is nothing," he said hoarsely, going towards the stairs.

"Is mamma's light burning?"

"You are not going to mamma's room," said Missy, earnestly, "at this hour of the night? You might make her very ill. I think you are very inconsiderate."

There came into his eyes for a moment a hungry, evil look. He looked at Missy as if he could have killed her.

"Then tell her why I didn't come," he said in an unnatural voice, taking a candle from her hand, and going up the stairs, shut himself into his own room.

Poor Missy was frightened. She wished she had let him go to his mother; as the light of the lamp fell on his face, it was dreadful. His clear blue eyes,

with their dark lashes, had always looked at her with
feelings that she could interpret. She had seen him
angry—a short-lived, sudden anger, that had melted
while you looked, but never malicious ; but this was
malice, despair. The habitual expression of his eye
was soft, happy, bright ; a good nature looking out.
She did not think he had lost his mind; she only
thought he might be losing his soul. His eyes were
bloodshot, his face of such a dreadful color.

"This is trouble," she said to herself, as with
trembling hands she put out the light, and went up
the dark staircase. At her mother's door she paused
and listened, and a voice within called her. How
gladly she heard it ! She went in, longing to throw
herself into her mother's arms and cry what is it?
But she controlled herself, and went softly to the
sofa where her mother lay, still undressed, the lamp
burning on the table beside her, her eyes shining with
an unusual lustre.

"I didn't know you were awake," said Missy, sitting down on an ottoman by the fire. "Your room
is cold," and she pulled together the embers, and put
on a stick or two of wood, her teeth chattering.
She knew quite well it was wasn't the cold that
made them chatter.

"Where is St. John ? " said her mother.

"He has just come in," returned Missy, looking
furtively at her—" and has gone to bed."

"Why didn't he come in to me?" asked Mrs. Varian,
anxiously.

"Because I thought that it—it was so late—you
ought not to be kept awake so long."

"Did you tell him not to come?"

"Well, yes."

Mrs. Varian sighed. "It would have been better not," she said.

Missy turned her face to the fire, which was beginning to blaze, and stretched out her hands to it. "Well, mamma," she said a little querulously, after several moments of silence, "I suppose you don't think that I care anything about St. John's trouble. I should think you might tell me without being asked to."

"O my child!" exclaimed her mother. "Forgive me. I have been so absorbed in him."

"O, I know that," retorted Missy, crying a little. "That isn't what I want to know."

"It won't take long to tell you. The girl to whom he was engaged, has fled from him and from her mother, and last night was married privately to a man for whom, it seems, she has long had a passion."

"Then why did she ever engage herself to St. John?" cried Missy, turning her pale and excited face towards her mother.

"I suppose it was the mother's work. The mother must be unscrupulous and daring. No doubt she worked hard for such a prize as St. John, and she found him easy prey, poor boy. Easier to manage than her daughter, whose passions are strong, and whose will is undisciplined. The girl could not conquer the thought of the old lover, though she had dissembled cruelly. I think she is but little to be preferred to her mother, inasmuch as her intention was the same; she meant to sacrifice St. John, and to satisfy her ambition. Only at the last moment, her passion conquered, and she broke faith both with her mother and him. O Missy, what wicked, wicked lives! Does it seem possible that there can be such women living?"

"I thank them from the bottom of my heart," said Missy, from between her set teeth.

"Yes," said her mother with a sigh. "It is right to feel that, I know. But oh, my boy; it is so hard to see him suffer. To have loved so, and been so duped. And he cannot, in his disgust and revulsion, conquer his great love for her. He is writhing in such pangs of jealousy. Think, last night this time he was dreaming happy dreams about her, as foolish and as fond as boy could be. To-night, she is in the arms of another—separated from him forever—leaving him with mockery and coldness, without a word of penitence or supplication. She flung him off as if she had disdained and loathed him."

"How did it come out—how did he hear it first?"

"This morning, he went for her to drive. They were to have had a very happy day. St. John, you know, is so nice and thoughtful about planning pleasures and expeditions. I think he must have had an insight into their characters, though he was so blinded. First, they were to go to see some pictures, then to the Park for an hour or two, then to Delmonico's for an early dinner; then to do some shopping before coming to the cars. The shopping meant letting her choose all sorts of expensive things to wear, to which she was unaccustomed, while he paid the bills. Poor boy, think of that not opening his

eyes. I asked if she never remonstrated, 'Yes, a little
perhaps, at first.' Well, they were to have had this
perfect day ; and St. John mounted the stairs to their
apartment without a misgiving.

"The moment the door was opened he felt what
was coming. The room was in confusion ; the mother,
wild and dishevelled, turned from him with a shriek.
It took but a moment, but it was a horrible moment,
to persuade her to tell him the truth.

"'Yes,' she cried, with a sudden impulse—perhaps it
was the first honest word she had ever spoken to the
poor boy—'Yes, you shall know everything. You
shall know all that I know. There is no good in keeping things back now. She has gone ; she is a deceitful, bad girl. She has left me to poverty and you to
misery. She has gone off with a wicked man, a man
who destroyed her sister, and left her, but whom she
has always loved. She has broken her promise to me
—she has deceived me, she has ruined me. What shall
I do ! how shall I pay her bills ! I shall have to hide
myself ; and I thought I had got through with being
poor ! She promised me, she promised me to bear
with you and to carry this out. Everything hung
upon it, every one was waiting—the landlord, the grocer
even knew that she was going to make a fine match,
and they were waiting. I had to explain it all to them.
You can't think how like heaven it seemed to have a
prospect of easy times. I have had a hard life, a hard
life, ever since I can remember. How I have worked for
that girl, and for her sister before her—what sacrifices
I have made ! You can't think, a man can't know. I
really enjoy telling the truth ; it's such a long time

since I've done it. Making the best of things—making
out that things were one way with us when they were
another—telling lies to every body—almost to each
other ! Oh, what shall I do without her ! I don't know
where to go or which way to turn ! She is a wicked
girl to have served me such a trick. She will be come
up with yet. She will hate that man—hate him worse
than she hated you. Nobody could say you were not
sweet and nice to every one, even if you were too
young. And he—he is an evil, deep, bad man. He will
break her heart for her, as he broke her sister's. And
he hasn't got a penny. And she, oh ! she has a fury
of a temper, and she must have her own way if she dies
for it. Well, she's got it, and I almost hope she will
be punished. I'd like to see her poor as poverty, and
come begging to the door.'

"And so on, Missy, in her wretched, selfish moan
of disappointed greed, while the poor boy stood stunned
and almost stupefied. It did not seem to him at all
real or true ; he felt as if he must wake up from it ; for
the girl had been a good actress ; and the mother,
though he had always felt a little uncomfortable with
her, had simulated the manners of a lady, and his refined
tastes never had been shocked ; at least never with
force enough to break the spell of the daughter's influence. Fancy what this revelation was to him ; the
woman, in her transport of anger, and in her despair of
further help from him, tearing away their flimsy
hypocrisies, and revealing their disgusting meanness.
It all seemed hideous raving to St. John, till she thrust
into his hand the letter that the girl had left. Then
the sight of the handwriting that had always given him

such emotions, and the cruel words, made an end of his dream, and he was quite awake."

"What did she write?" asked Missy.

"That he has not told me. He cannot seem to bring himself to speak the words. But I gather from him, it was a vehement protestation of what she felt for her old lover, and the contempt in which she held the poor boy, and perhaps some rude defiance of her mother. St. John, I think, could hardly have spoken many words during the interview. He emptied his pockets, poor boy, and left the wretched woman silent with amazement. She may well have repented of her reckless speech—how much she might have got out of him, if she had still played the hypocrite. He came down the stairs which half an hour before he had mounted, weak, like a person after months of illness. When he got into the carriage, his eyes fell on some lovely flowers which he had brought for her, and the sight and scent of them seemed to make clear the horrible reality. I think he really cannot tell what he did with the rest of the day. He told the man to drive to the Park, and there he wandered about, no doubt, for hours. I am sure he has not tasted food since morning. It must result in a terrible illness. How did he look, Missy, when he came in from the beach?"

Missy evaded ; and her heart smote her that she had not brought the poor boy to his mother, instead of turning him away from the only chance of comfort. "Shall I go and see?" she said. And going softly into the hall, she stood outside the door of his room and listened. "It is all quiet," she said, coming back. "Perhaps he has fallen asleep. He looked utterly worn out when he came in." Then she crept up beside her mother, and pulling a shawl about her, they sat talking, hand in hand, till the stars grew pale, and the chilly dawn broke.

CHAPTER III.

THE FIRST SERMON.

T was Sunday afternoon, a year and a half after this, and St. John had just been preaching his first sermon. Missy's dream of happiness was realized, and her brother was called to Yellowcoats parish—called before he was ordained ; and for three months the parish had been waiting patiently for that event, and living upon "supplies." St. John had not wished to come to Yellowcoats, his mother had not wholly desired it, but the fire and force of Missy's will had conquered, and here he was.

"I think it's a mistake," St. John had said. "Half the congregation will think I ought to be playing marbles yet, and wearing knickerbockers. Besides, it isn't the kind of work I want."

Then his mother had admitted, that it would be a great happiness to have him with her; and Missy had presented to his conscience, in many forms, that place and surroundings were indications of duty. It was not for nothing that he had been born and brought up

at Yellowcoats ; that there he had family influence,
and knowledge of the people with whom he was to
deal.   Was it not his home? Did he owe any
other place as much ?   And was it nothing that
a vacancy had occurred just as he was ready to
come ?

   " All the same, I doubt if it is well," he said, and
came ; for he was young and not self-willed, and the
kind of work he wanted had not come before him.
He consented to come and try. "But remember,
Missy, I do not promise you to stay."

   Upon one thing he was firm, he would not live at
home.   The rectory was in tolerable order, and there
he was to live, with one servant.   He never would be
happy unless he were uncomfortable, said his sister ;
nevertheless, she liked him better for it.

   St. John was changed, very deeply changed, since
that October night, a year and a half ago ; but he had
come to be again sweet-natured and natural, and they
loved him more than ever at home.   He had grown
silent, and never got back his young looks again.   He
had thrown himself into his studies with great earnest-
ness, and had worked, perhaps, more than was quite
wise.   Lent was just over, and his ordination ; and he
was naturally a little wan and weary from it ; but after
preaching that first sermon, there was a flush upon his
cheek.   The bishop had been there in the morning,
and had preached ; in the afternoon, he had had no
one with him, and had taken all the duty.   He was
alone with his people, and was fairly launched.   It
had been well known that he was going to preach, and
the church was very full.   Perhaps speculation about

the knickerbockers and the marbles had brought some. Perhaps affection and real interest in their young townsman had brought others. All the "denominations" were amply represented, and all the young women of the village who had smart spring bonnets, wore them, and came with their young men. In short, it was more like a funeral than an ordinary afternoon service; for a funeral in Yellowcoats was an improved occasion always. The church building was a very poor affair, shabby in detail as well as ungainly in plan, but it was well situated, in the midst of shade, with an old graveyard on one side, and the road that led to the door of the rectory, fifty feet back, on the other, and beyond some green grass and trees there were sheds for horses. The windows were of clear diamond-shaped glass, so that when the rattling old shades were rolled up, one saw lovely glimpses of the bay, and some green fields, and nearer, the delicate young green of the locust trees that stood thick in the inclosure. One could always look heaven-ward and sea-ward out of the windows of Yellowcoats church, and that was the only advantage it presented as a building.

Lent had come late that year; and the spring had come early. The air was soft and sweet, the verdure more advanced than is usual for the last of April. The earth was still sodden and wet, though the spring sun was shining warmly on it. The crocuses were peeping up about the stones of the foundation, and in the grass the Star of Bethlehem and the periwinkle were in blossom. The locusts, with their thin, high-up foliage, were just a faint green, their rough bark rusty from the winter's storms.

It is rather an ordeal to hear one's brother preach his first sermon, particularly if he is a younger brother, and one has more solicitude for his success, than confidence in it. Missy's heart beat furiously while he said the prayers—she very much wished he hadn't come to Yellowcoats. His voice soothed her; there was no indication in it that his heart was beating with irregularity. But then would dart in the thought of the coming sermon, and the trepidation would return. There was one thing to be thankful for, and that was, that mamma was not there. And when the sermon came, she scarcely heard the text; it was several minutes before she heard anything. By and by she got steadied by something in his voice and manner, not probably in the words. And after that, she renounced solicitude and assumed confidence. Yes, she need not be afraid for St. John. Though there was nothing wonderful in the sermon. The congregation had heard many a better, probably. But while it was simple, it was not trite. It was thought out, and definite, and well-expressed. The Rev. Dr. Platitude would have made three out of it, and thought himself extravagant. But what was it that held the people so silent, that made them follow him so? For Missy would have heard a leaf turned six pews off; would have felt it through and through her if a distant neighbor had even buttoned up her glove. No; nobody was turning pages, or buttoning gloves, or thinking of spring bonnets. St. John had them in his hand; they were his while he chose to hold them. There was an utter simplicity about him ; an absence of speculation about himself. Missy looked at him and wondered if it were indeed her brother.   There was a deep light in his eyes, that one sometimes sees in blue eyes ; there was a faint flush on his cheek ; there was a steady look about his mouth.   It began to dawn on Missy that he was going to be one of those men who are to preach from their hearts as well as from their brains ; who are to bring out from their own soul's labor, food for the hungry souls about them.   She began to feel that St. John's sermon had come somehow from the weary Lent that was just ended ; from the hard pressure of the past eighteen months ; from the cruel wound that had seemed to find his very life. But what were the people crying about ? Heaven knows. For they had heard many sermons before, and been like the pebbles on the shore for hardness and rattling indifference.   And they did cry, though St. John did not ; but his eyes were deep and earnest.

"Mamma," exclaimed Missy, throwing herself down by her mother's sofa, and hiding her face on her shoulder—"it was like Paradise—all the people cried."

"I didn't suppose they did that in Paradise."

"Oh, you know what I mean. It was like Paradise to me to see them cry. At any rate, you needn't have any fear about St. John."

"I never had any fear of him, that way," said the mother, quietly.

3

———◦◦———

CHAPTER IV.

THE PEOPLE NEXT DOOR.

T was a lovely July afternoon, and at five o'clock Missy had taken her work and a book down to the beach-gate, and sat there rather idly reading, while the tide, which was only a few feet away from her, was breaking on the pebbles with a sound that is dead against serious mental application. There was a drowsy hum of insects in the air, a faint whispering in the trees overhead. She took off the light hat that shaded her face, and threw it on the grass, and leaning back in the high-backed cane chair, thought what a comfort not to be in a hurry about anything. She was delicately and coolly dressed, just fresh from a bath and a sleep. Life seemed luxurious at that moment. She watched a sail-boat, almost as idle as she was herself, lolling across the bay, the faint west wind coming in light puffs that gave it but little impetus. Presently the plash of oars aroused her, and turning her head she saw St. John pulling up to the beach.

"Ah, that's nice!" she cried. "You've come to tea."

"Well, yes, but it is not tea time yet."

"Not for an hour and a half. This is very self-indulgent, coming home to tea twice in one week. I am afraid Bridget hasn't got the receipt for muffins quite through her head yet."

"Yes, Bridget does very well. I wish every one did as well as Bridget. . Myself, for instance."

"Oh, nonsense ; now you're moping again."

"No, I am not. Nothing as excusable as that. But I'm lazy. How can any one keep from getting that in this place, I should like to know ? "

"I don't know why this place must bear the blame of all one's moods," said Missy, much annoyed. "*I* don't get lazy here."

"But you see I do."

"Maybe you'd do that anywhere."

"I'll put myself where I sha'n't have any more chance to be lazy than a car horse ; where it won't be a question of whether I want to go or not. I gave you fair warning, Missy ; I told you this wasn't the life for me."

"Well, if you want to make me perfectly wretch-ed—" said Missy, throwing down her book.

St. John had come up from the beach, and had thrown himself on the grass, with his hands clasped under his head, his hat lying beside him.

"I won't talk of it if it makes you wretched. Only you mustn't be surprised when I decide upon anything you don't like."

"I'd rather be surprised once than worried out of my life all the time."

"Very well, it's agreed." And St. John was silent, which Missy did not mean him to be. She wanted to argue with him about his restlessness.

"Such a good work as you are doing," she said. "Think what every one says about you."

"I don't want to think about it, if you please."

"Think of all those Rogers children being baptised, and of old Hillyard coming into the church. I should as soon have thought of Ship Point Rock melting as his hard heart. Nobody ever heard of anything more wonderful. And the repairs of the church; how the people are giving. Think what it will be to see a recess chancel, and stalls, and a real altar."

"Yes," said her brother, with a sigh, "that will be very nice. But it will come on now anyway. Anybody can do it."

"Oh, St. John, you dishearten me. Already you want to do 'some great thing.' Isn't that a bad sign, for so young a man?"

He was silent.

"I wish," she said, with a shade of impatience, "I wish you'd tell me, if you don't mind, what sort of work you want to do? What sort of people, pray, do you want to have the charge of?"

"I like wicked people," he said, very quietly.

"You—St. John! Fie. What do you know about wickedness?"

"More than you think, perhaps," he said uneasily, getting up, and turning his back upon the blue water. "Come, we won't talk about this any more. What have you been doing since Tuesday, and how is mamma?"

"Mamma is as usual; we havn't done anything of interest. Oh, yes. I went to call on the new people next door; and we are much interested in making out what and who they are. I was not admitted. Madame is an invalid, I believe, and rarely sees any one.

The children are queer little things, the girl a beauty.
I see them often peeping through the hedge."

" How about the gentleman? have you seen
him ?"

" No ; the Olors know him slightly and say he's
nice. The wife seems to be a mystery. No one knows
anything about her. I am quite curious. They have
lived several years abroad, and do not seem to have
many ties here. At least no one seems to know much
of them, in the city."

"I hope they're church people ? "

"I don't know, indeed. I should not think it likely.
The children have an elfish, untamed look, and there is
such a troop of foreign-looking servants. What they
need of all those people to keep such a plain, small
house going, I can't imagine. I have no doubt they
will demoralize our women. Two nurses do nothing
but sit on the beach all day, and look at the two children who dig in the sand. The coachman never seems
to do anything but smoke his pipe from the time of
taking his master to the cars in the morning till the
time of going for him in the evening. They have a
man-waiter. I cannot think what for. He and the
cook and the maid all seem to be French, and spend
much of their morning in the boat-house. We have
the ' Fille de Mme. Angot,' and odors of cheap cigars
across the hedge. It isn't pleasant."

" How you do long to reconstruct that household ! "

" In self-defense. I shouldn't wonder if we had to
change every servant in our house before the summer is
over. Even Goneril does nothing but furtively watch

them from the upper windows and make reflections upon the easy times they have."

At this moment there was a splash in the water, and a cry. They had been sitting with their backs to the shell which St. John had left below on the beach, and a boy of five, the new neighbors' boy, had climbed into it, and, quite naturally, tumbled out of it. St. John vaulted over the fence, took two or three strides into the water, and picked him out.

"Heigho, young man, what would you have done if I hadn't been here?" he said, landing him dripping on the beach.

"Let me alone, will you!" cried the sturdy fellow, showing his gratitude and his shocked nerves by kicking at his benefactor. He did not cry, but he swelled with his efforts to keep from it.

"Of course I will," said his preserver mildly, looking down at him. "But I'd like to know what's become of your nurse. Where is she?"

"None of you's business," returned this sweet child, putting down his head. He was a dear little fellow, sturdy and well built, with stout bare legs, and tawny hair, banged on the forehead, and long and wavy behind. He had clear blue eyes, and a very tanned skin and very irregular features. He spoke with an accent of mixed Irish and French.

"I'm very sorry about it," said St. John, gently, "but I'm afraid you'll get cold. Better tell me where to find the nurse."

"None of you's business," returned the boy.

"There she is," said Missy in a low voice, "ever so

far beyond the steamboat landing, with the waiter. See if you can make them hear."

St. John put his hand to his mouth and called. But alas! they were too deeply engrossed for such a sound to reach them.

"The child will get a horrid cold," said Missy, "it won't do to wait. I'll take him up to the house, and send one of the servants home with him."

But Missy reckoned without her host; this latter declined to go to "her house," and planted his feet firmly in the sand.

"You'll have to carry him," she intimated *sotto voce* to her brother. Then he hit from the shoulder, and it was well seen that was not a thing that could be done. The shock to his nerves and the bath had already resulted in making his lips blue. The water was dripping from his hair to his neck, and it was fair to suppose he felt a little chilly, as the breeze was increasing a trifle.

"I'll tell you," said Missy, cheerfully. "You shall take me to your house, if you won't go to mine. I don't know the way, but I suppose you do. Through the boat-house?"

The boy lifted his eyes doubtfully to see if she were in good faith, glowered at St. John, and after a moment made a step towards the boat-house.

"What a nice boat-house you've got," said Missy, walking on in front of him. "I wish we had as big a one."

"Got my things in it," said the child, and then, frightened at his own part in the conversation, put down his head and was silent.

" Do you keep your toys here ? Why, how nice ! "
exclaimed Missy, pausing at the door.   " Why, what a
nice room, and here's a baby-house.   Pray whose is
that ? "

" That's Gabby's, and that's mine—and this is my
wheelbarrow—and that's her hoop—" And so on,
through a catalogue of playthings that would have set
up a juvenile asylum.

" I never saw so many playthings," said Missy, getting hold of his hand in a moment of enthusiasm over
a new velocipede.   " Have you got any more up at the
house ? "

" Lots," said the boy, succinctly.

" Won't you take me to see them ? "   And so, hand
in hand, they set off, St. John watching them from the
door of the boat-house with amusement.

Before they reached the house, Missy began to
have some misgivings about the proceeding.   She did
not enjoy the idea of taking the enemy in the rear.
What sort of people were they, and how would they
like the liberty of having her enter from the beach ?
Some people do not like to be indebted to their neighbors for saving their children's lives.   It's all a matter
of temperament, education—and they might not like
the precedent.   She wished she might find a servant to
whose care to commit him, and herself steal out the
way she had come in.   But, though there had seemed
to be nothing but servants visible every time she had
passed the house, or looked over at it from the upper
windows, there were none to be found to-day.   The
place was as silent as if no one lived in it.   She paused
at the kitchen door, and called faintly, and told the

boy to call, which he did with a good courage. But no
response. Then they went around to the front piazza,
and the boy, Jay, he said his name was, strutted up
and down it, and declined to go in, or to go up stairs.
He was getting bluer about the lips, and she knew he
must not be left. So she rang the bell, several times,
with proper intervals, but there was no answer. At
last she went into the hall, and taking a shawl she
found there, wrapped it around the child.

"Play you were a Highland Chief," she said, and
he submitted.

She rang once more, and then followed the tugging
of Jay's hand through the hall into the dining-room.
There the table was laid, quite in state, for one. From
the adjacent kitchen came an odor of soup, which was
very good, but there was no living thing visible in it but
a big dog, who thumped his tail hard on the floor. Then
they went back into the hall, and over the stairs came
a voice, rather querulous:

"Vell, vot is it—*Vite?* Vhere are all se servants?" Then, seeing a lady, the maid came down a
few steps and apologized. Missy led up the child and
explained the condition of affairs. Jay began to frown,
and fret and pull away, as soon as she approached him.
It was clear Alphonsine was not one of his affinities.
She was a coffee-colored Frenchwoman, with a good accent and a bad temper, and had been asleep when the
sixth ring of the bell had reached her. Missy began
to be pretty sick of the whole business, and to wish to
be out of it. So, rather peremptorily advising her to
change the child's clothes and rub him well, she started
to go away, boldly departing by the front gate, which

3*

was not a stone's throw from their own entrance. But
she had barely reached the gate when the French
woman came running after her, with a most voluble
apology, and a message from Madame, that if it would
not be asking too much of the young lady, would she
kindly come back for a moment and allow Madame to
express to her her thanks for her great goodness? The
woman explained that her mistress was an invalid, and
put the matter in such a light that there was no chance
of refusing to go back, which was what Missy would
very much have liked to do. The whole thing seemed
awkward and uncomfortable, and she turned back feeling as little inclined to be gracious as possible.

The woman led the way up the stairs, at the head
of which stood Jay, his teeth now chattering.

"Pray get his wet clothes off!" she said to the
woman. "I'll find my way, if you'll point out the
door."

The woman was not much pleased with this, and
showed it by preceding her to the door, and watching
her well into the room before she turned to push the
unwilling Jay into the nursery, and with deliberation,
not to say sullenness, take off his dripping clothes.

Missy found herself in a pretty room, rather warm,
and rather dark, and rather close with foreign-smellng
toilet odors. Before she had seen or spoken to the lady
on the sofa, she had felt a strong inclination to push
open the windows, and let in the glory of the sinking
western sun, and the fresh breeze of evening. She felt
a healthy revolt from the rich smells and the dim light.
A soft voice spoke to her from the sofa, and then, as
she came nearer, she saw the loveliest creature! Like

all plain women, she had an enthusiasm for beauty in her own sex. She almost forgot to speak, she was so enchanted with the face before her. It was, indeed, beautiful ; rare, dark eyes, perfect features, skin of a lovely tint. Missy was so dazzled by the sight she hardly knew whether she were attracted or not. The lady's voice was low and musical. Missy did not know whether she liked the voice or not. She could only listen and wonder. It was an experience—something new come into her life. She felt, in an odd sort of way, how small her knowledge of people was ; how much existed from which she had been shut out.

"I've lived among people just like myself all my life ; it's contemptible," she thought. "No wonder I am narrow. A woman lives such a stupid life at home."

She sat down and talked with Mrs. Andrews. Mrs. Andrews ! What a prosaic name for this exotic plant ; as if one called a *Fritallaria Imperialis* a potato. She began to wonder about Mr. Andrews. What was he ? Why had no one told her these people were remarkable ? She almost forgot to answer questions, and bear her part in the conversation. She did not yet know whether she admired or not. She only knew she was near a person who had lived a different life from hers ; who had a history ; who probably didn't think as she did on any one subject ; who was entering from a side door, the existence of which she had not guessed, upon a scene which had seemed to belong to Missy and her sort alone. From what realms did she come ? In what school had she been taught ? She could not make her out, while she was being

thanked for bringing Jay home. There was a languor
about her manner of speaking of the little boy, which
did not satisfy Missy, used to mammas who lived for
their children, and considered it the pride and glory
of life to know nothing beyond the nursery. This
was the first mother who had ever dared to be languid
about her children on Missy's small stage. She did
not understand, and perhaps showed her perplexity, for
her new acquaintance, with a faint sigh, said : " Poor
little Jay ; he is so strong and vehement, so alien.
I believe he terrifies me. I think it must be because I
am weak."

"I never liked a child so much ; he is a little man,"
said Missy, warmly.

"Ah, yes ! you are well and strong ; you are in
sympathy with him—but I—ah, well, I hope, Miss
Rothermel, you will never have to feel yourself useless and a burden."

"I hope not, I am sure," said Missy honestly, feeling a little hurt on Jay's account, but still a great deal
of pity for the soft voiced invalid. "Mamma could
understand you better. She has been ill many years."

"Ah, the dear lady ! I wish that I might know
her. But with her it is different in a way. She perhaps is used to it, if ever one can be used to misery.
But for me it is newer, I suppose, and, when young,
one looks for pleasure, just a little."

Missy colored ; she had forgotten that her mother
could seem old to any one, and then she saw how
very young her companion really was—younger than
herself, no doubt.

"It is very hard," she said. "Can't you interest

yourself in the children at all? They would be such
a diversion if you could."

"My little Gabrielle, yes. But Jay is—so different, you know—so noisy ; I believe he makes me ill
every time he comes near me."

"Gabrielle looks like you," said Missy. "I have
seen her on the beach sometimes."

Then the beautiful eyes lighted up, and Missy
began to be enchanted. She did not know that she
had produced the illumination, and that the beautiful creature was made happy by an opportunity to
talk about herself. She gradually—sweetly slid into it,
and Missy was wrapt in admiration. Her companion
talked well about herself, *con amore*, but delicately
and like a true artist. A beautiful picture was growing up before Missy. She would have been at a loss
to say who painted it. She did not even think her
egotistic, though she would have pardoned egotism in
one who seemed so much better worth talking of
than ordinary people. Her loneliness, her suffering,
her youth, her exile from her own people, her uncongenial surroundings—how had Missy learned so
much in one-half hour? And yet Mrs. Andrews had
not seemed to talk about herself. It was sketchy ; but
Missy was imaginative, and when a carriage driving
to the gate made her start up, she was surprised to
find it was half an hour instead of half a life-time
since she had come into the room.

"It is Mr. Andrews," she said, glancing from the
window, "and I must go."

"Don't !" said the invalid, earnestly.

"O, it would be better," said Missy, "it is so awkward. I know husbands hate to find tiresome friends

always in their wives' rooms when they come home."

"Yes, perhaps so, when they come to their wives' rooms when they get home."

There was a slight distension of the nostril and a slight compression of the lips when this was said. Missy flushed between embarrassment and indignation. Was it possible that Mr. Andrews was a brute, and was not at this moment on the stairs on his way to this lonely lovely sufferer?

Mrs. Andrews did not want her to go—she stayed at least ten minutes, standing ready to depart. As she went down the stairs, the servant passed through the hall, and she heard him announce dinner to his master, who promptly came in from the piazza, by which means, he and Missy were brought face to face in the hall near the dining-room door. Mr. Andrews probably felt, but did not express any astonishment at seeing a strange young lady in white muslin, without even the conventionality of a hat upon her head, walking about his temporary castle ; he merely bowed, and, being very hungry, went into the dining-room to get his dinner. As for Missy, she felt it was very awkward, and she was also full of resentment. She inclined her head in the slightest manner, and only glanced at him to see whether he was remarkable-looking, and whether he had any right to be a tyrant and a brute. It takes a very handsome man to have any such right as that, and Mr. Andrews was by no means handsome. He was not tall—rather a short man, and almost a stout man. Not that exactly, but still not as slight as he ought to have been for his height. He was not young either—certainly forty, possibly more. He had blue eyes, and hair and whiskers of light brown. The expression of his face was rather stern. He was evidently thinking of something that gave him no pleasure when he looked up and saw Missy, and there was perhaps nothing in the sight of her that induced him to cast the shadow from his brow. So she did not see that he had a good smile, and that his eyes were particularly intelligent and keen. She hurried past him with the settled belief that he was a monster of cruelty; the odor of the soup, which was particularly good, and the sound of the chair upon the floor as it was pushed up before the lonely table, and the clinking of a glass were added touches to the dark picture.

"I suppose he hasn't given her a thought," she said to herself, as the gate shut after her. "Dinner, imagine it, comes first. He looks like a gourmand; he *is* a gourmand, I am sure. That soup was perfectly delicious; I wish I had the receipt for it. But he is worse than a gourmand. Gourmands are often good-natured. He is a tyrant, and I hate him. Think of the misery of that poor young thing! How could she have married him? I would give worlds to know her history. *He* isn't capable of a history. I suppose she must have been very poor, and forced into the marriage by her parents. Nothing else can account for such a *mésalliance*."

When she entered the parlor, St. John was sitting by his mother's sofa. "How is our young friend?" he said. "Remember I saved his life; so don't put on any airs because you got him to go home."

"It was a great deal harder work," said Missy; "and you like hard work, you say. But, mamma, I have seen her, and she is the loveliest creature—Mrs. Andrews, I mean! She is confined to her room—never leaves it—a hopeless invalid. And he is a brute, an utter brute! I can hardly find words to describe him. He is short and stout, and has a most sinister expression. And now think of this—listen to what I say: *He went in to dinner, without going up to her room at all!* Can you think of anything more heartless?"

"Oh, yes," said St. John, commonplacely; "not sending her up any dinner would have been worse—not paying her bills—not taking her to the country."

Missy scorned to reply to him, but directed her conversation to her mother. "Her beauty is very remarkable, and she seems so young. The man is certainly forty. I really wish I could find out something about them. She is French, I think, though she speaks without an accent. She is so different from the people one sees every day; she gives you an idea of a different life from ours. And for my part, I am glad to see something of another stratum. Do you know, I think we are very narrow? All women, of course, are from necessity; but it seems to me I have led a smaller life than other women."

"I don't think you need regret it," said her brother, seriously; "it saves you a great deal."

"Pray don't say anything, you who like wicked people."

St. John was "hoist with his own petard."

" Then you think I might enjoy Mr. and Mrs. Andrews?" he said.

" Mr. Andrews would satisfy all your aspirations," returned Missy ; " but not his wife, unless it is wicked to be unconventional."

" But how did you find out she was unhappy ; I hope she didn't tell you so ?" asked Mrs. Varian.

" No, of course she did not ! I don't really know how I divined it ; but it was most easy to see. And then he did not come up to see her ! is not that enough ?"

" Perhaps he was hungry—unusually hungry ; or perhaps he is a victim to dyspepsia, and cannot go through any excitement upon an empty stomach. You know his doctors may have forbidden him."

" Really, St. John," said Missy, much annoyed, " it is not safe to find fault with a man in your presence. Your class feeling is so strong, I think you would defend him if he had two wives."

" Who knows but that may be the trouble ?" he said. " He didn't know which to go to first, and he may have had to send two dinners up. No wonder that he has dyspepsia ! That being the case—"

" You are rather illogical for a man. Who said he had dyspepsia? What does that stand upon? Mamma, I want to have the children in here often. Jay is a darling, and as to Gabby—"

" Gabby !" repeated her mother.

" Gabrielle," said Missy, blushing, and glancing anxiously at her brother, to see if he were laughing. " It was Jay called her Gabby—a horrid shortening, certainly. Gabrielle is a lovely name, I think. But what's the matter, St. John? What have I said now?"

"Nothing," said her brother, in a forced, changed voice, as he got up and walked about the room, every sparkle of merriment gone from his eyes.

"It is time for tea, is it not?" said Mrs. Varian.

"Yes, I suppose it is," returned Missy, wearily, getting up and crossing over to ring the bell, as if tea were one of the boundaries of her narrow sphere.

CHAPTER V.

GABBY AND JAY.

FTER that, there were daily visits to Mrs. Andrews, daily messages passing between the houses, daily hours with Gabby and Jay upon the beach. It became the most interesting part of Miss Rothermel's life. It was a romance to her, though she thought she was not romantic. Her dream was to do good, a great deal of good, to somebody, all the better if she happened to like the somebody. It was tiresome to do good all the time to Aunt Harriet, who was all the time there ready to be done good to. It was not conceivable that mamma could need her very much—mamma, who had St. John, and who really did not seem an object of compassion at all, rather some one to go to, to get comforted. She was "a-weary" of the few poor people of the place. They seemed inexpressibly "narrow" to her now. She

seemed suddenly to have outgrown them. She condemned herself for the time and thought she had bestowed upon them, when she counted up the pitiful
results.

"I suppose I have spent a month, and driven forty
miles, and talked volumes, if it were all put together,
to get that wretched Burney boy to go to Sunday
school. And what does it amount to, after all, now
that he does go? He carries things in his pockets to
eat, and he makes the other children laugh, and he sits
on the gravestones during service, and whistles loud
enough to have to be hunted away by the sexton every
Sunday. No; I shall let him go now; he may come
or not, as he sees fit."

It was certainly much pleasanter to sit on the beach
and curl Jay's tawny hair, and make him pictures on
shells, and teach him verses, and his letters. Gabrielle,
with her great dark, side-looking eyes, was not as congenial to Missy, but even she was more satisfactory
than the Burney boy, with his dirty hands and terrible
dialect. Children without either refinement or innocence are not attractive, and though Missy feared
Gabby was not quite innocent, she had a good deal of
refinement in appearance and manner. She spoke with
a slow, soft manner, and never looked one straight in
the eye. She had a passion for jewelry and fine clothes,
and made her way direct to any one who had on a
bracelet or locket of more than ordinary pretension,
and hung over it fascinated. It was sometimes difficult
to shake her off, and the questions she asked were
wearisome. Missy's visitors were apt to pet and notice
her very much at first and then to grow very tired of

her. She was a picturesque object, though her face
was often dirty, and her hair was always wild. She
wore beautiful clothes, badly put on and in wretched
order ; embroidered French muslin dresses with the
ruffles scorched and over-starched ; rich Roman scarfs
with the fringes full of straws and sticks ; kid boots
warped at the heel, and almost buttonless ; stockings
faded, darned with an alien color, loose about the
ankles. All this was a trial to Missy, whose love of
order and neatness was outraged by the lovely little
slattern.

For a long while she sewed on furtive buttons,
picked clear fringes, re-instated ruffles, caught up
yawning rents. She would reconstruct Gabby, then
catch her in her arms and kiss her, and tell her how
much better she looked when she was neat. Gabby
would submit to the caress, but would give a sidelong
glance at Missy's perfect appointments—yawn, stretch
out her arms, make probably a new rent, and tear
away across the lawn to be caught in the first thorn
presenting. She was passionately fond of fine clothes,
but she was deeply lazy, and inconsequently Bohemian.
The idea of constraint galled her. She revolted from
Missy's lectures and repairing touches.

Then Missy tried her 'prentice hand on the faithless servants. The faithless servants did not take it
kindly. They resented her suggestions, and hated
her.

Then she faintly tried to bring the subject to the
notice of the mother. This was done with many misgivings, and with much difficulty, for it was not easy
to get the conversation turned on duties and possible

failures. Somehow, it was always a very different
view the two took of things, when they had their long
talks together. It was always of herself that Mrs.
Andrews talked—always of her sufferings, her wrongs.
When your friend is posturing for a martyr, it is hard
to get her into an attitude of penitence without hurt-
ing her feelings. When she is bewailing the faults of
others, it is embarrassing to turn the office into a con-
fession of her own. Missy entered on her task humbly, knowing that it would be a hard one. She did
not realize why it would be so hard. She had a ro-
mantic pity for her friend. She would not see her
faults. Indeed, any one might have been blinded,
who began with a strong admiration. When a woman is too ill to be talked to about her duties even, it
is hard to expect her to perform them with rigor. When
Missy, baffled and humbled, returned from that unfortunate mission, she acknowledged to herself she had
attempted an impossibility. "She cannot see, she
never has seen—probably she never will be obliged to
see, what neglect her children are suffering from. She
is too ill to be able to take in anything outside her
sick room. The cross laid on her requires all her
strength. It is cruelty to ask her to bear anything
more. I am ashamed to have had the thought." So
she turned to the poor little children so sadly orphaned,
as it seemed to her, and with tenderness, tried to
lighten their lot, and shield them from the tyrannies
and negligences of their attendants. Little Jay lived
at his new friend's house, ate at her table, almost slept
in her bosom. He naturally preferred this to the cold

slatternliness of his own home, and he was rarely
missed or inquired for.

"He might have been in the bay for the past five
hours, for all the servants know about it," said Mrs.
Varian, to whom all this was an anxiety and depression. "Don't you think, Missy, you give them an excuse in keeping him here so much? They naturally
will say, if anything happens, they thought he was
with you, and that you take him away for such long
drives and walks, they never know where to find
him."

"My dear mamma," cried Missy, "don't you
think the wretches would find an excuse for whatever
they did? Is their duplicity to make it right for me
to abandon my poor little man to them?"

"At least always report it at the house when you
take him away for half a day."

So after that, Missy was careful to make known her
plan at the Andrews' before she took Jay away for
any long excursion. She would stop at the door in her
little pony-carriage, and lifting out Jay, would send
him in to say to a pampered menial at the door, that
they need not be uneasy about him if he did not come
back till one or two o'clock.

"We won't put on mournin' for ye before three,
thin, honey," said the man, on one occasion. Jay
didn't understand the meaning of the words, but he
understood the cynical tone, and he kicked the fellow
on a beloved calf. Then the man, enraged, caught him
by the arm and held him off, but he continued to kick
and hit from the shoulder with his one poor little un-
pinioned arm. The man was white with rage, for Jay

was unpopular, and Miss Rothermel also, and he hated
to be held in check by her presence, and by the puerile
fear of losing his place, which her presence created.

Now it happened on this pleasant summer morning
that Mr. Andrews had not gone to town, and that he
had not gone out on the bay, as was supposed in the
household, the wind having proved capricious. Consequently he was just entering from the rear of the house,
as this pretty tableau was being presented on the front
piazza. When the enraged combatants raised their
eyes, they found Mr. Andrews standing in the hall
door, and darkly regarding them.

"Papa! kill him!" cried Jay, as the flunky suddenly released him, dashing at the unprotected calves
like a fury. "Kill him for me!"

"With pleasure," said his father, calmly, "but you
let it alone. Come to the library at ten o'clock, I
will see you about this matter," he said to the man,
who slunk away, while Jay came to take his father's
outstretched hand, very red and dishevelled. By this
time Missy, much alarmed, had sprung from the carriage, and ran down the walk, just in time to confront
the father. He was beginning to question the boy, but
turning around faced the young lady unexpectedly,
and took off his hat. Missy looked flushed and as excited as the boy.

"I hope you won't blame Jay," she said, "for it is
safe to say it is the man's fault. They tease him shame-
fully, and he is such a little fellow."

Mr. Andrews' face softened at these words. It was
plain she thought he was severe with his children, but
that was lost in the sweetness of hearing any one plead

for his little boy with that intuitive and irrational tenderness.

"I want to hit him!" interrupted Jay, doubling up his fist. "I want to hit him right in his ugly mouth."

"Hush," said his father, frowning, "little boys must not hit any one, least of all, their father's servants. You come to me whenever they trouble you, and I will make it right."

"You're never here when they do it," said the child.

"Well, you keep quiet, and then come and tell me when I get home."

"I forget it then," said Jay, naively.

"Then I think it can't go very deep," returned his father, smiling.

"It will go deep enough to spoil his temper utterly, I'm afraid," said Missy, biting her lips to keep from saying more.

"I am sorry enough," he began earnestly, but catching sight of her face, his voice grew more distant. "I suppose it is inevitable," he added slowly, as Jay, loosing his hold of his father's hand, picked up his hat, straightened his frock, and went over to Missy's side.

"I am going to ride with Missy," he said, tugging a little at her dress. "Come, it's time."

"Perhaps your father wants you to stay with him, as he isn't often at home."

"O no," said Mr. Andrews, as they all walked towards the gate. "Jay is better off with you, I am afraid, and happier. And I want to thank you, Miss Rothermel, for your many kindnesses to the children. I assure you, I—I appreciate them very much."

"O," cried Missy, stiffly, and putting very sharp needles into her voice, "there is nothing to thank me for. It is a pleasure to have them for their own sakes, and everything that I can do to make Mrs. Andrews more comfortable about them, is an added pleasure."

Missy knew this was a fib the instant she had uttered it. She knew it didn't make Mrs. Andrews a straw more comfortable to know the children were in safe hands ; but she wanted to say something to punish this brutal husband, and this little stab dealt itself, so to speak. She was very sorry about the fib, but she reflected one must not be too critical in dealing with brutal husbands if one's motives are right. Mr. Andrews stiffened too, and his face took a hard and cynical look.

"Undoubtedly," he said, and then he said no more. Jay held the gate open for them.

"Come," he said, "it's time to go." Missy stepped into the low carriage—disdaining help, and gathered up the reins. Mr. Andrews lifted Jay into the seat beside her.

"And I guess I'll stay to dinner with Missy, so you needn't send for me," said Jay, seating himself comfortably and taking the whip, which was evidently his prerogative. Nobody could help smiling, even brutal husbands and people who had been telling fibs. "I haven't heard you invited," said the representative of the former class.

"O, Jay knows he is always welcome. I will send him home before evening, if I may keep him till then."

Mr. Andrews bowed, and the little carriage rolled

4

away, the child forgetting to look back at his father, eagerly pleased with the whip and the drive, and the sunshine and the morning air. Mr. Andrews watched them out of sight, and as they were lost among the trees in a turn of the road, he sighed and turned stolidly towards the house. It was a low, pretty cottage, the piazza was covered with flowering vines, there were large trees about it—the grass was green and well-kept, a trim hedge separated it from the Varian place; at the rear, beyond the garden, was the boat-house and then a low fence that ran along the yellow beach. The water sparkled clear and blue; what a morning it was; and what a peaceful, pretty attractive little home it looked. People passing along the road might well gaze at it with envy, and imagine it the " haunt of all affections pure." This thought passed through Mr. Andrews' mind, as he walked from the gate. It made his face a little harder than usual, and it was usually hard enough.

CHAPTER VI.

A PASSING SOUL.

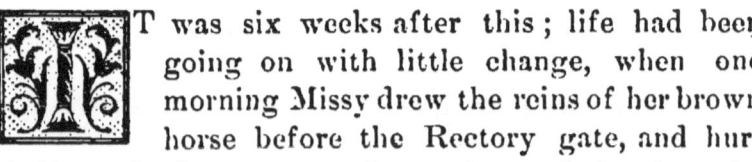T was six weeks after this; life had been going on with little change, when one morning Missy drew the reins of her brown horse before the Rectory gate, and hurriedly springing out, ran down the path, leaving the

carriage at the roadside. She had a vail tied close across her face; but she had no gloves, and her manner showed haste and excitement. St. John was in his study. She ran in, exclaiming, as she opened the door: "I wish you could come with me immediately, St. John. Get ready; don't stop to ask questions. I will tell you while you're going."

"Mamma?" he asked, with a sudden contraction of the face, as he started up and went across the room to get his hat.

"No! oh, thank Heaven! no. But don't stop for anything. Come; it is more to me than you."

Then St. John knew that it was something that concerned the Andrews'; but generously made all the haste he could in following her. As he stepped into the carriage after her, and took the reins from her hand, he said:

"Well!" and turned to listen.

"It is Mrs. Andrews," she said, tremblingly. "She is dying; she may be dead. I knew nothing of it till this morning, though her life has been in danger through the night. Those cruel servants did not send for us, and she has been in too much suffering to ask for any one. Now, she scarcely knows me, but at first turned to me eagerly. She had something to say; I don't know what. But she will never say it. Oh, St. John! Death is so fearful—the silence. I can never hear that word, whatever it is, of great or little moment."

"Her husband is with her?"

"That is the dreadful part. He is not at home. There is no one to do anything. How they got the doctor is a wonder; except there is a brute instinct, even in such creatures, that runs for the doctor. It was ages before I could find the address of Mr. Andrews in town. Ages before I could get any one off with the telegram. I came for you myself, because I could trust no one else to get you quickly. Oh, St. John, do drive a little faster!"

"And what am I to do; now that you have got me?" said her brother, in a low tone, gazing before him at the horse, now almost on a gallop.

"Do? oh, St John! save her! say a prayer for her! help her! What are such as you to do but that? I didn't think you'd ask me. Oh, it is so terrible to think of her poor soul. She is so unready; poor thing—unless her sufferings will stand instead. *Don't* you think they may? Don't you think God might accept them instead of—of spirituality and love for Him?"

"We're not set to judge, Missy," said her brother, soothingly. "Let us hope all we can, and pray all we can. I wish that she were conscious, if only for one moment."

"Well, pray for it," cried Missy, and then burst into tears. After a moment, she turned passionately to him, and said: "St. John, I am afraid it is partly for my own comfort I want her to speak and to be conscious for one moment. I want to feel that I have a right to hope for her eternal safety, and that I haven't been wasting all these weeks in talking of things that didn't concern that, when I might have been leading her to other thoughts. Oh, St. John, tell me, ought I to have been talking about her soul all this time, when it was so hard? She was—oh, I know you will understand me—she was so full of her sufferings, and—well, of herself, that I couldn't easily talk about what I knew in my heart she ought to be getting ready for. I didn't know it was so near. Ah, I wasted the hours, and now her blood may be upon my soul. St. John, there never was anybody so unready. It appalls me. I see it all now. Poor, beautiful thing. She seems to be only made for earth. Oh, the awe! St John, if I had been a very good person, utterly holy, I might have saved her, might I not? I should not have thought of anything else, and by the force of my one purpose and desire, I could have wakened her."

"Maybe not, my sister. Don't reproach yourself; only pray."

Missy twisted her hands together in her lap, and was motionless, as they hurried on. In a moment more they were standing at the gate. As Missy sprang out, little Jay met her, fretting and crying.

"Oh, why haven't they taken the children over to mamma, as I ordered?" she cried; but there was no one to make excuse. "Go, go, my dear little Jay," she pleaded. But Jay was all unstrung and unreasonable, feeling the gloom and discomfort. "See," she cried, hurriedly kneeling down on the grass beside him, "go to Mrs. Varian, and tell her you are come to pay her a little visit; and tell her to let you go to my room, and on the table there you will find a little package, tied up in a white paper; and it is for you. I tied it up for you last night. Go see what it is; you haven't any idea. It is something you will like so much!" Jay was on his way before Missy got into the house.

It was a warm morning, close and obscure. One felt the oppression in every nerve—an August suffocation. Low banks of threatening clouds lay over the island that shut in the bay from the Sound, and over the West Harbor. They boded and brooded, but would lie there for the many hours of morning and midday that remained. Not a ripple moved the sullen water ; not a leaf stirred on the trees ; the sun seemed hidden deep in clouds of hot, still vapor. The house was all open, doors and windows, gasping for breath. In the hall one or two servants stood aimlessly about, listening at the foot of the stairs, or whispering together.

St. John followed his sister closely as she entered the house. The servants made way for her, and they went quickly up the stairs. At the door of the sick room they paused. Another woman, wringing her hands, and listening with keen curiosity, stood gazing in. The room was in the most confused state. The coffee-colored Alphonsine moved stolidly about, and occasionally put a piece of furniture in its place, or removed a garment thrown down in the haste and panic of the past night ; but standing still, more often, to gaze back at the bed. She crossed herself often, in a mechanical manner, but looked more sullen than sympathetic. There was a bath in the middle of the room, cloths and towels strewn upon the floor beside it, mustard, a night-lamp flickering still in the face of day, a bowl of ice, some brandy. The windows were thrown wide open ; the bed stood with its head near one—another one was opposite to it. The light fell full upon the ghastly face of the suffering woman. Beauty ! had she ever been beautiful ? " Like as a moth fretting a garment," so had her anguish made her beauty to consume away. A ghastly being—suffering, agonized, dying—wrestling with a destroying enemy! Such conflicts cannot last long; the end was near.

As St. John and his sister entered the room, the doctor, who stood at the head of the bed, was wiping the perspiration from his forehead and glancing out of the window. He was troubled and worn out with the night's work, and was watching eagerly for a brother physician who had been summoned to his aid. He knew the new-comer could do no good, but he could share the responsibility with him, and bring back the professional atmosphere out of which he had been carried by the swift and terrible progress of his patient's malady. Above all things, the doctor wished to be professional and cool; and he knew he was neither in the midst of this blundering crowd of servants, and in the sight of this fiercely dying woman. He could have wished it all to be done over again. He had lost his head, in a degree. He did not believe that anything could have arrested the flight of life; all the same he wished he had known a little more about the case; had taken the alarm quicker and sent for other aid. He looked harassed and helpless, and very hot and tired. All this St. John saw as he came in the room.

Missy looked questioningly at him, and then as he gave a gesture of assent, came quickly to the side of the bed. She half knelt beside it, and took the poor sufferer's hand in hers. The touch, perhaps, caused her to open her eyes, and her lips moved. Then her glance, roving and anguished, fell upon St. John. She lifted her hand with a sudden spasm of life.

"A priest?" she said, huskily.

"Yes," said St. John, coming to her quietly.

"Then all of you go away—quick—I want to speak to him."

"There is no time to spare," said the doctor, as he passed St. John. Missy followed him, and the servants followed her. She closed the door and waited outside.

The servants seemed to be consoled by the presence of a priest; things were taking the conventional death-bed turn. Even the doctor felt as if the professional atmosphere were being restored in a degree. St. John, indeed, had looked as if he knew what he was about, and had been calm in the midst of the agitated and uncertain group, occupied himself, perhaps, by but one thought. Young as he was, his sister and the doctor and the servants shut him into the room with a feeling of much relief. The servants nodded, and went their ways with apparent satisfaction. The doctor threw himself into a chair in an adjoining room, and signified to Miss Rothermel that he would rest till he was called. And she herself knelt down beside an open window just outside the door, and waited, and probably devoutly prayed for the passing soul making her tardy count within.

She could not but speculate upon the interview. Now that the awful sense of responsibility was lifted off her and shifted upon her brother's shoulders, she felt more naturally and more humanly. She began to wonder whether it had been to ask her for a priest that the dying woman had struggled when she first saw her that morning. She was almost sure it was, for she had clutched at St. John with such eagerness.

It was probable she did not know him and did not associate him with Missy. His marked dress had been his passport. And Missy really did not know what her friend's creed was. It seemed probable she had been a Roman Catholic, but had dropped her form of faith in holiday times of youth and possible wrongdoing, and had never had grace to resume that, or any other in the weary days of illness—unprofitable so long as they did not threaten death. But now death was at the door, and she had clutched at the hem of a priest's garment. So, thought Missy, it is real when it comes to facts; for what fact so real as death? Everything else seemed phantom-dim when she thought of that face upon the pillow, with the wide-open window shedding all the gray morning's light upon it.

The moments passed; the still, dull, heavy air crept in at the window upon which Missy bowed her head; the leaves scarcely stirred upon the trees that stood up close beside it; a languid bird or two twittered an occasional smothered note. There were few household sounds. The servants, though released from their futile watching, did not resume their household work. Missy smelt the evil odor of the Frenchman's cigar, and was ashamed to find it vexed her, even at such a moment as this; she braced herself to endure the "Fille de Mme. Angot," if that should follow in a low whistle from under the trees. But it did not. The Frenchman had that much respect for what was going on within.

At last! There was a stir—a moan, audible even through the door, and Missy started to her feet, and signalled the doctor, who had heard it, too. Her brother opened the door and admitted them. But what a ghastly face was his ; Missy started.

He turned back to the bed, and kneeling, read the commendatory prayer,

"Through the grave and gate of death,
　Now the faint soul travaileth."

Ah, God help her ; it is over. He has brought to pass His act, His strange act, and only death lies there, senseless, dull death, corruptible, animal, earthy, where but a moment before a soul of parts and passions, had been chained.

Missy, new to death-beds, got up from her knees at last, weeping and awed, and, laying her hand on her brother's, said, "Come away, St. John, you look so ill."

St. John arose and followed her, going to the room and sinking into the chair lately occupied by the doctor. He looked ill indeed, but his sister could offer him no comfort ; quiet, and to be left alone was all he asked of her. At this moment the doctor summoned in consultation appeared ; both the professional men went professionally into the chamber of death, and Missy, clasping the inert hand of Gabrielle, who, whimpering, had refused to go up stairs, went sorrowfully home with the child, feeling that she had no more to do in the house of death that day.

St. John came home in an hour or two. Mr. Andrews had not yet arrived. Everything that could be done without him had, under the direction of St. John and the doctor, been done. The house was quiet and in order, he said. It was almost certain that Mr. An-

drews would arrive in the next train; the carriage
was waiting at the depot for him, though no telegram
had come. St. John threw himself on the sofa, and
seemed again to want quiet, so his sister left him, and
took the children to her own room. It was so close in
the house, and they were so restless, that after a while
she took them out upon the lawn. There was no sun,
and just a cool air, though no breeze, creeping in from
the water. It was comparatively easy to amuse them
there, or rather, to let them amuse themselves. Gabrielle was inquisitive and fretful, but little Jay seemed
to feel languid and tired by the morning's heat, and
crept upon her lap at last and went to sleep.

Missy, sitting in the deep shade of the trees near
the beech gate, soothed by the quiet, and worn with
the morning's excitement, almost slept herself. She
had gone over many times in imagination the arrival
of the husband, and his first moment at the bedside of
his dead wife. She felt sure all this had now taken
place, though she was too far from the house to hear
the arrival of the carriage from the depot. She wondered whether he would send in for the children at
once, or whether he would be glad they were away;
or whether he would think of them at all. She was
glad to remember she had no duty in the matter, and
that she did not have to see him, and it was rather a
comfort to her to feel she did not know the exact moment at which he was going through the terrible scene,
and feeling the first anguish of remorse. She kissed
Jay's tawny head, and with her arms around him,
finally slept, leaning back in the great chair. Gabrielle at first played at her feet idly, then went down to
the beach, and amused herself in the sand, but it was

hot, and she came back to the shade, and, lying on the rug at Missy's feet, slept too.

A small steam yacht, meanwhile, had come into the harbor, had put off a small boat, which was even now landing a gentleman near the boat-house of the Andrews' place. The boat returned to the yacht; the gentleman set down his bag on the steps of the boat-house, and looked around. All was quiet; no one seemed moving at either of the two houses. Certainly it was not a day to move if you could help it. The only hope was that those dark clouds in the west would move, and make some change in the stagnant state of things. The gentleman took off his straw hat and fanned himself and walked slowly forward, then, catching sight of the group under the trees, with something like a smile, turned back and approached them. He stood looking down upon them, before any of them moved. Certainly, a pretty enough group. Gabrielle was sleeping, face forward, on her arms, a graceful figure, on the dark rug. Missy, with her soft, pretty hair tumbled, and a flush on her cheek, lay nearly at full length in the stretched-out sleepy chair, her light dress swept upon the grass, and exposing one small and perfect foot with a gossamer stocking and a darling high-heeled low-cut shoe. And Jay, flushed and hot, with his tawny curls against her breast, and one brown hand in hers, lay across her lap; her other hand, very white by contrast, holding the brown bare legs in a protecting way; some picture-books, and a broad hat or two lay upon the grass beside them. There was something in the sight that seemed to move more than the spectator's admiration; but whatever emotion it was, was quickly dispelled, and commonplace greeting and pleasure came back into his face, as Gabrielle, aroused, got up with a cry of :

"Why, papa ! where did you come from ? I—I guess I was asleep."

Missy, with a start, sat up, bewildered. She had been dreaming, perhaps, of the scene in the upper room in the house next door, which haunted her imagination. And here she was, face to face with the man over whose remorse she rather gloated, and it would be difficult to say how any one could look less remorseful than he looked now. Certainly, more genial and pleasant than she had ever seen him look before. She felt that she must have been dreaming all the occurrences of the morning. Jay fretted and refused to wake. Her dress was wet where his hot little head had been lying ; he threw his arm up over her neck and nestled back.

"I—we—what train—have you just come ?" she stammered, trying to know what she was talking of, and to believe that there was no dead face on the pillow up-stairs.

"I did not come on a train, but in a yacht," he answered, putting his arms around Gabby's shoulders, and holding her little hands in his. "We started last night. Some friends of mine are on a cruise, and persuaded me to let them bring me here. But an accident to the machinery kept us over-night at our moorings, and interminable arrangements for the cruise put us back this morning. We have had a hot day of it on the Sound, and are just arrived. See, Gabrielle, there goes the yacht out of the mouth of the harbor. It is a pity we can't run up a flag from the boat-house ; but it is too hot for exertion, and I suppose all the servants are asleep."

"Then you haven't—" faltered Missy, "you—that is—you have not been to the house—"

"No," said Mr. Andrews, looking at her as if he did not mean to be surprised at anything she might say or do. "No, I am just on shore, and unexpected at home. I hope you are quite well, Miss Rothermel ;" for Missy was turning very pale. "I am afraid that boy is too heavy for you ; let me take him."

Missy was struggling to get up, and Jay was fighting to keep his place, and not to be disturbed.

"Let me take him. Jay, be quiet. What do you mean by this, my boy ? Come to me at once."

"No, oh no !" said Missy, regaining her feet, and holding the boy in her arms. He put his damp curls down on her shoulder, and both arms around her neck, and with sleepy, half-shut, obstinate eyes, looked down upon the ground, and up upon his father.

Gabrielle, seeing the situation, said, amazed : "*Don't* you know, papa?" and then stopped suddenly, and looked frightened.

"Hush, Gabrielle," cried Missy, trembling. For Gabby's heartlessness would be a cruel medium through which to communicate the news.

"There is some trouble ?" said Mr. Andrews, quietly, looking from one to the other. "Do not be afraid to tell me."

"Let us go up to the house," said Missy, hurriedly, taking a few steps forward with her heavy burden. Mr. Andrews walked silently beside her, looking upon the ground, with an expression not very different from the one he wore habitually, though very different from the one he had just been wearing. Gabby hung be-

hind, looking askance at the two before her, with min-
gled curiosity and apprehension in her face.

"You need not be afraid to tell me," he said, as
they walked on. "Has anything happened? I am
quite unprepared, but I had rather know. I suppose I
have been telegraphed, if I was needed—"

"I sent the telegrams to your office," said Missy ;
"the first one at nine this morning. My brother sent
the last one. The carriage has been at every train all
day."

"It was a strange mischance. They did not know
at the office that I was going home in the yacht."

"The servants were so heedless, and they did not
even send for us."

"You forget, I do not know," said Mr. Andrews,
in a controlled voice, as she paused, in walking as well
as in speaking. For her agitation, and the weight of
the sleeping child together, made her tremble so that
she stopped, and leaned against a linden tree on the
lawn, which they were passing.

"Oh, it is hard that it should come upon me," cried
Missy desperately, as she looked at him with a strange
pair of eyes, leaning against the tree, very white and
trembling, and holding the boy to her breast.

"Yes ; it is hard," said her companion, "for I
know it must be something very painful to move you
so. I will go to my house and learn about it there.
Come, Gabrielle ; will you come with me, child ?"

"Oh, stay," cried Missy, as he stretched out his
hand to the little girl, and was going away without her,
as she began to cry and hang back, taking hold of
Missy's dress. "It will be hard to hear it there—from
servants. It is the worst news any one could hear.

How can I tell you? The poor little children, they
are left—alone—to you."

And, bursting into tears, she sunk down beside
Gabrielle on the grass, and held her and Jay in one
embrace. There was a silence but for the sobs of
Gabrielle, for Missy's tears were silent after the first
burst ; they were raining now on Jay's head, and she
kissed his forehead again and again. " I have told
you very badly," she said brokenly, after a moment.
" I hoped you would not hear it all at once ; but it was
not my fault."

There was no answer, and she went on.   " The illness was so sudden and terrible, and there was no
hope, after we knew of it.   I feel so dazed and tired I
hardly know what to tell you of it.   It is several
hours since—since all was over.   I don't suppose anything could have been done to make it different ; but
it must be so dreadful to you to think you were not
here.   Oh, I don't know at all how you can bear
it."

She looked up at him as she said this.   He stood
perfectly still and upright before her, his face paler,
perhaps, than usual, hard and rigid.   But whether he
was hearing what she said, and weighing it critically,
or whether he did not hear or comprehend, she could
not tell.   There was no change of expression, no emotion in eye or mouth to enlighten her.   She had, in
her pity for him, and her agitation at being the one to
communicate the evil tidings, forgotten the rancor
that she bore him, and the remorse that she had wished
he might endure.   These feelings begán sharply to
awaken, as she glanced at him.   She felt her tears burn
her cheeks, looking at his unmoistened eyes.   She put

down Jay upon his feet, and disengaging herself from
Gabrielle, stood up, keeping Jay's hand in hers.

"My brother will tell you all the rest," she said,
slowly moving on, leading the children. Mr. Andrews mechanically followed her, looking upon the
ground. Missy's heart beat fast; she held the children tight by the hand; it seemed to her that this was
worse than all the rest. She was not much used
to tragedy, and had never had to tell a man the wife
was dead, whom he was expecting to meet within five
minutes.

The men and women she had known had loved
each other, and lived happily together, in a measure.
She was new to this sort of experience. She was thrill-
ing with the indignation that very young persons feel
when their ideal anything is overthrown. She was,
practically, in the matter of ideals, a very young person, though she was twenty-seven.

They were very near the house now. A few more
steps and they would be at the side door that led into
the summer parlor. There was a total silence, broken
by Jay's whimpering, "I don't want to go home with
papa; I want to stay with you to-night."

Gabby, who didn't have any more cheerful recollection of home to-day than he, chimed in a petition
to stay. She thought she would rather look over aunt
Harriet's boxes, and be a little scolded, than go home
to the ejaculations and whisperings of the servants,
and have to pass That Room. This was about the
depth of her grief; but she whimpered and wanted
to stay. When they reached the steps that led up to
the door, Missy paused and turned to Mr. Andrews,
who was just behind her.

"Shall I keep the children?" she said, facing him, her cheeks flushed, a child grasping each hand.

"Yes—if you will—if you will be so kind," he said. She had hoped his voice would be shaken, would show agitation. But it did not. It was rather low, but perfectly controlled, and he knew what he was saying. He "remembered his manners." He was recollected enough to be polite; "if you will be so kind."

"Come then, children," she said, trembling all over, voice included, as she went up the steps. He walked away without any further speech. Leaving the children in the summer-parlor, she ran through the house to one of the front windows, and pushing open a little the blind, sat down palpitating and watched him going down to the gate. He walked slowly, but his step was steady. He followed the road, and did not walk across the grass, like a man who does not think what he is doing. When he reached the gate, he did not turn to the right towards his own house, to the gate of which a few steps more would have brought him, but he walked up the road, with his head down, as if pondering something. Presently, however, he turned and came back, passed the Varians' gate, and went on into his own. And then Missy lost sight of him among the trees that stood between the two houses. She threw herself upon a sofa, and pressed her hands before her eyes, as she thought of that broken, pain-strained figure, rigid on the bed up-stairs. And if he did not cry for his coldness and cruelty, she did, till her head and her eyes ached

That night, after Missy had put the children to bed in her own room, as she went down stairs, she heard St.

John sending a servant in to ask Mr. Andrews if he would see him for a few moments.

"St. John," she exclaimed, in a low voice, joining him. "Why do you send in? It is his place to send for you. I would not do it, really. I—I hate the man. I told him you would tell him everything, and he has been here four hours at least, and has never sent for you. I don't believe he wants to hear anything. I have no doubt he has had a good dinner and is reading the paper. May be he will ask you to join him with a cigar."

"Don't be uncharitable, Missy," said her brother, walking up and down the room.

"But why do you send?" persisted his sister. "He doesn't want to see you, or he would have sent."

"But I want to see him. So, Missy, don't let us talk about it any more."

It was evident to his sister that St. John did not anticipate the meeting with much pleasure. He was a little restless, for him, till the servant came back with a message, to the effect that Mr. Andrews would be very glad to see Mr. Varian at once, if he were at liberty to come. St. John looked rather pale as he kissed his sister good-night (for he was not coming back, but going directly home to the rectory), and she felt that his hand was cold.

"He is young for such experiences," she said to her mother, as she sat down beside her sofa in the summer twilight.

"He doesn't seem young to me any longer," returned her mother.

"A few days such as this would make us all old," said Missy, with a sigh, leaning her face down on her mother's arm. "Mamma, I am sure this interview is very painful to St. John. I am sure he has been charged with something to say to her husband, *by that poor soul.* How I wish it weren't wrong to ask him what it was. But,"—with a sigh—" I suppose we shall never know."

"Never, Missy. But we can be charitable. And when you are my age, my child, you will be afraid to judge any one, and will distrust the sight of your own eyes."

At this moment Miss Varian came lumbering into the room, leaning on the arm of Goneril.

"I suppose," she said, not hearing the low voices, " that Missy is at her nursery duties yet. Are you here, Dorla? I should think she might remember that you might sometimes be a little lonely, while she is busy in her new vocation."

Missy scorned to answer, but her mother said pleasantly: "Oh, she is here; her babies have been asleep some time."

"I'm not surprised. I don't believe Gabby's grief has kept her awake. That child has a heart like a pebble, small and hard. As to little Jay, he has the constitution and the endowments of a rat terrier, nothing beyond. I don't believe he ever will amount to anything more than a good, sturdy little animal."

"He will amount to a big animal, I suppose, if he lives long enough," said Missy, with a sharp intonation of contempt.

"Well, not very, if he copies his father. Gabby has all the cleverness. I should call Jay a dull child, as far as I can judge; dull of intellect, but so strong and well that it gives him a certain force."

"Aunt Harriet!" cried Missy, impatiently, "can't

you leave even children alone? What have those poor little morsels done to you, that you should defame them so?"

"Done? Oh, nothing, but waked me up from my nap this afternoon. And, you know, deprived me and your mother of much of your soothing society for the past two months."

"I haven't begrudged Missy to them," said her mother, affectionately, drawing Missy's hand around her neck in the dimness. "I think the poor little things have needed a friend for a long while, and, alas, they need one now."

"It's my impression they're no worse off to-day than they were yesterday. There is such a thing as gaining by a loss."

Mrs. Varian put her hand over Missy's mouth; Miss Varian, annoyed by not being answered, went on with added sharpness:

"Goneril says the servants tell her all sorts of stories about the state of things between master and mistress in the house next door. I am afraid the poor man isn't to blame for snubbing her, as he has done. They say she—"

"Oh, my dear Harriet," said Mrs. Varian, keeping her hand on Missy's lips, "don't you think it is a pity to be influenced by servants. It is difficult enough to tell the truth ourselves, and keep it intact when it goes through many hands; and I don't think that the ill-educated and often unprincipled people who serve us, are able at all to judge of character, and to convey facts correctly; do you? I don't doubt two-thirds of the gossip among our servants is without foundation. Imagine Goneril describing an interview between us;

to begin with, she would scarcely understand what we said, if we talked of anything but the most commonplace things. She would think we quarreled, if we differed about the characters in a novel."

"Goneril! She would not only misunderstand, but she would misstate with premeditation and malice. That woman—" And on that perennial grievance, the lady's wrath was turned, as her sister-in law meant it should be, and Missy's feelings were spared. She kissed her mother's hand secretly, and whispered "thank you."

CHAPTER VII.

MISRULE.

MRS. ANDREWS died late in August. Late in September, one afternoon, Missy walked up and down at the foot of the lawn, and pondered deeply on the state of things. That anything could go on worse than things went on in the house next door, she felt to be improbable. That any children could be more neglected, more fretted, more injudiciously treated, she knew to be impossible. She did not mind it much that the servants plundered their master, and that waste and extravagance went on most merrily. But that her poor Jay should be reduced indeed to the level of a rat terrier, by the alternate coaxing and thwarting of the low creatures who had him in charge, was matter of different moment. It was very bad for Gabrielle, of course. But Gabrielle was not Jay, and that made all the difference. Still, even to save Gabrielle, Missy would have made a good fight, if she had known what way to go to work. The children were with her as much as ever; at least Jay was. Gabrielle was a little more restless under restraint, and a good deal more unfathomable than a month ago. She was intimate with one of the maids, and the Frenchman was in love with this maid, and petted and joked with Gabrielle, who seemed to carry messages between them, and to be much interested in their affairs. She was more contented at home, and less often came to look over Aunt Harriet's boxes of treasures and to be catechised by her as a return.

As to Jay, he was passionate and stubborn, and Missy's heart was broken by a fib he had just told her. The father came home at night, and always, she believed, asked for the children, and when they could be found, and made superficially respectable, they were brought to the table for a little while. But Jay fell asleep sometimes, with his head on the table-cloth, overcome with the long day's play. And Gabby, after she had got a little money out of his pocket, and a little dessert off his plate, preferred the society of the servants, and went away to them. In the morning, they rarely breakfasted with him. They were sometimes not up, and never dressed in time for that early meal. They took their meals before or after the servants, as those dignitaries found most convenient. Once, poor Jay wandered in hungry and cross at nine o'clock, and told Missy he had had nothing to eat, and that Gabby was dancing for the servants in the kitchen, while they ate their breakfast. They made such a noise, Jay said, they made his head ache, and he acknowledged to kicking one of the women who wouldn't go and get him his breakfast, and being put out from the festive scene in disgrace. He ate muffins and omelette on Missy's lap, that morning, but it did not probably make the other mornings any better. No one could advise anything. Mrs. Varian could see no way out of it, and painful as it was, could suggest nothing but patience. It was manifestly not their business to offer any interference. St. John, his sister appealed to in vain. Except the interview on the evening of the wife's death, and the few moments' preceding the funeral services, there had been no communication between them. St. John had called, but Mr. Andrews had been away from the house at the moment. On Sundays, he did not go to church— on week days, he was in the city. St. John told his sister, very truly, it would be impertinence to force himself upon a person so nearly a stranger, and she quite agreed with him. But Jay !

"Why isn't he my child, and why can't I snatch him up and run away with him," she cried, tossing a handful of pebbles into the water and wrapping her cloak closer around her as she walked away from the beach-gate. She could not understand eloping with a man, but with her tawny-haired mannikin she could have consented to fly, she felt.

It was a high September tide ; the water was lapping against the wall, the sky was blue, the wind was fresh. It was not yet sunset ; she suspected there were visitors in the house ; a carriage had driven up to the stable, from which she turned away her head, and

which she resolved not to recognize. Hastily following a path that led up to the little wooded eminence
that skirted the shore, she concealed her inhospitable
thoughts and was out of sight of the house. " I don't
really know who they were," she said to herself, when
she was safe in the thicket. "So many people have
bay horses, and I did not see the coachman. And
how could I waste this glorious afternoon in the
house ? They will amuse Aunt Harriet, and I could
not be with mamma if I were entertaining them. I
am quite right in making my escape."

The little path was narrow and close ; the thicket
almost met above her head. It was very still in there ;
the wind could not get in, and only the sound of the
waves, washing on the shore below, could.

> " Where, through groves deep and high,
>   Sounds the far billow,
> Where early violets die
>   Under the willow—"

she sang in a low voice, as from a little child she had
always sung, or thought, as she passed along this
tangled path. To be sure, it had the disadvantage of
being a low thicket of cedars, instead of a grove deep
and high. And the far billow was a near wave, and a
small one at that. But she had always had to translate her romance into the vernacular. She had grown
up in tame, pastoral green ways, in a home outwardly
and inwardly peaceful and unmarked ; and her young
enthusiasms had had to fit themselves to her surroundings, or she should have been discontented with them.
A good deal of imagination helped her in this. She
loved the scenes for their own sakes, and for the sake

5

of all the romance with which they were interwoven.
A sense of humor even did not interfere. She laughed
at herself as she grew older ; but she loved the places
just as well, and went on calling them by their ficti-
tious names.

Clouds of Michaelmas daisies bordered the path ;
purple asters crowded up among the dead leaves and
underbrush. She liked them all ; and the dear old
path seemed sweeter and more sheltered to her than
ever. Still, she felt a care and an oppression unusual
to her ; she could not forget little Jay, who was almost
always at her side when she walked here. She crossed
the little bridge, that spanned what had been a "ra-
vine" to her in younger days ; and climbing up the
hill, stopped on the top of a sandy cliff, crowned with
a few cedars and much underbrush. Here was the
blue bay spread out before her ; the neck of land and
the island that closed in the bay were all in bright
autumn yellow and red. Sweet fern and bayberry
made the air odorous ; the little purplish berries on
the cedars even gave out their faint tribute of smell
in the clear, pure air. There was a seat in the low
branch of a cedar, just on the edge of the bank. Here
she sat down and tossed pebbles down the sandy steep,
and thought of the perplexing question—how to rescue
Jay ; and Gabby, too, in parenthesis. Gabby was
always in parenthesis, but she was not quite forgotten.

Presently, on the still autumn atmosphere came the
faint smell of a cigar. At the same moment, the crash-
ing of a man's tread among the dry underbrush, in
the opposite direction from whence she had herself
come. Before she had time to speculate on the subject, Mr. Andrews stood before her, coming abruptly

out of the thicket. He was as much surprised as she, and perhaps no better pleased. It was impossible for either to be unconscious of the last interview they had had just one month ago. Mr. Andrews' complexion grew a little darker, which was an indication that he was embarrassed, perhaps to find he was on the Varian's land; perhaps that he was confronting a young woman who did not approve of him; perhaps that he was confronting any young woman at all. Who knows —these middle-aged men with thick skins may have sensibilities of which no one dreams, and of which no one is desired to dream.

Miss Rothermel's ordinarily colorless cheeks were quite in a flame. She half rose from her cedar seat, and then irresolutely sat down again. Mr. Andrews threw away his cigar down the sand bank, and without looking irresolute, possibly felt so, as he paused beside her. Her first word sealed him in his resolution not to raise his hat and pass on, as he would have done in an ordinary place. It was quite in character for her to speak first.

"I didn't know you were in the country to-day," she said with embarrassment. "You do not stay up very often, do you?"

Then she thought she couldn't possibly have chosen a remark more personal and unwise. She did not like him to think she knew his habits, and speculated about them. But here, she had told him the first thing.

"No," he said, "I do not stay up very often. I came home to-day in the noon train to give the children a drive this afternoon; but I found when I reached home, that they had gone off with the servants on a picnic. Perhaps you knew about it? I own I was surprised."

"No," said Missy, flushing more deeply, "I did not know anything about it, till they had gone away, and I disapproved it very much ; not that I have any right to approve or disapprove ; but I am very fond of Jay—and—and—oh, Mr. Andrews, I wonder if you would think it unpardonable if I said something to you !"

Mr. Andrews may have doubted whether he should think what she had to say very agreeable ; but he was too gentlemanly to intimate it. She looked so eager and interested, and it was all about his boy. So he said indefinitely, that she was only too good to the children, and it was impossible for him to think any- thing she said unpardonable.

Missy, with an underlying conviction that she was doing the precise thing that she had made up her mind not to do—rushed on with a hurried statement of the picnic facts ; how Gabby had known the plan for two or three days, and had closely guarded the secret ; how provisions had been put over night in the sail-boat, and the champagne carried down in the early dawn ; and how dear little Jay, carried away by the tide of excitement, and tutored by the infamous maids, had actually told her a falsehood, and explained to her the night before that she need not look for him in the morning, for he should be in town all day with his papa, who was going to take him to the dentist. Mr. Andrews uttered an exclamation at this last statement, and ground his cane into the ground at the root of the cedar-tree. "Poor little Jay," said Missy, looking ready to cry. "Think what a course of evil he must

have been put through to have been induced to say that.
Gabrielle I am not surprised at. She isn't truthful.
It doesn't seem to be her nature. I—I—didn't mean
to say that exactly."

"You needn't mind," said her companion, bitterly.
"I am afraid it is the truth."

"But Jay," said Missy, hurriedly, "is so sweet-
natured, and so clear and honest, I can't think how
they could have made him do it. It only shows me
how dreadful his temptations are, and how much he
must go through when he is at home."

"I don't see how it can be helped," said the father
with a sort of groan. "I can't be with them all the
time; and if I were perhaps I shouldn't mend the
matter. I suppose they must take their chance like
others."

"Very well, if you are satisfied," she said stiffly.

"But I am not satisfied," he answered. "I should
think I needn't assure you of that. But I feel helpless,
and I don't know what to do. I don't want to part
with the children just yet, you can understand that, no
doubt. And yet I don't see what arrangement I can
make to improve their condition at home. You must
see it is perplexing."

"Will you let me tell you what to do," cried Missy,
eagerly, twisting her fingers together as she spoke.

"Gladly," he returned, looking down at her.

"Turn away every servant in your house." He
looked blank and dismayed.

"They are as bad a lot as ever were brought together," she said. "They are neither honest nor truthful, nor in any sense respectable. There is not one of
them that is worth trying to reform. I don't wonder

you are dismayed at the thought of change. Men do
not know anything about such things, naturally; take
my word for it, you cannot keep them without danger
to your property, let alone your children."

"Are they worse than servants generally?" he
said, helplessly. "I thought they were always dishonest; mine have always been ever since I have had a
household."

"And we," said Missy, "have never had a dishonest
servant in our house a week."

"You have been very fortunate then."

"No," she said; "only we have had common pru-
dence, and have looked after them a little."

"Well," said Mr. Andrews, drawing a deep breath,
"if I knew how to go to work, I would get rid of them
all. But I don't really know anything about these
matters."

"If it were in your business, you would know how
to get rid of a dishonest clerk, I suppose."

"Oh, yes, that is a different matter. I could easily
deal with the men in this case. But the women—well,
really, you see it is uncomfortable. And I don't know
how to get rid of them, or where to get any better if
I do."

"Oh, that could be easily managed."

"Could it?" he said, earnestly. "Believe me, I
would do anything to—to—render the fate of my
children less unfortunate."

There was a touch of feeling in his voice that softened Missy.

"I wish you would be resolute about this then, and
make the change at once. I could—mamma could tell
you, perhaps, of good servants, and how to manage.

Believe me, it isn't so hard sending off servants and getting new ones. I wish you were as angry with these as I am. You would not find it hard."

Mr. Andrews smiled a little, but it was faintly, and he looked perplexed.

"If I only knew what to do," he said again. "If you will tell me the way, I will walk in it."

"Well, in the first place," said Missy, nothing loth, "I would take the horses at once and drive over to Eel Creek, where I understand the picnic party are, and capture the children—they may not get home till midnight, for you see the wind is against them, and these men know nothing about sailing. No doubt they meant to be home long before this time, starting so early, but they are not in sight. I have been watching for them. Then bring the children to our house; we will take care of them till matters are settled. Then, you know, when the servants get home, after being detected in such a scrape as this, they can expect nothing but to be dismissed. I am sure they would be much surprised at any other ending of the adventure, and they will take it very quietly."

"Oh, I'm not afraid of them, I believe," said Mr. Andrews, with a smile. "Only I don't exactly know how to go about it. What have they done? What shall I say to them? Is going on a picnic without permission sufficient ground to dismiss them all at once?"

"The champagne is, and the claret—and the chickens—and the deceit—and the children—and the sailboat!" exclaimed Missy, rather incoherently.

"I suppose you are right," said Mr. Andrews, with

a sigh. "They may well be glad to get off without any trouble."

"They may indeed. And if you call them together to-night, and speak severely to them, and tell them to pack their trunks and leave by the noon train to-morrow, they will think they have got off very easily."

"But what shall we do after they are gone?" asked Mr. Andrews, despondently.

"Oh, that is easy enough!" cried Missy, starting up and taking the path back to the house, her companion following her. "Mamma and I will take care of the children for a few days, till you are all settled. And there is an old servant of ours living in the village, who will go to you and take charge of things till you get your servants. She is quite capable—cooks well, and will do everything you need for a little while; and it is easy enough to get a man to look after the horses for a day or two, till you are suited with a coachman. One of the Rogers boys would do very well; they are honest, good people, all of them, and need work just now. They understand horses thoroughly; we had Tom ourselves for awhile. You needn't be afraid of them."

"They couldn't possibly be worse than Michael. I am sure I don't know how to thank you enough. The way really looks quite easy. But how about the new women? where am I to look for them?"

"Well, it depends," said Missy, "on what sort of service you want. Now, to be frank with you, Mr. Andrews, you have just twice as many servants as you need. But maybe you like to have a great many; some people do. I don't, you know. I can't bear to have a servant in the house who has no *raison d'être*.

Half your servants have no reasonable excuse for being in your house, except that they want your money."

"I always wondered," said Mr. Andrews, humbly, "why we needed so many; but there seemed no way of being comfortable with less."

"You see it is a small house," said Missy; "the work of keeping it in order is not great. And in winter—but I don't suppose you mean to stay in winter?"

"Yes, I mean to stay this winter. I think no place could be better for the children, if I can get the proper people to take care of them."

"Well, then you want to get—first, a cook. I don't suppose you'll have much company?"

"None, probably."

"Then you do not want a very pretentious one. A good plain cook—unless you want a great many *entrées* and great variety."

"Oh, as to that, I am thankful if I get three courses. The present cook began bravely, but has been cutting me down steadily. Yesterday we had no soup, and the day before, boiled rice and raisins for dessert."

"Oh," exclaimed Missy, indignantly, "that is an outrage, indeed! Well, I think if you could be patient under that, you could get along with a plain cook."

"Why must she be a plain cook?"

"Because," said Missy, artlessly, "if she is a plain cook and doesn't understand *entrées* and all that, she will help in the washing, and it would be *such* a blessing if you did not have to have a fourth woman in the house."

5*

Mr. Andrews looked bewildered, as he opened the gate for her to pass out.

"You see," said Missy, apologetically, "it is such a silly thing to have servants that you don't need. They are in each other's way in a small house. You need a good plain cook, and a waitress, and let these two do the washing and ironing. And then you need a nurse, or a nursery governess, a quiet, nice person, who will do everything for the children, including their mending. And then you need a coachman. And—well, of course you'll know whether it will be comfortable or not when you've tried it for a few weeks. But I am quite sure you will not lack anything that you have now, except disorder."

"I am sure of it," said Mr. Andrews, submissively.

"The most important of all," said Missy, as they crossed the lawn, "is the nurse—and I think I know the very person. I must ask mamma if she does not think she would do very well. She lives a mile or two out of the village; is a well brought up, well-educated girl, quite used to work, and yet quite capable of teaching. She has such a quiet, steady manner. I think her influence over the children would be so good. She manages her own little brothers and sisters well, I have noticed. Besides, she would probably come to you for very little more than the wages of an ordinary servant."

Missy colored after she said this. It seemed quite absurd for her to be economizing for her neighbor; but it was quite an involuntary action of her thrifty mind.

"I beg your pardon," she said, confusedly. "It seems very officious, but you know I can't help thinking it is a pity to spend money without thought.

Mamma laughs at me, but I can't help feeling annoyed at seeing a great deal spent to save the trouble of a little thought. That is why people go on multiplying servants, and paying whatever may be asked for wages, because they do not want to give themselves the trouble of thinking and planning about it."

"I think you are quite right," said Mr. Andrews. "And I beg you will not imagine that my household extravagances are with intention. I have always regretted that I could not have things managed differently, but I could not find a way to do it."

This was dangerous ground, and Missy wished herself off it, particularly as it was humbling to find herself on such familiar, counsel-giving terms with this brutal husband; but, in truth, she had been quite carried away by the near prospect of Having Her Own Way. She looked a little confused, and was silent as they walked along. It did not seem to be unnatural or uncomfortable to be silent with Mr. Andrews, who was essentially a silent man. Just before they reached the house, she gave a last look back towards the bay.

"I do not see them," she said, "they are not yet inside the harbor. I should not wonder if you caught them before they start from Eel Creek. Probably they were all day getting there."

"You are right, and I ought to hurry."

"You know the road to Eel Creek?"

"Well, yes, I think so; I am not quite sure, but probably I can find it. I have a general idea."

"If there is any doubt, take one of our men with you."

"Thank you, that won't be necessary. I will inquire my way. Miss Rothermel, you have been

very good—I don't know how I can thank you
enough."

"Oh, as to that, don't thank me till you have got
the other side of the trouble. Only don't give out—"

"You are afraid of me," he said with a smile.
"Well, I acknowledge I am rather a coward, when
it comes to the management of maid-servants.
But I will be firm."

They had now got to the steps that led into the summer parlor, and as she turned to go up them, she gave
a look at her companion, who was lifting his hat and
passing on. He looked so stalwart and so invincible,
that she believed he was anything but a coward, except where women were concerned. Somewhere,
however, there must be a loose scale in his armor.
He certainly was the sort of man tyrannized over
easily by women.

"And yet," thought Missy, correcting the conviction, "in one case we know he was a brutal tyrant.
But no matter. Anything to rescue Jay." So she gave
him a pleasant smile, and told him they should wait
tea for the children, and went into the house, while he
walked rapidly towards the gate.

CHAPTER VIII.

A TEA TABLE TRUCE.

WO hours later, Mr. Andrews drove up to the door, in the darkness, with a pair of sleepy children, and a pair of restless horses, and a coachman feeling deeply the surreptitious claret and champagne. Missy, hearing the turbulent voice of Jay, ran to the door, accompanied by Ann. The bright light from the hall came flooding on the piazza as the door opened, and Missy, reaching out her arms to take the sleepy boy from his father, looked like a good angel, to his eyes. Gabby was following up the steps and whimpering audibly.

"You will have your hands full, Miss Rothermel, I am afraid," he said gloomily. "The children are very cross. But I am thankful that I took your advice. The carouse was not nearly over. I believe the children would have been drowned, if I had not gone for them. The creatures were just embarking for the return voyage, all as drunk as lords. Heaven knows what might have happened if they had got off. I ordered them on shore, and put the sail-boat in charge of the man who lives near the beach, and the wretches are to come home on foot. The walk may sober them a little."

"Poor little Jay," cried Missy, hugging him. He slapped her, and then began to roar with remorse and headache combined, and to throw himself back and try

to fall out of her arms. They were now in the hall.
His father, horrified, began to reprove him.

"Oh, don't," cried Missy, "poor little man. He is
not responsible. To-morrow morning he'll be all right.
Come, Gabby, take off your hat, child."

"I don't know what I should have done with them,
if I had not had this refuge," said Mr. Andrews, looking careworn indeed.

"Oh, that is nothing," said Missy cheerily ; "we are
so glad to have them. And you, Mr. Andrews, mamma begs you will come in to tea."

"That will be impossible, I'm afraid ; thank you
very much," he said, looking anxiously back towards
the door, whence came the sound of stamping horses,
and an occasional mumbled ejaculation and a frequently snapped whip. "I have to look after the
horses, and this man."

"Let Peters do that," said Missy, bent on her own
way. She had determined to bury the hatchet and to
have Mr. Andrews stay to tea. She felt it was a gracious thing to do, though rather hard, and having
made up her mind to an act of magnanimity, objected
to being thwarted.

"Mamma wants to see you," she said. "Besides,
you have not had any dinner, and you will not probably get any at home, unless you cook it yourself. Let
Peters go in and attend to the stable. It is the only
thing to do."

"Perhaps you are right," he said, irresolutely.
"Well, as you are so kind, I will go home, and lock a
few of the doors, and return in a moment."

As he drove off, Missy heard him say a word or
two to the coachman, which convinced her he was not

afraid of men servants, whatever he might be of maid
servants. Ann was sent to call Peters. Gabby, who
was really ill from over-eating and over-fatigue, was
sent to bed in care of Goneril. Jay, who pled to stay
up to tea, was allowed to lie on the sofa beside the
fire, and get warmed after his long exposure to the
night air. Missy covered him with an afghan, and
kneeling down beside him, had just seen his eyes close
in unconquerable sleep, when Mr. Andrews came in.
He was half way across the room before her mother's
" Missy ! " started her to her feet. " Oh, I beg your
pardon ; I did not hear you. Mamma, let me present
Mr. Andrews."

Mrs. Varian half rose from her sofa, and Mr. Andrews thought her lovely and gracious, as every one
else did. He bowed to Miss Varian ; and, no doubt, he
thought they were all angels, as indeed he was excusable for thinking, coming from the dark and hopeless tangle of his own house. The cheer of the fire
and the lamp, the odor of the flowers, the grace of the
woman who had arisen to welcome him, the kindness
of the one who had been kneeling beside his little
outcast, the air of order, luxury, peace, all filled him
with a sense that he had been living in another world,
on the other side of the arbor-vitæ hedge. He was, as
has been said, a silent man, and one of those straightforward men who never seem to think that they need
to speak when they have nothing to say. He was not
silent from shyness, but from simplicity of motive,
from a native honesty ; consequently, his silence was
not oppressive, but natural. To-night, however, there
was much to say. There were the details of the
broken-up camp at Eel Creek, the various stages of hi-

larity and depression among the servants, the danger
of the children, the probabilities of a slow march, the
ludicrous side of the coming midnight court-martial.
When they were ready to go in to tea, Missy stayed
behind for an instant to tuck Jay's afghan about him
and put a chair beside him, and to feel whether his
pulse was quick. " Bless him," she whispered, giving
him a kiss, " better days are coming."

The tea table was as graceful and pretty as possible ; the things to eat rarely good, and Mr. Andrews,
poor man, had been fasting all day. He despised
lunch, and he hadn't had any chance to get a dinner ; so
no wonder he appreciated the tea that was set before
him. Miss Varian was in a good humor, and quite
sharp and witty, and whatever Mrs. Varian said, was always gracious and delightful. Miss Rothermel had
enough to do to pour out the tea, and she was quite
satisfied with the march of events, including Mr.
Andrews' appetite, and the complexion of the waf-
fles. She thought of the soupless dinner he had mentioned, and of the alms-house provision of boiled rice
and raisins, and she felt for a moment, what bliss to
keep house for a man with such an appetite and no
ascetic tendencies. St. John was a continual trial to
her. But then she checked herself sharply, and thought
how deceitful appearances were, and how cruel had
been the lot of the woman who had kept house for
him, till alas, a month ago exactly. It was a bitter
commentary on her fate, that he was able to enjoy
broiled oysters so unblushingly within thirty days of his
bereavement. Happily, behind the tea-kettle, Missy's
dark frown was hidden ; but she soon threw it off ;

she had made up her mind to be amiable for this one
evening, and she would not break her resolution.

After tea, when they were again around the parlor
fire, St. John came in. The sight of him changed the
expression of the guest's face ; the care-worn look
came back, and a silence. Before very long, he said,
rising, that he must go home, and make ready for the
reception of the criminals. This was plainly a thing
that ought to be done, and Mrs. Varian had been thinking so for half an hour. St. John went with him to
the door, and Missy heard Mr. Andrews say, as they
parted on the piazza : "I have wanted to see you. I
hope you don't think that, because our interview was
what it was, I shrink from further acquaintance.
Perhaps *I* should have gone to you, and said this.
I hope you will take it now. You can understand how
hard it is for me to say this."

"I do understand," said St. John earnestly ; "and
I hope that the painful association will not interfere
with our future intercourse. Perhaps *I* should have
gone to *you*, and said this."

She lost what followed—an irreparable loss. She
had been standing at the window, which was open, behind the curtain, and could not have helped hearing
what they said.

"Rather a high and mighty penitent," she said to
herself, indignantly, going over his words in her mind.
"And St. John is so young, and so—well, I am afraid
he's weak. It is natural for people to be weak when
they are young. He seemed only anxious to propiti-
ate him. I suppose he hopes in that way to get an influence over him. Of course, it must be hard to stand

up against a man of double his own age ; but I should
think being a priest would give him courage."

At this time, Jay woke up, and, in taking him to
bed, she missed St. John's return to the parlor, and
the remainder of his visit. "Mamma, what do you
think of him ?" she said, sitting down beside her mother's sofa late that night.

"I rather like him," was the answer.

"Yes, if one could forget everything. I think he
is gentlemanly, and unobjectionable in manner—almost pleasing. But I suppose I ought not to forget
what I know of his cruel neglect, and of the almost
trag·c end of it."

'Of course, that seems terrible—but—"

"But, mamma !" cried Missy, "I scarcely expected
you to say that. Oh, how true it is, women are cruel
to each other. Think—you know nothing in favor of
Mr. Andrews. Everything in his disfavor : nothing
against Mrs. Andrews : everything in her favor, and
yet you say, 'I rather like him ; all this is very
terrible—*but*—' "   .

"Well, you know I had never seen the wife. You
are influenced by admiration for her. I am influenced
by something that attracts me in the husband. We
really, Missy, do not know much of the lives of either
of them."

"I know that she was neglected, left alone. That
for days together she never saw her husband. That
his manner, on receiving the news of her death, was
more stolid and indifferent than mine would have been
on being told of the sudden and suffering death of a
total stranger. I know that she hated, feared him.

And she was impulsive, quick, and probably warm-hearted."

" Probably, Missy ? Well, I don't want to wound you—but—but her children did not seem very dear to her."

" Mamma, when one is suffering as she was, natur-ally, to an undisciplined nature, life centers where the suffering is. You cannot think of anything else. You just cry out, and bend your mind upon getting through with your pain as best you may, unless you have learned the higher lesson, which of course I know she hadn't. She had not in any sense learned the uses of her suf-ferings ; I don't deny that. But who heaped those suf-ferings upon her ? Who failed to make her better, if she was not perfect, child as she was, compared with him ? Think of the difference in their ages. Oh, it makes me bitter to think of it. No, nothing can excuse him, nothing."

" It is hard to say that. Wait till we know both stories."

" Those we never shall know. She can't tell us any more of hers, poor soul, and he never will, you may be sure. Or, if he did, I should not feel bound to believe him. I assure you, I am not impressed with him as you are."

" He seems very tender towards his children."

" Yes, tender, but weak and irresolute. Possibly a little remorseful ; we don't know how long this will last. He is undoubtedly sorry he broke their poor mother's heart, as sorry as such a stout, stolid thing can be, and he doesn't want the children to be drowned by the servants, or taught to swear or steal, just now, at any rate. He is willing to second our efforts to save them. He will not oppose us, at any rate. You must acknowledge it wouldn't look well, if he did."

"Now, Missy, you are uncharitable."

"No, mamma ; you are over-charitable ; this plausible gentleman has so worked upon you. Really I—I hate him. I always have, and your taking him up so only increases my aversion."

"Excuse me. My taking him up is imaginary.

"Oh, no, mamma, believe me, you have taken his side, unconsciously to yourself. And, equally unconsciously, you have, from the very first, set yourself against her, and deplored my infatuation. I have always seen it."

"I confess that some things you told me prejudiced me against her. I felt that her personal attraction must be great to make you overlook them."

"You mean her telling me things against her husband, even as early as our first interview."

"And her indifference to her children, Missy, and her great egotism."

"I can understand, mamma, how this would strike you. I am quite sure if you had known her, you would not have wondered, or blamed ; you would only have pitied. She spoke to me because she saw my friendship, and because, poor soul, she had seen no one but the servants for weeks or months. I shouldn't have wondered if she had told me her whole history the first time that I saw her."

"But she never did tell you her whole history, Missy. You know nothing of it really, notwithstanding all the time you spent with her."

"And that you find against her ! Really, mamma, you are hard to please. You reproach her for telling me so much, and you distrust her because she did not tell me more."

"Vague accusations, and complaints of injustice are easily made, Missy. I should think we were in a better position to judge of matters, if you had ever had a plain story of her life and its wrongs given to you."

"I wish, for.your sake, that I had ; but perhaps it was more noble in her to die without doing it. I am afraid, mamma, we shall never think alike about this. But if you can't sympathize with me, at least do not try me by too much approbation of this man. I will bear anything in reason ; but if you and Aunt Harriet and St. John all continue to pay homage to him as you did to-night, I shall think it rather trying."

"Oh, as to that, I think we were only civil ; and you were quite as amiable as we—which, my dear, you must continue to be, if you hope to keep any hold over Jay's fate. Poor little fellow ! do not, by an unnecessary show of rancor, throw him back into the arms of Alphonsine and Bridget."

"That is the only thing," said Missy, crossing the room to fasten the window for the night. "I mean to get my own way about him ; and I only hope it will not involve speaking many more words, good or bad, to his father."

CHAPTER IX.

THE SWEETS OF VICTORY.

HE next morning a little note came from Mr. Andrews. It was addressed to Missy.

"Dear Miss Rothermel—

"The woman named Alphonsine is very penitent, and begs to stay. Do you think I might allow her?   Very truly yours,

"JAMES ANDREWS."

Missy dashed off a reply on the other side of his sheet of paper in pencil.

"Don't keep her on any account. She is the worst of them all.   A. R."

As Missy twisted this up and handed it to the messenger, Mrs. Varian rather anxiously asked to see it. "Don't you even put it in an envelope?" she said glancing over the meagre slip. "Your notes are generally so nice; this doesn't look like you, and is hardly civil."

"Business is business," said Missy, twisting it up again, and going out to give it to the messenger. "I don't think it is worth while to waste monograms and London paper on such matters as these."

"What sudden thrift! Where are the children?"

"I am going to look for them," said Missy, drawing on her gloves. "I want to get them out of the

way, and keep them safe, till the hegira is over. I
haven't much faith in Mr. Andrews' having the nerve
to do it ; but perhaps I don't do him justice. If they
are not all got off by the noon train to-day, I shall
know it will never be done."

Missy carried the children out with her in the pony-
wagon ; she even took Mr. Andrews' intentions to be so
probable of execution, that she went two or three miles
inland to see the woman whom she had fixed upon in
her own mind, as the successor to Alphonsine in the
care of the children. She even stopped at the tin-
man's, in the village, to get the address of a good
substantial cook, whom she knew to be out of place,
who had a settled reputation for bread-baking, and
an honorable record in the matter of soup. She did
not say for whom she wanted her—she was a little
ashamed of taking it for granted, that her advice
would be acted upon. All the same, it was as well to
be prepared. She even drove to a house in one of the
bye-streets of the village, to see if a certain Ellen,
whose black eyes and white aprons had always met
her approval, was still out of a situation. All these
were at her command—cook, waitress, and nurse. It
was fascinating to have everything go so smooth.
How delightful to have your own way ; how heavenly
to make people carry out your plans. Through it all
there ran one little thread of doubt as to the steadfast-
ness of Mr. Andrews ; this only gave the matter zest.
She felt as if it were quite a stirring little vaudeville ; it
wasn't worth while to make tragedy out of it, and get
angry if she were disappointed—but altogether she liked
it. She liked driving about with her brisk little pony on
a bright September morning like this, doing her errands,

giving her orders, having people come out smiling to
their gates to speak to her.   She liked all this, even
when it was only her own errands she did, and her
own ordinary housekeeping that she looked out for.
It was a pleasure to secure the best butter and the
freshest eggs, and to drive to pretty, cool-looking farm-
houses for them ; to go for cornmeal and graham flour
just ground, to a romantic-looking old mill by the
edge of the woods, where the drip of the water and
the shade of the trees made a perpetual cool.   People
who had things to sell were always glad to see her,
for she bought a great many things and paid a good
price for them.   She was often called upon for favors
and for advice, and this pleased her.   The sight of the
pretty little carriage was a signal for many an in-
habitant of farm-house or village, to come out to the
roadside and have a consultation with the young lady
who drove it.   She was a favorite, and it is pleasant to
be important—and to have your own way.   She
generally had hers, even about other people's matters,
for it was a very good way, and a good way presented
in such a manner as was convincing.   Of course, she
had her disappointments ; the clam-man's daughter
did, on one occasion, marry the scallop-man's son,
against her advice—but they came to such speedy
grief, that it more than consoled her.   The miller's
wife was not willing, last Spring, to listen to reason
about her butter, and so had lost all market for it
among the people who paid high prices, and had to
carry it, finally, to the "store," and take what she could
get for it.   Missy lost the butter, but she had the
satisfaction of knowing, that the next year her advice
would be promptly taken.   All these things were sweet

to her, but how much sweeter it was to be feeling that she was managing completely a household in which she had no legitimate business to interfere ; that she was putting to rout a troop of worthless servants who had opposed her, and ill-treated her darling Jay. Above all, that she was making a very weak-kneed master stand firm. Oh, if she could be sure that he *would* stand firm ! It was this doubt, that made her feel as if it were all genteel comedy, and really quite exciting.

The children were pretty good that morning, notwithstanding the orgies of the night before. Gabrielle was subdued and a little ashamed, and Jay's memory was not burdened with any remorse, nor had he missed his sleep, nor omitted to make a very good breakfast in his new quarters. He was burly and jolly and good as ever. He liked the drive, and the stops, and the fresh cool breeze, and the bright September sunshine, and the holding the whip in his hand.

The roadside was bright with golden-rod and purple asters, the Virginia creeper was turning red on the fences and over the trees where it had flung itself ; catbrier, shining and glossy, cedar dark and dusky, sumach red and brown, all in mat and tangle of the luxuriant summer's growth, clothed the banks that edged the road. Jay stretched out his hand to catch the bright leaves when they passed near them ; the bottom of the carriage was filled with branches of red leaves, with bunches of Michaelmas daisies and asters already withering in the sun.

Missy looked at her watch ; it was just noon. Her heart beat high. They were on the road that led to the station. If the servants were sent off by the mid-

6

day train, they must meet them in the course of a few
moments. She now began to doubt whether it had
not all fallen through. It was impossible to say how
she despised Mr. Andrews when she thought it might
be that he had given in. Every rod of road they passed over added to this conviction. She looked at her
watch again. If they did not meet them within five
minutes there was no further hope.

"What's the matter, Missy ; why do you pull the
pony so ?" said Jay, looking up into her face. They
were going down a hill, where the road was narrow,
deep and sandy. At this moment they heard the
lumbering, and caught sight of a heavy vehicle coming
up the hill towards them.

"It's the stage !" cried Gabby, growing interested.
"And there's Léon, and there's Bridget, and there's
Alphonsine, and all of 'em."

Jay at this news set up a great shout, and started
to his feet.

"Sit down, Jay," cried Missy ; "don't you see
there isn't room for the stage to pass. I tell you to
be quiet." Missy had her hands full in managing Jay,
and getting the pony out of the road, with his head up
into the bushes. This was the only part of the narrow road where they could pass, so she had to draw
up on one side, and wait while the heavy stage crawled
up the hill. The information was soon telegraphed
through the gloomy ranks, who presented a sullen
front. The stage was driven by one Moses, who had
always driven it since any one could remember. He
sat bent up like a bow, with years of long and lazy
driving ; his hat pushed a little back on his head. He
nodded indifferently to Missy. It was all he did to

any one, so no one could complain. Beside him sat
Léon, dark and scowling ; behind them sat Michael,
red and wrathful ; behind him again, the dismissed
cook, laundress, nurse, and last of all, Alphonsine. It
was the wreck of a household, indeed. Missy felt a
momentary elation when she saw them all together.
She had not realized how many there were, before, and
to what a complete rout she had put them. It was
rather awkward, drawing up by the roadside, and having them all pass in review before her, as it were ; but
it could not be helped—the condition of a Long Island
road never can be helped. A heavy wagon, driven
by one of the sons of Moses, the stage-driver, filled
with the trunks of the departing servants, crawled on
after the stage. The boy was rather rakish-looking ;
he sat on one of the trunks and smoked a very bad
cigar, which he was not at the pains to remove from
his mouth when he approached the lady. She glanced
quickly at the trunks, and a wandering wish passed
through her mind that she might see the inside of
them, and estimate roughly the degree to which the
master had been plundered. She cast her eyes down
after this, or only allowed them to rest on her pony,
who did not like being crowded up into the bushes,
and did not stand quite still. It is very possible that
all might have gone well, if Jay could have behaved
himself decently ; but his old wrath returned when he
saw Michael, and saw him from a friend's side.

" Hurrah !" he shouted, getting on his feet on the
seat. "Hurrah ! You have got sent away, and it
was because you got drunk, and was bad yesterday,
and I am glad of it, I am."

Michael was too angry and too much the worse for

the last night's revel, to control himself. " You little
devil," he cried, and shook his fist at the boy.

Even then, if the boy could have been subdued, it is
possible that the habit of decent silence before their
betters, would have kept them all quiet till they were
out of hearing of the party in the pony carriage. They
all knew or suspected that Missy was their enemy, but
she was dignified, and no word had ever broken their
habit of respect to her. She flushed up and tried to
keep Jay quiet, and did not look towards the stage,
now floundering through the sand alongside. But she
had also the pony to keep under, and he required both
hands. Jay did not like to be called a little devil, and
there was no one to stop him, except by counsel, which
he did not ever much regard ; he made a dash with
the whip, and lurching forward, struck towards Michael
with all his small might. The end of the lash, fine
and stinging, reached that person's red, and sun-
scorched cheek.

"I'll teach you to call me little devil," cried Jay,
as he dealt the blow.

A howl of rage escaped the man, though it must
have hurt him very little. He made a spring for Jay.
The stage was going so slowly it was not difficult
for him to leap from it and land beside the little
carriage. Moses pulled up, much interested. Moses'
son, behind, pulled up, interested quite as much.
Michael caught the boy with a fierce hand. Missy
leaned forward, exclaiming, " Don't touch the child.
I forbid you. Don't touch him, unless you want to get
yourself in trouble ! "

A chorus of indignation burst from the crew in the
stage. Michael, backed by this, shook the child fiercely

in her very lap, boxed his ears, with one brutal hand
after the other, and then hurled him back upon her,
and swung himself into the stage again. A shower of
coarse and horrid words assailed poor Missy's ears, as
she caught him in her disengaged arm. It had never
been her luck before to be assailed by an Irish tongue,
loosed from the decency of servitude. She had never
had "words" with any of her mother's servants. This
was quite a new experience. She was white to her
fingers' ends. Jay did not cry. He was white too.
Not cowed, but overpowered by brute strength, and
stunned by the blows he had got. Missy never knew
exactly what they said; some horrid words always stuck
in her memory, but it was all a confused hideous jumble
besides. The women's tongues were the worst, their
voices the shrillest, the things they said the ones that
stuck in the memory most. Moses was so interested he
sat open-mouthed and gazed and listened. His son, infinitely delighted, gazed and listened too. At last,
Missy found voice to say, above the general babel :

"Moses, will you drive on, and let me pass ? You
will lose the train if you don't go at once."

This recalled to him the fact that he had the mail-
bag at his feet, and losing the train meant losing the
patronage of the Government of the United States.

"By Jingo, that's a fact !" said Moses, gathering
up the reins, and calling out "gee-up" to the lean
horses, who had been very glad to rest. The stage
lumbered on, and left the pony-carriage free to move,
after the baggage-wagon should have passed. But the
baggage-wagon was driven by Moses' son, and he had
no desire to shorten or renounce the fun. He did not
carry the United States mail. He was probably not

unfamiliar with Billingsgate, and was not shocked, only pleasantly excited, by the language employed. He even hurrahed a little, and laughed, and struck his hands upon his knees, as Jay was pitched back into the carriage, white and silenced. He liked a fight exceedingly, he did—any kind of a fight.

As the stage moved on, and the viragoes leaned back and shook their fists at the little carriage, and the two men roared back their imprecations at it, he had not the heart to move on, and let the pony out into the road. He knew how the little beast would dash away out of sight down the hill, under Miss Rothermel's whip ; they would be out of hearing in a second. No, he couldn't do a thing like that. It wasn't in him to spoil a fight. He laughed, and threw himself astride of the trunk, but didn't touch the reins, and didn't stir a step aside from blocking up the road. So it was that Missy got the full force of the parting maledictions ; so it was that she got the full tide of Irish, mixed with the finer-grained shafts of French invective ; so it was that she knew that Alphonsine had read the little note that she had sent in that morning to the relenting master, and that she was assured that she had made an enemy for life.

"We'll be aven wid ye yet !" cried Bridget.

"Mademoiselle shall hear from the 'worst of them all' again," sneered Alphonsine, darting a malignant look at her, from under her dark brows.

Then, and not till then, did the young driver of the luggage-wagon "gee-up" to his horses and move on, puffing the smoke from his villainous cigar into the faces of the pony-carriage party, as he passed them, and looking infinitely content as he jolted on. He was

not aware that he had done anything insolent or malicious. He did not know that the smell of his cigar,
and the keen amusement of his look, had been the last,
and perhaps most cutting, of the insults she had received. These wretches who had just disappeared
from her presence were strangers and foreigners, so to
speak ; but this low boy represented her home, her village, her place of influence. Poor Missy ! that was a
bitter hour. Her vaudeville was ending in a horrid
rout and rabble ; she was sore and sick with the recollection of it. She had been dragged through the mud
on the field where she had felt sure of triumph. What
was the triumph, compared to the mud ? She had succeeded in having them sent away ; but they had humiliated her, oh! most unspeakably. The degrada-
tion of having to listen to such words, and to sit,
impotent and silent before them, while they raged and
reviled her !

The pony dashed down the hill. They were out
of sight of the place of their defeat in a moment of
time; but she felt as if never, never could she get out
of sight of their leering faces, out of hearing of their
horrid words.

When they were at the bottom of the hill and had
turned into the main road, Jay began to recover from
the shock and fright, and to tremble and cry. Gabrielle never took her eyes off Missy's face ; she was full
of speculation, but such experiences were not as new
to her as to Missy. She, however, remembered, almost as well as Missy did, all those insolent words, and,
though not understanding them fully, kept them in
mind, and interpreted them in the light of events.

" Don't cry, Jay," Missy said mechanically. But she

was so shaken she could scarcely speak. She wanted
to get home and think it over; to get out of day-light,
to get breath and recover her voice again, and her self-
respect, her power of feeling herself a lady.

Jay's continued crying tortured her; Gabby's eyes
on her face angered her. She was trembling all over.
She had not made up her mind about anything, only
that everything was horrid and degrading, and that
she wished she had never seen or heard of any of the
name of Andrews—even little Jay.

As they approached the gate she saw that Mr. Andrews was walking slowly up and down before his
house, evidently watching for them. She tried to
drive quickly and pass him with a bow, but he came
up beside them as they passed through the gate, and
she had to pull up the pony and go slowly. He
walked beside the carriage and took Jay's hand, which
was stretched out to him.

" Well, I've got them all off," he said, with a sigh
of relief.

" We saw 'em all," cried Gabby, always glad to impart information. " We saw 'em all; and, oh, such a
time as we have had!"

"Michael beat me, and beat me," burst out Jay,
quite broken down at the thought of being sympa-
thized with.

"And, oh, the things they said to Missy!" exclaimed Gabby.

" And he called me a little devil, and I'll kill him!"
cried Jay, beginning to sob.

While these side-lights were being thrown upon
the occurrence, Mr. Andrews looked anxiously at

Missy, who was growing red and white, and trembling very visibly.

"Be silent, children," he said impatiently. "You have had some trouble, Miss Rothermel, I am afraid."

By this time they had reached the house; Missy threw down the reins, which Mr. Andrews caught.

"I hope nothing has happened to distress you," he said.

She did not wait to give Jay to his father, but getting out very quickly, and not noticing the hand that he offered her, said, in a voice not very steady, "I don't want to talk about it. It makes me ill to think of it. Call Peters, won't you, to take away the pony," ran up the steps and disappeared into the house. In another minute she would have cried.

He took the children out and drove the pony up to the stable. The children followed him, and he spent half an hour with them on the beach, trying to extract from them the history of the morning. It was rather difficult to get at the facts, but he got at enough to make him feel much disturbed in mind. The servant soon came down to take the children in to dinner, and to ask him to come in, too. But this he declined, wisely judging that his presence would not be very welcome now. He went back to his empty house, put the key in his pocket, and drove down to the village inn to get something to eat.

Late in the afternoon he went back to Mrs. Varian's, to ask for the counsel which had been before so freely offered him. He felt quite helpless, and could not move a step in reconstructing his household till he had been told what to do. The afternoon was quite clear, and since the sun had set, the fire on the

6*

hearth in the library looked very cheerful. The servant let him into that room. There he found the children playing together a game of checkers, and Goneril watching them. Ann went up-stairs to summon Miss Rothermel, but returned presently to say that Miss Rothermel was lying down with a severe headache, and begged that Mr. Andrews would excuse her. Miss Varian, who was in the adjoining parlor, dozing in a big arm-chair, roused at the sound of voices, and called to Goneril to come and lead her into the library. It was always an amusement to have a visitor, and she asked Mr. Andrews to sit down again, which he was very ready to do—his own house at present being a very uncheerful place to sit down in. She chatted briskly with him, and praised the children liberally. This surprised the children, who stopped their game to listen. They were much more used to hearing themselves scolded by Miss Varian. Then she came to the condition of his household, and asked him many questions. He was obliged to be very frank, and to tell her that he had sent the servants all away, according to Miss Rothermel's advice, and that now he was waiting further orders.

"Well, it's too bad," cried Miss Varian, with a laugh. "Missy has got you into this fix, and she's bound to help you out of it. I won't hear to her going to bed, and leaving you to starve. Why, what a predicament you're in ! Where did you get your dinner ?"

Mr. Andrews said he had had a very fair meal at the hotel, and seemed anxious to make the best of his position. "But who milks the cows, and takes care

of things at the stable? Horses can't be locked up
like chairs and tables."

"Oh!" answered Mr. Andrews, "Peters has found
a very decent man for me. I feel quite satisfied about
the horses and cows; and if it were not for imposing
these children upon you, I should not be in any trouble
about the house. It's more comfortable now than it
has been for some time, I assure you."

"All the same," said Miss Varian, "there is no
sense in your being kept in this unsettled state, just
because Missy chooses to set up a headache. It's a
new thing for her; she isn't the kind of young woman
that goes to bed with a headache whenever she's put
out. It's a wonder to me what has happened to disturb her. She was well enough at breakfast, but
wouldn't come down to her dinner. I never knew
her to stay away from dinner for a headache, or any
such nonsense before. Goneril shall go up and see
why she can't come down."

"I beg you won't take any trouble about it," said
Mr. Andrews, much disturbed. "I am sure she is ill,
she looked very pale. I would not have her annoyed
for anything. If it is not asking too much of you all,
to bear with the children, I will try to get some kind
of a household together to-morrow. I have no doubt
I could hear of some one in the village, or I could go
to the city in the morning and get some at an office."

"Heaven forbid!" cried Miss Varian, fervently.
"That would break Missy's heart, for she has been
longing to get these creatures away. And you wouldn't
be likely to get any better. You know men are always
imposed upon."

"That is true," said Mr. Andrews, with a sigh.

" Missy went to see about a cook this morning," put in Gabrielle, who had renounced her game and crept up to hear the talking. "And a waitress too. She said she had heard of a place for them, but she didn't say where. Maybe it was for you, papa."

" Maybe," said her father, absently.

" Alphonsine said in the stage this morning that she seemed to take a great interest in your affairs, you know."

" Hush !" said her father, with emphasis.

" How's that? Who's Alphonsine ? Your nurse? And what did she say ?" asked Miss Varian, with keen interest.

" Some impertinence of the servants after they were sent away, I suppose," said Mr. Andrews, threatening Gabrielle with a look.

" Did Missy hear it ?" asked Miss Varian, persisting.

" Papa says I mustn't tell," returned Gabrielle, hesitating.

" Oh," said Miss Varian, sharply. " It is always well to obey one's father."

" Gabrielle makes a great deal out of a very little," said Mr. Andrews, suppressing his annoyance. " She has had the misfortune to be a great deal thrown upon the care of servants. I shall be glad to get her into different ways."

" She ought to be sent to boarding-school," said Miss Varian.

" I am afraid you are right ; I must look about for a school for her in the course of the next few months."

Gabrielle gave Miss Varian a very bitter look, but Miss Varian was none the worse for that. Mr.

Andrews now arose to go, but Miss Varian protested he should not go till Missy had sent down the addresses of the persons she had recommended.

"I won't have you kept in such a state for anybody's caprice," she said, sending Goneril up with a message. And then Mr. Andrews knew that Miss Varian did not love her step-niece.

"Missy is very fond of managing," she said. "She must understand she can't lay down the reins whenever she chooses. She must carry out what she undertakes."

Goneril was gone a very long time, it seemed to Mr. Andrews; he really thought he was having a great deal of petticoat government. If it were not for the two children, he would have got clear of the whole sex, he thought. He would have taken bachelor apartments, and had not even a chamber-maid. He would have gone to a club for his meals, and not have spoken to a woman from year's end to year's end. But there was poor little Jay, with his tawny hair all unkempt, and his saucy sister with her sash ends in a tangle; for their sakes he must be grateful to these kind and dictatorial friends. Certainly he could not do without women while he had those two to care for. He must get used to women, he supposed; get to be half a woman himself; learn how to keep house; be a perfect Betty. He groaned, patiently, while Miss Varian kept up a brisk talk about his matters.

At last Goneril came back. Goneril was much interested in his matters too. She was so much interested, and so zealous, that he was quite abashed. He wondered how many more women would be needed to put his affairs *en train.* Goneril was a very tall, well-built woman, with an energetic tread. She had her own views on most matters, and was not withheld from uttering them by any false delicacy about a menial position. Wasn't she the daughter of an American farmer? So, when she came down to deliver Miss Rothermel's message, she added many of her own observations to the message, and quite bewildered Mr. Andrews. He did not know which was the original text, and which the comment on it; and Miss Varian's cross-fire did not render matters simpler.

"Here's the names of the persons Miss Rothermel was speaking of," Goneril said, giving him the paper; "and the places where you'll find 'em. But my opinion is, you'll have your trouble for your pains, if you go hunting up Melinda Larkins. She'll never come to you. She won't undertake to live in a family where there isn't anybody to look after things. Things go wrong in every house, more or less; but where there's only Help, the troubles are laid to the wrong door, and you never know what you'll be accused of."

"That is," said Miss Varian, sharply, "bad as a mistress is, it's worse without a mistress."

"I don't know anything about mistresses," retorted Goneril, with a toss of the head. "People that you live with may call themselves anything they like. That don't make 'em so. They might call themselves em-presses and prin-cesses, but it wouldn't make 'em so."

"And servants might call themselves Help, but that wouldn't make them so. As long as they draw their wages for the work they do, they are servants, and nothing more nor less than servants."

Poor Mr. Andrews felt as if he had got into a very

hot fire, and as if, somehow, he were guilty of having lighted it.

"I ought to be going to see about these—persons —I suppose ; if I can get them to-night it will be all the better," he said, rising, while the discussion about titles was still raging.

"Well, you won't get anybody on such short no- tice that's worth having," Goneril interrupted herself 'to say. "Melinda Larkins wouldn't think of taking a place, without going over to the island to see her folks about it. She has some self-respect, if she is obliged to live out."

"If she is obliged to go into service, you mean," said Miss Varian. "There won't be much difficulty about your getting her, Mr. Andrews, I am sure. All these people are very poor, and will do anything for money."

"Money isn't everything," began Goneril ; but Mr. Andrews had got to the hall.

"I can but go and see about them," he said, as he made his bow.

He heard a rage of tongues as he closed the door. He felt as if the flames were shooting out after him and scorching his very eyebrows.

He drew a long breath when he was out of hearing of the house, and under the trees in the night air. What bliss a world without women would be. Here he was embroiled with three, after his brave fight of the morning too, which should have won him their ap- plause. There was no pleasing them, and their tongues—their tongues. Pleased or displeased, he asked nothing better than to get away from them. He thought for a rash moment that he would steal

Jay and go away with him to some monastery, and
leave Gabby to her fate. But, poor little Gabby, he
was sorry for her, even if she did love to impart information and to make mischief. Yes, he must stay by
them, poor little mites, and try to help them out of their
dismal plight. So he went to the stable, and saddled
his horse, and threw a severe order or two to the decent man, of whom he was not afraid.

Then he rode into the jaws of fate, to see Melinda
Larkins, who couldn't make up her mind in a minute ;
to see the one proposed as nursery maid, who wasn't
in ; to see the waitress, who asked him a great many
questions that he couldn't answer. " What part of
the wash would be hers ? What evening could she
have ? Who was to get tea Sunday when the cook
was out ? Was there to be a regular dinner for the
children in the middle of the day, and a regular dinner again at night ?"

To all these questions, and many more as puzzling,
Mr. Andrews could give no well considered answer. He
felt the necessity of appearing to know a little about
the ordering of his household ; his dealings with men
had taught him that ignorance is fatal to authority, and
strangely and sadly as the sexes differed, there must
be some general points of resemblance. It would not
do to let this trim young creature, with her black eyes
and her white apron, respectful as yet, standing at
the gate in an attitude of attention, know that he had
never known who did the wash in his house, or
whether there was a regular dinner in the middle of
the day, or whether the cook ever went out, or how
many evenings belonged to the waitress. He said
rather lamely that he had only come to see if she

were disengaged ; he had not time to talk these details over. If she were at liberty, she might come the next morning at ten, and he would make final arrangements with her.

She respectfully consented to this, but it is highly probable that she saw through the maneuver, and knew that "time" was what her future master wanted, and that there was a good deal in her catechism that was new to him. He knew, or feared this knowledge on her part, and went slowly away on his milk-white steed, much humbled and perplexed.

The decent man took his horse and cared for it, but he let himself into the house with a feeling of his helplessness. He had matches, thanks to being a smoker, but he did not know how to fill a lamp, and of course all the lamps were empty. Every one knows that a candle does not give a cheerful light in a wide room. So he tried two candles, but they blinked at each other feebly, they were almost worse than one. It was almost impossible to read the evening paper ; he would conclude it was time to go to bed. So he poured himself out a glass of wine, not having the heart (or the chance) to eat a meal, and went upstairs. His bed had not been made ; there was no water in the pitchers. The windows had been closed, and the room was not fresh. He made up his mind that he could not sleep there ; he went into another room, entering into a calculation how many nights the beds would last, and when he should have to take to the sofas.

Another day dawned on this anarchy. He had no hot water for his shaving ; he did not know where fresh towels were, the keys of the closets being all at the bottom of the cistern. (A parting shot of malice from

Alphonsine, though he did not know it.) After a wretched bath, with towels in which he had no confidence, he went out into the damp morning, and getting on his horse, went down to the village barber, and then to the village inn for breakfast.

"This thing must not go on any longer," he said with firmness—but what use was there in being firm? He was helpless. What part of the wash *did* the waitress do? And what would bring Melinda Larkins to decision? And what questions would the nursery-maid elect be likely to ask him? He ground his teeth. A plague upon them all. He had made a fortune and lost it with less rack of brain than this business had occasioned him. If Miss Rothermel only would get over her little temper and come forward to the rescue. He couldn't blame her for being so indignant, but she needn't have vented it on him, who was not in the least to blame. There was the waitress coming at ten, and he had no answers to give her to her questions. He had not the face to go to the Varians' house again, indeed, he had not the courage, for Miss Varian and her iron maid were more likely to confront him than Missy was, who mighn't yet be through with her headache.

He rode slowly back from the village after breakfast, reflecting deeply. As he turned into the stable, he saw the welcome sight of Missy, in her shade-hat, going into the greenhouse, with a basket and some scissors. If he could only get her to talk to him for five minutes, all might be got into right shape. But what sort of a humor was she in? She had not the children with her—that was a bad sign. The dampness of the early morning had passed away, and the

sun had come out bright, though the dew was thick on
the grass. He hurried across the lawn and entered the
garden. Missy was busy at the door of the greenhouse, with a vine that seemed not to meet her approbation. Her basket stood at her feet, half-full of
the late blooming flowers that she had picked in the
garden as she came along.

"Good morning, Miss Rothermel," said Mr. Andrews, rather irresolutely, pausing behind her. She
had not heard his approach, and started. He felt that
it was unwarrantable, his coming in this way into
the garden; but starvation and perplexity and want
of shaving-water will drive a man to almost anything.
If he had gone to the house she would have refused
to see him. If she refused to speak to him now, he
should simply hang himself. She looked quite haughty
as she faced him; but he looked so troubled and so
humbled, it was impossible to be haughty long.

"I hope you'll excuse my coming to bother you
again," he said; "but upon my word, I don't know
how I am going to get my matters straight without
some help from you. I know it is quite unjustifi-
able, and you have quite a right to tell me so."

"No," said Missy, with rigid honesty, "I offered
you my advice. I remember that quite well. I have
only myself to blame if you give me any trouble."

"And I am sure I needn't tell you how very
sorry I am about the occurrence of yesterday. I
would have done anything to have saved you that
annoyance."

But Mr. Andrews saw that he'd better have left
the subject alone. All the softening vanished from
her expression.

"No one was to blame for that," she said. "It need never be thought of again." But it was evident the recollection of it had put her back into her armor.

Mr. Andrews felt a momentary indignation at her injustice ; but his straits were too sore for him to cherish indignation. "If it were not for the children," he said, "I would close the house at once, and go away. Gabrielle would be better off perhaps at boarding-school ; but Jay is such a baby. Still, I suppose that might not be a difficulty."

"He does seem rather young to send among strangers," she replied coldly, snipping down a fading branch of the climbing rose, and throwing it aside.

"But on some accounts, as I was saying to you the other day, I would much prefer keeping them together, and having them with me for the present."

"It would be pleasanter, perhaps," said Miss Rothermel, with distant but faint interest.

"What I want to ask you," he went on desperately, "is whether you think a household could be kept together, with any comfort or profit to the children, without any greater knowledge and experience on my part. I mean," he said confusedly, "could they get on without a governess, or a housekeeper, or some one to be at the head of affairs ? Could three or four women get on, that is, without some one in authority over them ? "

"Why, what is to prevent you from being in authority over them ?" said Missy, almost contemptuously. "That is, if you are willing to take the trouble of thinking about things."

"I am very willing to think about things, but I am sorry to say I am so ignorant that my thoughts are not likely to be profitable."

"Knowledge is power," said Missy, clipping another dry leaf off.

"That is very true, Miss Rothermel," he said, with a smile. "I am sure you feel yours. But be good enough to help me. Tell me, to begin with, what I am to say to the waitress, who is to come to see me in half an hour. She asks me questions that I don't know how to answer."

"Well, what are some of them, pray?"

"Why, as we are not to keep a laundress, what part of the washing she must do?"

"The fine clothes, of course."

"I don't believe we have any fine clothes in the house. I think everything is very plain."

"Oh, that is a technical expression. It means the starched clothes. Say that to her and she'll understand. The cook is to do the coarse washing."

"Ah, yes; I see. Well, she wants to know about dinner—am I to have a regular dinner, and are the children to have a regular dinner in the middle of the day? Now, what does a regular dinner mean when a waitress talks about it? and what ought the children to have for their dinner?"

"Why, it means," said Missy, "are the children to have scraps and a jumbled-up lunch, all on the table together—or, are they to have soup, and a nice steak, and some vegetables, and a pudding, and fare like Christians. I *hope* you settled that question for her."

"I will settle it, now that I know what she means. Thank you. And what wages is she to have? And who is to serve tea on Sunday nights? And how often must she go out; and when she goes out who is to do her work?"

"Tell her she is to go out every other Sunday, and the cook is to serve tea in her place on that night. And one evening in the week she can go out. And as the nurse will go out on one evening also, she must arrange with her what that evening shall be. And on the.nurse's evening out, she must sit up stairs and look after the children."

"Thank you. That looks plainer. I believe it was all she asked me. If I see the woman you thought might do for nurse, what questions will she be likely to ask me?"

"Why, I don't know; but you must be prepared to say, she is to do all the mending, and take the entire charge of the children, and of their clothes. And besides must teach them their letters and spelling every day for an hour, and must assist in waiting on them at their meals, for Jay needs some one every moment. But she is a sensible girl, and I am sure you will have no trouble with her. She won't be likely to ask you many questions."

"I am glad of that," said Mr. Andrews, growing lighter-hearted. "There is one thing more. You feel certain, Miss Rothermel, that three women can do the work? You know there have hitherto been five—"

Miss Rothermel looked contemptuous again. "That depends," she said, "entirely upon your wishes. Three women are all you need. You might have eight, but I don't think they'd add to your comfort."

"I am sure you are right," he said, apologetically. "All I mean is, will they be coming to me every day or two and saying they have too much to do, and excusing themselves in that manner for neglecting their work?"

" That depends, again, upon what you say to them, if they do come. If you never give in to any demands for more wages, and make them fully understand that you mean to keep three servants in the house and no more, you will not have any trouble. It will be an easy place ; they will be very glad to stay. These three that I have told you of, are all good servants. I don't see any reason that Jay—that you all—I mean—shouldn't be quite comfortable."

Mr. Andrews knew very well that all her solicitude was for Jay. He did not care, however. He was willing to get comfort, even over his son's shoulder.

"I can't tell you how much obliged to you I am," he said. " Your aunt's maid has rather frightened me about my cook elect. Do you think there will be any difficulty in getting her to consent to come ?"

"I don't know why there should be."

" Perhaps, if you would say a word to her, she might be influenced."

Missy grew lofty at once. She had evidently washed her hands of the matter.

"I don't know anything to say to her to induce her to come if she is not induced by the prospect of a good home and good wages. She will probably come."

" And the nurse ; is she not a sort of protegée of yours ? Perhaps if you would kindly give her some idea of her duties it might help her."

This Mr. Andrews said maliciously, for he had a man's contempt for caprice, and he could see nothing but caprice in Miss Rothermel's washing her hands of his affairs. Two days ago she had advised him, urged him, made up his cabinet for him. And now she only tolerated an allusion to the subject. It was not his

fault that the servants she had made him send away
had been saucy to her. He was not inclined to submit
to such airs (now that he had got his questions answered
and there was a reasonable prospect of hot water and
clean towels).

"She is not a protegée of mine at all," returned
Missy. "All I know about her, however, is in her
favor. She will, I think, take good care of the children. She will take her instructions best from you, and
she has intelligence enough to fill up details of which
you are ignorant necessarily."

Mr. Andrews bowed, and Missy filled up the gap in
the conversation by snipping off some more dead leaves.
There seemed really nothing for him to do but to go
away, and he was just preparing to do this when the
children rushed upon the scene. Jay pounced upon
Missy, and nearly threw her down ; she looked slight
and small, stretching up her arm to a high branch of
the vine, and the little ruffian probably felt his superiority and used it.

"You are a naughty boy," she said, picking up her
hat and the scissors which he had thrown to the ground,
but she did not say it very severely.

"Why did you go away without me ? " he said,
kicking at her glove, which lay upon the gravel walk.

"Because I didn't want you," she returned.

Gabrielle had crept up to her father, and was eying
Missy and Jay with sidelong observation. "Jay said
something very bad this morning," she said, including
her father in her circuitous glance. Her father naturally felt suspicious of Gabrielle's information ; it was
generally of a nature far from pleasing. He therefore
passed over her remark without notice, and putting out

his hand to Jay, said, "Well, you haven't spoken to me this morning. I think you have forgotten that you haven't seen me."

"Holloa! how are you?" cried Jay, catching at his father's hand with both his, and trying to climb up his leg. His hat fell off in the exertion, and his yellow hair, fresh from Goneril's brushing, blew about in the breeze.

"He said he didn't want to go home to you, papa," persisted Gabrielle.

"He didn't! there's affection for you," said the father, carelessly, with both hands now holding the boy, who chose to walk up him.

"He said—" and now Missy began to tremble. "He said he wouldn't go away from Missy."

"Thank you, Jay," said Missy, looking at the boy with a bright smile, and some relief. "They'd better let you stay with me if that's the way you feel."

"O no," cried the little viper, "we couldn't spare Jay. You could do like Alphonsine said you wanted to do, come to our house and live with us, and have things all your own way. You know she said that was what you were working for. Don't you remember, Missy? Just before Moses started up the horses."

Jay had made the ascent of his father and stood in triumph on his shoulder. Mr. Andrews with a rapid movement put him on the ground, made a step forward and brought his hand with force on Gabrielle's cheek, a hard stinging blow that made the child scream with pain and amazement, for he had never struck her before.

"Never repeat to me the words of servants," he said, in a voice terrible to her, and severe enough in

7

the ears of others, especially little Jay, who looked
awe-struck. There was a seat outside the greenhouse
door, and on this Missy had sunk down, trembling all
over. She opened her lips and tried to speak, but
literally she could not, the sudden agitation had taken
away her voice. Meanwhile Gabrielle had found hers,
and was crying passionately, very angry at the blow,
and very sure too, that crying was the way to get the
better of her father. But this time she was mistaken.
He took her hand almost roughly.

"Come with me," he said. "I have something more
to teach you."

His voice was rather unsteady from anger, his face
flushed, and his eye stern. No wonder Gabrielle's cry
sank into a frightened whimper, as she followed, or
was half dragged away by her father. Jay ran up to
Missy, and tried to climb into her lap. With an
impulse that the poor little fellow could not understand, of course, she pushed him away. It was the
first repulse he had ever had from her : though he was
still in petticoats, his pride and wounded affection
were strong ; he would not wait for a second rebuff.
He started down the path, crying, Papa. Missy saw
him overtake his father as he crossed the lawn, and
cling to his hand, hardly able to keep up with his rapid
walk. And so, with a child in each hand, he passed
out of the gate and disappeared from Missy's sight.

She sat still for a few minutes, and tried to collect
her thoughts. She felt as if some one had given her
a blow on *her* ear, and sent all the blood tingling to
her brain. Finally she got up, picked up Jay's hat,
which he had left on the field, and the scissors, and
the basket, which had been overturned in the mêlée.

She put the flowers back into it, angry and ashamed to see how her hand shook, and shutting the greenhouse door, slowly went out of the garden. Where should she go to get away from every one, and be by herself for a little while? If she went to the beach, thither the children might come in a few moments. If to the lawn, she was a fair mark for visitors and servants, and the walk through the cedars would bring all back—the interview there three days ago, whence all her troubles dated. Her own room was the best place for her.

She put down the flowers in the hall, and went up stairs under a running fire from Goneril, Aunt Harriet and her mother, dispersed about the lower rooms and hall.

It is astonishing how much unnecessary talking is done in a house, how many useless questions asked, how many senseless observations made. Just be very unhappy, overstrained or anxious, and you will find out how many idle words are spoken in an hour, if you happen to be bearing your burden among happy, unstrained, and careless people.

It seemed to Missy, calling out her answers in as brave a voice as she could, going through the house, that never were questions so useless, observations so senseless.

"Where are you going?" was among the last of her mother's.

"To my room; and don't let me be disturbed, please. I want to be quiet for awhile."

"Another headache?" cried Aunt Harriet from the hall below. "Really, this is becoming serious. I never knew you were capable of headaches."

"Thank you," said Missy, shutting her door and sliding the bolt. She sat down in a chair by the window and gazed out ; but she did not see the soft velvet of the lawn, nor the blue dimples of the bay against which the great trunks of the trees stood out.

There were some sails flitting about in the fresh wind, but she did not see them. She was trying to collect her thoughts and get over that blow on the ear that she felt as if she had had. It was new to her not to go to her mother and confide her trouble ; but this was a sort of humiliation she could not bring herself to talk about. She excused herself by saying it would only distress mamma. It would have distressed mamma's daughter so much to have given words to it that she never even allowed to herself that it might be a duty. It was all a punishment, she said to herself, for having received on terms of kindness a man who had behaved so to his wife ; that was a breach of friendship. It was something to bear in silence, to be hushed up, and forgotten, if it could be, even by herself. She wished that she might go away.

She got up and walked across the room—impulsively. Then sat down again, with the bitter reflection that it was only men who could go away. Women have to sit down and bear their disappointments, their mortifications, their defeats ; to sit down in the sight of them and forget them if they can. Men can pack their tender sensibilities into their valises, and go off and see that the world is wide, and contains other subjects of thought and interest than the ones they have been brooding over.

Go away ! No indeed ; she laughed bitterly when she thought of the commotion that would result from the mentioning such a plan. St. John might walk in any day, and say he was going on a journey. No one would question his right to go, or his right to decline giving any reasons for so going. He was seven years younger than she was, but he was free. She must account for all her goings, her doings; even the people in the village would sit in judgment on her, if she did anything that was not clearly explained to them and proved expedient. No—she was tied, bound to Yellow-coats. All their plans were laid to remain at home for the winter.

Since St. John had come to the parish, they had decided it was unnecessary to make their annual change; Missy had not cared for the winter in town, Mrs. Varian had been glad to be let off from it, Aunt Harriet had submitted to give it up. So here she was to stay, and here it was possible the Andrews' would stay, and here she must daily see the children and pass the house, and be reminded that she had been insulted, and had been a fool. It would be the village talk. All her past dignity and her grand disdain of lovers would pass for nothing. She had never entered the lists with other young women; she had prided herself on her determination not to marry. "I am not in commission," she would say loftily to the younger girls, making the most of her age.

The few suitors who, so far, had come to her, had been detestable to her. She did not deserve much credit for rejecting them, but she took a good deal to herself, feeling sure that she would, in the same way, have discarded princes. Of course, she had had her dreams about true love, but she had early decided that that was not to come to her, and that she

had a different sort of life to live. Being very fond
of plans and arrangements of all kinds, it was a great
satisfaction to her to feel she was building up the sort
of life that she was intended for, that she was daily
adding to its usefulness and symmetry. My will be
done, she was saying, unconsciously, in her daily
thought, if not in her morning and evening prayer.
Yes, it was a very beautiful, a very noble life she was
constructing, very devoid of self, she thought. She
was living for others ; was not that fine? She was
quite above the petty ambitions and humiliations of
her sex. She did not mean to marry, in deference to
the world's opinion, or in terror of its scorn. All the
same, she knew very well people held her very high,
and were not ignorant that she could have married
well if she had chosen. She did not think that this
was of any importance to her, till she found what pain
it gave her to think that people would now be of a
different mind. Had it come to this, that it could be
said she was only too ready to fall into the arms of a
month-old widower, stout and elderly ! Yes, that was
what the people in the village—the gentlemen going
down in the cars, the ladies in their morning drives—
would say. The scene with the stage load of servants
would be in possession of all these by to-morrow, if it
were not so to-day. She knew the ability of Yellowcoats to absorb news, as a sponge absorbs water ;—it
would look very fair and dry, but touch it, squeeze it,
ah, bah. Yellowcoats could take in anything, from
the smallest detail to the most exaggerated improba-
bility. She had spent her life in Yellowcoats, and she
knew it. From highest to lowest it craved a sensation, and would sacrifice its best and choicest to fill up

the gaping vacancy. She knew how good the story was, she knew how much foundation it seemed to have. What could she ever do to contradict it? Nothing. No word of it would ever reach her ears. She would be treated with the old deference, but she would know the laugh that underlaid it. She had no chance of contradicting what no one would say to her. And in action, what could she do? If she refused ever to see the children again, declined abruptly all intercourse with their neighbors, it would only be said, with more emphasis than ever, that she had met with sudden discouragement ; that the gentleman had become alarmed at her ardent interest in his household matters, and had withdrawn abruptly from even ordinary civilities. If she still went on as before, appearing daily with the children in the carriage, taking them to church with her, it would be said she was still pursuing the chase, was still cherishing hopes of promotion. Whatever she did, it was all one. She couldn't publish a card in the paper, she couldn't go about and tell people they had been misinformed, when they didn't acknowledge to any information at all. The only thing she could do was to marry some one else out of hand, and that she felt she was almost prepared to do, if any one else were to be had on a moment's notice. But all her few men were dead men, and there was not a new one to be had for the wishing.

It was surely a very trying situation, and Missy shed bitter tears about it, and felt she hated, hated, hated this strange widower, whom she persisted in calling stout and elderly, as if that were the worst thing that a man could be. She knew him so slightly, she hated him so deeply. What business had he to humiliate her so? Though, to do him justice, it had not been his fault; he had only been the instrument of her chastisement. These tantalizing thoughts were interrupted, in the course of an hour, by Ann, bringing her a letter. Missy sat down to read it, knowing it was from Mr. Andrews.

"It seems fated," he wrote, "that you are to suffer for your kindness to my children. It is needless for me to tell you how much mortification I feel on account of my little girl's misconduct. I am sure your kind heart has already made many excuses for her, and has divined how great my chagrin is at finding her capable of such wrong dispositions. I have to remind myself very often that her life has been what it has, through no fault of hers, else I might feel harshly towards her. I know very well that you will agree with me that it is best that the children should trespass no more on your hospitality, after the return that they have made. I have put them into the nursery. The servant who has to come to see me this morning, has engaged to return to me in an hour's time. I have no doubt she will be capable of taking care of them till I can secure the nurse and cook. At any rate, it is but just that you should be free from them, and I beg you will have no further thought about the matter, except to believe that I am deeply sorry for the annoyance that your generosity has brought upon you.

"Always faithfully yours,
"JAMES ANDREWS."

Missy's first feeling after reading this was, that he

had at least behaved well about it, and had put things in the best shape for her. It was the better way surely, for the children to stay away altogether now. She felt she could not bear the sight of Gabrielle, and the chance of having to meet Mr. Andrews himself was insupportable. Yes, it was the best way, and she hoped that they might never, never cross each other's paths again.

Perhaps he would close the house and go away. She hoped her precious protegées would not give him satisfaction, and then he would have to go away. But then came second thoughts, soberer and less hopeful. Was it best for the children to stay at home to-day? How explain to the household, beginning with her mother, this sudden change of base? What would Goneril say, the glib-tongued Ann, and all the rest? It looked like a quarrel, a breach, a sensation. Gabrielle would be questioned over the hedge; the whole story would get out. No; this would never do. The children's clothes were in the drawers of the spare room, their playthings all about the house. The packing these and sending them back so abruptly, would be like a rocket shot into the sky, a signal of sensation to all Yellowcoats.

And then, proving how real her affection for Jay was, there came a feeling of solicitude for him, shut up in that damp nursery. It always had been damp, and she had disapproved it; the worst room in the house, with trees close up to the window, and no sun in it.

The house had been shut up for several days, and in September, that does not do for country houses by the water. The Varians had fire morning and evening,

7*

and Jay had been dressed every day since she had had
the charge of him, by a bright little blaze of pine
and hickory.   It would be an hour before the woman
came, and what would she get together for their dinner.   Some poor baker's bread, perhaps, and some
sweetmeats.   Jay, poor little man, would be hungry
before this time, she was sure.   How he was fretting
and crying now, no doubt ; kicking his little bare legs
against the chair.

Missy yearned over him, and she thought, with a
pang, how she had pushed him away when he came
climbing into her lap.   If he were left there, with no
one to take proper care of him for two or three days,
she knew perfectly well he would be ill.   His hands
had been a little hot that morning, with all the care
that she had given him.   To-day was Saturday.   It was
not likely that the new women could be got into the
house before Monday.   No, she could not put poor
little Jay into all this danger, to save her pride.   So,
after a good cry, the result of this softened feeling,
she wrote the following little note to Mr. Andrews :

"I think you would do better let the children
come back and stay here till Monday.   By that time you
will no doubt have the servants in the house.   When
you are ready for them, please send me a few lines and
I will send Goneril in with them."

She hoped she had made it plain that *he* was to
keep out of the way, and as he had not merited stupid
in addition to stout and elderly, she felt quite confident he would understand.   She began several sen-
tences which were meant to imply, from a pinnacle,
that she did not blame him for the stings of his little
viper, and that no more need be said about it.   But

none of them satisfied her, and she put the note into
the envelope without anything but the bare statement
of facts recorded above. Then she took Jay's hat,
which she had brought in with her from the garden,
and calling Ann, told her to take the note and the
hat in to Mr. Andrews.

"The children are there, I think," she added carelessly, in explanation. "Jay ran off without his
hat."

She had bathed her eyes before she rang the bell,
that Ann might not see she had been crying. By
and by Jay came in, accompanied by the new waitress,
who explained from her master that Miss Gabrielle was
under punishment and was not to have any dinner.
She would come back at bedside. Jay looked a little
doubtfully at Missy. He had not forgotten his repulse. When the woman had gone out of the door,
she said,

"Come Jay, I think we'd better be friends, old
fellow," and taking him in her arms, kissed him a
dozen times. Jay felt as if a great cloud had lifted
off the landscape. Why had everybody been so
horrid? There must have been something the matter
with people. He gave a great sigh as he sank back
in Missy's embrace, but only said, "I want some
dinner."

CHAPTER X.

PER ASPERA AD ASTRA.

HE next day was Sunday, a chilly September day, threatening rain. Missy quite wished it would rain, and then there would be an excuse for omitting the children's church-going. But church time approached. It did not rain, indeed, looked as if it were to be a prolonged sulk, and not a burst of tears. So the carriage was ordered, the children made ready, and Miss Varian and Goneril, armed with prayer-books, waited on the piazza. The children looked very pretty in their mourning. Gabrielle was so handsome, she repaid any care in dressing her, and Alphonsine had really exerted herself to make up a pretty black dress, and trim a hat for her. There is always something pathetic in the sight of young children in mourning, and Missy had almost cried the first time she saw Jay in his little black kilt and with that somber cap on his yellow curls. She was quite used to it now, and did not feeling like crying from anything but vexation, as she came out on the piazza when she heard the carriage wheels approaching. She was going to church, to be sure, and that ought to have been soothing to her feelings. But she was also going to face the little populace of Yellowcoats, and that was very ruffling to them. She felt it was a pity she could not make herself invisible, and that her neighbors could not make themselves invisible too. She was sure they would say better prayers if that could be the case. How they would gaze at her as she walked down the aisle! How glances would be exchanged, and nudges given, as the little black-clad children came in sight. It is all very well to say, don't think of such things if you know you're doing right. It takes a very advanced saint not to mind what people think, and Missy, poor Missy, was not that. She longed to say her prayers, and felt she had never needed to say them more ; but it was as if a thousand little devils, with as many little prongs, were busy in a swarm around her. To add to all her fretting thoughts, Aunt Harriet was particularly trying, Goneril was more audacious, the children were exasperating, even sitting still and in their Sunday clothes.

As the carriage rolled up to the church gate, Missy felt her face growing red and white with apprehension of the eyes that would in a moment more be looking at it. The bell had stopped ringing, and she heard the organ. Of all moments, this was the worst to go in.

"What are you waiting for?" said Miss Varian, sharply, as Missy paused, irresolute.

"Nothing," said Missy with a groan, and she went forward, bidding the children follow. Goneril, of course, was a dissenter, and had to be driven to the other end of the village to say her humble prayers. I think she objected to stopping even at the church gate, and to riding with people who were going there. She always had a great deal to say at the Sunday dinner, about forms and ceremonies and a free Gospel, but as her fellow-servants were most of them of a more advanced creed themselves, she did not get much sympathy, or do much injury to any one.

So Goneril went her way, and Missy, with her blind
aunt on her arm, and the children following in her
wake, went hers. Certainly it was the way of duty,
or she never would have walked in it.   If she had
dared to do it, she would have stayed from church
that morning, and said matins among the cedars on
the bank. But as she did what was right, and what
was hard, no doubt, her poor distracted prayers got an
answer, and her marred, distorted offering of worship
was accepted.

St. John was not yet in the chancel; they had
fallen upon the moment when they would naturally
be most conspicuous and attract most notice from the
congregation. Miss Varian always would walk slowly
and heavily ; the children gazed about them, and met
many curious eyes. Missy looked haughty enough ;
she was never particularly humble-looking. When
they reached the pew-door (and it seemed to Missy
they would never reach it), Miss Varian was a long
while getting through the kneeling cushions, and accepted no help from any one.

"Well, I hope they all see the children and are
satisfied of my intentions," said Missy bitterly to herself, as she stood thus a mark for the merry eyes of
Yellowcoats. At last, Aunt Harriet made her way to
the end of the pew, and Missy followed her, letting
the children take care of themselves.

St. John's voice; well, there was something in it
different from other voices. There must have been a
dim and distant echo of that company who rest not
day nor night. It did not recall earth and vanity. It
made a lift in the thoughts of those who heard it.
Missy, amidst distraction and vexation, heard him, and

in a moment felt that it was very little worth, all that
had caused her smart and ache. When St. John read,
people listened, whatever it was. Perhaps it was
what is "sincerity" in art. He read in a monotone
too, as does his school. He did not lift his eyes and
look about him ; he almost made a business of looking
down. It was very simple ; but maybe those who
would analyze its power, would have to go far back
into fasts and vigils and deep hours of meditation.
Missy drew a long breath. She didn't care for Yellowcoats' gossip now, while she heard St. John's voice, and
poured out her fretted soul in the prayers of her childhood. Perhaps she never knew how much she owed
her brother, and those disapproved austerities of his.
We do not always know what the saints win for us,
nor how much the fuller we may be for our holy
neighbor's empty stomach. And the children tumbled
and twisted about on their seats, and Jay went to
sleep, and Gabby eyed her neighbors, and Missy did
not mind. It was well that she did not, for if she had
reproved them, Yellowcoats would have whispered,
what a step-mother is that, my brothers. And if she
had caressed them, they would have jeered and said,
see the pursuit, my sisters. But as she simply let them
alone, they could say nothing, and settled themselves
to listen to the sermon after the prayers were said.

And in the sermon there was a word for Missy. It
was an old word, as most good words are ; Missy remembered copying it out years before, when it had
seemed good to her, but now it seemed better and fuller :

"Let nothing disturb thee, nothing surprise thee :

"Everything passes :

"God does not change :

" Patience alone weareth out all things :
" Whoso holds fast to God shall want for nothing :
" God alone sufficeth."

And " the benediction that followeth after prayer "
seemed to her more than ever

"A Christian charm,
To dull the shafts of worldly harm."

Even though the arm stretched out to bless were
that of the young brother whose steps she had so often
guided in their days of childhood.

As they went in, Missy had seen, somehow, with
those quick, light-blue eyes of hers, that Mr. Andrews
was in the church, in a pew near the door. She knew it
was the first time he had been in the church since his
wife's death. She began instantly to speculate about
his reasons for coming, and to wonder whether he
would have the kindness to go off and leave them
to get into the carriage by themselves after service.
Then St. John's voice had broken in upon the fret, and
she had forgotten it, till they were at the church door,
coming out, before chattering little groups of people on
the grass outside. It did not yet rain, but the sky
was gray as granite, and the air chill.

Jay's warm little hand was in hers, unconsciously
to them both. Miss Varian was leaning heavily upon
her other arm. Half a dozen persons came up to speak
to them as they made their way to the carriage. At
the carriage door stood Mr. Andrews. Jay made a
spring at him. Mr. Andrews gravely lifted him in.
Missy felt an angry agitation as she saw him, but the
words of St. Theresa's wisdom stood by her for the

moment. He scarcely looked at her as he put her into the carriage. Gabrielle, very subdued, followed, and Mr. Andrews closed the door, lifted his hat, after some commonplace about the weather, and the carriage drove away. All Yellowcoats might have seen that. Nothing could have been more unsensational.

That evening St. John came to tea, very tired and silent. He sat alone with his mother an hour before tea, and Missy saw tears on her cheeks as she brought in the light. She came into the library and lay on her sofa, but could not join them at tea. Those tears always gave Missy a jealous feeling. These long talks with St. John now always brought them. At tea the children chattered, and St. John tried to be amusing to them, and after tea, as they sat around the library fire, while the rain outside dashed against the windows, he took Jay on his lap, and told him a story. Jay liked it, and called for more, and Gabby drew near to listen.

"Why didn't you tell us a story to-day at church," he said. "Stories are a great deal nicer than talking the way you did."

"Goneril says it doesn't do us any good to go to church when we don't want to," said Gabby. "Does it, Mr. Varian?"

"People don't go to church to be done good to," said Missy, who had no patience with Goneril, and less with Gabrielle.

"Don't they?" asked Gabrielle, ignoring Missy, and turning her great eyes up appealingly into St. John's face, as she leaned on the arm of his chair.

"No, I should think not," said St. John, slowly, putting his hand on hers.

"Translate it into words of one syllable, St. John," said Missy, poking a pine-knot into blaze, " that people go to church for worship, not for edification."

"Well, children," he said, "no doubt you have always been taught to go and say good-morning to your father, and give him a kiss, haven't you? And you generally do it, though it doesn't do you any particular good, nor, for the matter of that, very much to him. But he likes it, and you always ought to go. Maybe sometimes you don't want to go; sometimes you're busy playing, or you're hungry for your breakfast, or you're a little lazy. But if you always give up your play, or put off your breakfast, or get over being lazy, and go, no doubt you have done right, and he is pleased with you. Now, going to church is a service, a thing to be done, to be offered to God; it isn't that we may be better, or learn something, or get any good, that we go. It is to pay an honor to our Heavenly Father; it is something to give to Him, an offering. I think we should be glad, don't you? There are so few things we can give Him."

Gabrielle was not convinced, and offered objections manifold, but Jay said "All right, he'd go next time without crying, if Goneril didn't brush his hair so hard."

"You mustn't get her into an argument, then," said Missy. "The faster she talks, the harder she brushes."

"You won't be here another Sunday, Jay," said Gabby. "You'll have your own nurse, and maybe she'll brush easy."

The children were soon sent to bed, and then St. John went away.

"I have something to tell you, Missy," said her mother. "Come to my room before you go to bed."

Missy's heart beat faster. Now she should know the explanation of her mother's tears, and St. John's long silences.

"Well," said Missy, sitting down by her mother's sofa, before the fire which blazed uncertainly. She knew from the clear shining of her mother's eyes, and from the faint flush on her cheek, that it was no trifling news she was to hear, and that before that pine log burned away, they should have gone very deep. She felt a jealous determination to oppose.

"You don't know how to begin, I see," she said, with a bitter little laugh. "I wish I could help you."

"Oh," said her mother, "it is not very difficult. St. John says you told him never to talk to you about going away ; and so it was best not to talk about it till everything was settled."

"Certainly ; he has only kept his promise. I did not want to be stirred up with all his fluctuations of purpose."

"I do not think, Missy, you can justly say he has fluctuated in purpose. I think he came here almost under protest, giving up his will in the matter to please us—to please you. In truth, I think he has had but one purpose, that has been strengthening slowly day by day."

Missy lifted her head. "I don't understand exactly. I know he has been getting restless."

"I don't think he has been getting restless."

"Well, at any rate it looks so, going from one parish to another in six months."

"But, he is not going from one parish to another."

Missy started. "What do you mean, mamma? I hope he isn't—isn't giving up the ministry."

"Oh, no; how could you think of such a thing."

"Well," cried Missy, impetuously, "please remember I am outside of all your counsels. Everything is new to me. St. John is going away; is going to make some important step, and yet is not going to a new parish, is not forsaking his vocation. How can you wonder I am puzzled?"

"He isn't forsaking his vocation; he is only following what he is very sure is his vocation in its highest, fullest sense."

"You don't mean," cried Missy, turning a startled face to her mother, "that St. John has got an idea that he is called to the religious life? Mamma, it isn't possible. I can't believe you have encouraged him in this."

"I have had nothing to do with it, alas, my child. One must let that alone forever. We can give up or deny to God, our own souls; but 'the souls of others are as the fruit of the tree of knowledge of good and evil; we must not touch them.' I had my own soul to give, and I did not give it."

Missy turned coldly away while her mother pressed her hands before her face. There was a silence, in which a bitter flood of thoughts passed through the mind of the younger one.

"I am a reproach to you, mamma," she said. "Perhaps I ought not to exist. There are moments when I feel the contradictions of my nature to be so great, I wonder if it were not wrong, instead of right, that I was born—a broken law, and not a law fulfilled. I know—you need not tell me—you had always thought of the religious life yourself. We have not talked much of it, but I have had my thoughts. Your first marriage bound you to the world, because it left you with me. I suppose if I had not been born you would have entered a sisterhood. Then, mamma, you need not evade it, you would have missed the real love, the real life of your heart. You have never told me this, but I know enough to know you did not love my father. It cannot be your fault ; but it was your fate. Do not contradict me, we never have gone so deep before. Yes, mamma, *I* bound you to the world. I was the unlovely child who stood between you and heaven. How could I help being unlovely, born of duty, not of love? I don't reproach you, except as my existence reproaches you. St. John is not a contradiction ; his nature is full and sweet ; he might live a happy life. Why do you sacrifice him? You say you have had no hand in this—mamma—mamma—you moulded him ; you bend him now. You do not know how strong your influence upon him is. It is the unconscious feeling of your heart that you are making reparation. You are satisfied to give him up who is all the world to you, that Heaven may be propitiated. It is I who should have been sacrificed ; I, who have been always in your way to holiness—a thorn in your side, mamma—a perverse nature, not to be bent to your path of sacrifice and immolation."

"Do not talk of sacrifice, my child, of immolation. It is a height, a glory, to attain to. I cannot make you understand—I will not contradict you."

"No, do not contradict me. I am contradicted enough. I am not in your state of fervor. I see things as they are, I see plain facts. Believe me, this enthusiasm cannot last. You will find, too late, that you have not counted the cost; that you cannot bear the strain of feeling—a living death—a grave that the grass never grows over. Time can't heal a wound that is always kept open. You are mad, mamma, you are mad. We cannot bear this thing. Look at it, as you will when your enthusiasm cools."

"I have looked at it, Missy, for many months, through silent nights and days. It is no new thought to me. My dear, I have many lonely hours; I have much suffering, which abates enthusiasm. Through loneliness and suffering, I have had this thought for my companion. I know what I am doing, and I do it almost gladly. Not quite, for I am very weak, but almost, for God has been very gracious to me."

"It is infatuation, it is madness, and you will both repent."

"Hush, my child," said her mother, trying to take her hand, "the thought is new to you, that is why it seems so dreadful."

But Missy drew her hand from her mother's and turned her face away. Her heart was pierced with sorrow at the thought of parting from her brother. It was the overthrow, too, of all her plans for him, of all their joint happiness and usefulness. But, to do her justice, the bitterness of her disappointment came from the idea of separation from him. She loved him a great deal more than she acknowledged even to herself. Life would be blank without him to her, and what would it be to her mother? This sudden weight of woe seemed unbearable, and it was a woe worse than death, inasmuch as, to her mind, it was unnecessary, unnatural, and by no law of God ordained. She felt

as if she were smothering, stifling, and her mother's
soft voice and calm words maddened her.

"I need not talk to you," she cried, "for you
are in this state of exaltation you cannot understand
me. When your heart is broken by this sorrow ; when
you sink under the weariness of life without him, then
we can talk together in one language, and you can
understand me. But it will be too late—Oh, mamma,
hear me—but what is the use of talking !—remember
how young he is, how little of life he knows ! Think
how useful, how honorable, his work might be. I cannot comprehend you ; I cannot think what magic there
is about this idea of the monastic life. Why must St.
John be better than other men of his generation?
Why cannot he serve God and live a good life as
better men have done before him ? I see nothing in
him so different from others; he is not so much worse,
that he needs such rigor, nor so much better, that he
need set himself apart. Believe me, it is the subtle
work of a crafty enemy ; he cannot be contented with
the common round, the daily task ; he is not satisfied
to do justice, love mercy, and walk humbly ; he must
do some great thing."

"We shall see," said her mother, gently. "His
vocation will be tested. You know it will be long before he is permitted to enter the order he has chosen.
He may not be accepted."

"Not accepted !" cried Missy. "A man with
money, influence, talent—Oh, we need not flatter ourselves. He will be accepted soon enough. They may
coquet about it a little to save appearances, but
they will not let him escape them, you may be quite
sure."

"Missy, I must beg, if you cannot spare me such things, you will at least not wound St. John by saying them before him."

"Oh, you may be sure I will not wound his saintly ears by such profanity. But you—I did not think you had yet left the world. I fancied there was yet one of my blood to whom I might speak familiarly. You and St. John are all I have ; and when he is a monk, I shall be obliged to be a Trappist—are there female Trappists?—excuse my ignorance of such matters—or offend you occasionally by my secular conversation."

"Missy, we won't talk of this any more till you have got over your bitterness a little. I hoped you would not take it so. I have dreaded telling you for the pain it would give you, but I did not think you would so misapprehend him. By and by, I am sure you will see it differently, and though you may not fully approve, you will yet admire the fullness of his faith, and the sweetness of what you call his sacrifice."

"Never, never," cried Missy. "I love truth and right and justice too much to admire even the most beautiful perversions of them. I may be reconciled so far as to hold my peace. More you cannot ask of me. Mamma, remember, you and I have always thought differently about these things. St. John took your faith, and has always been dearer and nearer to you than I. I cannot help the way I was made ; we are not responsible, I suppose, for the shape of our minds any more than for the shape of our bodies. St. John always loved to hear about miracles and martyrdoms ; I never did. It wasn't his merit that he liked them, nor my fault that I didn't like them. Such as I am by nature, you must be patient with me."

"Such as we are by nature, my dear, would draw little love to us from God, or men. Our corrections and amendments make our worth. I love you for what you have made yourself, in spite of passion and self-will, and St. John, for the conquest he has made of faults that lie deeper and more hidden. Ah, my dear, we may go to prisons and reformatories to see how attractive people are by nature."

"You know," said Missy, coldly, "I never could feel as you do about this making over, 'teaching our very hearts to beat by rule.' You see it is—just one part of our difference. St. John will always please you. I am afraid I cannot hope to do it, and as we are to spend our lives alone together, it is to be regretted."

" Oh, Missy, Missy, do not try to break my heart !"

"If it is not broken now, by this cruel separation, nothing I can do will break it. Mamma, forgive me, if I am not as humble and reverent as I should be, but you have laid a great deal on me. All this is, as you say, quite new to me. It is as if you had taken me by the hand, and led me to the room where my brother lay dying and had said to me, 'See, I have mixed the poison, and given it to him ; we have talked it over for months together ; we are both convinced that it is right and good Death is better than life. Be content, and give thanks for what we have done.'"

" My child, you cannot surely be so blind. How is it that you do not perceive that it is not death, but life, that I have led you in to see ? That I have shown you your brother, girded with a new strength, clothed with a new honor ; set apart for the service of God forever.

8

Missy, he is not lost to us, dear, while we believe in the Communion of Saints."

"Mamma, I don't believe in it! I don't believe in anything. You have overthrown my faith. You have killed me."

"Listen to reason, Missy, if not to faith. St. John is happy; happier than I ever knew him, even as a child; he is happy, even in this time of transition and suspense. If he is blessed with this great gift, if he has sought peace and found it, even in what may seem to you this hard and bitter way, let us be thankful and not hinder him. This is not of an hour's growth, and he will not waver. He is slower than we are, Missy, slower and deeper. St. John is steadfast, and he is fully persuaded in his own mind of what he wants to do and what he ought to do. I know no one with so little natural enthusiasm—the fire that burns in him is not of nature. And he has counted the cost. He knows what he gives up, and he knows what he gains. He knows that he is sure of misconception, reprobation, scorn, and I do not think it weighs a straw with him. What would weigh with you, and possibly with me, is literally of no force at all with him. You know he never thought at all what the world might say about him, not from disrespect to the opinion of others, but from deep indifference, from perfect unconsciousness. That is nature, and not grace, but it makes the step less hard The separation from us, Missy, the giving up his home, that has been a battle indeed; but it has been fought, and, I think, will never have to be gone over, in its bitterness, again."

"I don't know how you can have any assurance of that; excuse me for saying so."

" Well, I cannot explain it to you. I am afraid I could not make you understand exactly. ' The heart hath its reasons, which the reason cannot comprehend.' "

" No doubt. I am not right in asking you to cast these spiritual pearls before me— "

" Missy !"

" But I may ask for some plain husks of fact. I am capable of understanding them perhaps. If it isn't bringing things down too much, please, when does my brother go away—where does he go to, when he goes ?"

" I suppose he will go next month ; he will offer his resignation here to-morrow at the vestry meeting."

" Then will begin the strife of tongues," said Missy, with a shudder. " I suppose he will think it his duty to tell these ten solid gentlemen ' with good capon lined,' fresh from their comfortable dinners, why he goes away."

" Assuredly not, Missy. St. John is not Quixotic. He has good quiet sense."

" He had, mamma. Excuse me. Well, if I may hear it, where is he going, and is it to be unequivocally forever—and—I hope he remains in our own communion ? I don't know whether I ought to ask for such low details or not, but I cannot help a certain interest in them. I suppose an ecstasy has no body ; but a resolution may have."

" Surely, Missy, you will not say things like these to St. John ? Save your taunts for me. It would wound him cruelly, and he would not know, as I do, that they spring from your suffering and deep love to him."

" Truly, mamma, you are too tender of the feelings of your ascetic. If I wound him, that is a part of what

he has undertaken ; that is what he ought to be prepared for, and to ask for. You can't put yourself between him and his scourge. Think of it ! how the
lash will come down on his white flesh ; and St. John
has always been a little tender of his flesh, mamma.
Well—is he Roman or Anglican? For I confess I
feel I do not know my brother. Please translate him
to me."

"I don't know why, having seen no wavering in
his faith, you should insult him by supposing he has
any intention to forsake it. But let us end this conversation, Missy. I feel too ill to talk further to-night,
beyond telling you he hopes to enter an order in Eng-
land, and that he will be gone, in any event, two
years. After that, it is all uncertain. If he is received, he is under obedience. He may be sent to
America ; he may end his days in India. We may
see him often, or we may see him never. It is all
quite one to him, I think, and I pray he may not even
have a wish."

Mrs. Varian ceased speaking, and lay back on
her sofa quite white and exhausted.

"I suppose I'd better not keep you awake any
longer, then," said Missy, rising. "Is there anything
I can do for you? Call me if you need me. Good-
night." She stooped over her mother and kissed her
lightly. She would not touch her hand, for fear she
should show how cold hers was, and how it trembled.
She went across the room to see if the windows were
closed, and then to the fire to see that it was safe to
leave for the night, and with another word or two,
went out and shut the door. A tempest of remorse
for her unkindness came over her when she was alone

in her own room. She knew what her mother was suffering, had suffered, and though she reproached her for having influenced her brother's decision, she reproached herself for having added one pang to her already too great sorrow. She had, indeed, cruelly wounded her, and left her to the long night watches without a word of repentance.

Missy would have given worlds to have been on the other side of the door she had just closed. *Then* it would be easy to let the tears come that were burning in her eyes, and to throw herself into her mother's arms, and be silently forgiven. But in cold blood to go back, to reopen the conversation, to take back what she had said, to humble herself to ask forgiveness for what was true, but which ought not to have been spoken—this was more than she had grace to do. She longed for the time to come when she should have a sorrow to bear that was not mixed up with repentance for some wrong-doing of her own. This loss of her brother, cruel as it was, would always be made crueller by the recollection of her jealousy of him, of her unkindness to her mother, of the way in which she had rejected her sympathy and taunted her with the share she had had in what had happened. It all seemed insupportable, the wounded love, the separation, the remorse, the jealousy, and the disappointment. What was her life now? St. John was woven into every part of it. What was her work in the parish, with him away; what her home without his presence? The world, she had given up as much as he, she thought; in it she could find no amusement. Study had been but a means to an end; there was nothing left her but duty—duty without peace or pleasure. She had her mother still, but her mother's heart was with St. John. Missy felt that there was a barrier between them which each day's suffering would add to. She should reproach her mother always for having influenced St. John. (She never for a moment altered her judgment of the error that had been made, nor allowed that there might be a side on which she had not looked.) She was certain that her mother would be unable to endure the separation, and that the months, as they wore away, would wear away her life. She would see her mother fading away before her eyes ; and St. John, in his new life, leaving his duties to her, would be sustained by his mother's praise, and the approbation of his perverted conscience. She would be cut off from the sympathy of both mother and brother ; equally uncongenial to both. She thought of them as infatuated ; they thought of her as worldly-minded ; she looked down upon their want of wisdom ; she knew they looked down upon her unspiritual sordidness. It was all sore and bitter, and as the day dawned upon her sleepless eyes, she thought, with almost a relenting feeling, that if St. John had found peace *anywhere,* he was not to blame for going where it led him.

CHAPTER XI

MY DUTY TO MY NEIGHBOR.

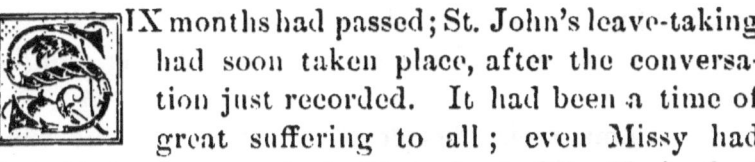IX months had passed; St. John's leave-taking had soon taken place, after the conversation just recorded. It had been a time of great suffering to all; even Missy had found it harder than she had imagined. Miss Varian had taken it very much to heart, and in her violence Missy had become calm. Her natural place was, of course, in opposition to this member of the family. It seemed improper for her to be fighting in the ranks beside her aunt. This, and her great pain in parting from her brother, hushed her outward opposition. She felt she was, at least, justified in supporting him in the eyes of his deserted parish—and thus, Yellowcoats believed always that Missy had been the chief instrument in depriving them of his services; so correct is popular information. Her mother, Missy did not understand. The actual moment of parting was as full of agony as she had anticipated; for an hour after, there really seemed a doubt to others than Missy, whether the poor mother would ever come out of the swoon which had followed the last sound of the carriage wheels outside. But when, after a day or two, the physical effects of the emotion passed away, Mrs. Varian seemed to grow content and quiet; a deeper peace than before filled her eyes. The yearning, pining weariness which Missy had anticipated, did not come. She seemed to heed neither companionship nor

solitude ; her solitude seemed peopled with angelic company ; while her face welcomed all who came near her, far from angelic as they might be. Her health seemed stronger. It was all a mystery to her daughter.

"Mamma seems better than for years, this winter," she was obliged to say, when asked about her mother's health. She did not talk much about St. John, even with Missy, but when she did talk of him, it was with simplicity and naturalness. His letters never threw her into depression, nor was she deeply anxious when they did not come. She always gave the letters to Missy to read, which had not been the case before. They were short, affectionate, plain as to fact, expressing nothing of inward emotion. Missy felt sure that this was understood between them, and that the outpouring of heart which had been so dear to both, was part of the sacrifice.

The new clergyman came, and parish matters in their new light had to be talked over. This was acute pain to Missy, to whom it seemed St. John's work alone. It seemed to give no pain to her mother, and her interest in affairs connected with the village church was unabated. The only thing that seemed to pain her, was the adverse criticism upon the step her son had taken, which Miss Varian took pains should come to her ears. People opened their minds on the matter to *her*, knowing she was strongly opposed to it, and she felt it to be her one source of consolation, to repeat these confidences to her sister-in-law.

After a time, it became Missy's business to thwart her in obtaining interviews with her mother, and to have always a servant in the room. Before a servant,

Miss Varian would not talk on family matters, even when she was very bitter, and Goneril had a comfortable corner of the room where she was not loth to do her sewing, and where she saved Mrs. Varian many a sharp stab. The children, too, came often to the house, almost as often as in the summer time, and they and their nurse made a wall of defense as well.

After all, the winter wore away not unpeacefully to the Varian household, and all the desponding anticipations seemed to have been unwarranted. The children went and came ; Jay's warm little hand was often in Missy's when she walked and rode ; she had much occupation in the house, not as many interests outside. Time seemed to be healing the wound made by her brother's departure ; she had read systematically, she was in fine health, the winter had been steadily cold and bracing. Yes, it had been a quiet, peaceful time to them all since Christmas. She blushed when she remembered how persistently she had prophesied evil, refusing to be comforted. "I must be very commonplace," she thought. "I am not even capable of suffering consistently." On the whole, however, it was a relief to be contented and comfortable, and she did not reject it exactly, though she took it under protest, and with a certain shame. She had, too, got over the violence of her feelings in the matter of her neighbor. She remembered her keen emotions with mortification. A good many things had contributed to this, principally the fact that St. John's going had eclipsed all other events, and that, in that real sorrow, the trifling sting was forgotten. Besides, the gentleman himself had had the kindness to keep entirely at home.

It was now May, and since November Missy had

8*

not spoken to him once. His household matters seemed to have been working smoothly. The servants, Missy learned through Eliza, the nurse, were contented and industrious. Mr. Andrews, she said, was the nicest gentleman to work for. He seemed as comfortable as a king, and was pleased with everything they did for him. He read his paper after dinner, and then talked with the children, and after they went to bed, read or wrote till after all were sleeping in the house. Two nights in the week he stayed in town ; he did not seem to mind going back and forth. Sometimes he brought a gentleman home with him, but that was not very often. He seemed to think the children much improved, and he took an interest in their lessons, and made them tell him every night what they had been learning. As Eliza was herself their teacher, this gratified her very much. She was a steady, sensible young woman, and was in reality a protegée of Missy's. Missy had had her in her Sunday-school class, had prepared her for confirmation, and had never ceased to look after her and advise her ; and had told a very naughty "story" when she denied to Mr. Andrews that the nurse elect was any protegée of hers. But in certain crises the most virtuous of women will say what is not true.

At first Missy tried to repress Eliza's devotion to her, and not to listen to the details she insisted on giving of her daily life and trials ; but it was too alluring to give advice, and to manage Jay by proxy ; and after a month or two, Missy ruled as truly in the Andrews nursery as she did in her own home. She was not without influence, either, over the other servants in the widower's establish-

ment. They knew they owed their places to her,
and they were anxious to obtain her good opinion.
Through Eliza many hints were obtained how to manage about certain matters, how to arrange in certain
delicate contingencies.

"Why, if I were in your place, Eliza, I should tell
the cook she'd better speak to Mr. Andrews about
Martin's coming in so late. It is always best to be
truthful about such matters."

" Of course I don't know anything about it ; but it
seems to me the waitress would do much better to put
up all the silver that is not in use, and ask Mr. Andrews to have it packed away. It only gives additional work, and can do no one any good ; and it is
really rather unsafe to have so much about, Mr. Andrews is away so many nights."

This had all come about so gradually, Missy would
have denied indignantly that she had ever put a finger
in her neighbor's pie ; whereas, both pretty little white
hands were in it greedily, all ten fingers, all the time.
Dear Missy, how she did love to boss it !

It was only when Gabrielle turned up her eyes,
with the expression that she had had in them that horrid day by the green-house door—though she discreet-
ly held her tongue—or when by rare chance Missy
passed Mr. Andrews in driving, that she stiffened up,
and felt the angry aversion coming over her again.
As long as he kept out of sight it was all very well ;
and he had been wise, and had kept out of sight all
the winter long.

It was now May ; and perhaps he began to think it
would be very rude not to make a call upon his neighbors, after all their kindness to the children ; perhaps

he began to grow a little tired of his freedom from the
tyranny of women; perhaps his evenings were a trifle
dull, now that he could not sit, with his book, between
a wood fire and a student lamp. Perhaps he came
from duty; perhaps he came because he wanted to
come; but at all events he came, one soft May evening, in the twilight, and walked up the steps of the
piazza, and rang the bell that he had not rung for six
long months of frost and snow. It is certain he
felt a trifle awkward about doing it; his manner
showed that. Missy was alone in the library, writing
a letter by the lamp. She looked up, surprised, when
he entered—indeed, more than surprised. They were
both so awkward that they were silent for a moment—
the worst thing to be.

"It seems a long while since I have seen you, Miss
Rothermel," said Mr. Andrews; and then he began to
see how much better it would have been not to say
it. It was so absurd for people living side by side
not to have spoken to each other for six months. It
couldn't have happened without a reason; and the reason came, of course, to both their minds.

"Yes, I believe it is," returned Missy, uncomfortably. "I think I caught sight of you, one day last
week, coming from the cars. The new time-table is a
great improvement, I should think. I suppose you get
home now quite early, don't you?"

She was naturally the first to get command of herself, and by and by they got upon safe ground. But
Missy was uneasy, stiff; Mr. Andrews wished the visit
over many times before it was, no doubt.

"I will call my aunt," said Missy, "she enjoys
visitors so much."

"Which is more than you do," thought Mr. Andrews as he watched her cross the room and ring a bell. But Miss Varian was long in coming.

"Don't you think Jay is growing nicely?" asked Mr. Andrews, trying to find a subject that was safe. He dared not mention Gabrielle, of course.

"Yes, he seems very well this spring. And he is a good boy, too, I think—for him, that is."

There was a certain pretty softening of her face, when she spoke of Jay, that never escaped Mr. Andrews. He liked to see it, it amused him as much as it pleased him. "Jay has made his first conquest," he thought. "This severe little lady is perfectly his slave."

"I am afraid he troubles you with his frequent visits. His nurse tells me he insists on coming very often," he said aloud.

"Oh, he never troubles me ; sometimes I do not even see him. He is great friends with mamma."

"Mrs. Varian is well, I hope? I have thought very often your brother's absence must try her very much."

Most unreasonably the tears rushed into Missy's eyes at the allusion to her brother. The letter on her lap was to him, and she was rather less composed than usual.

"We bear it," she said, "as people bear what they cannot help. It was what mamma wanted for him, and so, in some ways, it seems easier to her than to me. Though of course the loss falls heaviest on her." This was more than she had ever said to any one, and

she could not understand, a moment after, how she
could have said it.

"It was," he said thoughtfully, "a grave step for
him to take; I confess I cannot understand his
motives, but, young as he is, one feels instinctively his
motives are more entitled to respect than those of most
men."

"I cannot respect motives that give me so much
misery," she said, in a voice that trembled.

At this moment Miss Varian came in. While Mr.
Andrews was speaking to her, and while the severe
hands of Goneril were arranging her a seat, Missy had
time to recollect how near she had been to making
Mr. Andrews a confidant of her feelings about her
brother. Mr. Andrews, who had broken his wife's
heart; a pretty confidant. She colored high with
shame and vexation. What had moved her to so
foolish a step. She was losing all confidence in herself; people who habitually do what they don't mean
to do, are very poor reliance. "I always mean to treat
him with contempt, and I very rarely do it," she
thought. "It is amazing, and a humiliation to me to
recall the way in which I always begin with coldness,
and end with suavity, if not with intimacy."

Pretty soon, Miss Varian began to ask what sort
of a winter he had had. He said it had been very
quiet and pleasant, and that spending a winter in the
country had been a new experience to him.

"You must have found it very dull," she said. "I
hate the country when there's nobody in it, and I
wonder you could want to stay."

"But there was somebody in it," said Mr. Andrews, with a frank smile, "for me. A little boy and

girl that are of more importance than kings and crowns, God bless them."

"With all my heart," said Miss Varian, "but I didn't know you were so domestic. I'm glad to be able to say, I've seen a man who would give up his club and his comfort for his children. Not but that you had some comfort here, of course. It wouldn't do to say that before Missy, who organized your cabinet for you, didn't she? How do your servants get along?"

"Very well, thank you," said Mr. Andrews uncomfortably.

"And have you taken the house for another year?" went on the speaker.

"Oh, yes, it agrees so well with the children here," answered Mr. Andrews apologetically. "I did not know where they would be any better off."

"Well, we must be grateful to them for keeping you, I suppose. I don't think you have been a very valuable neighbor so far, however. You haven't lived enough in the country to know what is expected of neighbors, perhaps."

"No, I must confess—"

"Why, neighbors in the country have a serious duty in the winter. They spend evenings very often together; they play cribbage, they bring over the evening paper; they take watches to town to be mended; they mail letters, they even carry bundles."

"I should think Mr. Andrews would give up the lease of his house if you put much more before him as his duty for next winter."

Missy said this quite loftily, having grown red and white, possibly a little yellow, since her aunt began

to speak.   Her loftiness, perhaps, piqued Mr. Andrews
a little, for he said, turning to her :

"Hasn't a neighbor any summer duties ?   I hope
Miss Varian will make me out a list."

"With pleasure," cried Miss Varian, scenting mischief in the air.

"My aunt's ideas of duty are individual, pray let
me say," Missy put in, in not the most perfectly suave
tone.

"A neighbor, in the summer," went on Miss Varian, as if she had not spoken, "a neighbor in the summer comes across after dinner, and smokes his cigar
at the beach gate, if any of the family are sitting on
the lawn.   In rainy weather he comes over for a game
of cards ; occasionally he comes in time for tea ; if he
has a sail-boat, he takes his neighbors out sometimes
to sail ; he brings them peaches, the very first that
come to market, and he never minds changing a book
at the library in town."

"But these are all privileges ; you were going to
tell me about duties, were you not ?"

"As to that, you may call them what you please,
they are the whole duty of man in the country, and I
can't see how you ever came to overlook them for such
a length of time."

"You shan't be able to reproach me any more.
Peaches are not in market ; and my sail-boat is not
out of winter quarters.   But I might change a library
book for a beginning.   Haven't you got one that I
might try my hand upon ?"

"To be sure I have," said this hateful woman, with
great enjoyment of her niece's anger ; "I have a vol-
ume of Balzac that Goneril has just got through,

under protest, and I'd like to have another, to make
an utter end of her. It's my only chance of getting
rid of her, and you would be a family benefactor."

"Please, let me have the book," said Mr. Andrews.
" Is it this one on the table ?"

" No," said Miss Varian. " I don't think it is
down-stairs. Missy, ring the bell for Goneril to get
it ; will you ?"

Missy had been sitting with her head turned away,
and her lips pressed together. After her aunt spoke,
she sat quite still for a moment, as if she could not
bring herself to execute the order ; then, without
speaking, got up and walked across to the bell, and
rang it, sitting down when she came back, a little further from the light, and from the two talkers.

" Missy, you've got through with the book yourself, haven't you ?" said her aunt, determined to make
her talk, as she was sure her voice, if she could be
made to use it, would show her agitation.

That was Missy's calamity. Her voice was very
sweet and pleasant ; the nicest thing about her, except
her feet and hands. But it was a very unmanageable
gift, and it registered her emotions with unfailing ac-
curacy. Missy might control her words, occasionally,
but she could not control her voice, even occasionally.
It was never shrill in anger, but it was tremulous and
husky, and, in fine, angry. So now, when she answered her aunt that she had not seen the book, and
did not know its name, and did not want to read it,
the words were faultless, but the voice, alas, betrayed
the want of harmony between aunt and niece. That
Mr. Andrews had suspected since his earliest acquaintance with them.

"Oh, then, I won't keep it out for you," Miss Varian said blithely. "But, maybe you'd like Mr. Andrews to take back your Lecky ; I heard you say at breakfast you had finished it. It wouldn't be much more trouble to take two than one, would it, Mr. Andrews ?"

"Neither would be any trouble, but a great pleasure," said Mr. Andrews, civilly.

"Thank you ; but there is no need to put it upon you. We have not left our books to chance bounty ; the expressman is trusty, and takes them regularly."

"We sometimes have to wait three days !" cried Miss Varian, annoyed to have her errand look like a caprice.

"Well, I shall try to be more prompt than the expressman. Perhaps you'd better make out your list, that there may be no mistake."

"Missy, get a card, will you, and make out a list."

Missy again got up, after a moment's hesitation, looked in her desk, and got the card and pencil, and sat down as if waiting for further orders. In the meanwhile Goneril had come in, and was waiting, like a suppressed volcano, for information as to the cause of this repeated interruption of her evening's recreation. Miss Varian sent her for the book, and then said, "Missy, I wish you'd get the card."

"I have been waiting some time," said Missy.

"Well, then," said Miss Varian, pleasantly, "write out a list of Balzac, beginning with 'Les Petites Misères de la Vie Conjugale'—translated, of course, for Goneril can hardly read English, let alone French. I *ought* to have a French maid."

"Surely," said Missy, "if you want to read Balzac."

"I do want to read him, every line," returned her aunt. "'Les Petites Misères.' Well, let me see—what else haven't I read of his?"

Missy paused with her pencil suspended over the paper after she had written the name. She disdained to prompt.

"Can't you think, Missy?" said her aunt sharply.

"I can't," said Missy, quietly.

"Well, you're not often so short of words, whatever may be the cause. Mr. Andrews, I beg you won't think ill of my niece's intelligence. She is generally able to express herself. You have read ever so many of Balzac's books aloud to me, you must know their names."

"I don't recall them at this moment," returned Missy, using her pencil to make a little fiend turning a somersault, on the margin of the evening paper which lay beside her.

"Can't you help me, Mr. Andrews," said Miss Varian, a little tartly.

"I, oh, certainly," said Mr. Andrews, recalling himself from what seemed a fit of absentmindedness. "Some of the names of Balzac's books. Let me see, 'César Birotteau,' 'Le Père Goriot'—"

"Oh, I don't mean those. I've read all those, of course. I'd like some of the—well, some of the ones I wouldn't have been likely to have read, you know. Missy, there was one you were so horrified about, but you were fascinated too. Can't you think what it was? It occurs to me I'd like to try it again. You're not generally so stupid, or so prudish, whichever it may be." Missy's lips grew tight; she made another little fiend on the paper, before she trusted herself to answer.

"Perhaps," she said, handing the card across the table to her aunt, "you had better leave it to Mr. Andrews and the librarian. Maybe between them they can find something that will please you."

"Well, Mr. Andrews, then I'll *have* to leave it to you. And if you bring me something that I have read before, it will be Missy's fault, and you'll have to hold her responsible for it."

"I hope I shall be able to suit you; but in any case, I have quite a lot of French books at the house, which are at your service."

"But, you see, my maid can't read French, and so I have to have translations."

"Oh, I forgot. Well, perhaps, Miss Rothermel, some of them might suit you, if you'd let me send them in to you."

"You are very kind," said Missy. "But I have my reading laid out for two months to come, and it would be impossible for me to take up anything more."

Mr. Andrews bowed, and got up to take his leave. Miss Varian gave him the card and her hand too, and said an effusive and very neighborly good-night. Missy half rose, and bent her head, but did not offer to put out her hand.

"The caprices and the tempers of women," he thought, as he went home under the big trees and looked back at the friendly or unfriendly lights gleaming from the library window. "Their caprices and their tempers and their tongues!"

Nevertheless, he found himself speculating upon which of Balzac's books Missy had been fascinated with and horrified about. He did not like to think of her as reading Balzac, and being ashamed to own it too. He always thought of her as a "severe little lady;" she seemed to him, with all her caprice and temper, and even her sharp tongue, as the embodiment of all the domestic virtues. He had liked her face that day she came out of church, with her blind aunt on her arm, and little Jay close at her side; surely she was a good woman, if there were good women in the world. Nevertheless (as he lit his cigar), he could have wished she had a better sense of justice, and did not vent on him the anger engendered by the faults of others.

The next evening promptly upon the arrival of the carriage from the train, Eliza and Jay brought over "Les Petites Misères," and another of Balzac for Miss Varian from the library, and the last "Saturday Review," "Revue des Deux Mondes" and "Punch" for Miss Rothermel. Missy would not even take them off the table where her aunt had laid them down. She considered it quite humbling that he could not understand his literature had been refused. She had quite prided herself on the decision with which she had nipped in the bud that neighborliness, and here he was persistently blooming out into politeness again.

"This shall be put an end to forever," she thought. "They shall go back with their leaves uncut to-morrow, and that he cannot misconstrue."

CHAPTER XII.

FIRE AND SWORD.

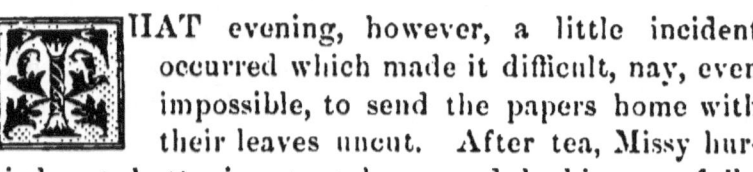HAT evening, however, a little incident occurred which made it difficult, nay, even impossible, to send the papers home with their leaves uncut. After tea, Missy hurried out, buttoning a sack on, and looking carefully around to see that she was not followed by neighborly notice. It had been a warm and lovely day ; May was melting into June ; the evening was perfect, the sun not quite below the hills as yet. Missy went across the lawn ; the tide was high, and there was little wind. She pulled in the anchor of a little boat that rocked on the waves, and stepping in, took the oars and pushed out. No one was looking ; Mr. Andrews was no doubt taking his solid and comfortable dinner, and had not yet ventured to accept Miss Varian's invitation to come and smoke his cigar at the beach gate. Missy had resolved that he should find no one there to bear him company, even if she gave up her favorite after-tea hour on the lawn, all summer. She pulled out into the bay, with a sense of getting free which is one of the pleasures of a woman on a horse or in a boat by herself. Some of ' Missy's happiest hours were spent skimming over the bay like a May-fly. No one could recall her to duty or bondage till she chose. She almost forgot Aunt Harriet when she was across the harbor ; housekeeping cares fell from her when she pushed off into the water,

and only came back when the keel grated on the shore again. To-night she drew a long breath of freedom as she pulled herself, with light-dipping oars, far out on the serene blue bay, and then, resting, held her breath and listened. How sweet and placid the scene !

Fret and headache, sin and temptation !—it was difficult to believe in them, out here in the cool and fresh stillness, palpitating with the gentle swell of the tide, fanned by an air that scarcely moved the waters, transfigured by the glorious hues that overspread the heavens and colored sea and land. " It is good to be here. Why must I ever go back again ?" she thought, and then scorned herself for the unpractical and senti-mental longing. " At any rate, I shall have time to go over to the West Harbor, before it is night, and per-haps get a look across Oak Neck into the Sound."

The village looked tranquil and sweet as she passed it ; the smoke rose from a chimney here and there ; the faint sounds came out to her like a dream ; a little motion attracted the eye now and then, where the road was not hidden by the trees ; a boatman moved about on the shore, but slowly, musically. The rich verdure of the early summer fields crept down to the yellow strip of sand, upon which the waters plashed ; two or three spires reached up into the rosy sky ; pretty cottages peeped through the silent trees, green lawns lay with the evening shadows stretching across them. It was hard to believe that there, in that tranquillity, nestled sin and sickness ; that there people went to law with each other, and drove sharp bargains, and told lies. That there indigestion and intemperance had their victims ; that lust laid its cruel wait beneath that shade, that hypocrisy there played its little part.

"I will believe only what I see," thought Missy, gliding past. "All is lovely and serene." It was a long pull to the West Harbor. The pink had faded from the sky and from the waters before she turned towards home. She paddled along the shores of the little island that lies opposite Yellowcoats, and shuts in its pretty harbor from the Sound, and watched the changing of the sky from rose color to gray, and from gray to deep, dark blue, and the coming out of a silver thread of moon, and of a single star. Then one by one she saw lights glimmer in the distant village, and one, a little brighter and sharper than the rest, that even made for a moment a light against the sky.

"Lady Bird, Lady Bird, fly away home,
    Your house is on fire, and your children will burn,"

she sang to herself as she rowed across the bay, with her back to the place she was going to, as is the sad necessity of rowers. She neared the shore just below Ship Point, and then, turning around her head, stopped involuntarily to listen, as she heard the sound of a bell. It must have been a fire, after all, she thought; for while she rowed across the bay, she had forgotten the sudden light that made her think of Lady Bird, and the sound of her oars had kept her from hearing the bells which had been ringing for some time, no doubt. Her first impulse was to spring on shore, and run up the lane towards the houses that lay on the out-skirts of the village, and hear what was the matter. Then she reflected that she could do no good, and that her absence and the fire together might upset her mother; so she soberly turned her boat towards home, speculating nevertheless, upon the chances of the fire, and wondering whose old barn or out-house had fallen victim to the heel of its owner's pipe. She certainly had no feeling of personal interest in the matter, further than as all Yellowcoats was of personal interest to her.

But as she neared the steamboat landing, and came opposite a stretch of road that was clear of trees, she could hear voices, and see people moving along it.

A sudden feeling of fright came over her, for beyond the steamboat landing were but two houses, their own, and Mr. Andrews'. She pulled with all her strength and her boat shot through the water, but it seemed to her she crept, and that she had time to go through scenes of misfortune and trouble enough to turn her gray. She could see no blaze, but the bells down in the village were still pealing forth their call. There was just light enough to see motion upon the road, and hear voices, and there must have been a multitude of them to have been audible above the dash of her quick oars.

She scarcely dared look around when she felt the keel touch the stones ; no, it was not the Andrews' house ! What a sight on their own lawn ! Volumes of smoke covered the house ; a score of people thronged the place ; men with lanterns were calling and shouting ; piles of what looked like furniture lay about ; women were flitting here and there on the outskirts of the crowd, she could see their light clothes through the haze. It was all so dim, she felt more terror than if a great flame had towered up and showed her all. Springing from the boat, she ran to the beach gate, now lying off its hinges on the sand.

9

"What is it?" she said faintly to the first person she encountered. One of the maids, hearing her voice, ran towards her from a group where she had been standing uselessly telling her story over and over.

"What is all this, Ann?" she said, hurrying forward to meet the girl.

"O Miss Rothermel! Oh! Oh!" she cried, and bursting into tears ran off, throwing her apron over her head. Missy's limbs shook under her. Her one thought was, of course, her mother. She struggled forward through the crowd, on this part of the lawn, all men.

"Keep back now, keep back. We don't want no women here," cried a man, pushing her away, without looking at her. They were working stoutly at something, she didn't know what. The crowd were being pushed back. The smoke was suffocating, the ground uncertain; ladders and furniture seemed under her feet at every step. She could not speak, she did not recognize the man who pushed her back, nor could she, through the smoke, see any face clearly enough to know it. She heard a good many oaths, and knew that the crowd were very much in the way, and that the men at work were swearing at those who hindered them. Still she struggled to get nearer. Every moment she seemed to grow weaker, and every moment the horror of failing to get to her mother, seemed to grow stronger. At last she saw what they were trying to do, to get a rope stretched round the house, to keep back the crowd, perhaps from danger, perhaps from plunder. She heard above the noise, Mr. Andrews' voice in com-

mand ; the crowd seemed to obey him. A line was
stretched across the lawn, some thirty feet from the
house, and the idle people were pressed back behind it.
Missy by a desperate effort writhed through the
crowd, and caught at the rope, and held by that,
though pushed and swayed up and down, and almost
crushed between her taller and more powerful neighbors. Mr. Andrews, passing along inside the cleared
space, was calling out some orders to the men. He
passed within a foot or two of where she stood, and
she found voice enough to call to him and make him
hear.

"Where are you ?" he said, hurriedly, coming
towards her through the darkness.

"Let me come to where you are," she gasped,
stretching out one hand to him, but keeping the other
fast closed over the rope.

"Let Miss Rothermel pass there ; fall back, won't
you, quick."

They obeyed him, falling back, and in a moment
Missy stood free inside the rope, holding desperately
to the hand Mr. Andrews had stretched out to her.

"Mamma—" she said, brokenly, "tell me if she is
hurt."

"She is safe—all right—I took her, at the first
alarm, to my house. You'd better get to her as
quickly as you can. Come with me, I will get you
through the crowd ; it is less on this side of the house."

He hurried her forward ; she stumbled and nearly
fell over a roll of carpet, and seemed to be walking
over an expanse of books and table-covers and candle-
sticks.

"Don't worry about any of these things," he said,

"they'll all be safe, now the crowd are all behind the rope."

"I don't worry about anything," she said, "but mamma."

"You can be easy about her; there, I can't be spared here, I think you can get on now. Tell her the fire is all out, and there is nothing to worry about. I will see to everything. Ho, there, let Miss Rothermel through, will you?"

She crawled under the rope, and the people made way for her very promptly. It was so dark, she could not recognize any of them, but she heard several familiar voices, and offers of assistance. She was soon out of the press, and then ran fleetly through the gate and out into the road, and then through the gate of the Andrews' cottage, and in a moment more was kneeling by her mother's side. Mrs. Varian, at the sight of her, broke down completely, and sobbed upon her shoulder. She had been perfectly calm through all the excitement, but the relief of seeing Missy was more than she could bear. No one had known where she was, and there had been unspoken terror in the mother's mind. A few hurried explanations were all that she could give. An alarm of fire had reached her in her room, about twilight, and an oppressive odor of smoke and burning wood. She had heard cries and exclamations of fright from the servants, and Goneril, in all haste, had run for Mr. Andrews. In a moment he was on the spot, and no words could express her gratitude for his consideration, and her admiration for his energy. Before anything else was done save to send the alarm to the village (which was the work of an instant, as a horse was saddled at the door), he had insisted upon bringing her here ; she had walked down the stairs, but the smoke and the excitement had overcome her, and he had lifted her in his arms, and carried her out of her house into his own. After a little time Goneril had appeared, leading Miss Varian, and bringing a reassuring message from Mr. Andrews. The people from the village, she said, had got there in an incredible time. All Yellowcoats, certainly, had gone in at that gate, Miss Varian said, coming into the room at that moment, guiding herself by the door-posts and wainscoting in the unfamiliar place. Certainly she should alter her opinion of the extent of the population after this. And every man, woman and child in all the town swarmed round the place ten minutes after the alarm was given, and were there yet, though the fire had been out for almost half an hour.

"And," she went on, addressing Missy, "if it hadn't been for this neighbor of ours, that you have been pleased to snub so mightily, I think we shouldn't have had a roof over our heads, nor a stitch of clothing but what we have upon our backs. Such a crowd of incapables as you have in your employ. Such wringing of hands, such moaning, such flying about with no purpose. And even Peters lost his head completely. If Mr. Andrews and Goneril hadn't set them to work, and kept them at it till the others came, there would have been no help for us. Mr. Andrews insisted upon my coming away, ordered me, in fact. But I forgave him before I had got out the gate, though I was pretty mad at first."

"I wonder if I ought not to go and see if I can be of use," said Missy, irresolutely, rising up.

But the start and flutter in her mother's hand made her sit down again.

"It's my advice to you to stay where you are," said her aunt. "We are a lot of imbeciles, all of us. We are better out of the way. It isn't very pleasant to think of the linen closet emptied upon the lawn, and all Yellowcoats tramping over it, but it's better than being suffocated in the smoke, or crushed to death in the crowd."

Missy gave her mother a reassuring pressure of the hand, and did not move again. They were indeed a company of useless beings. It was a strange experience to her to be sitting still and thinking the destruction of her household goods a light misfortune. That linen closet, from which the unaccounted-for absence of a pillow-case, would have given her hours of annoyance; the book-cases, where order reigned and where dust never was allowed ; the precious china on the dining-room shelves, only moved by her own hands—for all these she had not a thought of anxiety, as she felt her mother's hand in hers. The relief from the fears of that quarter of an hour, while she was making her way through the crowd, had had the effect of making these losses quite unfelt. Subdued, and nervously exhausted too, she sat beside her mother, while the noises gradually subsided on the grounds adjoining. The house was but a stone's throw from the road, and from the Varians' gate, and Miss Varian, with keen ear, sitting on the piazza outside, interpreted the sounds to those within.

"Now the women are beginning to go home," she said. "The children are fretting and sleepy ; there, that one got a slap. Now the teams, hitched to the

trees outside, are unhitched and going away. I wonder
how much plunder is being stowed away in the bottom
of the wagons. I feel as if my bureau drawers were
going off in lots to suit pilferers. There now, the boys
and men are beginning to straggle off in pairs. You
may be sure there isn't anything to see, if *they* are
going. Talk of the curiosity of women. Men and
boys hang on long after *their* legs give out. Ah ! now
we're beginning to get toward the end of the entertainment, I should think. I hear Mr. Andrews calling
out to the men to clear the grounds, and see that the
gates are shut ; ah, bang goes the front gate. Well,
I should think the poor man might be tired by this
time. I should think he might come in and leave
things in charge of some of those men who have been
working with him."

The clock in the parlor struck ten, and then half-
past. Eliza, who had been watching the children, and
making up some beds above, now came down and
begged Mrs. Varian to come up and go to bed, but she
refused. The other servants, who had been over at
the fire, possibly helping a little, now came in, bringing a message from Mr. Andrews, that he begged they
would all go to bed ; and that everything was safe and
they must feel no anxiety. It might be some time before he could get away. Missy persuaded her aunt
and her mother to go up. Eliza conducted Miss Varian
to a small "spare" room. Missy felt a shudder as she
put down her candle on the dressing-table of the room
where she had seen Mrs. Andrews die. She hoped her
mother did not know it.

While she was arranging her for the night, she had
time to observe the room. It was very much changed

since she had last been in it ; the pictures were taken
from the walls, the position of the furniture altered,
she was not sure but that it was other furniture. Certainly the sofa and footstool and large chair were
gone. Mr. Andrews himself occupied the small room
on the other side of the house that he had had from
the first. This room, the largest and best in the house,
had been kept as a sort of day nursery for the children through the winter. Missy had often thought of it
as calculated to keep alive the memory of their mother,
but now it seemed, as if with purpose, that had been
avoided, and as if the whole past of the room was to
be wiped out.

It could be no chance that had worked such a
change. There were holes still in the wall where a
bracket had been taken down. A new clock was on
the mantelpiece ; there was literally not a thing left the
same, not even the carpet on the floor. It gave her a
feeling of resentment ; but this was not the moment to
feel resentment. So she went softly down the stairs,
telling her mother to try to sleep, and she would wait
up, and see if she could do anything more than thank
Mr. Andrews when he came in. This was no more
than civil ; but strangely, Missy did not feel civil, as
she sat counting the minutes in the parlor below. She
felt as if it were odious to be there, odious to feel that
he was working for them, that she must be grateful to
him. All her past prejudices, which had been dying
out in the silence of the last few months, and under
the knowledge of his steady kindness to his children,
came back as she went up into that room, which, to her
vivid imagination, must always bring back the most
painful scene she had ever witnessed. She had never

expected to enter this house again, at least while its present tenants occupied it, and here she was, and certain to stay here for one night and day at least. She had had none of these feelings as she sat during the evening silently thankful beside her mother; all this tumult of resentment had come since she had gone upstairs. The memory of the beautiful young creature, whose dreadful death she had witnessed, came back to her with strange power; and the thought that she had been banished from her children's minds made her almost vindictive. How can I speak to him? how have I ever spoken to him? she thought, as her eyes wandered around the room, searching for some trace of her. But it was thoroughly a man's apartment, "bachelor quarters" indeed. Not a picture of the woman whose beauty would have graced a palace; not a token that she had ever been under this roof, that she had died here less than a year ago. The nurse had come into the room as Missy sat waiting, and, seeming to divine her thought, said, while she put straight chairs and books:

"Isn't it strange, Miss Rothermel, that there isn't any picture of Mrs. Andrews anywhere about the house? I should think their father would be afraid of the children forgetting all about her. I often talk to them about her, but I don't know much to say, because none of us ever saw her; and Mr. Andrews never talks about her to them, and I am sure Jay doesn't remember her at all. There was once a little box that Jay dragged out of a closet in the attic, and in the evening after he found it, he was playing with it in the parlor by his father, and Gabby caught sight of it, and cried, 'That's my mamma's box; give it to me, Jay.' They

9*

had a little quarrel for it, and Gabby got it, and then Jay forgot all about it, and went to play with something else. But," went on Eliza, lowering her voice, " that evening I saw Mr. Andrews, after the children had gone to bed, empty all Gabrielle's things out of the box, and carry it up stairs, and put it away in a locked-up closet in the hall."

"Probably he wanted to punish her for taking it away from Jay," said Missy, insincerely, feeling all the time that it was not the thing for her to be allowing Eliza to tell her this.

"No," said Eliza, " for he brought her home a beautiful new box the next evening, and he wouldn't have done that if he had wished to punish her, I think."

"Eliza, don't you think you'd better see if the fire is good in the kitchen? Mr. Andrews might want a cup of coffee made, or something cooked to eat. He must be very tired."

Eliza meekly received her dismissal, and went into the kitchen. At half-past eleven o'clock Missy heard the gate open, and went forward to meet Mr. Andrews at the door.

"You are very tired," she said, falteringly.

"I believe I am," he returned, following her into the parlor. She was shocked when she saw him fully in the light of the lamp. He looked tired indeed, and begrimed with smoke, his coat torn, his arm tied up in a rude fashion, as if it had been hurt.

"Sit down," she said, hurriedly pulling out a chair. He stumbled into it.

"I really didn't know how tired I was," he said, laying back his head.

"Can't I get you some coffee, or some wine? You ought to take something at once, I think."

"I'd like a glass of wine," he said, rather faintly. "Here's the key. You'll find it in the sideboard."

But when he attempted to get the hand that wasn't bandaged into his pocket, he stopped, with a gesture of pain.

"Confound it!" he said; "it's a strain, I suppose;" and then he grew rather white.

"Let me get it," said Missy, hurriedly.

"The inside pocket of my coat—left side," he said.

She fumbled in the pocket, rather agitatedly, feeling very sorry that he was so suffering, but not sorry enough to make her forget that it was very awkward for her to be bending over him and searching in his inside pocket for a key. At last she found it, and ran and fetched the wine. He seemed a little better when he drank it.

"What is the matter with your arm?" she said, standing by him to take back the glass.

"A ladder fell on it," he said.

"And you sent for the doctor, did you?"

"The doctor, no! What time has there been to be sending off for doctors?" he returned, rather impatiently, turning himself in the chair, but with a groan. Missy ran out of the room, and in two minutes somebody was on the way to the village for the doctor. Eliza came back into the room with her.

"Can't you get on the sofa? and we'll make you easier," said Missy, standing by him.

But he shook his head. "I think I'll rest a little here," he said, "and then get to my room."

"I know; I've sent for the doctor, but I am afraid

it will be some time before he comes. I thought I might be doing something for your hand that's strained, I am afraid to meddle with your arm. Do you think your shoulder's out of place, or anything like that?"

"No, I hardly think it is," he said. It's more likely nothing but a bruise; but it hurts like—thunder!"

This last came from an attempt to get out of his chair. Missy shook up the pillows of the sofa.

"See," she said, "you'll be more comfortable here; let Eliza help you." He submitted, and got to the sofa. "Now, before you lie down, let us get your coat off," she said. She felt as if he were Jay, and must be coaxed. But getting the coat off was not an easy matter; in fact, it was an impossible matter.

"It's torn a good deal," she said; "you wouldn't care if I got the scissors and cut it a little?"

"Cut it into slivers!" he said, concisely. He was evidently feeling concisely, poor man!

Eliza flew for the scissors; in a moment Missy's pretty fingers had done the work, and the poor mutilated coat fell to the floor, a sacrifice to neighborly devotion. "Now run and get me a pail of boiling water, and some flannels—quick. In the meantime, Mr. Andrews, turn your hand a little; I want to get at the button of your sleeve. Oh, dear! don't move it; I see. Here go the scissors again. I'll mend the sleeve for you, I promise; it's the least that I can do. There! now it's all right. Now let me get this towel under your wrist. Ah! I know it hurt; but it had to be done. Now here's the hot water. Eliza, kneel here by Mr. Andrews; and as fast as I hand you the flannel, put it on his wrist—see, just there."

Missy withdrew, and gave her place to Eliza ; but the first touch of her hands to the flannel which she was to wring out made her jump so, she felt sure she never could do justice to them.

"You'd better let me wring out the flannels, Miss Rothermel, and you put them on," said Eliza. "My hands are used to hot water." So Missy went back to her place, and knelt beside her patient, taking the steaming flannels from Eliza's hand, and putting them on his wrist. Before she put each one on, she held it up against her cheek, to see that it was not too hot. She was as gentle and as tender and as coaxing as if she were taking care of little Jay. It is a question how much sentiment a man in severe pain is capable of feeling. But certainly it ought to have been a solace to any one to be tended by such a sweet little nurse as this. Who would think that she could spit fire, or snub her neighbors, or "boss" it, even over servants?

Missy was a born nurse. She was quick-witted, nimble-fingered, sure-footed, and she was coaxing and tender when people were "down." She was absolutely sweet when any one was cornered or prostrate, and couldn't do any way but hers.

The hot cloths, which had stung him a little at first, soon began to relieve the pain in his wrist.

"There, now, I told you it would. You were so good to let us do it. Do bear it a little longer, please."

Missy's eyes had wandered to the clock many times, and her ears had been strained to catch the sound of the doctor's steps outside. But it was now an hour since the messenger had gone, and it was very certain he could not have been at home. When he might come, how many miles away he was at this moment, it was impossible to guess. She knew very well that the other arm was the real trouble; and she knew, too, that leaving it for so many hours unattended to might make it a bad business. Her experience never had gone beyond sprains and bruises, but she had the courage of genius; she would have tackled a compound fracture if it had come in her way.

"That tiresome doctor," she said, sweetly. "I wonder when he'll get here. See, I've muffled up the wrist in this hot bandage. Now suppose we try if we can't do something for this arm over here. I'll be ever so gentle. Now see, I didn't hurt you much before."

Mr. Andrews' face contracted with pain as she touched his wounded arm, even in the lightest manner. In fact, he was bearing as much pain as he thought he could, without having it touched. But it wasn't in nature to resist her, and he turned a little on his side, and the scissors flew up his sleeve and laid bare the bruised, discolored arm.

"You see," she said, softly getting a piece of oil-silk under it, "if it is only bruised this will help it, and if it's broken or out of joint or anything, it will not do any harm. It doesn't hurt you when I touch it here, does it?" she went on, watching his face keenly as she passed her hand lightly over his shoulder.

"It hurts everywhere," he answered groaning, but he did not wince particularly.

"I don't believe there's any dislocation," she said cheerfully, though not too cheerfully, for she knew better than to do that, when any one was suffering. "I don't believe there's any dislocation, and if there isn't,

I'll soon relieve you, if you'll let me try." Eliza came back with more hot water, and again for a patient half hour the wringing of flannels and the application of them went on. At the end of that time, Missy began to think there was something besides sprain and bruise, for the patient was growing pale, and the pain was manifestly not abating. She gave him some more wine, and bathed his head, and fanned him, and wished for the doctor. There was no medicine in the house with which she was familiar. Her own beloved weapons were now out of reach, and she could not bring herself to give opium and the horrid drugs in which this benighted gentleman still believed. Ignatia, camomilla, moschus! Ah, what she might have done for him, if she could have known where to lay her hand on her tiny case of medicines. She gave him more wine ; that was the only thing left for her to do, since he would probably not submit to letting her set his arm, which she was now convinced was broken. She felt quite capable of doing it, or of doing anything rather than sitting still and seeing him suffer. She privately dispatched Eliza to get bandages, and her work-basket, and to replenish the fire in the range.

At last, at a few minutes before two o'clock, the welcome sound of the doctor's gig driving to the gate, met her ear. She let him in, while Eliza sat beside the patient. He looked surprised to see her, and they both thought involuntarily of the last time they had been together in this house.

"You are a good neighbor," he said, taking off his hat and coat in the hall.

"We have had a good neighbor to-night in Mr. Andrews," said Missy, with a little stiffness. "He has made himself ill in our service, and we feel as if we could not do too much in taking care of him."

"Certainly," said the doctor, searching for his case of instruments in his pocket. "You have had a great fire, I hear. How much damage has been done?"

"I do not know at all. I had to stay with my mother, and Mr. Andrews is in too much pain since he came in, to answer any questions. I am very much afraid his arm is broken."

"Indeed," said the doctor, comfortably, shaking down the collar of his coat, which had been somewhat disarranged in the taking off of the superior garment. It seemed as if he were trying how long he could be about it.

Missy fumed.

"Now," he said, following her into the room. He seated himself by the patient in a chair which Missy had set for him when she heard the gate open, and asked him many questions, and poked about his arm and shoulder and seemed to try to be as long in making up his mind as he had been in getting ready to come in.

"Well?" said Missy at last, feeling she could not bear it any longer.

Mr. Andrews' face had expressed that he was about at the end of his patience several minutes before.

It was hoping too much, that he should tell them at once what was the matter; but by and by it was allowed them to infer that Mr. Andrews' arm was broken in two places; that the shoulder was all right, and that the wrist was only sprained, and was much the better for the treatment it had had. He praised Missy indirectly for her promptness, told her Mr. Andrews might thank her for at least one hand—which he could undoubtedly have the use of in a few days. Mr. Andrews' face showed he wasn't prepared for being helpless for even a few days. The pain, great as it was, could not prevent his disgust at this.

"And how long before my arm will be fit to use?" he said shortly.

"Better get it into the splints before we decide when we shall take it out," said the doctor, with complacence, taking out his case of instruments.

He enjoyed his case of instruments, and there was so little use for it at Yellowcoats. It was on his tongue to say something discouraging about the length of the confinement probable, but Missy gave him a warning look, and said cheerfully, "a broken arm is nothing; I've always thought it the nicest accident that any one could have. Besides, it is your left arm. You won't mind the sling at all, if you do have to wear it for a few days longer than you might think necessary. St. John broke his arm once when he was a boy, and it was really nothing. We were surprised to find how soon it was all well."

Missy spoke as if she knew all about it.

"Then you know how to help me with the bandages?" the doctor said.

"Oh, yes, I remember quite well."

By the time that the arm was set, and the patient helped into his room by the doctor and Eliza, Missy had decided that Mr. Andrews bore pain pretty well for a man, and that the doctor was even stupider than she had thought. She also arrived at the conclusion that the whole situation was as awkward as possible, when the door closed upon the object of her solicitude, and she realized that she could do him no further good.

It was only then that she became aware that she was
deeply interested in the case.   To do her justice, if it
had been Eliza's arm she would have suffered a pang in
giving it up.   She was naturally a nurse, and naturally
enthusiastic.   She had made up her mind to disregard
the doctor's orders totally and give the patient homeo-
pathic treatment, according to her lights.   But here was
conventionality coming in.   She must give him up, and
he was no doubt to be shut up in that room for a day or
two at least, to be stupefied with narcotics, and then
dosed with tonics.   Missy clenched her little tired
hands together.   Why could Eliza go in and take care
of him, and she not ?   She could not influence him
through Eliza, or Melinda, or the waitress.   She must
give up conventionality or homeopathy.   It was a
struggle, but conventionality won.

<hr />

CHAPTER XIII.

MINE HOST.

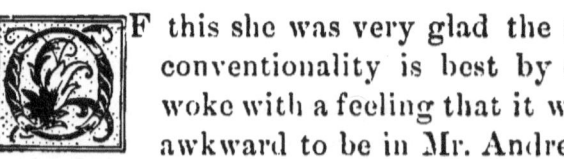F this she was very glad the next morning :
conventionality is best by daylight.   She
woke with a feeling that it was exceedingly
awkward to be in Mr. Andrews' house, and
to have no house of her own to go to.   When she
came down-stairs, Eliza was just putting Mr. Andrews'
breakfast on a tray.   She said he had had no sleep,
and seemed to be uncomfortable.   The breakfast-tray
did not look very inviting, so Missy reconstructed it,

and sent it in, brightened with some white grapes that the gardener had just brought to the door, and three or four soft-looking roses, with the dew upon them.

"Tell Mr. Andrews I hope he will let us know if there is anything we can do for him," she said, half ashamed, as Eliza went up-stairs with the tray.

By this time Miss Varian had come down-stairs, and Goneril, very tired and cross, twitched some chairs and a footstool about for her; and Anne, looking oddly out of place, came in to know if she should carry Mrs. Varian's breakfast up to her. It was all very strange and uncomfortable. The servants had evidently spent much of their time in talking over the incidents of the fire, and Melinda was late with her breakfast. Missy couldn't imagine where they had all slept; but here they all were—two cooks in the kitchen, two waitresses in the dining-room, two maids in the parlor, and no breakfast ready. Miss Varian felt very irritable; the children had waked her by five o'clock with their noise, and she could not go to sleep again. The absence of her usual toilet luxuries exasperated her, and all the philosophy which she had displayed the night before forsook her. She scolded everybody, including Mr. Andrews, who was to blame for having such a hard bed in his spare room, and the cook, who was so late in getting breakfast ready. Missy disdained to answer her, but she felt as cross, in her way. The children, who had been sent out of doors to allow Miss Varian to go to sleep again, now came bursting in, and made matters worse by their noise. They were full of news about the fire, and, to judge by their smutty hands and aprons, had been cruising round the forbidden spot.

"Jay, if you love me," said Missy, putting her hands to her ears, "be quiet and don't talk any more about the fire. Let me eat my breakfast, and forget my miseries."

But Gabrielle could not be silenced, though Jay, when the hominy came, gave himself to that. She always had information to impart, and this occasion was too great to be lost. She told Missy everything she didn't want to hear, from the destruction of the flower-beds by the crowd, to the remarks of the boys at the stable, about her father's broken arm.

"They said he was a fool, to work so hard for nothing; they expected to be paid, but he didn't. Then Peters said 'maybe he expects to be paid as well as you,' and then they all laughed. What did they all laugh for, Missy, and do you suppose my father does expect to be paid?"

"I suppose you were where you had no business to be," said Missy, shortly. "Now, if you will eat your breakfast, and be silent, we shall thank you."

Then Gabby retired into the hominy and there was a silence if not a peace. It was a dull morning—much fog, and little life in the air. Missy hadn't even looked out of the window. She dreaded the thought of what she was to see on the other side of the hedge. If it had been possible, she would have delayed the work that lay before her; but she was goaded on now by the thought that if she did not hurry, they must spend another night here, and eat another breakfast to the accompaniment of Gabby's information and observation. It was ten o'clock before she could get away, leaving directions to the servants to follow her.

It was a dismal scene ; the faultless lawn trampled and torn up, the vines torn from the piazza and lying stretched and straggling on the ground. The windows were curtainless, the piazza steps broken, the piazza piled with ladders and steps and buckets ; the front door had a black eye. There was at this side of the house not much evidence of the fire, but at the rear it was much worse. The summer parlor was badly damaged, the sashes quite burnt black, the ceiling all defaced. The flames had reached the room above, Missy's own room, and here had been stayed. The windows were broken out, a good deal of the woodwork charred, and the walls much damaged with water. These two rooms were all that were seriously injured. It was quite wonderful that the damage had gone no further ; there had been no wind, and Mr. Andrews had been on the spot ; if they had not had these two things in their favor, the house must have gone. Peters had shown himself a respectable donkey, and none of the women but Goneril proved to have any head in such an emergency. Missy tried to be comforted by the smallness of the material injury. But the desolation and disorder of the pretty rooms ! In her own, Missy fairly cried. She felt completely *dépaysée.* A few hundred dollars and a few weeks would put it all in order again, but Missy was not in a philosophic mood. She felt herself an outcast and a wanderer, and turning bitterly from the scorched spot, vowed never to love anything again.

By this time the clumsy Peters and the headless maids had come up to be set to work. So turning the keys on the damaged rooms, she followed them out and began to try roughly to get the furniture back into the rooms to which it belonged. Her ambition, at present, was to get her mother's and her aunt's rooms in order to have them return that night, and the kitchen so far reconstructed that the servants might do their work. But at night-fall, the prospect was so dismal, the hall so encumbered with unbestowed goods, the workmen so tardy, the progress so small, that Missy reluctantly acknowledged she would be cruel to her mother, if she insisted on bringing her back to such a scene of desolation. She must be contented to accept Mr. Andrews' considerate hospitality. He had sent over Eliza with a message at lunch time, in which he took it for granted that they were to stay there for the present, and covered all the ground of an invitation, and was less offensive. It was understood and inevitable, and so she tried to take it.

The rain came down heavily at six o'clock ; as she locked herself out of the front door, and wrapping her waterproof around her, went down the wet steps, and out on the soaking ground, feeling tired and heartsick, she could not but contrast the scene with that of last evening, when, under the smiling rosy sunset, she had come down the steps on her way out to her stolen row upon the bay. It seemed a year ago, instead of a day. Ann followed close behind her, with various articles for the comfort of her mother. At the door of the Andrews' house Ann took off her mistress' waterproof and overshoes.

"I am almost too tired to speak, Ann," she said. "I shall go up-stairs and lie down, and you may bring me a cup of tea. I don't want any dinner."

But once up-stairs, Missy found she must change

her plans, and forget her weariness. Her mother was quite unable to go down to dinner; indeed, was only waiting for her tea, to try to quiet herself with a view to getting a tolerable night. Miss Varian had a violent attack of neuralgia; the whole house had been laid under tribute to alleviate her sufferings. She was to have her dinner in bed, and had ordered the house to be kept perfectly quiet after she had partaken of that meal. Eliza, the waitress, no less than Goneril, had been actively running up and down stairs, to take her orders to the kitchen. Melinda had received directions from Mr. Andrews to cook an unusually elaborate dinner, to do honor to the guests. Ann had confided this to Mrs. Varian in the afternoon. She thought it such a pity, for she knew nobody would eat it. And now, when Missy told her mother, as she took off her hat, that she was going to lie down and have a cup of tea, Mrs. Varian made an exclamation of regret.

"The meals that have gone up and down stairs to-day in this house!" she said. "Mr. Andrews, poor man, doesn't eat much, but it has to be carried to him. And your aunt has had her lunch in many varieties, and now her dinner. And I, alas! And now, if you can't go down, my dear, and the fine dinner has to go off the table without any one even to look at it, it will be unfortunate. You don't think you could go down just for the form of it, and try to eat something? Eliza has had to get out some of the silver that has been packed away, and I have heard much consultation outside about table-cloths. It does seem very awkward. Three guests, and all demanding to be served with dinner in their own rooms. Poor Missy, it always comes on you. There now, don't mind a word of what I've said, but stay here and rest, I know you need it."

For Missy had thrown herself down into a chair, and looked just ready to cry. She was quite over-strained, and if ever any woman needed a cup of tea and the luxury of being let alone, that woman was Missy.

"Of course I can go down," said Missy, with something between sobbing and spitting fire. "I can do anything in the world—but hold my tongue," she added, as she saw her mother look distressed. "Oh, of course I'll go down, I don't really mind it. I shan't have even to smooth my hair. For as there will be no critics but the children and the waitress, I may be saved that effort. I suppose I must praise the dinner liberally, to make Melinda happy. Oh, I *am* so tired. My hands feel as if they were full of splinters and nails, and I can't go across the room to wash them. I wonder if the waitress would care if I didn't wash them. I'm sure I shouldn't. By the way, I must ring for Ann and tell her I am going down to dinner, or the best table-cloth will be taken off before I see it."

Ann took down the message in time to stay the spoliation of the table, and when dinner was served, came up to say so to her mistress. She was too tired to do more than wash her hands ; she did not even look in the glass. She felt hysterical as well as weary, and said to herself, if Gabrielle says anything hateful, I shall certainly make a scene. The lights hurt her eyes as she went into the dining-room. Jay laid hold of her hand, and kissed it with fervor, and then pulled a bow off the side of her dress, to make up for the caress.

"So we are to have dinner together, are we, you

and I and Gabby," she said, sinking into her chair,
and pointing Jay to his.

"And papa," said Gabby, with a keenly interested
look. "Didn't you know he was coming down to
dinner ?"

"No," said Missy, feeling herself grow red. "I
thought he wasn't well enough."

At this moment, the door opened, and Mr. Andrews came in.

"I did not think you were able to come down,"
Missy said, rather awkwardly, rising. "You must
excuse me—for—for taking my seat before you
came."

"It was so tiresome staying up stairs," said Mr.
Andrews simply, and they took their places silently.

The two children's seats had been placed opposite
to Missy. But Jay refused to submit to this arrangement, and kicked against the table legs and cried till
he was carried around to sit by Missy. He certainly
behaved very badly, and made them all uncomfortable. Then, when they had got partly over this, and
were trying to talk a little, Gabby took occasion to
say, when there was a pause in the rather forced conversation, critically looking across at Missy :

"If you had known papa was coming down, would
you have brushed your hair, do you think, Missy ?"

The waitress, Missy was sure, suppressed a sudden
giggle. Missy was so angry, and so agitated, she grew
pale instead of red.

"I am sure I should," she said, deliberately, looking at her. "And perhaps, have put another cravat
on, for this one, I am afraid, is rather dusty."

"Why didn't you put it on any way," said Jay.

10

"Why, because little children are not supposed to know or care ; but for grown people, we have to try to be polite."

These brave words over, Missy felt she had done all that was possible in self-defense, and began to feel as if she should cry at the next assault. Poor Mr. Andrews looked bitterly annoyed. He was so pale and ill-looking, and had made such an effort to come down and be hospitable, that Missy's heart was softened. She resolved to make it easy for him, so she began to talk about the condition of the house and to ask questions and get advice. But the poor man was too ill, and too straightforward to talk about anything he wasn't thinking about. The presence of Gabrielle made him nervous as a woman ; every time she opened her mouth, if only to ask for a glass of water, he was sure she was going to say something terrible. Such a dinner. Melinda's nice dishes went away almost untouched, almost unseen. At last Gabrielle, reassured by the subjection in which she found her elders, ventured upon that which lay nearest her heart, namely, the topic of discussion in the stable that morning.

"Papa," she said, in a very insinuating voice, and with a glance around, "*do* you expect to be paid for—"

But Missy was too quick for her. She started to her feet, the color flaming to her face.

"Gabrielle, I forbid you to speak another word while I am in the room. Mr. Andrews, you must excuse me—I am very sorry to make you so uncomfortable, but I cannot--stand it—any longer," and with an hysterical choke she sprang to the door.

When she was gone, I wouldn't have been in Gabby's place for a good deal. Fortunately the waitress was out of the room when the fracas occurred, and when she came back, she was at liberty to suppose that the furious punishment bestowed upon Gabrielle was in consequence of an overturned glass of wine which was bedewing the best table-cloth. Some gentlemen are so particular about their table linen. She had not seen this side of Mr. Andrews' character before, but then, to be sure, they had never used the best linen since she had been in the family.

When Missy, panting and hysterical, reached the top of the stairs, she didn't know exactly what to do. She knew very well if she took refuge in her mother's room (which was her own, too), she destroyed all chance of sleep for her mother that night. She couldn't go into the nursery, where Gabby would probably be sent for punishment. She couldn't seek the sweet shelter of Miss Harriet Varian's sympathy, and it wasn't dignified to sit on the stairs. What was she to do? Just at this moment, Goneril came softly out of her mistress' room.

"Is Miss Varian asleep?" asked Missy, in a low tone.

"Heaven be praised, SHE IS!" returned Goneril, with great fervor.

"Then I will go and sit by her till you get your dinner," she said, going past her into the room. Here was refuge and darkness, and she sat down in an easy chair near the door. How little consolation there was in being quiet, though, and thinking. She was so enraged—so humiliated. She had fought clear of the embarrassment and disgrace of last autumn, and had

flattered herself she had conquered both herself and
gossip ; and now it was all to be done over again.
She had no heart to begin again. She was going
away. She would go away. There was no reason
she should not have her way, sometimes. There was
a good excuse for a summer's absence. They would
leave the carpenters and painters in the house—she
didn't care for the house now, and what they did to it
—and they would go to the mountains till she had got
over this miserable sensitiveness, and till the Andrews'
had got tired of Yellowcoats. Oh, that that might be
soon ! She never wanted to see one of the name
again, not even Jay. (She had had these reflections
before, and had thought better of them, at least as
concerned Jay.) By and by, while she was still
solacing herself with plans for flight, she heard the
children come up-stairs, Jay fretting, as if he felt the
discomfort in the air. Gabrielle was very silent.
Eliza was rather hurried ; she was human, though a
good nurse, and there was a large and cheerful circle
sitting down around the kitchen table to an unusually
good dinner. It was rather hard lines to be putting
the children to bed, when they ought to have stayed
up, as they always did, until she had had her dinner.
Now everything seemed out of joint for some reason,
and the children as troublesome as possible. Eliza,
excellent servant though she was, was but a servant,
and to sit pat-patting Jay, while the festive circle
down-stairs were getting through the choicest bits of
pastry and of gossip, required more patience than she
had. The children were hustled into their night-
clothes rather hastily. Gabrielle, sulky and white,
offered only slight petulant resistance, but Jay cried

and grew worse-tempered every minute. At last Eliza got them both into bed and turned down the lamp.

"Now go to sleep, like a good boy," she said, tucking in the clothes of Jay's crib ; but there was restlessness in her very tone, and though she sat down, she did not convey the idea of permanence, and Jay grew wider awake every moment, watching lest she should go away. At length, starting up impatiently, she cried :

"There's reason in all things. You're big enough to go to sleep by yourself. I must have my dinner."

And without a look behind, she hurried from the room. This had never happened before. She had always occupied herself in putting away the children's clothes, and in moving softly about the room, and singing in a low voice ; and so Jay, without being absolutely coddled, had always fallen asleep with a sense of protection and companionship. But to-night everything was going wrong. Here was papa in such an awful way, and Missy running away from the table crying, and Gabby scared to death and punished—and now his nurse getting cross, and going down and leaving him all alone in the dark. There had been vague and terrible stories of what came in the dark, during the reign of Alphonsine and Bridget, which had not been quite obliterated.

Jay lay mute with amazement for a moment ; and then, sitting up in bed, and looking into the dimness surrounding him, began to cry piteously, and to call upon Eliza to come back. But Eliza was out of reach of his cries now, and Gabby, stubborn and wicked, would not open her lips. He cried and sobbed till his throat felt sore and his head burning.

"Missy, Missy! I want you, Missy!"

Missy had listened, with vexation at Eliza, but with no intention of taking up her duties, till that plaintive cry smote her heart and melted it. The poor little lonely child, with no love but the unsteady love of hirelings! She started up and stole into the nursery. The cry with which Jay flung himself into her arms made him dearer to her than ever before. He clung to her, all trembling and beating, his wet little face buried in her neck.

"You won't go away and leave me, you won't, promise me, Missy, you won't go."

"No, Jay, my own little man, I won't. Lie down; I promise you, I'll stay."

Every one else had failed him, but he still believed in Missy. So he was pacified and reassured, and after awhile lay down, holding both her hands. She let down the side of his crib, and sitting beside him, laid her head on his pillow; he put one hand on her throat, and held the other tight in one of hers, and so, after awhile, he fell asleep. But a ground-swell of sobs still heaved his breast after such a heavy storm. Missy held the little warm hand tight, and kissed him in his sleep. She had promised not to go, and she dared not move his hand from her neck, nor stir her head from the pillow for fear of waking him.

The room was still and dim, and she was very tired; by and by the troubles of the day melted into dreams, and she slept. How long, she could not tell. A light gleaming in her face aroused her; she started up in sudden consternation, for Mr. Andrews stood looking at her, in, it must be said, equal consternation. He had moved the screen from the nursery lamp, and coming up to the bed to look at his boy, had seen the not unpretty, but very unexpected picture of the two sleeping in this close embrace.

Missy's first feeling was one of anger; but surely Mr. Andrews had a right in his own nursery, and, as usual, she was in the wrong—she was where she had no business to be; her bitter vexation showed itself on her face.

"I beg your pardon," he said, stepping back, "I—I didn't know you were here."

"Jay cried so, I came in to pacify him," she said, "and he would not let me go."

"You are very kind to him," said the father earnestly.

"Not particularly," she returned, fastening up the side of the crib, and laying him softly further over on his pillow. "One doesn't like to see a child imposed upon, and Eliza was very wrong to leave him."

"Miss Rothermel," said Mr. Andrews, still earnestly, and Miss Rothermel prepared herself for something she did not want to hear, "I have no words to express to you the annoyance that I feel about Gabrielle."

Missy waved her hand impatiently.

"But I have words to express a resolution that I have formed this evening, and that is, that it shall be the last time that you shall suffer from her. I shall send her away to boarding-school as soon as I can make the necessary arrangements; and that I hope will be within a week, at furthest."

It was now Missy's turn to be in earnest.

"I hope you won't do anything of the kind, Mr. Andrews, on my account at least. I can only assure you, it would be far more annoying than anything she has ever done. I should never forgive myself for having caused you to do what I am quite sure would be the worst thing for her. She is very well situated now. You have good servants, she has the free country life she needs, and no bad companions. If she can't improve now, I'm afraid she never will."

"I'm afraid she never will, wherever she may be," answered Mr. Andrews, with almost a groan. "I could tell you something of her, if—if—"

"I am sure of one thing," rushed on Missy, not heeding what she might have heard if she had listened; "I am sure of one thing, I should never have a moment's peace, if I felt I had been in any way the cause of sending from her home such a desolate little child. I cannot forget that I had a friendship for her mother, and I should be always followed by the thought of her reproach."

Mr. Andrews' face changed; he bent his head slightly. The change was not lost on Missy.

"Besides that feeling," she said, with a touch of bitterness, "which, I have no doubt, you look upon as a weak piece of sentiment, I don't see what difference her going or staying can make to me. It would be a pity to do her an injury which would do no one any good. I shall not necessarily see her half-a-dozen times, before we go away, which, I hope, we shall do for the summer, very shortly. And when we come back Jay will have forgotten me, or you will all, perhaps, have left the place. It is really too much said already on a subject which is very insignificant, though it has proved sufficiently disagreeable." And she moved as if to go away.

"I quite agree with you that it has been very disagreeable; but I don't entirely see that what you have said alters my duty in the matter. I think she has deserved to be sent away; I am not sure that the discipline of a school would not be the best thing for her. I am quite sure that it is not my duty to destroy my own peace, or deprive my little boy of friends or kindness, by keeping her at home."

"Not your duty, Mr. Andrews!" cried Missy. "Well, of course we look at things from such different points, it's no use discussing—"

"We will waive the discussion of my duty," said Mr. Andrews, not urbanely; "but I should be very glad to know why you think it would hurt Gabrielle to send her to a good school?"

Like all home-bred girls, she had a great horror of boarding-schools, and with vivacity gave a dozen reasons for her horror, winding up with—"I believe it would make her a hundred times more deceitful than she is now. It would establish her thirst for intrigue; it would estrange her from you; it would deprive her of the little healthy love that she has for out-door life and innocent amusement. If you want to ruin Gabrielle, Mr. Andrews, *pray* send her to a boarding-school!"

"I don't want to ruin Gabrielle, but I want to have a little peace myself, and to let my neighbors have some, too."

"Your neighbors' peace needn't be considered, after—after we go away from the house; and I am sure you have frightened her enough to-night to make

10*

her behave better while we are obliged to stay with you."

As soon as the words were out, Missy shivered at their sound. She did not mean to be so rude.

"I beg your pardon," she said, not with successful penitence; "but you know we did not impose ourselves upon you from choice."

"I know you would not have come if you could have helped it, certainly. I am not to blame for that, however."

"Well, I'm sure I didn't mean to blame any one. You must excuse me; I am very tired to-night. Only let Gabrielle's matter be considered settled, won't you? I shall thank you very much, if you will promise me she shan't be sent away."

The father glanced at the small white bed, where Gabrielle lay motionless, with her eyes shut and her face turned from them, presumably asleep.

"I won't take any step about sending her away, if you feel so about it—for a little while, at least."

"Very well; thank you! Then it is settled. Good night." And Missy went away, not exactly, it must be owned, as if she had received a favor, but as if hardly-wrung justice had been obtained for Gabrielle and Gabrielle's dead mother. That, at least, was how she felt—and Mr. Andrews wasn't altogether stupid. He sighed as he bent over Jay's crib, and smoothed the hair back on his pillow, screening the light from his eyes, and turning down the lamp; but he did not go near the bed of the offending Gabrielle, and left the room without another glance in her direction.

CHAPTER XIV.

YELLOWCOATS CALLS TO INQUIRE.

HE next morning, Missy managed to get away without encountering any one more formidable than Jay and the servants. Mr. Andrews probably made an intentionally late breakfast, and Gabrielle was more than willing to keep out of sight. Matters at the house she found in worse confusion than ever. The only plumber in the village was more eminent for good-nature than for skill. He doctored furnaces and ranges, cooking stoves and "air-tights," but it must be said he was more successful with the latter. Water-backs, and traps, and reservoirs had grown up since he learned his trade, but, like a good-natured creature, he put his hand to whatever was asked of him, and sometimes succeeded in patching up leaks, and sometimes didn't. He was the worst berated man in Yellowcoats, but in the greatest demand. No one's wrath lasted out the first glance of his good-humored face. He never thought of keeping his word ; indeed, it would have needed a great deal of principle to do it. The one that was first, got him, whether prince or peasant, and generally found it necessary to mount guard over him till the job was finished. He was willing to work all day, and all night, irrespective of meals or sleep. Such good-nature could not fail to be rewarded, and so every one "put up" with him, and he was not supplanted.

His yesterday's work at the Varians', however, had
not been a success. He had left the range in a lament-
able condition; something very distressing was the matter with the water-back, and the fire could not be made.
The house-cleaners were all at a loss for hot water ;
trusting in his promise to be on hand the first thing
in the morning, they had all waited for him, without
sending in to Miss Rothermel. Upon inquiry, it was
found that a magnate in the horse-and-cow business,
some miles distant, had come to grief in the matter of
his tin roof, and had captured Mike at an early hour,
and was probably even now mounting guard over him,
and it was believed that no threats or entreaties would
induce him to give him up till the roof was water-tight.
As it was a very bad roof, and had been in Mike's hands
for years, it seemed probable that nothing short of a
day or two would answer for its repair. Still, several
hours of Peters' time was taken up in going over to
appeal to the sense of honor of the horse-and-cow man.
In the meanwhile, it was deplorable to see what a
motive power hot water was, and how difficult it was
to get it, when once one has come to depend upon a
boiler. Very little could be done except in the small
matter of putting drawers and closets in order. The
women sat about the kitchen and berated Mike, unable even to get a bit of dinner cooked.

At three o'clock, Peters returned to say that
there was no hope. The horse-and-cow man had
taken the ladder away from the roof, and declared
Mike shouldn't come down till the leaks were stopped,
if it took him till November. Of course the house
could not be habitable till the range was in order.
Missy with a groan acknowledged her fate, and de-

cided it was meant by destiny, that she should stay at
Mr. Andrews' till everybody in the village was
saturated with the intelligence.

She had been away from her mother all day, and
Ann had reported her as was not feeling quite so well,
so at half past three o'clock, she had turned her back
upon the desolation, and leaving the servants to do
what little they could or would, went back to sit with
her mother for the rest of the afternoon, which had
turned out fine and sunny.

Mrs. Varian was suffering quietly, as usual, but
was very glad to have her daughter for a little while.
The room was quiet and cool, and in an easy chair by
the window, Missy found a little rest. She read aloud
to her mother for awhile ; but there soon began to be
distractions.

"Mamma, here are the Wellses going in at our
gate. I hope they'll enjoy the sight of the battered
steps and the trampled lawn."

"It is but civil of them to come and leave a card,
at all events."

"Ah, and here goes somebody else. Who is it,
with such a pretty pony phaeton, and a puny little
footman, and a pug dog? It must be the Oldhams.
I didn't know they had come up. Well, I hope Ann
has on a respectable cap, and that the bell wires are
not broken, as it seems probable all Yellowcoats will
call to inquire for us to-day."

"I am sure it is very kind of Yellowcoats. Why
do you speak so, Missy? You surely can't resent it."

Missy bit her lips ; she had a resentment that she
had never let her mother share. Yes, she did resent
it. It was bitter to her to know that they were all

coming, and that every one would know where they had found asylum, and that all the old story of last September would be revived. She was quite correct in thinking that all Yellowcoats was on its way there that afternoon. Ann must have had a lively time answering the bell and the questions.

It was now the third day since the fire. The second day had been a stormy one, and the sunshine seemed to have come on purpose to disseminate the gossip. Missy, from behind the blinds, watched the carriages drive in. There were Oldhams, country Oldhams and city Oldhams, a family far reaching and intricately entwined in Yellowcoats' connections. It was not safe to say anything anti-Oldham to any one in Yellowcoats, for they were related to everybody, gentle and simple, in the place. There came the Roncevalles, who had two men on the box, and were debonair and rich and easy-going. There were the Sombreros, in a heavy, not recent carriage, driven by a man who did not even hold himself straight, and who couldn't have been dragooned into a livery. But the inmates of the carriage held themselves straight, and other people had to walk straight before them. If the object of mankind is to secure the respect of its fellows, they had attained that object. People of manifold more pretension quailed before their silent disapprobation. They "rode their sure and even trot, while now the world rode by, now lagged behind." Missy felt a sharper pang of wonder what the Sombreros had heard about her, than what the people with the two men on the box, or the black ponies and the pug dog had heard ; she felt that the Sombreros would never change their minds, and minds that don't change are to be held in awe. She saw them drive away with a heavier sense of apprehension than she had felt before. But they did not turn and look towards the Andrews' cottage, as the others did. Missy felt sure the two men on the box of the Roncevalles' carriage nudged each other ; the two ladies in the carriage certainly did turn and look that way ; very gently and decorously, but still they turned.

By and by a carriage coming out met a carriage driving in, directly before the Andrews' house. They stopped. The ladies bent eagerly forward and talked in low tones ; more than one glance flashed towards the closed blinds of the widower's house. Missy's cheeks were scarlet and her breath came quick ; but she was fascinated and could not look away. It was gentle Mrs. Olor and her pretty young daughters—who could dread anything from them ? Stirring Mrs. Eve was just giving them the information that she had received from the waitress at the Varians' door. She was the kindest and busiest person in Yellowcoats, but she had a sense of humor, and she also was very particular about her own daughters, one of whom was with her in the carriage. Who could doubt what view she took of Miss Rothermel's aspirations ? Missy watched breathlessly the faces ; the mammas alone talked, the daughters listened, with smiles and rather pursed-up mouths. Superior the whole party seemed to feel themselves, as people always seem to feel when they have a little story against their neighbors, not reflecting that their own turn may come next. Missy had felt superior for twenty-seven years, though she hadn't talked more gossip than most other well-disposed and well-bred persons. Still, she had felt superior, and it was horrid to be made to feel inferior, and she bit her lips, and angry tears came up into her eyes. Her mother lay watching her silently on the bed.

"Well, Sister Anne, Sister Anne, do you see anybody coming?" she said at last, gently.

Missy forced herself to speak indifferently, "Only the Olors and the Eves. They have met just outside the gate, and are mincing us quite fine, I should judge from their animated looks."

"Well, I hope they haven't anything worse to say of us than that we've had a fire, and that the place looks sadly out of trim."

"Mamma," said Missy abruptly, as with wreathed smiles the friends parted and the carriages drove away, "what do you say to a journey this summer? I'm sadly cut up about this fire. I never shall have the heart to get things in order before autumn; I'm tired of Yellowcoats for the first time in my life, and—I want to go away."

"Go away, Missy! How could we do that? I fear I am not strong enough; and your Aunt Harriet— you know we resolved two years ago, we'd never try it again. She is so hard to please, and you remember what a trial we found the whole three months."

"It would be less of a trial than staying here. I, for one, would be glad to risk it. And as to you, I sometimes feel sure you need a change more than anything."

Mrs. Varian shook her head. "I need rest more than anything."

"Invalids always feel that, and yet see what benefit they get from journeys that they have dreaded."

"Besides," said the mother rather hesitatingly,

"you know there is always a chance of St. John's return."

"I didn't know," said Missy, a little coldly.

"You know as much as I do," returned her mother. "You saw his last letter. He says all depends upon his being accepted. He may come back at any time."

"Oh, as to that," cried Missy, "I think there is no danger that he will not be accepted. It would surprise me very much if he escaped. A man with a handsome income is generally found to have a vocation."

"You have been reading too much Browning and Balzac, I am afraid," said her mother with a sigh.

"I have been reading life, and hard, common sense," cried Missy. "I ought to have been prepared to find we were all to sit meekly waiting at home, while the saint of the family was on probation. It ought to be honor enough. But I allow I would like to have a voice in my sacrifices, and to make them self-denials."

"It is new to me to imagine you finding your pleasure anywhere but at home. Since you feel so about it, I am sure—"

"Oh, don't say anything more about it," cried Missy, thoroughly unhinged. "I can stay here, I suppose. I really am not quite new at doing what I don't like, even if I am only secular."

"You are tired, Missy. Now go and lie down, and don't think anything more about this matter. When we are both fresher, we will talk it over, and you shall decide what shall be done."

At half-past five o'clock she got up, and dressed carefully for dinner, bracing herself for the ordeal with much philosophy. At dinner, she found her philosophy quite superfluous, for Mr. Andrews did not make his appearance, and Gabby scarcely lifted her eyes from her plate.   This young person had been awake the night before, and an attentive listener to the conversation between her father and Missy, and it had naturally made a profound impression on her.   It is difficult to say why Missy felt annoyed that Mr. Andrews did not come to dinner.   She ought to have felt relieved ; but on the contrary, she felt vexed.   It is always disagreeable not to act your part when you have rehearsed it, and feel well up in it.   But it was a great vexation to her to think that she was keeping him from his own dinner-table by reason of that unpleasant speech of the night before.   She had only realized that he wasn't at breakfast at the time, with a sense of relief.   She now remembered it with a sensation of chagrin.   Also, she recalled his pallor and weariness of expression last night, which in her misery about herself, she had forgotten.   It was possible he was really suffering to-day.   It was only three days since he had met with a serious accident, all in their service.

"How is Mr. Andrews feeling to-day ?" she asked of the waitress.

"Not quite so well, Miss, I think."

"Has he kept his room ?"

"Oh, no, Miss, but he doesn't seem to have much appetite, and I believe the doctor told him he mustn't think of going to town for several days yet.   He had been telling the doctor he was going down, and would stay away perhaps a week, and promised to keep very quiet there.   But the doctor wouldn't hear of it, and said the hot weather might come on suddenly, and make him very sick, and besides, he wasn't fit to bear the journey."

Missy was quite chagrined by this information. Mr. Andrews had felt so constrained and uncomfortable in his own house, he could not bear it any longer. Or else he had so honorably desired to put her at her ease while she had to stay, that he had wanted to go away. Either view of the case was bad enough ; but it was undeniably an awkward situation, and if he persisted in keeping away from the table for another meal, she should feel that it was unendurable, and they must go away, range or no range, order or disorder.

Jay followed her from the table, clinging to her skirts. She went directly to her mother, where the child's prattle covered her absent-minded silence.

It was a lovely June evening, fresh after the rain of yesterday, and she sat by the window watching the pink clouds fade into gray, and the twilight make its way over the fields and roadside. Jay babbled his innocent babble to inattentive ears ; by and by he grew sleepy. Eliza came, and he was sent away.

It was about half-past eight, when the servant came up, and said that there was a person below who wished to see Mrs. or Miss Varian. Missy struck a match and looked at the card. It was the agent of the insurance company, in which the house had been insured.

" Why could he not come in the daytime ! I absolutely can't talk business to-night."

The servant explained that he came up by the evening train, had been at the house, and was to go away by an early train in the morning.

There was no help for it ; Missy dismissed the pink clouds and the soft creeping twilight and her thoughts, and went down stairs to the parlor. The room was lighted only by a lamp which stood on the table in the middle of it, by which the agent sat. He was a trim, dapper, middle-aged man, not at all aware that he was not a gentleman, and very sharp about business matters, while he was affable and explanatory, as became a business man dealing with a young lady. His manner annoyed Missy, who would have got on much better if he had been simply business-like. She knew he had the better of her in his knowledge of matters, and her memory was very unusually faulty about the things she ought to have remembered. The papers were all in her room at home, and for aught she knew, had been lost or destroyed when that room was torn to pieces to save it from the flames. She certainly had not been wise enough to think of looking for them since the fire occurred.

"You will have to come again," she said ; "I really am not prepared to-night to talk it over."

He seemed disposed to take advantage of this, and rather pressed an immediate decision on some question.

It was not till this moment that Missy knew that Mr. Andrews was in the room. He was lying on a sofa in a corner, and a screen stood before him, shielding him from the light.

"Mr. Andrews, I beg your pardon," she said, getting up. "I am afraid we are disturbing you. I didn't know you were here. We will go into the dining-room if this gentleman has anything more to say."

"I don't think he has," said Mr. Andrews, raising himself a little on his elbow. "Don't think of going to the dining-room, or of discussing the matter further, for I am sure you are too tired to-night. Perhaps I can attend to the matter for you."

An inquiring look towards the agent had a very salutary effect upon him. It was quite amazing to notice how his manner changed when he found he had a man to deal with. Missy sat by humbled, while she listened to their talk.

Why couldn't she have been business-like ? Why couldn't she have said what Mr. Andrews was saying, without "losing her head," and getting nervous ? It was her affair, and she certainly ought to know more about it than he did.

When the man was fairly out of the door, she gave a sigh, and said :

"I am very much obliged to you, Mr. Andrews, for helping me out of it."

"I think the man is rather a sharper, and I'm afraid you are not a business woman, Miss Rothermel."

"I am afraid not ; and I always meant to be."

Then there was a pause. Mr. Andrews laid his head back on the pillow of the sofa, and seemed not to have anything more to say. Missy had a great deal to say, but she didn't know where to begin. She was full of contrition and purposes of amendment ; but the situation was most embarrassing, and Mr. Andrews was not inclined to help her. Time pressed. It was insupportable to sit still by the lamp, and not say anything. Mr. Andrews was lying down, too. What if any one should come in, and find her sitting there, entertaining him ? She wished for Aunt Harriet—for any one ; but she must say her say ; and she rushed at it.

"I am afraid," she said, in a voice that showed agitation, "I am afraid you are not so well to-day, Mr. Andrews."

"I have had an uncomfortable day ; but I don't

suppose I am materially worse—at least the doctor doesn't tell me so."

Then another pause. Certainly he did not mean to help her.

"I am afraid," she said, getting up, and laying down upon the table the paper-cutter that she had been turning and twisting in her fingers, "I am afraid our being here makes you very uncomfortable. And it ought to be just the other way. We are so much indebted to you! You have been so good—and—and—"

She made a step toward him, and standing behind the screen in front of his sofa, which came up to her waist, leaned on it for a moment, looking down—then said, "I don't know how to express it, exactly; I hope you'll understand. I know I haven't behaved well about—about—things—but I suppose I had some excuse. It is so hard to remember one's own insignificance, and to think only about other people! I have thought of no one's discomforts or miseries but my own. I haven't been nice at all; I've been horrid. I never should have believed it of myself. At my age it seems so paltry and undignified to be minding what people may say or think, if only you know you're doing right. I have resolved I will never let it come into my mind again, nor affect my conduct in any way. And I hope you will excuse my rudeness, and the discomfort I have caused you, and will let me make up for it in some way, while we stay with you."

He lay looking at her as she stood behind the screen, leaning a little toward him on her folded arms. The only light in the room was behind her, shining through her fair, fine hair, now in a little curling disorder ; all her face was in shadow. It is possible she looked to the lonely man almost a " blessed damosel," leaning to him out of Heaven.

" You have made up for it," he said, " very fully. I hope we shall always be friends, if you will let me."

" It shan't be my fault if we are not," she said. Then, hurriedly saying good-night, she went away. There was a clock in the hall, which struck nine as she passed it. It had a peculiar tone, and she never could forget it. It had been striking as she passed it on the gloomy morning last summer, when she had hurried to that fearful death-bed.

It gave her a pang to hear it now. It seemed sharply to accuse her of something. It recalled to her all her prejudices, all her resolutions. It brought to her mind his manner when she had told him of his wife's death, his absence of feeling in all the days that followed. It revived his banishing the mother's memory from the children's minds ; his ready purpose to send away her favorite Gabrielle. And then she thought of what she had just been saying—of what he had just said, and in what an earnest way ! Her face burned at the recollection.

" Am I never to have any peace in this tiresome matter," she said to herself as she shut herself into her room. " I will not think of it any more, while I am obliged to remain in this house. I will honestly do all I can to make things comfortable ; he has done enough to make that proper. Afterwards I will keep my promise by being kind to the children, and by really serving them when it is in my power. It does not involve me in any intimacy with him. You can stand a person's friend, and not see him once a year. I will never do anything to injure or annoy him. That is being an honest friend, as we are bidden to be, even to our enemies. I have put myself and my pride away. I will do all I can to forward the comfort and pleasure of every one in the house, and there is the end of it."

CHAPTER XV.

A MISOGYNIST.

ACTING upon this wise resolution, Missy came down the next morning a little late, to breakfast. She was not going to escape any one. She had on a fresh cambric morning-dress, and some roses in her belt. The breakfast-table looked quite populous when she entered, for Mr. Andrews was at the foot of the table, and the two children on one side, and Miss Varian on the other, in the seat that had been placed for Missy. Miss Varian's coming had been rather a surprise to every one, for she had been nursing her neuralgia so assiduously, no one imagined it would go away so soon. Mr. Andrews got up when Miss Rothermel came in, and Jay shouted a welcome from out of his hominy plate.

Aunt Harriet said, " Well, Missy, I suppose you didn't expect to see me."

" You've got Missy's place," said Jay, without ceremony.

" Oh, no matter," cried Missy, turning a little pale, for she foresaw that her fate would be to sit at the head of the table and pour out the tea. Nobody sat there ordinarily, and the waitress poured out the tea. But the table was not very large, and Aunt Harriet had spread out herself, and her strawberries, and her glass of water, and her cup of coffee, and her little bouquet of flowers, over so much of the side on which she sat, that it would have caused quite a disturbance to have made a place for Missy there.

"Where will you sit, Miss Rothermel?" asked the waitress, with her hand on the chair, looking perplexed, and glancing from the encumbered neighborhood of Miss Varian, to the freer region behind the urn and tea-cups.

"Oh, anywhere, it makes no difference," said Missy, determined not to fail the first time she was put to the test. "Here, if it is more convenient."

The servant placed the chair at the head of the table, which Missy promptly took. Mr. Andrews, who had been standing with rather an anxious face, as if he saw his guest's struggle, sat down with a relieved expression.

"You are just in time to reconstruct my coffee," said Miss Varian. "Among her other good qualities, Mr. Andrews, your waitress does not number making good coffee. Mine is tepid, and the cream was put in last, I am sure. You must let Missy make you a cup; I am afraid you have forgotten what good coffee is, if you have been drinking this all winter."

Missy bit her lip, and then shrugged her shoulder, and gave Mr. Andrews a comical glance, as the only way of getting over her aunt's rudeness. She also gave the servant a smile, and a little shake of the head, as she handed the hot cup of coffee to her. The woman

11

was very red and angry, but this mollified her. Miss
Varian had the most artless way of insulting servants.
Nothing but the general understanding, that it was
her way, and the certainty that she would give them
a good deal of money at Christmas, kept the servants
at home respectful to her.

"Yes, Missy does understand putting a cup of
coffee together, even when it's only tolerable to begin
with," she said, tasting it with satisfaction. "I think,
Missy, if you showed the cook your way of making it,
to-morrow morning, Mr. Andrews would bless you
every day of his life."

"Why, my dear aunt, the coffee is excellent," cried
Missy, "I don't know what you are thinking of.
Next you'll be criticising these muffins, which are
perfect. Shall I give you one?" Soon after this, the
servant left the room, ostensibly to get some hot
muffins, but really to pour out her wrath to the cook.
While she was gone, Missy perceived that Mr. Andrews had neither tea nor coffee, and was eating very
little breakfast. "Are you not going to have coffee?"
she said.

"If you will give me some, I think I should
like to judge whether Miss Varian is right." So Missy
made him a cup of coffee, very hot and nice, and as
there was no waitress in the room, got up and carried
it to him herself, before he knew what she was
doing.

"I beg you'll say it's good," she said. "Now, Jay,"
as she passed him, "you surely *have* had hominy
enough. Don't you want some strawberries." So she
got him a plate from the side-board, and gave him
some strawberries, and a kiss, and put the muffins

within Gabby's reach before she sat down. Mr. Andrews' anxiety quite melted away, and he began to enjoy his breakfast.

"While you are up, Missy," said Miss Varian, just after she sat down, "give me a glass of water."

Missy laughed, and so did Jay and even Gabrielle, who looked alarmed as soon as she had done it. Could a person be sent to boarding-school for laughing in the wrong place, she wondered. Missy gave her aunt the glass of water, and arranged things so that she could find them near her plate. And so, the breakfast that had begun so threateningly, ended quite peacefully. The morning was warm, but lovely.

"I think, if you will take me to the piazza, I will sit there awhile, Missy, but you will have to get me my shawl and hat, or go off on a cruise to find Goneril, who is never where she ought to be."

"Oh, we'll indulge Goneril with a little breakfast to put her in a good humor for the day, and I'll find the shawl and hat," said Missy, taking her aunt's hand to lead her from the room.

Jay came to make her give him her other hand, and Gabby, allured by the sight of a new bauble on Miss Varian's watch-chain, followed them closely. Miss Varian was established on the front piazza, sheltered from the sun and wind (and conspicuous to the passers-by), Gabby was nailed to her side in fascinated contemplation of the trinket, which, it was quite probable, the capricious lady would end by giving her, and Missy was free to go to her mother for a little while. In half an hour she came down ready to go to her work in the dismantled house. She went into the parlor to find her parasol, and there was Mr. Andrews

with letters and papers before him, trying painfully to
write with his stiff left hand. "Oh, you must let me
do that for you," cried Missy, pulling off her gloves.
"If they are business letters, that is," with a little
hesitation, for she caught sight of a woman's handwriting, among the letters before him.

"The business ones are the pressing ones. It would
be a great kindness, if you could. But you are needed
at the house, perhaps."

"I can write for half an hour or so. I have sent
the women over, with their work laid out for them for
all the morning. I am quite used to this. I write Aunt
Harriet's letters every evening, till I go almost to sleep."

"I shall not let you go to sleep," said Mr.
Andrews, "over mine." So Missy wrote, and Mr.
Andrews dictated, for half an hour at least. "That
is all that is needed now; I am very much obliged
to you."

"There are a good many more before you yet,"
she said, glancing at the heap.

"They will do as well another time. Perhaps, if
anything comes to-day that has to be attended to, you
will be kind enough to write me a few lines to-night."

"Yes, of course; and if you want anything for
the afternoon mail, don't fail to send over for me."
Then she went away, feeling very virtuous.

In the afternoon, as she came down the steps to go
back to see if her mother wanted her, she saw Mr.
Andrews' just entering at the gate. It was the first
time that he had been out, and he showed his four
days' confinement to the house. As she met him, he
said, with a little hesitation, "I have come to see if
you won't go out for a little drive with us this after-

noon. It is too fine a day to be shut up in the house."

Her heart sank. A drive *en famille* with the Andrews', in the teeth of all that had happened in the last few days! How could she brave it? Her color changed a little and perhaps he saw it.

"Don't go if you don't fancy it," he said.

"Oh, it's just the afternoon for a drive. But I was going back to sit with mamma, who has been alone all day."

"I sent up to Mrs. Varian's room to see if there were any chance that she would go with us, and Goneril came creeping out on tiptoe to say she had just fallen asleep, and must not be disturbed."

The last hope was extinguished ; she made just one more cowardly attempt. "But you," she said, "are you well enough ? Isn't it rather against the doctor's orders ?"

"No, he gave me permission himself this morning, finding me very much improved."

Then Missy said to herself, "I should think the man could see—" And aloud she said, "Oh, there is nothing in the way. I'll go to the house for my gloves and vail."

When she came back the open wagon stood before the gate of the cottage. Jay was already in it, brandishing the whip and shouting, much to Michael's displeasure, who stood by the horses' heads. Mr. Andrews was coming from the house. Gabby stood behind a post of the piazza, showing a face lead-color with sullenness and disappointment. She had no hat on, and was evidently not to be of the party.

"Isn't Gabby going ?" said Missy to Jay.

"No," cried Jay, in selfish satisfaction, "Papa says there isn't room."

"Poor Gabby! why, that won't do," she said, going to meet Mr. Andrews in the path. "Won't you take Gabrielle?" she said. "There is plenty of room for the two children with me on the back seat."

Miss Rothermel enjoyed being magnanimous so much, Mr. Andrews hadn't the heart to refuse her.

"Which way are we going?" he asked, as Michael drove slowly. Jay clamored for a drive, which took them through the village. Miss Rothermel, of course, would give no vote. Gabrielle, when questioned, agreed with Jay. Mr. Andrews admitted it was a pretty drive. "The greatest good of the greatest number," thought Missy, while Michael drove that way.

They took the road through the village, where the men sat thick on the store steps, and where the young village maidens were taking their afternoon saunter. They met the Sombreros, they met the Oldhams and the Olors—whom did they not meet, enjoying or enduring their afternoon drive? Mr. Andrews had his arm in an unnecessarily conspicuous sling. It was malicious of Goneril to put on that glaring great white silk handkerchief. He was labeled hero, and people could not help looking. Missy did not blame them, but it was horrid all the same. However, when they were out of the village, and there were comparatively few people to meet, the influence of the charming day and the absence of charred remains and disordered rooms began to brighten her, and she almost liked it. They drove along a road by the bay. The tide was high, and was breaking with a contented little purring sound against the pebbles; little boats bent idly with the in-

coming tide and pulled lazily at their anchors. The
bay was as blue as the sky ; some white sails drifted on
it, for scenic effect, no doubt, for what else ? for there
was no wind, but only a fresh cool air that came in
puffs and ripples across the water. Beside them,
on the other side of the road, were green and flowering banks, where Jay saw wild roses and anemones
and little nameless and beloved wild flowers. There
was privet budding and hawthorn fading, and barberry and catbrier and wild grape, in fresh June coloring. Little dust came here in this narrow road, and
with this constant dampness from the bay. Nobody
pulled down the vines, and they hung in undisturbed
festoons from the cedars and the stones.

"I like this," said Jay, with a sort of sigh, after a
long moment of silence.

"So do I," said Missy, giving him a kiss.

The sun was behind the cedar and barberry and
catbrier banks. They went as far down the Neck as
there was a road to go, and then turned back, "the
gait they cam' again." The children were exception-
ally good, and no one talked much. It was not
the sort of hour when one talks much, good or bad,
or thinks much, either. Enough bliss it was to be
alive,

> "But to be young was very heaven."

Jay liked it, and Missy liked it too, though she
was twenty-seven. And Mr. Andrews, possibly,
though he did not say anything about it.

When they came up the steep little hill by the old
mill, Jay felt the spell of the water and the wild-

flowers broken, and began to clamor to be taken over on the front seat between papa and Michael. He was cold, he said, and he wanted to see the horses, and he didn't want to stay where he was, in point of fact. It was rather a serious thing to contradict Jay, and to carry him howling through the village, like a band to call attention to the arrival of a circus. It was well to afford entertainment to one's neighbors, but Missy did not think it necessary to court occasions of sacrifice, so, with her pleasure much diminished, they stopped, while Mr. Andrews managed to put out his one stiff hand, and then she proceeded to push the hopeful boy over the back of the seat, and establish him between his father and the coachman.

"I must say, Jay, you are a spoiled child," she exclaimed.

"That's so!" cried Jay, complacently, making a lunge towards the whip.

"If you say 'that's so' again, I shall be angry with you," said Missy. "Mr. Andrews, won't you try to stop the children from talking this vulgar slang. Jolly, coquettish, bizarre slang I don't mind, once in a very great while, from children, but this sort of kitchen and village boy vulgarity they never will get over, if they keep it up much longer."

"I have done my best," said Mr. Andrews.

"Well, I hope you'll excuse me for saying I don't think you have covered yourself with glory."

"Jay, we're a bad lot; we must reform at once," said the father, putting his stiff arm around his boy, and giving him a hug. "Miss Rothermel will give us up if we don't."

"That's so!" cried Jay, boisterously, kicking the

shawl off his legs, and nearly tumbling off the seat in his enthusiasm.

"I *have* given you up," said Missy. "Don't put yourselves to the trouble of reforming on my account."

Nothing seemed to disturb the tranquillity of Mr. Andrews this evening. He looked around and saw Missy's face darken as they found themselves meeting carriages arriving from the cars, but it did not seem to depress him; on the contrary, he seemed quietly amused.

"The cars are three-quarters of an hour late!" exclaimed Missy, unguardedly; "I thought we should have escaped them."

"There is no dust to-night," said Mr. Andrews; "so they don't do us any harm."

"No, of course not," murmured Missy, bowing stiffly to Mrs. Eve and her placid-looking son, who swept past them as if they were fugitives from justice.

"There was racing and chasing on Cannobic Lea!"

It was amazing why every one who came from the cars by the late train drove as if pursued by fate.

When they reached home, there was another trial awaiting Missy. A long-legged, good-looking man was sitting on the piazza, with his feet higher than his head, and a meerschaum in his mouth. He came forward briskly to meet the arrival and welcome his host; but he was aghast to find a well-dressed young lady getting out of the carriage, and could scarcely command words to explain that he had only that day heard of his friend's accident, and had hurried up, by the just-arrived train, to learn its extent. He was

11*

evidently one of Mr. Andrews' bachelor friends—a woman-hater, like himself; and his thorough chagrin at seeing Miss Rothermel, after an introduction, go into the house, would have been amusing to any one less intimately connected with the surprise. Just as Missy—followed closely by the children, and, at a little distance, by the two gentlemen—was entering the house, a second female cavalcade, headed by Miss Varian, attended by two maids bearing bathing-clothes and towels, came from the direction of the water, and met them upon the piazza.

"Is that you, Missy?" said her aunt; "I have been trying my first bath of the season; and I assure you it was cold." As if this were not enough to try the nerves of the poor misogynist, Mrs. Varian at this moment descended the stairs, accompanied by Anne with her shawl and book.

"I thought I would give you a surprise, Missy," she said, with her sweet smile, "and be down-stairs to meet you."

Missy kissed her, and tried to look as if it were an agreeable surprise. The cup of the guest's amazement was now apparently full. Here were six strange women gathered on his friend's threshold to meet him, all evidently at home. Had Mr. Andrews' accident affected his reason, and had he begun a collection of these specimens, that had lately been his abhorrence? What had occurred, to turn this peaceful abode of meerschaum and Bourbon into a clear-starched and be-ribboned country house, where shooting-coats and colored shirts were out of place? What should he do about his boots? Was there a train to town to-night? or ought he to stay, and look after poor Andrews?

Wasn't it his duty to telegraph to some one in town at once for medical advice? He had always heard that people turned against their friends when the brain was involved; and, most likely, this was a case in point, and Andrews had turned toward his enemies, as well.

All these thoughts rushed through his mind (and it wasn't a mind that could bear rushes through it, without showing its disturbance), while Mr. Andrews, with unusual urbanity, was bowing to Mrs. Varian, and making her welcome. It was the first time she had been down-stairs since she had been in the house, and it seemed to give him a great deal of pleasure. She always called out in him, as in every man who met her, the highest degree of chivalry that was in him.

But the guest did not look at her; he only looked at his friend, transformed into a ladies' man, a Chester-field—everything that he wasn't before. He stag-gered in his gait as he looked on, and took hold of the door-post for support. Missy was glad Mr. Andrews did not observe his agitation; but none of it escaped her, and she longed to give a chance for explanation.

"What can he think of us?" she reflected miser-ably. But no moment for explanation arrived. The dinner-bell rang, with sharp promptness, as they stood in the doorway. It was Melinda's night out, and no grass was allowed to grow under the family's feet when that night came round. The children were hungry too, and rushed ahead into the dining-room; so nothing remained for Mr. Andrews, but to lay down his hat, give his arm to Mrs. Varian and follow them in. Miss Varian exclaimed she wasn't ready for dinner, just coming from the bath, but Missy dreaded her disturbing them by coming in later, and begged her to come at once. She was hungry, and consented. The guest, whose name seemed to be McKenzie, had nothing to do but to follow. There were places enough arranged at the table, but by a villainous, vicious contrivance of fate, every one got a seat before Missy, who had to place her aunt at table, and she was left staring at her enthronement at the head. "I don't think I'd better sit here," she faltered rather low to Mr. McKenzie, who was stranded beside her, "I think there may be something to carve, and I'm not much at that."

"Oh, by no means," he exclaimed, hurriedly, "I couldn't think of it—that is—I am sure you belong there—I—I—you—that is—"

"Oh, very well," said Missy, seeing that Mr. Andrews was looking rather anxiously in their direction, and sank into her seat.

"I want to sit next to Missy," cried Jay. "Even if she was cross to me, I love her all the same, don't you, papa?"

"All the same," said Mr. Andrews, smiling, and not looking disconcerted, as he took the stopper out of the decanter by him. Missy was very angry for a moment. Why had he not been disconcerted, as she most unhappily was? But in a few moments she thought better of it, and was ashamed of herself. There was poor mamma, who had made such an effort to come down; she must have a cheerful hour at all events. And the miserable man next her must be put at ease. The room was rather warm, and his heat increased his agitation. His soup almost choked him, and Missy at one time thought she should have to introduce him to his napkin, he seemed too ill at ease to find it, though it was beside his plate. She put the salt within his reach, but he didn't see it, and a water bottle, but he was even beyond that. So she filled his glass and pushed it towards him. He saw it at last, and drank it off at one gulp.

"Mr. Andrews," said Missy, "can we have the door a little open? It is rather warm at this end of the room."

"Certainly, Miss Rothermel," exclaimed Mr. Andrews, getting up to open it. "Why didn't you speak before?"

"Heavens! Missy, what are you thinking about! The door open on my back. I should be ill with neuralgia in half an hour. Mr. Andrews, I beg you'll have a little mercy on us. Missy will kill off all the household if you let her have her way about ventilation."

"Oh! *n'importe*," cried Missy, as Mr. Andrews stood irresolute and embarrassed. "Mr. McKenzie and I may die of asphyxia, but that would be better than Aunt Harriet's getting neuralgia. Pray sit down, Mr. Andrews, I really am used to it."

"And I," said Miss Varian, going on uninterruptedly with her dinner, "am quite familiar with these cases of asphyxia. Pray don't be disturbed, Mr. Andrews. Miss Rothermel has them two or three times a week."

It was so ludicrous, the uninterrupted calm of Miss Varian, who knew she was going to have her own way, and the heat and agitation of the others; that, as Mr. Andrews reluctantly took his seat, they all laughed·

"It is quite true," said Mrs. Varian, wishing to reconcile him. "You know, Missy, you are very imprudent. I believe your aunt has saved you from a great many colds."

"From an early grave, no doubt," said Missy, fanning herself, and giving Mr. McKenzie another glass of water, while he was looking amazed from Mrs. Varian to her sister-in-law. He was still quite incapable of helping himself.

"If he has apoplexy, it will be on my conscience," thought Missy. So, after the discussion, she signalled the waitress to open a window near. This was quietly done, and Miss Varian never knew it, not being as sensitively organized as she thought she was. In the meanwhile, something had come on the table which had to be carved, and it had been put before Mr. Andrews.

"This is a hard case," said the host, "but a man with ' never a hand ' can't carve. McKenzie, I believe I must put it upon you."

This was exactly the last straw. The wretched man actually gasped. He writhed, he tried to speak.

"Can't Melinda?" said Missy, quite forgetting that it wasn't her place to make suggestions. She felt sure Mr. Andrews had not seen the purple shade of Mr. McKenzie's complexion.

"Melinda has no gift," said Mr. Andrews. "I have tried her more than once, but she can't carve."

"Then let me try," cried Missy, springing up. "You'll see *I* have a gift."

"Missy!" murmured her mother, deprecatingly, at

this boldness. She evidently had not seen the state the guest was in.

"Mamma," cried Missy, "you know I've had to carve, and make tea, and do a hundred things that didn't belong to me, ever since I was twelve years old, and now you blame me for wanting to show off my accomplishments, when I'm quite of a proper age to display them. I've been imposed on by the family all my life, and now—the ingratitude of republics."

As Missy finished her speech, she stood by Mr. Andrews, who had reluctantly got up, and was glancing rather sternly at his friend.

But the friend did not look at him, he was gazing bewildered at Missy. The familiarity and complete at-home-ness of the whole party made him doubt his senses. It was bad enough to see the women so at ease, though he could believe anything of them. But Andrews evidently liked it, and was pleased with all the liberties they took. It was impossible to account for the state of things by any theory but that of brain disorder. How he got through the rest of the dinner, Missy never quite knew. He had no one to pour out glasses of water for him, and put the wine within reach, for she quite washed her hands of him and sent Gabrielle to take her place, while Mr. Andrews took Gabrielle's; and Missy remained to carve. When they came out from the dinner-table, Mrs. Varian went up stairs, and Missy went into the parlor to gather up some of her aunt's things, of which there were always plenty to gather up. The two gentlemen went on the piazza. She heard them talking as they sat down beside the window, and prepared to smoke.

"I must say, Andrews—"

"Yes."

"That—well. I was a little taken aback to find things—so—a—so—well—so altered with you."

He was beginning to breathe freer and to gain courage, now the atmosphere was clear of women.

"I don't quite understand," returned his friend. "You mean I'm looking badly? You might have thought so a day or two ago, but I'm quite myself to-day, thank heaven."

It seemed to Mr. McKenzie that that was just who he wasn't, but he only smiled derisively, and said, "No; I didn't mean that. I don't think you looking much amiss. On the contrary, you seem uncommonly jolly."

"Jolly!"

"Well for you—that is. Look here, Andrews, if there's a train back to town to-night, I guess I'll take it. I'm not a lady's man, you know. You see I didn't have any idea of what you expected of your friends. I'm not prepared."

"Prepared, for what? We didn't have a dinner-party, did we? I hope you don't mind meeting these neighbors of mine, who have been burned out of their own house, and have taken shelter for a few nights in mine."

"Neighbors," repeated the guest, who was a very good fellow, but not the quickest in the world.

"Why, yes—from the house next door, where the fire was. You knew there had been a fire, I take it, since you had heard about my accident."

"Yes."

"Well, those ladies, as I said, were obliged to leave their own house in flames, and I brought them in here."

" Oh !"

" They seem to be very much obliged to me for what they think I did for them on that occasion, and we get on very well together."

There was a pause, during which Mr. Andrews lighted his cigar, and Mr. McKenzie appeared to be digesting the intelligence.

" All the same, it seems a little queer," he said, after a good deal of deliberation.

"Queer? I must say I don't see it."

" Well, considering how you feel about such things, I mean. I don't suppose there's any real objection, if anybody likes it. There are enough of 'em to make it proper, I've no doubt."

" O yes, I don't think there's anything improper ; you needn't be uneasy, in the least, McKenzie."

There were a good many puffs before the new-comer spoke. He was evidently thinking deeply.

" I'm not uneasy about it, but I suppose you know what people will be saying. I know better, of course ; but they'll say it, all the same."

" Come, now, McKenzie, who cares for what they say? When you get a little older you won't mind, you know."

This was a club joke, for McKenzie wasn't very young. He had a way of turning red, however, very youthfully, and did care what people said about him, if it had anything to do with the sex opposed to his.

"Ah, bah ! that's all nonsense. You'll care, I guess, as much as anybody, when you find what everybody, these ladies here into the bargain, expect of you."

"That's your opinion, is it? Well, come now, I'll set you at rest. These ladies are remarkably sensible. The youngest of them, who is the only one you'd be likely to want me to marry, has a great contempt for me; thinks I'm a brute, and all that. She's fond of the children, and is only civil to me because I happen to be their father and her host."

"Ah, bah!" cried McKenzie, with infinite contempt.

"It's the truth, McKenzie. And I'll tell you something more; she's a spit-fire, and I've been so afraid of her I haven't been near the house all winter."

"You've made up for it this summer, then. No, Andrews, don't you tell me any such stuff. I'm not so young as *that*, you know."

Andrews laughed a little comfortably, as he smoked. "Well, there's no use in talking, then. But it's a hard case. You'd better not let her know your suspicions."

"Let her know! Heaven forbid! No, I don't think there's any danger."

"McKenzie, upon my word, I believe you're afraid of her too."

"Not in just the way you are."

"She's so little, she couldn't hurt you."

"Not just the way she's hurt you."

"You don't believe me yet. Well, now, let me tell you seriously. This young lady is not the marrying kind; she is too sensible by half. I wouldn't ask her for the world. And you know—well, you know I'm not likely to try it again very soon. We won't talk any more about this; but you may make your mind easy on the subject."

Missy heard as far as this ; it wasn't strictly honorable, but she did. She had been sitting in a chair by the window, the easier to pick up a lot of chessmen, which were scattered on the window sill and under it. She had her lap full of the rattling things, when she became interested in the conversation on the piazza. She could not move for some seconds, being fascinated by the sound of her own name. Then, when she wanted to go, she was terrified by the fear of being discovered ; the chessmen made such a rattling if she moved an inch ; she felt it certain that Mr. Andrews would start and come to the window and look in to see who was eavesdropping, if he heard a sound. He would be sure to think it was Gabrielle, till he found it was the virtuous Missy. How she trembled. How angry she was, and how ashamed. But after this last pleasant declaration she started up, chessmen or no chessmen, and darted out of the room. Mr. Andrews did hear a noise, and did look in, and did think it was Gabrielle ; but he could not see who it was that fled ; and though Missy heard him sternly calling the little girl in the hall, she was not virtuous enough to go out and tell him, over the balusters, who had overheard his flattering remarks. This omission would probably have rankled in her conscience if she had not seen Gabrielle, from the window, come in at the front gate with Jay at the same moment. So the father must be assured that the children were neither of them the offenders. He could think what he pleased of the servants, that was no matter of hers.

She was too angry to go down-stairs again. She would have found it difficult to say why she was so angry. She knew she was sensible, she knew she was a spit-fire ; she knew Mr. Andrews did not mean to ask her to marry him. All this was no news ; he had a right to say what he had said, to an intimate friend. She could not expect to be considered sacred. Why shouldn't Mr Andrews talk about her to his friend ? He had not been absolutely disrespectful ; he had only mentioned facts—a little jocosely to be sure ; and a woman hates to be spoken jocosely of between two men, even if admiringly. And Missy hated to be spoken of, at all. She felt that she was sacred, though she knew she hadn't any right to feel so. Poor thin-skinned Missy ; it was so hard for her to keep from being hurt ; everything hurt her, she was so egotistical.

In the morning it was a joyful sound to her to hear Michael driving to the door for the early train ; it was comforting to see the guest drive away alone, and to know that further confidences were over between them for the present. Friends ! Imagine calling such a creature your friend, thought Missy, turning away from the window.

It would have been a blessing if he had stayed away. It is difficult even for a humble-minded young woman to be amiable and easy with a person who has called her a spit-fire ; it was almost impossible for Missy. Going down to breakfast was like facing a battery ; she went to the door two or three times before she had the resolution to open it, and feel herself launched upon the day's embarrassments. Once at table, Mr. Andrews was so commonplace and un conscious, she felt herself strengthened by his weakness. It was a great advantage to know what he did not know. She knew exactly what he thought of her; he did not know that she knew this, nor did he know what she thought of him; Heaven forbid! So she could hold these two advantages in her hand and use them. The result was that she was a little shy and a little silent, and weighed her words very carefully, for a day or two. But bah! when did ever a woman made as Missy was, do anything unnatural to her for longer than a day or two. It was quite in character for her to lay out new parts to act, but equally in character for her to throw them aside impatiently, and fall back into her standard *rôle*. She not unfrequently declared to herself, I will be this, I will be that, but she always ended by being Missy. So that it was not surprising that when at last the house was ready for its occupants, and they moved bag and baggage out of the Andrews' cottage, the young lady was as unaffectedly herself as if Mr. McKenzie had not drawn that unhappy statement from his friend. Not that she had forgotten it, exactly. But she had let it drop into that crucible of injuries and misconceptions, an egotistical mind, and it was melted up into something that hurt no longer; in fact, even gave a little pleasure. She had been so natural and so pleasant, that the house seemed dreary to all the family but Gabby, when she was gone. She also missed the excitement herself, and it seemed rather tame the next morning to breakfast with Aunt Harriet alone. The tented field unfits one for the pastoral life; she found herself bored by the security and stupidity of the day on which she was entering. But that did not last long. She was in an hour or so, too busy to be bored.

CHAPTER XVI.

ALPHONSINE.

OR the second day, the only visitors from the cottage were Jay and Eliza. Gabby only looked askance at the house, from over the arbor vitæ hedge ; it was a foregone conclusion they would not be troubled much by her. Mr. Andrews had now begun his daily journeys to town. Though still obliged to wear his arm in a sling, he was quite able to go to business. No doubt he had there some clerk who could write letters for him as well as Missy, though it is just possible he found it more amusing to have her do it.

June was now in full reign. If Yellowcoats were not perfect to the senses now, it never would be. The days were so long, the nights so soft and moonlit, the air, night and day, so full of fragrance. The ladies sat late on the lawn, by the beach gate. Even Mrs. Varian had ventured to come down, leaning on her daughter's arm, and sit, carefully wrapped, and with a rug spread over the grass, to watch the beauty of the sunset. The second evening after their exodus from his roof, Mr. Andrews found them so sitting, as he strolled down to the beach after dinner. The dinner had been good, the wine had been good, his cigar was good ; but there was an indefinite something wanted, a flavor of companionship and human interest. He looked longingly over the hedge ; he wondered if Miss Rothermel would remember how angry she had been, when Miss Varian told him, it was one of his duties to his neighbor, to come and smoke an after-dinner cigar on the lawn. He was quite interested in this speculation—how good was Miss Rothemel's memory? Sometimes he thought it very strong, sometimes he wondered at its non-existence. As he never forgot anything himself, and generally did what he meant to do, Missy was naturally a puzzle to him. She evidently had forgotten about the observation of Miss Varian, for she looked up with a very pleasant smile, when the grating of the beach gate on its hinges, caused her to turn her head. She pulled forward upon the rug a chair which had been standing beside her with books and a shawl upon it. These she put on the bench at her feet, and Mr. Andrews took the chair.

"You are sitting with your back to the sunset," she said, after the subsiding of the froth of welcoming talk among the little party.

"Well, so are you," he said.

"But I have a reason, and you haven't."

"No reason, except that you put my chair just where it is, and I didn't dare to move it."

Missy frowned; it reminded her that she had heard it stated by this gentleman, that he was afraid of her.

"A plague upon it, what have I said now," he thought.

"I am watching that boat," went on Miss Rothermel, letting drop his remark about the chair, as if it had not been worth answering. "Do you see how she is shilly-shallying there in the mouth of the harbor? There is a good breeze to bring her in, and she will lose it, if she doesn't look out. A little while ago she ran in—crept along the Neck a way, then stood out again, and now, nobody can guess what she means to do, except that she evidently doesn't want to go away. I have been watching her since five o'clock."

"Whose boat is it?" asked Mr. Andrews. "Does she belong about here?"

"No, I am sure not; I think I know all the boats that belong in the harbor, and she has an odd, unfamiliar look."

"Let's have a look at her through my glass," said Mr. Andrews; and he got up and went back to his boat-house, returning with a telescope. "This will show us the whites of our enemy's eyes," he said, adjusting it on its stand, by the beach gate. Missy got up eagerly, and went up to it. It was some moments before she got it fitted to her eye, and then a moment more before she found her craft.

"Ah! here she is," she cried. "It's a capital glass. It's almost like boarding her; it really is uncanny. There is a woman on board, and two men; and see—they have a glass! And—well, I could affirm they are looking at us. See, see, Mr. Andrews! Oh, what a funny effect! It is as if we were staring at each other across a parquet."

"Well," said Mr. Andrews, taking her place at the glass, "it is as if the opposite box didn't like being stared at, and were pulling down their curtains, and putting their fans before their faces. Upon my word, they have gone about, and are getting out of reach of our glass, just as fast as they can."

All the party were now as much interested as Missy had been. Miss Varian clamored to be told exactly what course the little vessel took; Goneril, who happened to be behind her chair, had some unnecessary comment to offer. Mrs. Varian even watched her breathlessly.

" It is very odd," said Missy ; " from the moment we put up the glass, they made off. Look ! they are half way across to Cooper's Bluff. In five minutes they will be out of sight."

It was quite true. In less than five minutes the little sail had shot out of range of the glasses and eyes upon the Varian lawn, and all that could follow it was very vague conjecture. It occupied the thoughts of the little party till the sunset took its place, and then, the apprehension of dew and dampness for Mrs. Varian, and then the moving up to the house. Mr. Andrews carried some shawls and a book or two, and stopped at the door of the summer parlor, as the others went in. He consented, not reluctantly by any means, to go in with them.

" For I assure you," he said, as he entered, " I find it quite dismal at home since you all went away."

Miss Varian seemed to take this as a personal tribute, and made her thanks. " I had supposed," she added, " that Jay was the only one who felt it very much ; but I'm glad to know you shared his amiable sentiments."

" By the way, where is he to-night ?" asked Missy, putting a shade on the lamp.

" The children were bribed to go to bed very early to-night. Eliza asked permission to go home this evening, and stay till morning ; and so, I suppose, they were persuaded to be sleepy early to suit her."

Late that evening, as Missy looked out, before shutting her window for the night, she thought again of the little vessel that had excited her curiosity. She

rather wondered that she had bestowed so much speculation upon it ; but again, when she awoke in the night,
she found herself thinking of it, and wondering how
there happened to be a woman in the party. Oyster-
men and fishermen do not burden themselves with
women when they go out into the Sound ; and this
little vessel had not the look of a pleasure boat. She
had rather a restless night, waking again and again ;
she heard all sorts of sounds. Once the dog at the
barn began to bark, but stopped shortly after one
sharp snarl. At another time, she was so sure she
heard a noise upon the beach, that she got up and
opened the window and looked out. The night was
dark—no moon, and but faint light of stars. A light
fog had gathered over the water. She listened long ;
at one moment she was certain she heard the voice of
a child, crying ; but it was only once, and for the space
of a moment. And then all was silent. The wind
among the trees, and the washing of the tide upon the
shore she still could hear, but could hear nothing else.
She went back to bed, feeling ashamed of herself. It
was like Aunt Harriet, who heard robbers and assas-
sins all night long, and called up Goneril to listen,
whenever a bough swayed against a neighboring
bough, or a nut dropped from a tree.

"At any rate, I won't tell of it at breakfast,"
thought the young lady, determinately, putting her
face down on her pillow. By and by she started up,
not having been able to "boss" her thoughts, and get
asleep. That was not imagination, whatever the
child's cry and the dog's bark had been. There was a
sound of oars, growing gradually fainter as she listened. Well, why shouldn't there be ? Men often had

to go off to their sloops, to be ready for an early start
when the wind served; maybe it was almost day-
break. But no, as she reasoned, the clock struck two.
On such a dark night, it *was* unusual, at such an hour
as this, for any one to be rowing out from shore. If
there had been a man in the house, she would have
risked ridicule, and roused him to go out and see that
all was right. But the men slept at the stable—there
was absurdity, and a little impropriety, in her going out
alone at such an hour to call the men. It would rouse
Mrs. Varian, no doubt, and give her a sleepless night.
And as for Miss Varian, it would furnish her a weapon
which would never wear out, if, as was probable,
nothing should be found out of order about the place,
or on the beach. No one likes to be laughed at; no
one less than Miss Rothermel. She shut the window
again, and resolutely lay down to sleep. But sleep
refused to come. It is impossible to say what she
feared; but she seemed to have entered into a cloud
of apprehension, vague as it was bewildering. It
was useless to reason with herself, she was simply
frightened, and she should never dare to scorn Aunt
Harriet again. Was this the way the poor woman
felt every night after the household were all at rest?
Well, it was very unpleasant, and she wasn't to be
blamed for waking Goneril; if Missy hadn't been
ashamed, she'd have waked somebody.

It was not till dawn fairly came that she was able
to go to sleep. From this sleep she was confusedly
wakened by a hurried knock at her door. The sun
was streaming into the room. She felt as if she
hadn't been asleep at all, and yet the misgivings of
the night seemed endlessly far off in time.

"Well, what is it?" she answered, sitting up and pushing back her pillow, and feeling rather cross, it must be said.

"They've sent over from the other house to know if Jay is here," said the waitress, out of breath, showing she had run up-stairs very fast.

"*Here!*" cried Missy, springing to the door and opening it. "How should he be here? Do you mean to say they cannot find him?"

"Oh," gasped Ann, putting both hands on her heart, "Eliza's in a dreadful way. She's just got in from spending the night at home, and went up to the nursery to dress the children, and opened the door softly, and there was Jay's crib empty, but Gabby sound asleep."

"He'd gone into his father's room, no doubt," said Missy, pale and trembling.

"No," cried the woman, "she ran right off to Mr. Andrews' door, and he called out the child wasn't there, and in a terrible fright, she came over here. When I told her no, I knew he wasn't, she flew back."

"Go there, quick, and tell me if they find him in the kitchen or dining-room ; maybe he missed Eliza and crept down-stairs and fell asleep on the sofa in the parlor."

This mission suited Ann exactly ; she ran as her mistress bade her, but failed to come back with news. Missy dressed in a moment of time. She saw it all ; she knew what she had heard in the night ; she knew what the boat had meant hovering about the harbor, shooting out of sight. She knew what was the explanation of the fire, for which no one had ever been able satisfactorily to account. She began to realize what it was to have an enemy. The thought of that child's cry, so suddenly smothered last night, sent a pang through her. She scarcely knew how she got her clothes on ; her hands shook as with an ague. When it came to opening the front door to let herself out she found they were as weak as if she had had a fever. Half-way across the lawn she met Ann, who shook her head and wrung her hands, and turned back, and followed her. Ann liked to be in the proscenium box when there was a tragedy on the boards ; it would be dull laying the breakfast table when all this excitement was going on next door (though a trifle more useful). She ran after her mistress, who did not stop till she reached the gate that led into the Andrews' yard. There she found herself face to face with Mr. Andrews, who had come hurriedly down the path with the confused air of one who had been waked from sleep by a sudden and stunning blow.

" What does it mean," he said to her, as she came into the gate.

" You haven't found him ?" she said, as they went together towards the house. " Where are his clothes —what has been taken—what doors were open ?"

" His clothes are left—only a blanket from the bed is missing—no doors were open—a ladder was against the nursery window. I am bewildered. I don't know what it means at all."

" It means Alphonsine," cried Missy, leaning against the door for support. " It means revenge and a reward. The boat we watched last night—the sounds I heard in the night—ah, ah, don't let us waste a moment. It was two o'clock when I heard the sound of oars—it is seven now—and a good breeze blowing.

Oh, my poor little Jay, where have they got you by this time !"

"You suspect that woman," said the father, "that I sent away last autumn? But what motive—what provocation—what could have prompted such an act? I confess I cannot follow you—"

"Believe me, and don't waste a moment," cried Missy. "Rouse the village, ring the bells, get out your boat, send for the Roncevalles, telegraph to town to the police. The Roncevalles will take their yacht, she came in yesterday—you know she's fast. Why do you look so doubtful? Mr. Andrews, I love him as well as you do. I am sorry for you, but I shall hate you if you are not quick. Every moment that you doubt me is a moment lost. Jay is in the hands of wicked people. You will never see him again, if you are not prompt. Those creatures have stolen him—they will board some French ship outward bound ; don't look for motive—they know you have money—they want revenge for being sent away. Oh, my little boy ! What have I brought upon you !"

And with a burst of tears, Missy hid her face. The poor man groaned and turned away. He walked to the door and back, as if trying to steady his brain and to think.

Missy recovered herself in a moment, and making a step forward, with a passionate gesture of the hands, "Do something," she cried. "Do not, do not waste a moment."

Then, seeing he still had not admitted her theory, but was weighing it with a troubled mind, she exclaimed, "Send in a hundred different directions if you will, but send my way first. You have no other plan;

follow mine till something better comes before you ; it is better to be doing something than nothing."

"You are right," he said, with sudden resolution, starting towards the library door—"Send a woman over to Captain Perkins ; tell Michael to saddle Jenny."

From that moment there was no lack of speed in carrying on the search. In half an hour, the bells were ringing in the village steeples ; the telegraph wire was talking hotly into the Police Headquarters of the city ; men and boys were swarming on the beach. The good yacht Ilia, which had loafed in yesterday, with no intention but to spend a few hours in harbor, was ready at a moment's warning. In a hasty conclave of half a dozen gentlemen, it had been decided that Miss Rothermel's suspicions were quite worth acting upon, *faute de mieux*. There were others who had seen the mysterious little craft ; and one man who had come upon a foreign-looking group encamped upon a lonely point of the Neck, the day before. There were two men and a woman in the party, and they had evidently shunned observation. There were foot-marks upon the sand, a little below the Andrews' boat-house, and a track that the keel of a boat had made when pushed off, in the falling tide. It was more than probable that the child had been stolen with a view to the largest reward, and that the matter had been well arranged ; and Miss Rothermel's idea, that out on the Sound some homeward-bound French ship was expected to come along, which would take them on board, and put them beyond reach of pursuit for many weeks at least, found favor. There was, of course, a possibility of their having failed to meet their ship, or of their not

having such a plan ; and all the neighborhood of the
Necks, and the shores along the Sound must be instantly
searched ; it was even possible that their plan had been
to secrete him in the city. Jay had been a well-known
and rather favorite little person in the neighborhood—
Mr. Andrews was understood to be rich—the people
were naturally kind-hearted—the occurrence was quite
beyond the ordinary; in short, it was a day unparalleled
in Yellowcoats for excited feeling. Men were scouring
the woods on horseback and on foot, and patrolling the
shores in boats ; mothers were leaving, equally, wash-
tubs and piano-fortes, to hug closer their own children
and mourn over the dangers of poor Jay, and listen
for the latest news. People drove aimlessly about from
house to house ; all day long there were groups on the
steamboat wharf, and along the shore that led to Mr.
Andrews' house ; the telegraph office was besieged.
Little work was done. I almost think there was no
dinner cooked in more houses than the Andrews' and
the Varians'.

When the Ilia sailed gallantly out of the mouth of
the harbor, the foremost and fastest of all the pursuing craft, people cheered and wept, and prayed for the
continuance of the stiff breeze that had been blowing
since day-break. But the stiff breeze was a two-
edged sword that cut both ways ; while it helped the
pursuers, it helped the pursued.

At first, it was decided Mr. Andrews should not go
on the yacht, but should be on the spot to direct, and
order the search in different quarters. A hastily
sworn-in officer was taken on board, and several gentlemen who had full authority to act for him. But
when the last boat load was about to push off, a cer-

tain fierce impatience seemed to seize him. He had taken up Missy's theory, it seemed, at last, and felt that he could not let them go without him. He signalled them to wait, and hurried across the lawn to Missy, who stood with a rigid face, watching the vessel's sails filling with the breeze.

"I believe I'm going with them," he said, "there is nothing I can do here. If anything comes up, you will decide. The fact is, I can't stand it, all day in suspense."

"Then don't keep the boat waiting," said Missy, with ungraciousness. The truth was, she wanted to go so wildly herself, she hated him for being able to do what she could not. What was the suspense more to him than to her, she thought. She must count all these dreadful hours at home, while he could feel he was nearer, every moment, to some certainty, good or bad, which must be so many hours further off from her. In a moment more he had sprung aboard the little boat, and they were off.

All this while Gabrielle had been wandering about, silent and eager. At first she had been questioned, with few results, as to her knowledge of the events of the night. She had denied, generally, having been awake or knowing anything till Eliza had waked her up in her fright at finding Jay's crib empty. Then, in the hurry and panic, she had dropped out of notice. Missy found her standing beside her on the lawn, watching the boat go off. A sudden doubt came into Missy's mind as she saw the child's keen, silent face.

"What was Alphonsine's last name?" she said to her, without preface.

12*

"Gatineau," she answered, promptly.

"When did you see her last?" she asked, looking at her narrowly.

"I—I—don't know—" faltered the child, turning her eyes away.

"Yes, you do know, Gabby," said Missy, firmly. "Tell me quickly. Did you see her yesterday?"

"I promised not to tell," returned the child, faintly.

"Come into the house with me," said Missy, taking her by the hand with no uncertain grasp. "I want to talk to you about all this."

There were groups of people upon the lawn, and Missy felt afraid to trust herself to talk before them, afraid, also, that the presence of strangers would weaken her power over the child, who followed her unwillingly into the house. When there, she shut the door upon them, and sat down, drawing Gabrielle towards her.

"We all feel very unhappy about your little brother," she said, looking directly into the oblique eyes of Gabrielle; "this is a terrible day for your father and for us all."

"They won't hurt him," faltered the child, uneasily.

"They say they won't, but they may. They tell lies, those French people. Alphonsine told lots of lies when she was here. We can't believe her, even if she says she won't hurt Jay."

"I know she won't," said Gabrielle.

"We'd give anything to get him back," said Missy. "Tell me all that happened; you shall not be punished."

"I promised not," said the child, looking down,

and glancing towards the clock uncomfortably. Missy caught the direction of her glance.

" Why do you look at the clock ?" she asked.

Gabrielle hung her head lower than before, and looked convicted.

" When did she tell you you might tell ?" demanded Missy, with keen sagacity.

" Not till after ten o'clock," murmured the girl.

Missy's heart sank ; it was just forty-five minutes past eight o'clock. They had felt sure of safety if the child could be kept silent for that length of time, and had no doubt set an outside limit to her silence.

" You are quite right," said Missy, " in not breaking your promise. " I suppose she thought you would be punished to make you tell, and she told you you must hold out till ten ?"

Gabrielle nodded, perplexed at this reading of her mind.

" Always keep your word, even to wicked people," said Missy, getting up and smoothing out some papers that were lying open on the table. " You know *I* think Alphonsine is a wicked woman, but you must keep your word to her all the same, you know."

Gabrielle was quite reassured by this, and drew a freer breath.

" She told me I might tell after ten o'clock if I couldn't help it, and she'd give me—the—the—"

" I understand," said Missy, " the reward she offered. Well, now, I'll go and see about some things up-stairs, and you can come with me and put my ribbon box in order. And at ten o'clock I'll call you to come and tell me all about it."

Gabrielle brightened. She had rarely had access

to Missy's sashes and ribbons ; she longed to get at them, even at this agitated moment. While she was shut in Missy's room in this congenial occupation, Missy went down stairs and rapidly turned forward an hour the hands of the hall and parlor clocks ; then waiting fifteen minutes in breathless suspense, called up to Gabrielle to come to her. She was sure the child would not have any correct estimate of time, and saw her glance without surprise at the clock on the mantelpiece, which pointed at ten.

"Now, I suppose you may tell me all about it," she said, trying to speak very indifferently. "Tell me when you first saw Alphonsine."

"Day before yesterday," she said. "After dinner, when papa had taken Jay to drive, and left me all alone."

"Oh, where were you ? "

"I was down on the beach below the cedars. I heard somebody call me softly up on the bank, and I looked up and saw Alphonsine beckoning to me. So I went up, and she took me behind the bushes and talked to me."

There was a long pause.

"Well," said Missy, trying to smooth out her voice as she smoothed out the creases in a piece of work she had in her hand. "Well, what did she say ? "

"I don't know," murmured Gabby, getting uneasy, and twisting around on her heels, and getting out of range of her interlocutor's eyes. "I don't know—all sorts of things."

"Oh, I suppose she talked about me, and asked whether your papa came to our house often, and all that."

Gabby gave her a doubtful, sharp look.

"Ye—es," she said.

"And you told her about that, and then she said—?"

Gabby, relieved to have this most delicate part of the conversation so passed over, went on to state that Alphonsine had coaxed her to tell her all about Eliza, the nurse, and when Eliza went out, and all about the ways of the other servants in the house. And when she knew that Eliza was going out to stay away till morning, the next night, she had told Gabby she had a great secret to tell her, and made her promise to keep it. She then told her, Jay was the cause of all her (Gabrielle's) trouble, and that if he went away she wouldn't be snubbed so, and her papa would give her plenty of money and buy jewelry for her, instead of laying it all up, as he did now, for Jay. This part of her communication Gabby made with much shame-facedness, and many oblique looks at her companion. This latter was discreet, however, and helped the narrative on with many little questions which took off the edge of its badness. Gabby admitted that Alphonsine had given her a ring at this stage of the interview, and that she had said she was going to give her something else, if she did what she asked of her. Then she said she had been getting married to a German sea-captain, who was rich, and wanted a little boy. And she liked Jay, and was going to see if she couldn't get Jay to come away and live with her. But, of course, Jay mustn't know anything about it, for he was so little he would tell it all to his papa, and that would spoil everything. She would come that next night, after Eliza had gone out, and talk to Jay herself about it. But Gabby must promise to get up softly as soon as Eliza went away, and unfasten the window that opened on the shed, if it should be shut, and also promise to lie quite still, and not speak till she was spoken to, if she heard her come. Then, at that visit, she would bring her a locket and a fine sash, which she had bought for her. And then, with many flattering words, she sent her away, staying herself till some one came for her in a boat, she said.

All the next day, Gabrielle felt very important, having this secret, and knowing what a visitor they were going to have in the night. She watched Eliza go off that evening with much satisfaction. It grew dark, and very soon Jay was fast asleep, and she got up and opened the window, and there lay awake and waited for Alphonsine. Hours passed. She heard her father come in and go to his room, and all the house shut up. Then she thought Alphonsine wasn't coming, and had been laughing at her. So she went to sleep at last and didn't know anything more till she heard Jay make a cry, and then heard somebody hush him up and put something over his mouth. She sat up in bed and saw, by a light put in one corner, and shaded, that Alphonsine had Jay in her arms, bundled up in a blanket, and that somebody was waiting half-way in at the window. This was a man, Gabrielle knew when she saw Alphonsine hurry to the window and put Jay in his arms, for he spoke German in a low, hoarse, man's voice. She was frightened at seeing Jay taken away out into the darkness in a strange man's arms, and she began to cry. Alphonsine uttered a bad word, and told the man to go on, she must settle this stupid. She spoke in German, but Gabrielle knew German. Then she came back to Gabrielle, and was very coaxing, thrust-

ing into her hand the package she had promised, but
telling her she had a pair of bracelets that matched the
locket, that she had meant to bring her, but would send
her, if she held her tongue until after ten in the morning.

"No matter what they do to you," she said, "hold
your tongue till then, and you will never need be sorry.
I shall know, for I have somebody here that tells me
all about what's going on. And if I hear you haven't
told, you'll have your bracelets by express on Thurs-
day. You see I keep my promise ; look at the locket,
and see if it isn't beautiful, and the bracelets are worth
ten of it."

Then, with hurried words of caution, she left her—
only looking back to say, "Tell Madamoiselle next
door if she finds out I have been here, that I have not
forgotten her. I would do a good deal for the love of
her."

The window Gabrielle closed, because she was a
little afraid, but the lamp she put out in obedience to
Alphonsine's injunction, after she had looked at the
locket, which was very big, and very gay with garnets.
The sash, too, was quite magnificent, showing that Alphonsine was playing for high stakes. She had wrapped
these two treasures up, and, together with the ring, they
were tightly concealed in the bosom of her dress. She
had not had time to admire them as they deserved,
not having dared to bring them out till she should be
alone. Now, however, she yielded very willingly to
Missy's invitation to unbutton her dress, and brought
them to the light. Missy took them with trembling
hands ; they were the price of blood, and she almost
shuddered at the touch of the little monster who

pressed close to her to gaze with delight upon her treasures. Not one word in the narrative had indicated remorse, or sorrow for being parted from her little brother. The servants, and the children in the street, seemed to have more feeling. After Missy had looked at the showy French locket, she unwrapped the sash, thinking, as she did so, how much reliance could be placed on the woman's statement that she was married to a German sea-captain. The paper in which the sash was wrapped first she had not noticed. The inner paper was a plain white one. Some writing on the outer paper, which had been loosely round the parcel, caught her eye. It was a part of a bill of lading of the Hamburg barque Frances, bound to Valparaiso, and it bore date three days back, and was signed by G. A. Reitzel, captain. Alphonsine had not meant to leave this trace ; in her hurry, perhaps, she had pulled this paper out of her pocket with the package. Gabrielle said it had not been wrapped around it, but had been with it when in the hurry and the darkness she had thrust it into her hand. Missy sprang up in haste. This was an important clew. How should she get the news to the Ilia? She left the astonished Gabrielle and flew down stairs. One or two gentlemen were on the beach below the house, talking, and scanning the harbor with glasses. She ran down to them and communicated her news. It might make all the difference, they said, and they estimated its importance as highly as she did. It was of the greatest moment that they should be warned to look for a German barque and not a French one ; besides the difference of the course she would take for Valparaiso if she got out to sea before they overhauled her. Missy shivered.

"Don't talk of that," she said. "The suspense would be unbearable. I look for them back to-night."

The elder of the gentlemen shook his head. "You must remember they had nearly seven hours the start of us," he said, "and a good stiff breeze since daybreak."

"But the delays," said Missy, "and the uncertainty of coming up with the vessel at the right moment. I count on their losing hours in that."

"But then," returned the other, "the woman must have had good assurance of their arrangements to have taken the embargo off the child at ten."

"How shall we overtake them and get this news to them?" asked Missy, finding speculation very tiresome which did not lead up to this. No one could suggest an answer. The Ilia was the quickest vessel anywhere about, and it would be an impossibility to overtake her.

"Can't you telegraph to some station a few miles further down the Sound than she can yet be, and tell them to send out a boat and watch for her, and board her with the message?" said Missy. This was finally decided on, and carried out with some variations.

About two o'clock, a message was received that the Ilia had been boarded, and was in possession of the intelligence. She had evidently sighted no Hamburg bark, or she would have sent back word to that effect, nor had she made quite as good time as they had hoped she would. The wind was slackening, and varying from one quarter to another. It would not hold out much longer, every one agreed in thinking. And so the afternoon wore on. Some of the gentlemen went in to the Varians and got a glass of wine and some lunch in the dining-room. Others drove away and came back again. Always there were two or three on the lawn, and some one was always at the glass by the beach gate.

Missy shut herself into her own room. Even her mother's sympathy was no help. She wanted to be let alone ; the suspense was telling on her nerves. She had hardly eaten at all, and there had scarcely been a moment till now, that she had not been using her wits in the most active way. Poor wits ; they felt as if they were near a revolt. But what could she do with them for the hours that remained, before a word, good or bad, could come from the slim little yacht and her gallant crew? Hours, she talked about. She well knew it might be days. One of the gentlemen on the lawn had said, of course she would return if by midnight they had met with no success ; they were not provisioned for a cruise ; and at best would never think of going out to sea. This gentleman was elderly, and had a son on board the Ilia. Missy scorned his opinion—now that Mr. Andrews had gone, there would be no turning back. She did not say anything, but she felt quite safe, provisions or no provisions. The days did wear away—as all days do.

> " Be the day weary, or never so long,
> At last it ringeth to evensong."

Evensong, however, brought its own additions to the misery. If it were hard to think of the betrayed child, alone with such cruel keepers, when the sun shone, and the waves danced blue and white, it was little short of maddening when the twilight thickened, and the long day died, and the thick, starless night set in. Missy could not stay in the house after dark ; it seemed to her insupportable to be within four walls. She paced the beach below the lawn, or sat under shelter of the boat-house, and watched the bonfire which the men had made a few feet off, and which sent a red light out a little way upon upon the black waters.

A little way, alas, how little a way ! Missy's eyes were always strained eagerly out into the darkness beyond ; her ears were always listening for something more than the lonely sounds she heard. It seemed to her that it would be intolerable to watch out these hours of darkness and silence ; she must penetrate them. She felt as if her solicitude and wretchedness would be half gone if the night were lifted, and the day come again. Ten o'clock struck—eleven—the outsiders, one by one, dropped off. There were left two or three men who had been hired by some of the gentlemen to watch the night out by the bonfire ; Mr. Andrews' own man, the Varians' man, and Missy and Goneril. Eliza, the nurse, worn out and useless, had gone to bed. Of course, Ann was expended, and no one but Goneril had nerve and strength left to be of any service. She had a real affection for the little boy, with all her ungraciousness, and felt, with Missy, that the house was suffocating, and sleep impossible. She had got Miss Varian into her bed, and then told her she must fight her burglars by herself, for Miss Rothermel needed her more than she. This put Miss Varian in a rage, but Goneril did not stop to listen. She went to Mrs. Varian's room, and soothed her by taking down warm wraps for Missy, and promising to stay by her till she consented to come up and go to bed. She also carried down coffee and biscuits to the men, and made Missy drink some, and lie down a little while inside the boat-house door. It was surprising how invaluable Goneril was in time of trouble, and how intolerable in hours of ease.

Midnight passed, and in the cold, dreary hours between that and dawn, poor Missy's strength and courage ebbed low. She was chilled and ill; her fancy had been drawing such dreadful pictures for her they were having the same effect upon her as realities. She felt quite sure that the child never would be restored to them; that even now, perhaps, his life was in danger from the violent temper of the wicked woman in whose hands he was; that if she found herself near being thwarted in her object, she was quite capable of killing him. Her temper was violent, even outstripping her cunning and malice. Poor little boy! how terrified and lonely he would be, shut down, perhaps, in some dark hole in the ship. "I want you, Missy! I want you, Missy!" he had cried, heartbroken, in the darkness of his own nursery. What would be his terror in the darkness of that foreign ship. She felt such a horror of her own thoughts that she tried to sleep; failing that, she made Goneril talk to her, till the talking was intolerable.

The men around the fire smoked and dozed, or chatted in low tones; the wind, which had come up again, made a wailing noise in the trees, the rising tide washed monotonously over the pebbles; a bird now and then twittered a sharp note of wonder at the untimely light of the fire upon the beach. These were

the only sounds; the night was unusually dark; a
damp mist shut out the stars, and there was no moon.

It was just two o'clock; Missy had bent down for
the fiftieth time to look at her watch by the light of
the bonfire; Goneril, silent and stern, was sitting with
her hands clasped around her knees, on the boat-house
floor, when a sudden sound broke the stillness, a gun
from the yacht as she rounded into the harbor. The
two women sprang to their feet, and Missy clutched
Goneril's arm.

"If those milk-sops have come back without him,"
said the latter between her teeth, answering Missy's
thought. Surely they would not have come without
him; the father was not a man to give up so; and yet
it was earlier than any one had supposed it possible
they could return; and the wind had been so variable,
and the night so dark. Could it be that they had come
in, disheartened and hungry? feeling the barque was
beyond their reach upon the seas, and excusing themselves by sending after her steam instead of sail?

The men around the fire sprang up at the sound of
the gun, and in an instant were all alertness. One
threw a fresh armfull of wood on the fire "to make it
more cheerful-like;" two others sprang into a small
boat and pushed out to meet the yacht.

"It'll be a half hour before they can anchor and
get off a boat and land," said Goneril, impatiently.
"It'll never occur to 'em that anybody on shore may
want to know the news they've got. As long as they
know themselves, they think it's all that's necessary."

Missy felt too agitated to speak. The long excitement had taken all her strength away, and a half hour
more of suspense seemed impossible to bear. Goneril

also found it intolerable ; she had not lost her strength
by the day's agitation, but she had no patience to
stand still and wait for them.

"I'll run up and tell the cook to have some coffee
ready for the gentlemen, and some supper. Most
likely they've come in for that. Men don't work long
upon an empty stomach. The boy wouldn't be much
to them if the provisions had given out."

With this sneer she hurried away, and left Missy
alone. She came back, however, before the sound of
oars drew very near the beach. She had caught up a
lantern from the hall table as she passed it, and lighted
it at the fire. It gave a good light, and shone up into
her handsome face, as she paced up and down restlessly upon the beach.

"Well, they'll soon be here," she said, standing
still and listening to the regular stroke of the oars, and
the sound of voices out in the darkness gradually coming nearer. "They can't be much longer, if they don't
stop to play a game of euchre on the way, or toss up
which shall stand the supper. Much they care for anything but that. If they could smell the coffee it would
hurry them. Men are all alike."

The voices came nearer ; Missy's eager eyes saw
the boat's prow push into the circle of light that went
out from the bonfire, but the mist made it impossible
to discern what and who were in her. She made a
step forward, and the water washed against her feet ;
she clasped her hands together and gazed forward,
scarcely seeing anything for her agitation. Goneril
stood just behind her, on the sand, holding up the lantern, which shone through Missy's yellow hair. Missy

saw some one spring ashore; she heard the captain's
hearty voice call out :

" All right, Miss Rothermel ; you put us on the
right track ; we've brought the little fellow back, safe
and sound, to you."

Then some one else stepped out upon the sand ;
some one else, with something in his arms, and, in a
moment more, a little pair of arms, warm and tight,
hugged her neck, and a fretful voice cried :

" Let me go to Missy—I want Missy—" and Mr.
Andrews hoarsely said, trying to take him back, seeing
her stagger under his weight,

" Let me carry you ; you shall go to Missy in a
moment, and you shan't be taken away from her again."

They were within a few steps of the boat-house ;
Missy, with the child clinging obstinately to her,
staggered into it, and then—well, it was all a blank
after that ; for the first time in her life, and the last
in this history, she fainted dead away.

Jay stopped his crying, Goneril dropped her
lantern, Mr. Andrews started forward and caught her
in his arms. The other gentlemen, directed by
Goneril, had already gone towards the house ; Goneril,
in an instant, seeing what happened, called to one
of the men on the beach, to run for water and some
brandy, and kneeling down, received Missy in her
arms, and laid her gently down upon some shawls.
Mr. Andrews caught up the lantern, and anxiously
scanned the very white face upon the shawls. It
looked dreadfully like a dead face ; poor Jay was
awestruck, and crept close to his father's side. Goneril
chafed her hands, loosened her dress, fanned her,
moved the shawls and laid her flatter on the floor.

But it was an obstinate faint ; even Goneril looked up alarmed into Mr. Andrews' alarmed face.

"I wish we had the doctor, though he's an ass," she said. "Send your man there for him, quick as he can go ; but don't you go away yourself, I might want you—I don't know what is going to happen."

It was a moment's work to despatch the man, who was helping haul up the boat, which half a man could have done. The brandy and the water soon arrived, but failed to produce any apparent effect. "You take that hand, rub it—don't be afraid—rub it hard," said Goneril, as Mr. Andrews, kneeling on the other side, set down the lantern. "I don't like this sort of thing. I've seen a dozen women faint in my life, but they came to as quick as wink, if you dashed water on 'em. I've heard people do die sometimes of their feelings—but I never believed it before. But then, I needn't wonder—this has been an awful day, and she's looked, poor thing, like dead for the last four hours or more. Heavens, there ain't a bit of pulse in her. Just you put your ear down : *I* can't hear her heart beat—why *don't* that idiot hurry ; not that he'll do any good by coming, but, my conscience, I don't want her to die on my hands. I've had enough of this sort of business. I wouldn't go through such another day. I've heard of people losing their heads when they were most wanted—I—I don't know what to do—I believe I've lost mine now—" and Goneril dropped the hand which she had been fiercely chafing, and starting up, stood with her arms upon her hips, gazing down on Missy.

Poor Goneril, the day had been a hard one, and she was made of the same clay as other women, though a little stiffer baked. She had lost her head, and her nerves were shaken, for once in her experience. Mr. Andrews' day certainly had not been less hard, but he had a man's strength to go upon, and not a woman's.

"Let us see," he said, lifting Missy and laying her where the wind blew fresh upon her from the door, then hurrying to another door pushed it open violently with his knee—"Hold the lantern down," he said— "Now give me the brandy," and he forced a drop or two into her mouth. The change of position, or the stimulant, or the fresh wind in her face, started her suspended powers into play—and a slight movement of the lips and a flutter in the pulse on which Mr. Andrews' hand was laid, showed him Goneril had been in a panic, and Missy was only paying the penalty of being an excitable woman. I hope he didn't think it was a nuisance, considering it was all about his boy. Goneril was quite ashamed of herself for having lost the head on which she so prided herself. She was almost sharp with the young lady, when, after more rubbing and more brandy, she opened her eyes and looked about her.

"I didn't know you was one of the fainting kind or I should have been prepared for you," she said, raising her up and putting some pillows and shawls behind her. The pillows and shawls she had twitched into place with asperity, the tone in which she spoke was not dulcet.

"You have given us a great fright," said Mr. Andrews, drawing a long breath as he stood up ; and, taking off his hat, passed his hand over his forehead.

"It doesn't take much to frighten a man," said Goneril tartly. "Please to shut that door. Cold's as

13

bad to die of as a fainting fit, and it's like a pair of
bellows blowing on her back."

"What are you talking about, and where am I?"
murmured poor Missy, a sickened look passing over her
face, as her eyes fell on Mr. Andrews. He wasn't slow
to understand it, and kneeling down beside her, said :

"You have had too much excitement to-day, and
getting Jay back made you faint. Now, don't think
any more about it, but let me assure you, he is well
and safe."

For Master Jay, like a valiant little man, had
slunk out of sight at the occurrence of the fainting fit,
and stood outside the door-post, around which he
gazed furtively back upon the group, prepared to depart
permanently, if anything tragic came about. He was
thoroughly masculine, was Jay ; he never voluntarily
stayed where it wasn't pleasant.

When Missy heard Mr. Andrews' words, and knew
that her keen suspense had ended, she began to cry hysterically. Everybody knows that the physical sensa-
tions of coming back after a faint are not joyful, no matter what news you hear. It was all horror and suffering,
and Missy wept as if her heart were broken instead of
being healed. Goneril chided her with very little regard to distinction of class ; but they had been fellow-
sufferers for so many hours, she seemed in a manner
privileged.

"I can't think what you're taking on so about," she
said, spreading the shawl out over Missy's feet, picking
up the lantern, and tidying up the boat-house as a
natural vent to her feelings. "There might have been
some sense in it if they had come in without the child,
as we thought they would ; or if he'd been your own

child, or if it had been any fault of yours, that he got
carried off. There's nothing ever gained by bothering
about other people's troubles ; folks have generally got
enough to do in getting along with their own. The
Lord gives you grace to bear what He sends you—at
least He engages to ; but there ain't any promises to
them that take on about what they've taken up of
themselves. Don't set your heart on other people's
children unless you want it broken for you. And don't
go to managing other people's matters unless you want
to get into the hottest kind of water. You burn your
fingers when you put 'em into other people's pies.
Every man for himself and every woman for herself,
most emphatic. Keep your tears till the Lord sends you
children of your own to cry about ; goodness knows
you'll need 'em all if you ever come to that."

Goneril had had two children in her early disas-
trous marriage ; one had died, and one had lived
to go to destruction in his father's steps, so she always
bore about with her a sore heart, and the passionate
love of children, which she could not repress, she
always fought down fiercely with both hands. Her
sharp words did not soothe Missy much. She cried and
cried as if there were nothing left to live for, and the
fact that Mr. Andrews was there and was trying to
make her hear him above Goneril's tirade, did not help
matters in the least.

"If you'll take my advice," said Goneril to this
latter person, dashing some more brandy and water
into a glass, and speaking to him over her shoulder as
she did it, " If you'll take my advice, you'll go away
and leave her to get over it by herself. She's just got
to cry it out, and the sight of you and the boy'll only

make it worse. Take him home and put him to bed, and let's have a little common sense."

"Oh, go away, go away, everybody," cried poor Missy, smothering her face down in the shawls.

"Take this," said Goneril, sternly, holding the brandy and water to her lips, which she had no choice but to take, and it was a mercy that she didn't strangle amidst her sobs. But she didn't, and found voice to say,

"I am better. I don't want anything but to be by myself," before she began to sob again.

Thus adjured, it was natural that poor Mr. Andrews should think it best to go away. Nobody wanted him, evidently, and he had been ordered away by two women, when one was always quite enough for him. So he took Jay by the hand and went out into the dim path that led up to his own house. It was, no doubt, time to put the child to bed! The clock in the hall was just proclaiming three in its queer voice, as he went in, and stumbled through the darkness up to the nursery, where he had to go through another scene with the nurse, who woke up and was hysterical.

But Jay soon battered the hysterics out of her. He had been fretful before, but now he was fiendish, and it was as much as they could do to get him into bed. I am afraid it passed through her mind that he'd better have got to France, and it took all the paternal love of Mr. Andrews to keep from inaugurating his return home by a good thrashing. The tragic and comic and very unpleasant are mixed in such an intimate way in some cups.

CHAPTER XVII.

ENTER MISS VARIAN.

'IE next day about noon Mr. Andrews, with Jay by the hand, walked up the steps of the Varians' house. He had got a few hours of sleep after daylight, and had just swallowed a cup of coffee and called it breakfast, and now, looking haggard and weary, had, as was proper, come over to see about Missy and her hysterics.

She too had just come down-stairs, and was sitting in a great chair by the window in the parlor, with foot-stool under her feet and an afghan spread over her. The day was cool and brilliant ; all the fogs and clouds of the night had been blown away by a strong north wind ; the sun was coming in at the window, and Missy was trying to get warm in it, for she felt like Harry Gill in the story-book, as if she should never get warm again. She was pale, and lay with her head back in the chair, looking a disgust with life and its emotions. From this attitude she was roused by the unexpected entrance of Jay and his father, whose approach she had not heard. She changed color and tried to stand up, and then sat down again.

"Don't get up," said Mr. Andrews, lifting Jay to kiss her. "There, Jay, now you'd better go away. Find Goneril and play with the kittens a little while, and then I'll take you home."

He opened the door for Jay, who was very willing to go, not feeling quite at home with Missy yet, since the fainting-fit. He looked askance at her as he went out of the door, as at one who had come back from the dead.

"He wasn't worth all I went through for him yesterday," thought Missy. And then she took it back, and thought, in an instant, he was worth a great deal more—which was a way of hers.

Mr. Andrews sat down on the other side of the window, and said, with a weary laugh, as he leaned back in his chair, "I'm glad it's to-day, instead of yesterday."

"Ah!" said Missy, with a shiver.

"I don't know how much you've heard of our adventures—"

"I haven't heard anything. I have just come down-stairs, and last night I wouldn't let them tell me. I only wish I could forget it all. I cannot bear to think of it."

"I don't wonder. It was bad enough for us, who were doing something all the time, but for you, who couldn't do anything but wait, it must have been— well, there's no use going over it. We've got him, Miss Rothermel, and that's enough to think about. Only let me tell you this, if it hadn't been for you, we should not have him now."

"If it hadn't been for me, you wouldn't have lost him at all," said Missy, bitterly.

"I don't understand—you mean the woman's hostility to you? I really think that had very little to do with it. She is such an evil creature, she would have done the same, or worse, without that for an excuse. You may, rather than reproach yourself for that, congratulate yourself upon having been the means of sending her away, before the child was totally corrupted. When I think what danger he—they—were in from her, and how little I suspected it, I am more than ever convinced that I am not fit to have the care of him. Believe me, you did me, as well as the children, an inestimable favor, when you advised me to send those creatures away ; and to you I owe a year of comfort and peace, and Jay owes, I don't know what."

Missy flushed painfully, and her companion saw it, but he went on ruthlessly, " You never will let me allude to this, Miss Rothermel ; but I want to say one thing about it, now we are on the subject, and then I will promise not to trouble you again. You are so over-sensitive about this matter you have made yourself uncomfortable, and—well—though it's not of much importance—you've made me uncomfortable too. If you will believe me when I say I shall always consider you did me the greatest favor when you induced me to send those servants away, and if you will bear in mind the benefit you did the children, you will surely be able to be indifferent to the tattle of a set of people whose tongues are always busy about their betters, in one way or another. If they were not talking about this, they would be talking about something else ; it was only the accident of your hearing it that was unusual. I have no doubt in our kitchens every day are said things that would enrage us, but luckily we don't hear them. This has been such a barrier between us, Miss Rothermel ; won't you be good enough to make way with it to-day, and promise not to think of it again ? You have given me a new cause for gratitude in what you did for Jay yesterday. Surely, after what

we both went through we can never be exactly like—
like strangers—to each other. I hope you'll let me come
a little nearer to being a friend than you've ever permitted me before, though if I recollect, you made a
very fair promise once about it."

"Why haven't I kept it? I can't remember having—"

"Having snubbed me badly since that night. No,
I acknowledge that you have kept your resolution
pretty fairly. But then, you know, it was impossible
not to see it was an effort all the time. If you could
forget all this about the servants, and let us be the
sort of friends we might have been if Gabrielle had
never meddled, you would lay me under another obli-
gation, and a more binding one than any of the others,
great as they have been."

Mr. Andrews was talking very earnestly, and in a
manner unusual to him. One could not help seeing
that nothing short of the events of yesterday could
have made it possible for him to speak so. His heart
had been jarred open, as it were, by the great shock,
and had not yet closed up again. It wouldn't take
many hours more to do it ; Missy realized that perhaps he wouldn't speak so again in his life; the moment was precious to her, because, whether she liked
him or not, there is a pleasure in looking into reserved
people's hearts ; one knows it cannot happen every
day.

And that was the moment that Miss Varian chose
for coming into the parlor, with Goneril and Jay and
the kittens. She had heard his voice, and she naturally
wished to hear all about the affair of the pursuit.
Goneril was nothing loth, and Jay was quite willing

to go if the kittens went, so here the party were. Missy involuntarily bit her lips. Mr. Andrews' forehead contracted into a frown as he got up and spoke to Miss Varian, who settled herself comfortably into a chair. •

"Now," she said taking her fan from Goneril, and getting her footstool into the right place, "now let us hear all about it."

Mr. Andrews, with a hopelessly shut-up look, said he didn't think there was much to tell.

"Not much to tell!" she echoed. "Why, there's enough to fill a novel. I never came so near to a romance in my life. I positively wouldn't have missed yesterday for a thousand dollars. It gives one such emotions to know so much is going on beside one, Mr. Andrews."

Mr. Andrews didn't deny her statement, nor a great many others that she made, but he seemed to find it very difficult to satisfy her curiosity. In fact, she got very little out without mining for it. She asked the hour when they first sighted the barque, and she got it. Two o'clock. Then the course they took, and the changes of the wind, and the deviations that she made, and the reasons that they did not gain upon her for an hour or more. All this might have been interesting to a sea-faring mind, but not to Miss Varian's. She asked questions and got answers, but she fretted and didn't seem to find herself much ahead. Missy knew Mr. Andrews had come over to tell *her* all about it—but not Miss Varian. He really did not mean to be obstinate, but he couldn't tell the story with the others present. Missy gathered a few bald facts, to be filled out later from the narrative of others. She didn't feel a con-

13*

suming curiosity. Jay was here, the woman wasn't. That was enough for the present. She felt a far greater interest in those few words Mr. Andrews had been interrupted in saying. They went over and over in her mind. She only half attended to Miss Varian's catechism.

" Well," cried Goneril, who was hopelessly jolted out of her place by the events of yesterday, " well, one would think you'd had a child stolen every other day this summer, by the way you take it. Captain Symonds, over on the Neck, made twice the fuss about his calf, last autumn. I don't believe yet he talks about much else."

Miss Varian gave her maid a sharp reprimand, and asked Mr. Andrews another question in the same breath.

" How did the French woman act when the warrant was served on her ? "

" Oh, well, just as any Frenchwoman would have acted under the circumstances, I suppose. You know they're apt to make a scene whether there's any excuse for it or not."

" But did she cry, or scold, or threaten, or swear, or coax, or what ? "

" Why, a little of all, I think ; a good deal of all, indeed, I might say. She tired us out, I know."

" But did she seem frightened ? How did she take it ? What was the first thing she said when she saw the officer ?"

" Upon my word, I have forgotten what she said. I heard Jay's voice in the cabin, and I was thinking more about him, I suppose."

" But what excuse did she make for herself ? How did she put it ? "

" Oh, a woman never has any trouble to find excuses. She seemed to have plenty."

"But what possessed you to be so soft-hearted as to let her go ? "

" What did I want of her ? I was only too happy that she should go, the further off the better."

" I must say I think you were ridiculously weak."

" That is just possible."

" And she, and the wretch she called her husband, all are on their way to South America ? "

" I hope so, I am sure."

" What did the captain say ? How could he answer for stopping to take up the party in the night ? Did he pretend to be ignorant of what they were about ? "

" Yes, he assured us he was ignorant, and I should not wonder if he spoke the truth—French truth, perhaps ; but I don't believe he suspected more than a little smuggling venture, or an un-actionable intrigue of some kind. He knew the man somewhat, and made a bargain to lay outside the harbor for a few hours, and pick them up if they came out before daylight. The man told him it was his wife and child, who had been detained in the country by the illness of the child, and that he would pay him fifty dollars, besides the passage money, if he'd wait for them. No doubt the captain suspected something, but, as I say, nothing so serious as the job they'd undertaken."

"The wretch ! He ought to have had his ship brought back to port, and have been kept there for a month, at least, and lost his cargo, and been put to no end of loss and law. You were ridiculously weak,

Mr. Andrews, to let him go, and worse than weak to
let the woman go."

"Maybe so, Miss Varian, maybe so. It wouldn't
be the first time, at any rate."

"To think of that horrid creature going off and
doing what she chooses!"

"I'd rather think of her in South than in North
America. And as to doing what she chooses—she'll
do that, whichever continent she's on—for she is a
woman."

"You should have shut her up in prison, and made
that captain suffer all that the law could put upon
him. You wouldn't appear against them because you
are too lazy, Mr. Andrews, and that is the English of
it. And so other people's children may be stolen, and
other vessels go prowling around our shores, and this
sort of thing be done with perfect impunity, Mr. Andrews, with perfect impunity."

"I am very sorry, Miss Varian, but I hope it won't
be as bad as you anticipate. There are not many
women as wicked as Alphonsine, and I don't think she
will try it again."

"Try it again! Why, she will try something
worse. She will never rest. I shan't sleep easy in my
bed. I do not think we are safe from her attempts,
any one of us."

Thereupon Goneril laughed, a most disrespectful
laugh, though a suppressed one, and her mistress, in a
temper, ordered her out of the parlor. She obeyed
the order in the letter, but not in the spirit, pausing
to talk to Jay about the kittens, and then inviting him
to the piazza, where, the windows being open, she
could hear the conversation within as well as before.

This episode broke the thread of Miss Varian's cate-chism, and she forgot Alphonsine in her wrath against Goneril. Meanwhile, a carriage drove up with vis-itors ; Mr. Andrews hurried to depart, Missy disap-peared into the adjoining room, and Miss Varian, being left to entertain them, soon forgot her maid's offenses. Visitors were a balm for most wounds, with her.

CHAPTER XVIII.

AT THE BEACH GATE.

 FORTNIGHT after this, Mr. Andrews was smoking his post-prandial cigar with the Varians at the beach gate, and watching the sunset. It had been a fortnight of not very varied experiences. Mr. Andrews had chiefly learned from it how difficult it was to see much of his neighbors without making it a formal business. It was in vain to ask Miss Rothermel to drive ; equally un-fruitful to ask her to sail. So many evenings of the week proved rainy, or foggy, or cold, that this was only the third cigar he had smoked on their lawn since the evening when they watched the boat which was lying in wait for poor Jay. It was impossible to deny that the evenings were lonely, and that meer-schaum companions were scarce, and that Mr. Andrews, since his stirring adventure, had rather hankered for some one to speak to. This evening he said, rather awkwardly,

"Mrs. Varian, I am expecting some visitors this week. I am going to ask you to call on them, and—and show them some attention."

Missy, who was making some pictures on a slate for Jay on the ground at her feet, suddenly looked up with a face of amazement.

"I hope it isn't Mr. McKenzie, for he'd rather be excused from our attentions," she said with a laugh.

"No," said Mr. Andrews, looking embarrassed, "it isn't any of my boorish men, Miss Rothermel. It is—some ladies."

"Oh!" said Missy, and she dropped her eyes on Jay's pictures, and did not say another word. What she thought, it would be unwise to conjecture. For she felt a keen, fine tingle of anger all through her, and she knew, as she looked at Jay's yellow mane lying on her lap, that he was going to be taken away from her more surely than by Alphonsine, and that there were breakers ahead, and her short-lived peace was going to founder. She went through it all in such a flash that she felt her fate was settled when Mr. Andrews spoke again.

"I have asked my cousin, a charming person, Mrs. Eustace, whom I am sure you'll like, to come with her daughter and spend the remainder of the summer with me. They are without a home of their own at present, and are drifting, and it seems to suit them very well."

"No doubt," said Miss Varian, with keen interest. "I'm sure they'll have a nice time. Is the daughter pretty?"

"I believe so, rather," returned Mr. Andrews, beginning to feel uncomfortable. "It is two or three years since I have seen her. They have been living abroad some time."

"I am sure," said Mrs. Varian, with gentle sympathy, "it will be a very pleasant thing for you. You may depend upon us to do all we can to make the ladies satisfied with Yellowcoats. I am sure they can't help liking it if they do not care for gayety."

"I am certain that they don't. They seem to me the very persons to be happy here. They are cultivated; I'm *sure* you'll like them, Miss Rothermel, and the daughter has quite a talent for drawing, and they are cheerful and always ready to be amused, and are generally very popular."

"Well, well," cried Miss Varian, "now that sounds pleasant. They are just what we want here. Missy needs somebody to stir her up a little, she is a trifle set and selfish, and I tell her she never will be popular till she gets over that and goes into things with a little dash of jollity. It doesn't do to be too dictatorial and exclusive and superior; people leave you behind and forget that you're anything but a feature of the landscape. It's always been your mistake, Missy. Now we'll see if it's too late to mend, and whether this young lady and her mother will not teach you something."

"I am sure," said Mr. Andrews, uncomfortably, "Miss Rothermel doesn't need to be taught—anything. I should think it was rather the other way."

"Thank you," said Mrs. Varian, with a smile, covering up Missy's silence. "I hope it need not be a matter of instruction either side. I can quite understand neither young lady would enjoy that."

"I don't know anybody would enjoy it less than

Missy," cried Miss Varian, sharply, for she scorned the making of peace. "But what we need, is not always the thing we enjoy."

"When do you expect your guests?" said Mrs. Varian, anxious to create a diversion.

"The latter part of the week, I should think; I don't quite know what day. The children will be so much the better for having them, I shall be glad when they are here. I shall feel so much safer about Jay, when I am in town. You can understand for the last two weeks I have had a continual feeling of uneasiness when I am away from him."

Considering that he had spent every day since that fatal time, in Missy's care, this did seem a little hard. She did not reflect, that perhaps he did not know it—her bitter feelings did not favor calm reflection.

"Tell us something more about our future neighbors," said Miss Varian. But Mr. Andrews had no ability to tell things when he was uncomfortable, and the atmosphere was palpably uncomfortable, murky and lowering. He didn't know what he had done, poor man, he had thought he had done such a fine thing. But in spite of Mrs. Varian's gentle courtesy, and Miss Varian's cheerful bantering, he knew he had made a mistake. He wished himself well out of it, and was glad when Mrs. Varian found it chilly and got up to go into the house. He had found it chilly for some time.

CHAPTER XIX.

FIVE CANDLES.

THE week passed away; a good deal of it was spent by Mr. Andrews in the city. The expected guests seemed uncertain in the matter of appointments; either they didn't know their own minds, or they were trying the mettle of their future host's temper. More than one night he had stayed in town to meet them and to bring them up, but after a shower of telegrams, no guests had come. At last, on Friday morning, he had gone to town, and told the servants he did not know when he should be back; till he sent a telegram they need not make any preparation for the visitors.

This day was Jay's birthday. With a sore heart, Missy had been preparing for it. She was making this week a sort of valedictory. Every day might be the last; Jay would never be hers after this. And he had never been so sweet; he was gentle and good and loving, and never wanted to be out of her sight. This birthday they had been talking of for many weeks. She had planned an ideal treat for him; when, on this fatal Friday morning, she woke up to the news that one of their own servants had come down with what might be a case of scarlet fever. The girl was carefully quarantined. Missy had not been near her, and did not propose to go near her, but it broke up poor little Jay's party. It was impossible to allow children to come to the house. She took him out for a drive, and all that, but there was the birthday cake, and there were the candles, and there were all the pretty little gifts that were to come out of the simulated charlotte russe. They must have a feast, nothing else could take its place. So that afternoon she took a sudden resolution. She would make a sacrifice of her own feelings. She would go to the Andrews' cottage and give Jay his fête there.

"Do you think it's wise, Missy?" said her mother faintly.

"It's kind, at all events," returned Missy. "The poor baby is going to have hard times enough with the new cousins, it's but fair his last birthday without them should be festive. I've sent to have the children I'd invited for him come there. Now, don't look serious, mamma. One must not be always thinking of one's self. And what is a fiction of propriety, compared with Jay's happiness?"

"Compared with his permanent happiness, nothing, but compared with an afternoon's pleasure, a good deal, and you've been so rigid yourself about it, Missy. You've eschewed that poor cottage like a pestilence. I didn't suppose anything would tempt you into it. You felt so bitterly about our staying there, though you didn't tell me ; and I'm sure you've never crossed the threshold since."

"And I shouldn't cross it now, but that the master himself's away, and—and in fact, I haven't the heart to disappoint the child, and circumstances seem to make it my duty to give up my whim. In short, mamma, it is too late to be sorry, for I've sent word to the children, so don't, please, worry any more about it."

At five o'clock the children came, two stout little girls with hair in pigtails, and three freckled little boys with shaved heads; they were the hopes of illustrious families.

Missy contrasted them with Jay, and wondered that any one could endure creatures so commonplace, and that patience could be found to provide them nourishment and clothing.

Jay, however, seemed to like them very much, and that gave them a certain importance in her eyes. Gabrielle interested herself deeply in the attire of the little girls, and the "party" proceeded with great success through its various stages of shyness, awkward advances, rough responses, good fellowship, to hilarious riot, and open warfare. They had a series of games in the boat-house till six, then races on the lawn till nearly seven, when Missy, tired of adjusting differences and pinning collars, left them in Eliza's care, and went in to superintend the arrangement of the tables and the darkening of the windows, so that the candles might be lighted at half-past seven o'clock. She thought less well of human nature than usual at the moment. Even in its budding infancy it could be so disagreeable, and its innocence was so far from pleasant, what would not its mature development be. Jay himself had tired her out. He had been willful, selfish, wanting in love to her; his party seemed to have turned him into somebody else. She again concluded he wasn't worth it all; but since she had begun the fête, she must go through with it. It gave her rather an uncomfortable feeling to be going into the house she had forsworn so vehemently. It was doubly hard now that Jay's naughtiness had taken away the last excuse she had; he cer-

had not enjoyed himself very much, had not, in fact, had so many fits of crying and got into so many passions in the same number of hours since Alphonsine went away last autumn. It certainly had been an ill-starred birthday. When the waitress came to her for directions about the table-cloth, she felt sure she detected a smile on her decorous mouth, and when the cook put her head in at the door and begged to know if Miss Rothermel wished the cold chicken sliced or whole, she felt all through her that there was a shade of disrespect in the woman's tones.

"I am sure," she said, "I know nothing about all that. I suppose you will give them something for tea, as every day, and I will arrange for them the cake, and the things that have been sent over from my house. Only be as quick as you can, for it is getting late."

The servants snubbed, Missy proceeded to arrange the bonbons. This necessitated going to the china-closet for a dish to put them on. She hated this. She wished herself out of the place ; her cheeks grew scarlet, stumbling about among *his* plates and glasses, his decanters and soup tureens. She heard low talking and laughing in the kitchen. What a fool she had been to put herself in this position ! What did Jay have a birthday for, and tempt her out of her resolution? And then she remembered the poor young mother, the anniversary of whose sufferings they were keeping without a thought of her. She seemed to be fading out of the memories of all, loving and unloving, among whom, only a year ago, she had had her place. She was no more than a name now to her children. Who could tell whether her husband remembered her departure with relief or remorse, or remembered her at

all ? New servants moved about the house which she
had left ; new household usages prevailed ; nothing of
her seemed left. Here was one who had called herself
her friend, who had thought of her for the first time
to-day—this day, which her throes should have made
sacred to her memory.

Missy tried to catch at the shadow which seemed
passing away from her ; tried to realize that this
woman of whom she thought, had been, was, the wife
of the man whom she had grown to like, to listen to,
to wonder about. She tried to remember that this
dark-eyed, pure-featured picture was the mother of
tawny, snub-nosed, ruddy Jay ; but it was all a picture, an effort of the brain, it was no reality. The
reality seemed, Jay, in the flesh, she who felt she
owned him, and the father about whom she could not
keep her resolution, and the household which she had
reconstructed.

The bonbons looked less pretty to her than when
she bought them ; she wished the fête was over, and
she herself out of this uncomfortable house. The
waitress, having ended her little gossip in the kitchen,
came in and laid the cloth and closed the windows,
and lighted a lamp or two. Missy arranged the bonbons and the flowers, and the deceitful charlotte russe,
with its cave of surprises. It was nearly half past
seven o'clock, and she put the cake upon the table,
and proceeded to arrange the five candles around it.
Now, every one who has put candles around a birthday
cake knows that it is a business not devoid of difficul-
ties. The colored wax drips on the table-cloth, the
icing cracks if you look at it, the candles lean this
way and that, the paper or the match with which you

have lighted them, drops upon the linen or the cake, and makes a smutty mark. All these things happened to Miss Rothermel, and in the midst of it, in trooped the impatient children, headed by Jay, who had burst past Eliza, declaring that he wouldn't wait a minute longer. The sight of the table was premature; she did not mean to have him see it till it was perfect. He dragged a heavy chair up beside her, climbed up on it, tugged at her dress, pushed her elbow, shrieked in her ear. The moment was an unhappy one; Miss Rothermel was not serene, the provocation was extreme; she turned short upon him, boxed his ears, took him by the arms and set him down upon the floor.

"You're such a little torment," she said, "there is no pleasure in doing anything for you."

Jay roared, the sudden, short roar of good-natured passion; the children crowded round. Missy told them to stand back, while she bent forward to rescue a candle, tottering to its fall. Jay hushed his howls, intent upon the candle; the children were all around Missy, with their backs to the door. Gabrielle had gone around to the other side of the table, facing the door, and was leaning forward on her elbows, gazing silently, not at Missy, but beyond her. The candle nodded over the wrong way, a great blot of green wax dropped upon the table-cloth. Jay screamed with excitement, and made a dash forward to get his hands in the wax.

Missy stamped with her foot upon the floor—ah! that it must be told!—and slapped his hands and pushed him back. And then the sudden green gleam in Gabby's eyes made her start and look behind her.

There in the door stood—Mr. Andrews and two ladies.
How long they had been there, who can tell? There
was a look of amusement on his face, a look of eager
curiosity on the faces of the strangers. The hall was
not lighted, the parlor was not lighted—the dining-
room was, in contrast, quite brilliant, and the decorated
table and the group of children quite a picture. Missy
was not capable of speaking, for a moment. She
caught the candle and blew it out, and tried to find
her voice, which seemed to have been blown out, too.

"What a charming picture," cried the young lady.
"This, I know, is Miss Rothermel—and which are my
little cousins?—ah, this must be Jay—he is your image,
Mr. Andrews," and she flew upon him with kisses,
while the mother, singling out a stout, little girl, with a
pigtail, not unlike him in feature, embraced her as
Gabrielle. While this mistake was being rectified,
and the correct Gabrielle being presented to her cousins, Missy recovered herself enough to turn to Mr.
Andrews and tell him she did not think he was coming
home that night.

"The telegram wasn't received then? I sent it at
ten o'clock this morning."

No, no telegram had been received. The waitress
was standing by, the picture of consternation, and cor-
roborated the statement incoherently. Missy then explained as well as she could, her presence in the house,
but nobody seemed to listen to her; the ladies were so
engrossed with caressing the children, they did not
heed. Mr. Andrews himself seemed not at all to be
interested in any fact but that the children were having a good time, and that to balance it was the companion fact that there was no dinner ready.

The cook was looking through the kitchen door, which was ajar, with a bewildered face. The birthday cake and the bonbons were a mockery, no doubt, to the hungry travelers. Missy wished the cake and the travelers in the Red Sea together.

"How charming," said Miss Eustace, rising from her knees before Jay, and looking at the table. "How charming it is, and how good of you, Miss Rothermel. Mamma, is she not good? Think of giving up all that time for a little child who never can repay you !'

"Miss Rothermel is unselfish," said the mother, releasing Gabby from a final embrace. "Jay ought to love her very much. Jay, you do, I know. Tell Miss Rothermel you love her."

"And thank her for the party," cried the daughter, stooping over him with irrepressible fondness, again.

"I won't," said Jay, stoutly, pulling himself away. "It's none of you's business."

"Jay !" cried his father.

But Missy moved forward, as if to protect him, and said, "He only means that he and I can settle our accounts together. Can't we, Jay?"

Jay did not answer otherwise than by clutching at her gown and scowling back at the honeyed cousins. How sweet it was, that little fist tight in her dress; Missy felt it almost made up for the whole affair, and gave her resolution to make another and more definite apology for being there.

"I am sure," cried Miss Eustace, "you are unselfish, indeed. There isn't one young woman in a hundred would have done it ; taking all that trouble, and coming over here by yourself,—without a lady in the house, I mean, you know, and all that—and not

minding about us, and not standing on conventional-
ities, and such tiresome things. Oh, Miss Rothermel,
I am sure we shall be friends. I *hate* proprieties, and
I love to do what comes into my head. I am so bored
with the restrictions that mamma is insisting on forever."

Miss Rothermel changed color several times during
this speech. It seemed to her she had never been so
angry before ; one's youngest grievance is always
one's greatest, however. Perhaps she had hated people as much before, but it did not seem so to her. She
could not say anything, but she moved towards the
door, stooping down to loosen Jay's hands from her
dress.

" I am very sorry," she said to Mr. Andrews, " to
have been the means of interfering with your dinner.
I hope the cook will be able to get something ready for
you."

" You are not going away ?" said Mr. Andrews,
anxiously.

" The children will be so disappointed," said Mrs.
Eustace. " We are not used to them enough to make
them happy, yet. Do stay, Miss Rothermel. It is no
matter at all about dinner. I was thinking if the cook
would make some tea and an omelette, and put some
plates on for us, we could all sit down, birthday and
all, and make our meal. I think I'd better go out and
speak to her about it—or—or—perhaps you will go,
Miss Rothermel ?"

Missy bit her lip, and did not answer, but passed
on towards the door, and her hand was unsteady as she
opened it. Jay set up a howl, feeling that things
were wrong. But putting it upon his desire for cake,

14

Miss Eustace darted forward, and gave him a handful of bonbons, to pacify him, and taking up a knife, was going to cut the cake. But Jay, who had correct feelings about the cake, only howled the louder, and struck out at her so handsomely that she was fain to give it up. She overcame, with great discretion, a very angry look that came into her eyes, and laid down the knife, and, wreathed in smiles, threw him a kiss, and said they would be better friends to-morrow. She was afraid of attempting to offer the kiss more practically, as Master Jay's fists were heavy, for fists which had only been at it for five years. Nobody but Missy knew why he was howling, or what he meant by his incoherent demands.

"Oh, I see," she said, turning back with a smile. "He thinks no one else should cut his cake. Well, Jay, I'll cut it for you, and be sure you tell me to-morrow who has got the ring."

Jay's screams subsided, and in a silence born of expectation, Miss Rothermel stepped forward and took up the knife. It was inevitable that the new-comers were taking her measure. And it is pleasant to relate that, pleased by Jay's loyalty, her face was bright, and almost pretty at the moment, and she was always graceful and her figure admirable. She leaned over the table, and cut the cake, and gave Jay his piece, and with great promptness, withdrew to the door again, leaving Miss Eustace to take her place, and put the remaining pieces of cake into the greedy hands held out for them.

"I don't want you to go away from me," cried Jay above the stillness, with his mouth full of cake, and his eyes full of tears.

"Oh, but I must," said Missy, giving him a kiss,

"and remember to tell me who gets the ring. Good-night."

With a sweeping good-night to all the party, she went out before he could get up another roar. Mr. Andrews followed her, though she was half-way down the path before he overtook her. It was nearly August, and the days were already begin-ning to show the turn of the season. It was quite dark, coming from the lighted room.

"I must beg you won't come any further with me," said Missy, at the gate. "It is quite light, and I am in the habit of walking all about the place at night."

"You must allow me," said Mr. Andrews, not go-ing back at all.

"I think you are needed to keep the children in order, and I am sure you ought to go back and see about some dinner for those ladies, since you've brought them here," said Missy firmly, pulling the gate after her, and looking at Mr. Andrews from the other side of it

"I have no doubt they'll see about it themselves, they know more about it than I do. And I want to thank you, Miss Rothermel, for remembering Jay's birthday, for I am ashamed to say I had forgotten it myself. The poor boy would have had a dismal time if it had not been for you. I'm always having to thank you, you see."

"I don't see why you should be at that pains. I didn't do it for—for anybody but Jay, and he and I can settle our little account between ourselves, as I told the new cousin just now. Good-night," and before Mr. Andrews could open the gate, she was swallowed up by the darkness and the shrubbery, and

he was obliged to go home, which he did slowly and in
some perplexity. He could only hope his cousins
would not be as difficult to comprehend as his neighbor was.

As for Missy, she came in with flushed cheeks and
threw herself down on the seat beside her mother's
sofa.

"Aunt Harriet has not come down? That is the
first thing that has gone right to-day. I've got so
much to tell you. Mamma, they've come—the new
cousins, I mean—right in the midst of the birthday
party, and no dinner ready for them, and everything
about as bad for me as it could be."

"Now, I suppose you wish you had been contented
to stay at home as I advised you. It *was* unfortunate.
Did Mr. Andrews come with them, and how did it
happen that they were not expected?"

"Oh, the telegram never was delivered, and they arrived in the last train, without any carriage to meet
them, and trundled down four miles in the stage, and
arrived hungry and tired, to find all the house dark
but the dining-room, and a table full of bonbons and
birthday fripperies, in place of the solid cheer that the
solid host delights in. Jay met them with howls, and
kicked the young lady till she could have cried; but
Gabrielle made up in sweetness for the party, in-
genuous child that she is!"

"I suppose there is no use in asking if you like
them; you had made up your mind on that point long
before you saw them!"

"I hate them. I didn't suppose I could detest any
one so much. They are ready to open the war at once.
They haven't even the grace to wait and see whether I

mean to make fight or not. They are bent upon one thing, making a conquest of the stout Adonis, and securing themselves permanently in charge of his establishment. They flew upon the children with kisses before they had seen whether they were oafs or angels ; they opened their batteries on me before they knew whether I was an enemy or not. The mother assumed the charge of the house before she had been five minutes in it ; the daughter had flattered Mr. Andrews and both the children *ad nauseam* before she took her bonnet off. Jay is to be Mademoiselle's pet, by arrangement, because they have discovered that he is his father's favorite. Gabrielle falls to Madame's share, and a nice time may she have of it, petting a green snake. They had heard enough of me to know I might be dangerous ; and they hadn't sense to wait and to see whether I were or not. It is war to the knife, and now I don't care how soon they bring on their heaviest guns."

"Your metaphor is a little mixed, my dear ; I am afraid you are not as cool as could be wished."

"Ice wouldn't be cool in such a company. You are long past hating any one, I know, but even you would have had some difficulty in keeping yourself charitable if you had heard that young woman's oily insolence to me. She is sure we shall be such friends, for she too is unconventional and fond of improprieties. *She* would think it a fine lark to be free of a gentleman's house while he was away from it ; she is so artless, no one knows what she might not do if she had not dear mamma to watch her. Gushing young thing ; she needs such care. She looks twenty-five, but I am prepared to celebrate her eighteenth birthday before the sum-

mer passes. I heard her telling Jay to guess how
many candles she would have to get for her cake. I
am afraid he said more than she thought compliment-
ary, for she changed the subject very quickly, and
told him that she had some candy for him in her
trunk. He had just had a surfeit of candy, and
he told her, to my delight, he didn't want her candy,
that he had plenty of his own. Wasn't it nice of him?
That's what I call a discriminating child, mamma. It
isn't every boy of five who knows a possible step-
mother when he sees her. I am proud of Jay. I wish I
were as confident of his father's discretion. Poor man,
how he will be cajoled! How he will learn to rever-
ence the opinion of Mrs. Eustace, how he will dote on
the airy graces of the daughter. I wish you could see
them, mamma. They rather affect the attitude of sisters. If it were not for the superior claims of the
daughter, I am sure the mother is capable of aspir-
ing to the post herself. I should not wonder if it were
left an open question with them, which one of them
should have him. Mrs. Eustace certainly is young-
looking, but she is stout. The daughter is ridiculously
like her; you seem to jump over twenty years as you
look from one to the other; the same figure, but a little
stouter, the same hair, but a little thinner, the same
eyes, but gone a little deeper in, the same complexion,
but a little thickened, the same smile, but a little
more effort in getting it to come. They are about the
same height, and they wreathe their arms about each
other, and smile back and forward, and pose and
prattle like a vaudeville."

"Really, my dear, you made good use of your

time. How many minutes were you in their company, I should like to know ?"

" They arrived about twenty minutes before eight, —it is now ten minutes past. That is just how long I have known them."

" Well, dear, for half an hour, I think you are rather venomous. But though I don't take your judgment of them altogether, I wish they hadn't seen fit to accept Mr. Andrews' invitation, or that Mr. Andrews hadn't seen fit to offer them an invitation. Don't let it all bother you, Missy. It has been rather a muddle from the beginning. I think you'll have to make up your mind to let Jay go, though it will be pretty hard."

" Hard !" cried Missy, bitterly. " But of course, I've made up my mind to it. I went through it all that evening on the lawn, when Mr. Andrews told us that they were to come. It is but with one object that he brought them, it will have but one end."

" I don't believe that he brought them with this object, but I acknowledge that it may possibly end in giving the poor little fellow a stepmother. I am afraid he is the sort of man that is easily taken in."

Missy's face expressed scorn.

" Yes, he is just that sort of man, and if he didn't drag poor Jay in with him, I should say I was glad he had got the fate that he deserved."

" Hardly that, Missy. He has always been very nice to you, and I can't think why you feel so towards him. But I've always felt it was a mistake for people to garner up their hearts in other people's children, and I've wished, from the beginning, that you cared less for the boy. Give it up now, dear, and make up your mind to interest yourself in other things."

"That's very easy to say. I've made up my mind so a hundred times in the last week, but it doesn't stay made up, and I shall go on caring for him till he's taken away from me, and a good while after, I'm afraid."

————————◆◆————————

CHAPTER XX.

THE HONEYED COUSINS.

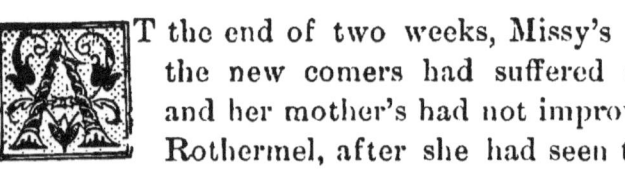T the end of two weeks, Missy's opinion of the new comers had suffered no change, and her mother's had not improved. Miss Rothermel, after she had seen them drive out one day, took occasion to go to the house and leave Mrs. and Miss Varian's cards, and her own. This visit had been very promptly returned by the two ladies, whom Missy had not been as happy in escaping in her own house, as in theirs. Mrs. Varian also saw them; they were effusive, cordial to suffocation, adroit; they had evidently changed their minds about the war, and meant to know the ground better before they engaged the enemy. She found them clever and amusing; they had traveled a good deal, and seen much of the world. They were also superficially cultivated, and were familiar with some of the outposts of art and literature. They had studied and read just enough to make them glib, and they had tact enough not to go beyond their depth. Many a deep and quiet

student had been abashed before the confident facility
of the pretty Flora in the ateliers where she had
studied abroad ; and at home, it is needless to say she
overwhelmed her cotemporaries with her advantages
and her successes. What she could not decently relate,
herself, of these and of her social triumphs, her mother
related for her. The daughter, in return, told of her
mother's wonderful abilities and influence ; of the
Countess This's friendship for her, the Lady That's
indebtedness ; there was nothing wanting to fill up
the picture. They did not spare details ; in fact, after
awhile, the details became a great bore, though at first
they amused everybody, whether everybody believed in
them or not. In short, they were not first class artists
in puff, only clever amateurs ; but in a country where
this art is in its infancy, they imposed upon a good
many.

Missy often had occasion to wonder whether Mr.
Andrews was imposed upon or not ; he of course
might want to marry his cousin, without believing that
so many other people had wanted to. But she longed
to know whether he saw through their palpable little
feminine schemes, whether he knew them for the cheats
they were, and was just going into it because he was
fascinated with the young woman's pretty looks and
sprightly ways, and because the older woman knew
how to order him good dinners and keep the children
quiet.

For, that he was going into it, she would not permit
herself to doubt. He looked rather preoccupied and
uncomfortable when she saw him. He had come over
one evening alone, to propose some drive or expedition,
in which she had promptly refused to take part. An-

14*

other evening, he had come accompanied by Miss Flora, who had made a jest of her unconventionality, and had been pert and lively to an astonishing degree, but who had wished herself away many times before the call was over, and who had said bitter things to her escort about the stiff household, on her way home. The evenings at the beach gate were at an end; the distance between the two houses had grown into a chasm. The children, ah! that was the hardest part, came less and less frequently, and Jay was as spoiled and changed as Missy, in her greatest despondency, had imagined. Continued petting and present-giving had established a certain tie between him and his cousin, and the sight of Missy always seemed to stir up all the evil in him, or perhaps all the contradictory good. At all events, he was so palpably bad with her, that he gave a text that Mrs. Eustace was not slack in preaching on—to wit, her pernicious influence upon him. Mr. Andrews was a silent man; he did not say amen to any of these comminations, neither did he contradict them.

The chasm between the two houses hourly grew in breadth. Miss Rothermel had never called after the first. All the advances had to be made by the new-comers. Miss Varian had, indeed, been rather troublesome, and had invited the young lady to read to her, and that had been the excuse for several morning visits. But even her persistence was not proof against the coldness of the young lady of the house, and finally she ceased to come at all. The people in the neighborhood had called upon them, and they had been invited to whatever was going on, which, though it was not much, was enough to keep their spirits up. They were quite popular, the mother was called a charming person, the daughter extremely clever, playing like an artist, painting like a genius, and with such lovely manners, too. Of course, every one said Mr. Andrews would marry her, or break his heart about her. They wondered how Miss Rothermel would take it, and Miss Flora was not slow to express to everybody to whom she had a chance to express it, her regret that Miss Rothermel did not seem to like her, and her innocent wonder what could be the cause.

"For I am not used to being snubbed," she would say. "I don't know why it is, but people generally seem to like me. I suppose it's because I'm good-natured, and don't make any trouble. I know, of course, it's nothing in me different from other people ; it's only that I'm happy and all that. But Miss Rothermel seems to hate me, actually. She really is quite rude ; and I may say it to you, scarcely lady-like in her treatment of me. Mamma is so incensed about it, and I think it troubles Mr. Andrews, who is so kind, and wants our summer here to be without a cloud. But it isn't worth thinking about. I can't help being happy, and having a beatific time, even if she isn't pleased about it."

Sailing parties, and drives, and whist and sketching parties had all been refused by the severe little lady next door ; but at last there came an invitation which she made up her mind to accept. It was to dinner, and Mrs. Varian had said it must be done. She was troubled a little at the attitude in which Missy had placed herself, though she could not help sympathizing with her in her dislike of the two strangers.

"Am I fine enough, mamma?" said Missy, presenting herself before her mother, at seven o'clock, one evening the latter part of August. She was fine, indeed, in a pale grey dress, with a train that was imposing, and sleeves to the elbow, with beautiful lace, and an open throat with lace, and lovely stockings, and the most bewildering little shoes. She had a string of pearls around her neck, and gloves with no end of buttons, and a great color on her cheeks, and a deal of light in her pale eyes.

"Am I fine enough, mamma?"

"Fine enough, my dear? you are actually pretty; I wish you did not have to go away. I should like to look at you all the evening."

Miss Flora was not able to wear pearls of that magnitude, nor lace of that value; she dressed strikingly, but of necessity, rather cheaply, and her cheap finery galled her, in the presence of such elegance. Missy looked much better than usual; Flora looked much worse, having sailed with Mr. Andrews all the morning, till she had a red tinge on her nose, and a swollen look about her eyelids and lips. The wind had been very strong and the sun very bright, and Miss Flora had forgotten to put on a veil. She had had a very nice sail, but—it was unfortunate that there was to be dinner company that evening. Darkness and cold cream would have put her all right, if she could have taken refuge in them instead of facing all that light and all those people.

The mother also was a little fretted at some of the domestic arrangements. The cook had given warning that morning, and the waitress was doing her worst; the gardener had insulted her point-blank, and the grocer and the butcher hadn't kept their word. Mr. Andrews liked a good dinner and no bother; it was but too probable that he wouldn't have the one to-day, and would have the other to-morrow, when the servants came to him with their grievances. When to this was added the inflamed state of Flora's complexion, she felt as if her cup were full, and her eyes were spiteful as they dwelt on Missy, though her smiles were bountiful.

Mr. Andrews was silent, after he had spoken to Missy on her arrival, and they all stood about the room aimlessly, before dinner was ready. If Mrs. Eustace had stood in a nearer relation to him, what a sharp little shot he would have had in his ear for not talking to his guests ! He had been talking, quite respectably, for him, to one of the Miss Olors, when Miss Rothermel came in. Since that occurrence he had been silent, and Flora had had to speak to him twice before he could be made even to look at her. This gave a sharp little ring to the young lady's laugh, but he did not remark it, probably.

When dinner was announced, he went straight to Miss Rothermel and offered his arm. But Mrs. Eustace pressed forward and told him he had forgotten, and that he was to take Miss Olor in. She laughed and told Miss Rothermel she hoped she would excuse him ; he was the most absent of men.

" Dear Mr. Andrews," she said, " never remembers the claim of young girls ; Flora and Lily Olor sat by themselves all last evening while he entertained Mrs. Eve and her sister. Duty is always first."

" Oh, then I am duty ?" murmured Missy, drawing back, hardly knowing what she said. Mr. Andrews stood speechless with an awkwardness worthy of a

younger man, waiting to know whom he was to take if
he was not to take Miss Rothermel.

"I don't mean, dear Miss Rothermel," she cried,
"that it wouldn't be a pleasure to take you. We all
know nobody can talk half so well or knows half so
much. But Dr. Rogers is to have that pleasure, and
Miss Lily falls to Mr. Andrews' share. You know, dear
Mr. Andrews, we talked it all over this morning, but you
are so forgetful."

Mr. Andrews said to himself, "We didn't do anything of the kind;" but it wasn't exactly the thing to
say aloud, and he was obliged to content himself with
taking pretty Miss Olor and seeing Miss Rothermel
made over to the doctor, who had already diffused
an odor of paregoric and rhubarb through the room.

Now the doctor was not a man generally invited
out to dinner at Yellowcoats. He was underbred and
elderly, and rather stupid. He did not expect to be invited, and nobody could have been more surprised than
he to receive this invitation. He was indebted to his
middle-agedness for it, and to his stupidity. Mrs.
Eustace thought he would be a charming neighbor for
Miss Rothermel, and the fact that he was a widower
made it a beautiful satire.

The clergyman of the parish took in Mrs. Eustace
to dinner ; next to him came Missy, and then the doctor. Opposite, were a mamma and a papa of the young
people at the other end of the table—a mamma, that
is, of one, and a papa of another. At Mr. Andrews'
end of the table they were all young and vivacious :
two young Olors, two young men from town, and Miss
Flora, who was youth itself. They were very vivacious
—a thought too much so, for beings who were out of

school. They laughed and talked about things which seemed to have grown up during their mushroom summer intimacy. Nobody could have seen any thing to laugh at in what they laughed about ; their manners put every one else outside. Mr. Andrews seemed to be within the circle ; he had heard the jokes so often, he seemed to understand them, and though it was possible that he was bored, he recovered himself sufficiently to be civil. Mrs. Eustace's end of the table was a notable contrast, as it was meant to be. She had been obliged to ask Missy (for whom in fact the dinner was given), but she had planned to make her as uncomfortable as possible.

The reverend gentleman was not a conversationalist, the medical one was heavier than lead. The mamma and papa were solid and undertook their dinner materially. Mrs. Eustace made talk diligently. She questioned the clergyman about his Sunday school, the doctor about his patients, she appealed to Miss Rothermel and the mamma opposite about subjects of domestic interest. She treated Missy as the cotemporary of herself and this mamma ; she spoke in extenuation of the " young people's" shortcomings at the other end of the table ; she begged these two mature ladies not to tell anybody in Yellowcoats what a noisy set they were. Dear Mr. Andrews, she said, enjoyed it so much. It was such a boon to him to have a cheerful home. He was like another man ; only that morning he had told her he had not realized what a miserable life he had been leading till they came. And the children, poor neglected darlings, she could not bear to think of what they had had to endure for the past few months.

"I have dismissed their nurse," here she turned
to the mamma. "I have found her a most untrusty
person. She goes to-morrow. I have been so fortunate in securing a servant I have had at different times
for several years. She is a capable, uncompromising
creature, and admirable in the government of children.
But here I am running on about the children ; I beg
you will excuse me, I know it isn't table-talk. Dear
Miss Rothermel, tell me about your aunt's rheumatism."

The blow about Eliza's going away had been almost
too much for Missy's fortitude. Mrs. Eustace looked
at her critically, while she waited for the report of Miss
Varian's rheumatism.

"I am afraid that isn't table-talk either," she managed to say ; but at the moment the darlings in question came into the room, and all eyes were turned to
them. Flora opened her arms for Jay to spring into,
which he did with considerable roughness. Gabrielle
sidled up to Mrs. Eustace, who embraced her with a
warmth most beautiful to see, and made a place for her
beside her, for dessert was on the table. The children
had left off their mourning, and Gabrielle was braw
with sashes and trinkets. As soon as Jay caught sight of
Missy, he began to fret ; not to go to her, but she evidently made him unhappy, and he kept looking at her
furtively, and dashing about the glasses and making
plunges for things out of his reach, and acting as the
worst kind of a story-book boy acts, who is held up as
a warning. Flora kept her temper admirably, and
bore his kicks and pushes with a beaming sweetness.
He also tore her lace, which, though cheap, was her
own, and possibly her all.

" He always acts so badly when Miss Rothermel is near," she said, sotto voce, to her neighbors. " I don't know what it is. I suppose sensitively organized children feel the influence of temperament, don't you suppose they do? And really, don't laugh, but that's just the way Miss Rothermel always makes *me* feel— restless and fretful, and as if I'd like to break things, and maybe kick somebody."

This made them all laugh, even Mr. Andrews, who turned such an admiring, smiling gaze upon the sun- burned Flora, as to fill her with genuine courage.

" Dear Jay," she said, caressing him, " they're laughing at me."

" They ain't," said Jay, loud enough for all the table to hear, " they're laughing at Missy, and you made 'em."

" O, fie," cried Mrs. Eustace, half frightened and half pleased. " Your Flo never did anything so naughty. Little boys sometimes misunderstand."

Missy felt as if she wanted to cry ; it was such an enemy's country she was in. She was generally quite ready to defend herself, but this time she had not a word to say ; her eyes fell, and her sensitive face showed her pain. Everybody tried not to look at her, but did look at her, of course, and then they tried to talk of other things so diligently as to be apparent. The dinner was wretched after this ; a sort of damp crept over every one, even in the youth's department, as Flora called their end of the table. Mr. Andrews never said a word, good or bad, to any one, and that is not a convivial example for a host to set. The dinner had not been a very good one, although pre- tentious, and Mrs. Eustace had secret stings of apprehension from his silence. She did not know whether it arose from annoyance about the disrespect to Missy, or from disapprobation of the ducks, which were dried up and skinny, and one could fancy had a taste of smoke. The dessert was tame, and the coffee tepid. Contrasted with the perfection of the ménage next door, it was a very shabby dinner, and Mrs. Eustace felt really vicious when she watched Miss Rothermel, scarcely attempting to taste the successive failures set before her. But if the truth were known, it was not contempt for the failures, but real inability to eat. She had been galled and wounded beyond her power to show fight ; she only asked to get out of it all, and to be let alone. Even Mrs. Eustace saw she had perhaps gone too far, as she heard the quiver in Missy's voice, when called upon to answer some question at a time that everyone was listening. Mr. Andrews might think she had as much transcended her part in insulting his guest, as she had fallen below it in not preparing him a good dinner ; she telegraphed to Flora to discontinue. Flora, in alarm, discontinued, but the ship did not right itself. The mamma and the papa could not recover themselves, the doctors of medicine and theology were helpless in the emergency, the young people were in confusion, Mr. Andrews was struck speechless ; it was a total wreck.

The ladies got into the parlor somehow—the gentleman got through their smoking somehow. When they met there afterward, it was to find a very silent party ; the young ladies were yawning and declaring themselves worn out with the sailing party of the morning. Missy was sitting in a chair by the window, her face away from the rest of the party. Jay was

standing in a chair beside her, pulling at the drapery
of the window, and talking in a very big-boy tone,
but in reality very much comforted by being with her.
She had one hand stretched up to take hold of his skirt,
for he was rather in danger of tumbling, notwithstanding his grand talk. Missy understood him, and was
satisfied of his affection. Mr. Andrews walked straight
up to her, not noticing anybody else as he came into
the room. She felt herself color fiercely before she
turned her face around, for she knew that he was
coming.

"Have you and Jay made friends?" he said, un-
fortunately.

"I did not know we had quarreled," she returned.
She would have resented anything he said, not having
forgotten his approving glance at Flora, when she
made them all laugh at her.

"I am awfully sorry," began Mr. Andrews, in a low
tone, looking at the carpet. But Missy didn't permit
him to finish the sentence.

"Oh, Mr. Andrews, that is such an old story. You
are always being awfully sorry, but it never prevents
things happening. I think the only way is not to give
them a chance to happen. I want to go home now, if
you will see if my maid is come."

Mr. Andrews went to see if the maid had come.
She had, and was having a beautiful time in the
kitchen with the servants. What Mr. Andrews was
thinking of when he came back into the parlor it was
difficult to guess from his face. He might have been
angry, he might have been bored, he might have been
wounded. He certainly wasn't in a good humor. He
merely said to Miss Rothermel that her servant was in

the hall, and then stood aside as she moved away, only
bowing as she said good-night, and, with a kiss to Jay,
and as few words as possible to the others, passed out
of the room.

"The only way is not to give such things a chance
to happen," she said to herself, all in a quiver, as she
went out into the night, and the door shut behind her.
She heard a not very suppressed noise of laughter in the
parlor, as she passed the windows going off the piazza.
She had crossed that threshold for the last, last time,
she said to herself.   And this time she kept her resolution.

CHAPTER XXI.

MRS. HAZARD SMATTER.

HE two houses were now at open war, at
least the female part of them.   Jay was forbidden, without any secresy, to go into his
neighbor's grounds, Gabrielle was in an
ecstasy of gossip all the while, and brought Flora news,
true and false, continually.   She spied through the
hedge, and found the new servants and her high-
minded cousins ready to receive a report of all she discovered, *i. e.*, if it were reported in a whisper.   Mr.
Andrews seemed to have given up all attempts to reconcile the contending parties.   He never went to the
Varians' now, nor made any effort to exchange neighborly courtesies.

Missy was very bitter and unhappy, about these days. She knew what all Yellowcoats was saying about Mr. Andrews and his cousin, for they said that to her openly. And she surmised what they did not say openly to her, to wit : that the cause of her own unhappy looks was her disappointment in the matter. How can one help unhappy looks ? One can help unhappy words ; one can do all sorts of things that are meant to mean happy acts, but how to keep the cloud off one's face at all hours and moments, is an art yet in the bowels of time. Missy knew she looked unhappy, and she knew she could not dissemble it. She knew, by this time, that she was jealous, and jealous not only in the matter of Jay. She knew that, deride him as she might, the silent widower was an object of interest to her. She did not yet acknowledge to herself that she cared for him, but she did acknowledge that it was important to her that he cared for her, that he gave her a certain sort of admiration. Alas ! she felt a doubt now whether he gave her even a small degree of respect. For who can respect a jealous woman ? And she had been jealous, even before she saw her rival, or knew more of her than that she might be her rival.

There is nothing kills self-respect like jealousy. Missy hated and despised herself from the moment that she knew she was jealous. She felt herself no longer mistress of her words and actions. Begin the morning with the best resolutions in the world, before noon she would have said or done something that upset them all. She had such evil thoughts of others, such an eating, burning discontent with herself. She remembered her childish days, when her jealousy of her stepfather made her a little fiend. "I was brought up on it, I learned it with my alphabet,—it is not my fault, it is my fate," she said to herself with bitterness.

It was very fortunate perhaps, as she could dissemble so ill, that the two houses saw so little of each other. Flora was not of a jealous nature, and it seemed as if she had very little to be jealous about. She was having it all her own way apparently, and she longed to flaunt her triumphs in her rival's face. That was the one thing that she felt she was not succeeding in. She could not be sure Missy knew it, every time she went out to drive with Mr. Andrews, and that took away half the pleasure. Miss Rothermel kept herself so much out of reach of criticism it was unsatisfactory. Pure speculation grew tiresome. It was the longing of Flora's heart to have another meeting, and to display Mr. Andrews, but Missy baulked her. At church it could have been accomplished, but most unhappily Mr. Andrews wouldn't go to church (at least with them). His amiable and accomplished cousins could make him do a good deal, but they couldn't make him do that. Neither could they make him talk about his neighbors nor laugh at any of their sarcasms.

About this time, Miss Varian had a friend to stay with her. Mrs. Varian was always rather shy of her sister's friends ; they were apt to be strange cattle. This one, however, Mrs. Varian remembered in her youth, and had no doubt would be of an unobjectionable kind. Mrs. Hazard Smatter had been an inoffensive New York girl, not considered to carry very heavy guns, but good-looking and good-natured. That was the last Miss Varian knew of her. In the revolution of years she turned up again, now a middle-aged woman, with

feeble gray hair, and misgivings about revealed religion. She had married a Bostonian, and that had been
too much for her. She despised her former condition so
much as not to desire to allude to it. She was filled with
lofty aspirations and cultivated herself. There was
nothing that she did not look into, though it was
doubtful whether she saw very much when she did
look. Having begun rather late, she had to hurry a
good deal to know all that was to be known about
History, Science, Art, Theology, and Literature ; and
as these rivers of human thought are continually flow-
ing on, and occasionally altering their channels, it was
perhaps excusable that while she kept up, she sometimes lost her breath, and was a little unintelligble.
If it had only been one river, but there was such a lot
of them, and of course a person of culture can't ignore
even a little boiling spring that has just burst out.
There's no knowing what it may develop into ; one
must watch its course, and not let it get ahead of one.
Taking notes on the universe is hard work, and Mrs.
Hazard Smatter felt that her gray hair was so to be
accounted for. It was her one feminine weakness, the
one remnant of her pre-cultured state, that led her to
call it premature.

What with dress reform, and want of taste, she
was not a woman to reproach with personal vanity.
She was rather a little person. She had pale blue eyes
somewhat prominent ; a high forehead, which re-
treated, and a small chin, which did, too. She attri-
buted these defects to her place of nativity, and drew
many inferences about the habits and mental peculiar-
ities of her ancestors, which wouldn't have pleased
them if they'd known about it. She had a very candid

mind, and of course no family pride, and it was quite
surprising to hear her talk on this subject.

Mrs. Varian was quite frightened the first evening.
Miss Harriet was delighted. She always had liked
the dangerous edge of things, and had felt herself
defrauded in being forced to live among such conventional people as her sister's friends. Mrs. Smatter was
so unexpectedly changed from the commonplace com-
rade of her youth, that she could not be thankful enough
that she had sent for her. The first evening they only
got through Inherited Traits, the History of Modern
Thought, the Subjection of Women, and a few other
light and airy themes, which were treated, of course,
exhaustively. To Miss Varian, it was a foretaste of
rich treats in store.

"Mamma," cried Missy, when she was alone with
Mrs. Varian, "what kind of creature have we got hold
of?"

"I can't classify her," said her mother. "But I
am afraid it will be very hard to use hospitality without grudging towards a woman who talks so about
her grandfather, and who knows so much more than
we do about the sacerdotal systems of the prehistoric
races."

"I'd much rather she'd talk of things I don't understand, than of things I do. How long do you suppose she is going to stay?"

"I am afraid Harriet will never be willing to let
her go, she seems so charmed with her."

"Don't you think she might be persuaded to take
Aunt Harriet home to Boston with her, to live? Fancy,
a few minds to tea two or three times a week, and on
the alternate nights, lectures, and clubs, and classes.

It is just what Aunt Harriet needs, indeed it is. See if you can't lead up to it, mamma."

The next morning, when Missy passed the guest's room, the door of which stood open, she was surprised to see a complete revolution in the furniture. The rugs had all been taken away, the curtains, unhooked and folded up, were lying on a chair, the sofa and two upholstered chairs were rolled away into the adjoining chamber. The bed, pushed out into the room, stood in a most awkward attitude at right angles with nothing. On the pillow was pinned a pocket compass, which indicated due north. Goneril, who was putting the room in order, with set teeth, explained that it was by the lady's orders, who had instructed her that her bed must always stand at exactly that angle, on account of the electric currents.

"I take it," said the woman, "she doesn't like to ride backwards."

The rugs were liable to contain disease germs, as well as the upholstered furniture, and she had intimated that she would like the walls rubbed down with carbolic once or twice a week.

"I told her," snapped Goneril, "that we weren't a hospital, no more were we a hotel."

It was well that the duster was not made of anything sterner than feathers, or the delicate ornaments of the dressing-table would have had a hard time of it, for she brushed with increased vehemence as she got worked up in talking. "She told me she would have preferred straw for her bed, but it was no matter now, as it was all made up. Straw was the only thing for beds, she said, and to be changed once a week. I'm sorry I didn't take her at her word. I know she

15

enjoys the springs and the new mattress, and if it hadn't been for the trouble, I'd have given her her fill of straw, and lumpy straw at that. I told her I was used to clean and decent Christian folks, who didn't need to have their beds burned once a week, and who didn't carry diseases about with them, and who could get along without carbolic. And as to carrying up water enough to flush a sewer every night and morning, I wouldn't do it for her nor any other woman, clean or dirty. And as to being called up at twelve o'clock at night to look at the thermometer and to close the window an inch and a quarter, and to spread a blanket over her feet to keep the temperature of her body from going a little bit too low—and then being called up at five to look again, and to take the blanket off, and to see that it didn't get a little too high,—it's just a trifle more than I can bear. I hope the new woman will like it, when she comes. *I'm* going next week, Wednesday, and that's the end of it."

"I am ashamed of you, Goneril; you're not going to do anything of the sort. Don't upset Miss Varian by talking so to her. Let her have a little peace, if she likes Mrs. Smatter."

"I'm the one to talk about being upset. It's bad enough to wait on an old vixen like Miss Varian, but when it comes to waiting on all her company, and when her company are fools and idiots, I say it's time to go. I've put up with a good deal in this house. I've come down in the world, but that's no reason I should put up with everything. It's one thing to say you'll be obliging and sleep in a room that's handy, so you could be called if anything extraordinary happened, where the person you're looking after is afflicted of

Providence. But it's another thing to be broke of your rest two nights running to keep count of the thermometer over a well woman who hasn't sense enough to know when she's hot and when she's cold. It's bad enough to be Help anyhow, but it ain't worth while to be walked over. I can stand folks that's got some sense, even if they've got some temper. But people like this, jumbling up almanacs and doctors' books, and free thinkin' tracts ; them I can't stand, and what's more, I won't stand, and there's an end of it."

There wouldn't have been an end of it, though, if Miss Rothermel had not got up and walked away. There is a limit beyond which even American Farmers' Daughters must not be permitted to go, and Goneril had certainly reached that limit, and as she would have talked on for an hour in steadily increasing vehemence, there was nothing but for Missy to go away, with silent disapprobation, and wish the visitor well out of the house. The visitor she found at the breakfast-table, blandly stirring her weak tea, and waiting for her oatmeal to have an additional fifteen minutes on the fire. The cook had been called in and acknowledged that the oatmeal had only had two hours of cooking. Mrs. Smatter had explained, on exact scientific principles, the necessity of boiling oatmeal two hours and thirty-five minutes, and the wheels of breakfast stood still while this was being accomplished. The cook was in a rage, for oatmeal was one of her strong points, and she always boiled it two hours. Miss Varian was growing distrustful of everything. Mrs. Smatter had raised her suspicions about the adulteration of all the food on the table. Even the water, she found, wasn't filtered with the proper filter, and there was salt enough in the potatoes to destroy the tissues of a whole household.   She desired the waitress to have a pitcher of water boiled for her, and then iced ; and she would be glad if she would ask the grocer where he got his salt.

By dinner time Miss Varian's usual good appetite was destroyed ; she was so engaged in speculating about the assimilation of her food, that she had a bad indigestion.   When evening came, she was so fretful she was almost inclined to quarrel with her new-found friend.   As they sat around the lamp, Mrs. Smatter became a little restless because the conversation showed a tendency to degenerate into domestic or commonplace channels ; she strove to buoy it up with æsthetic, speculative, scientific bladders, as the case might be. Missy pricked one or two of these, by asking some question which wasn't in Mrs. Smatter's catechism ; but, nothing daunted, she would inflate another, and go sailing on to the admiration of her hearers.

A letter had come from St. John, in which he gave some hope that he might return in the autumn, though he entered into no explanation of the reason for such a change of plan.   Missy was all curiosity, and her mother was all solicitude, but they naturally did not talk much to each other about it, and of course did not wish it alluded to in Mrs. Smatter's presence. Miss Varian, however, asked questions, and brought the subject forward with persistence.   It seemed to Miss Rothermel profanation to have her brother's name spoken by this woman.   What was her dismay to hear Mrs. Smatter say, settling herself into a speculative attitude :

"I hear, Mrs. Varian, that your son is in one of

those organizations they call brotherhoods. I should like very much, if you don't mind, if you would tell me something about his youth, and how you brought him up, and what traces you saw of this tendency, and how you account for it."

"I don't understand," faltered Mrs. Varian. "Do you mean—his education—or—or—"

"I mean," said Mrs. Smatter, "was he physically strong, and properly developed, and did you attend to his diet? I should have thought oatmeal and fish and phosphates might have counteracted this tendency; that is, of course, if you could have anticipated it."

"He has always been in very fine health," said the mother.

"Indeed! That seems inexplicable. I have always felt these things could be accounted for, if one were inclined to look into it. It *must* be the result of something abnormal, you know. If we could look into the matter, I am sure we should find the monastic idea had a physical basis."

"Indeed!" said Miss Varian, tartly. "Well, I shouldn't have thought it had anything of the kind. No more than that the culinary idea had a spiritual basis."

"I have always thought," remarked Mrs. Smatter, ignoring the interruption, "that science would do well to study individual cases of this kind, to ascertain the cause of the mental bias. It would be useful to know the reason of the imperfect development of the brain, for instance, of this young man, who represents a class becoming, I am told, quite numerous. Do you remember, dear Mrs. Varian, any accident in childhood—any fall?"

"I really think you've got beyond your depth," cried Miss Varian, under the spur of indigestion and family feeling. "If I were you I would talk about things I understood a little. St. John Varian isn't down in your books, my dear. You can't take him in any more than you can the planet Jupiter, and you'd better not try."

"Indeed," said Mrs. Smatter, a little uneasy. "Is he so very remarkable an entity?"

"I don't know anything about his entity, but he has a good brain of his own, if you want to know that, and he didn't fall down stairs when he was a child, any more than St. Charles Borromeo, or St. Francis Xavier, or Lacordaire did. But then, perhaps you think they did, if it were only looked into. Fancy what a procession of them, bumping down the stairs of time, or tumbling out of trees of knowledge that they'd been forbidden to climb up."

Missy laughed, a little hysterically, and that irritated Miss Varian, whose indigestion was really very bad, and who was naturally opposed to Missy, and who was ashamed to find herself tackling her guest in this way and upholding the unpardonable step of St. John in the hearing of his mother, who was to blame for it It was exasperating, and she didn't know who to hit, or rather, who not to hit, she was so out of patience with everybody.

"If you'd give up the phosphates," she said, "and inquire into the way he was brought up, you might get more satisfaction. How he was drilled and drilled and made to read saints' lives, and told legends of the martyrs when he was going to bed, and made to believe that all that was nice and jolly in life was to be given up almost before you got it, and that all the sins in the decalogue were to be confessed, almost before you'd committed them ; if you'd look into *this*, you might get a little light upon your subject."

" Ah !" said Mrs. Smatter, interested, "perhaps that might account—"

"Aunt Harriet," cried Missy, getting up, and letting her work fall on the floor—spools, thimble and scissors dispersing themselves in corners—"Aunt Harriet, there is a limit—"

"A limit to what? Superstition and priest-craft—maudlin sentiment and enervating influence—"

"Mamma, won't you go up stairs with me ?" cried Missy, and there was no time given Mrs. Smatter for further speculation, or Miss Varian for further aggression. After the door closed behind them, Miss Varian's wrath rose against her inquisitive friend, and family feeling carried the day.

"You'd better drop the subject of St. John, permanently," she said with decision.

And Mrs. Smatter accommodatingly offered to read her a treatise on the Artistic Dualism of the Renaissance, with which the evening closed.

CHAPTER XXII.

A GARDEN PARTY.

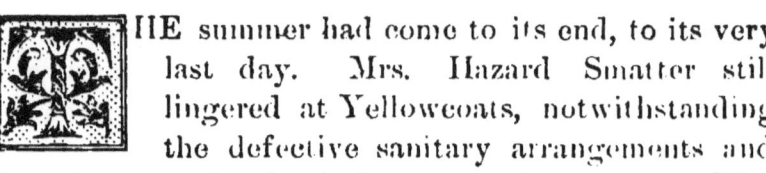HE summer had come to its end, to its very last day. Mrs. Hazard Smatter still lingered at Yellowcoats, notwithstanding the defective sanitary arrangements and the absence of stimulating mental contact. Miss Varian had felt considerable mortification that her friend should know she lived in such an atmosphere, and was always speaking of it apologetically and as temporarily stagnant. She had however given Mrs. Varian no rest till she had consented to see that it was her duty to provide some social entertainment for Mrs. Smatter, something, of course, inadequate to the mental needs of that lady, but something that would show her that she was still in the midst of civilized life. A lady who used familiarly the names that Mrs. Smatter did, could not of course be dazzled by the doctor or the rector. But she could be made to see that they had a good many young women who dressed well and several men who were good style. And there were two painters, and a stray architect or so, and a composer, staying in the place. These were not much, to make a show against the minds to which Mrs. Smatter was accustomed, but they were better than nothing. Therefore, Mrs. Varian must have at least two headaches, and Missy at least three days' work writing her invitations and getting up her garden party.

Now, a garden party is a charming thing when

everything is favorable. All the neighborhood was delighted at the prospect, for invitations to garden parties were not rife in Yellowcoats, and the Varians' place was unusually nice for such a thing.

The weather had been close and warm for several days, and the deep shade of the trees upon the lawn and the cooling ripple of the water beyond had entered into the picture everyone had drawn of the projected garden party. But on the morning of that day, a cold east wind set in, and dashes of rain fell about noon— then the sky grew leaden from having been gusty and mottled, and though no more rain fell, the wind was as raw as November, and the chill was something that ate to one's very marrow. A garden party ! the very idea became grotesque. A warming-pan party, a chimney-corner party, a range, a furnace-party, would all have been more to the purpose.

But people came, and shivered and looked blue. They huddled together in the house, where fires were lighted, and gazed out of windows at the cold water and the dreary lawn. A few daring spirits braved the blast, and went out to play lawn-tennis and a little feeble archery. But their courage did not keep them long at it in gaze de Chambery and India mull. One by one they dropped away and came shaking back into the house.

Mrs. Smatter was quite above being affected by the weather. She expected to hold high carnival with the painters and the architect, who were of course presented to her at once. The composer, a grim, dark man, looking like a Mexican cut-throat, held off. He preferred young women, and did not care to talk about Wagner out of office hours. The architect was a mild

15*

young person, not at all used to society, and he very soon broke down. Mrs. Smatter was a little agitated by this, and did not discriminate between her painters; she talked about the surface muscles to the landscape man, and about cloud effects to the figure painter. This confused everybody, and they severally bowed themselves away as soon as they could, and Mrs. Smatter ever after spoke with great contempt of the culture of Yellowcoats. She was obliged to content herself with the doctor and the rector, who did not dare to go away while she was asking them questions and giving them information, which she never ceased doing till the entertainment ended.

As to Missy, the whole thing was such a vexation and disappointment she scarcely knew how to bear it. The bright fires and the flowers, and the well-ordered entertainment redeemed it somewhat, but it remained a burlesque upon a garden party, and would never be what it was meant to be. The people from next door had come—Miss Flora in a new gown, and the mother all beaming in a bonnet crowned with buttercups ; Mr. Andrews very silent and a trifle awkward. There were too many people to make it necessary to say many words to them when they came in, and they were presently scattered among the crowd.

An hour later, Missy, with her cheeks flushed from the talking and the warm rooms, went out of the summer parlor and across the lawn to a pair of young people who had been silly enough to stay there till there was danger of their being made ill by the cold. She had promised an anxious mamma by the fire to see that her daughter had a shawl or came in, and had just delivered the message and the shawl and turned away from the obdurate little idiot, who would not give up her flirtation even to escape pneumonia, when she saw that Mr. Andrews had followed her.

"It is a very unlucky day for my garden party," she said, as he joined her. "The sky and the water like ink, and a wind that actually howls."

"I wanted to speak to you a moment," he said, as if he had not noticed what she was saying. "Will you take cold here for a moment?"

"No," she answered, feeling her checks burn.

"This has been an unlucky summer in some ways, Miss Rothermel, but now it's over; and before we part, I want to say a few words to you."

"Certainly," said Missy, distantly. "I hope you're not going away soon?"

"I've taken passage for the 6th, that is a week from to-day, and I don't know when we shall return—very possibly not for several years."

There was a pause, while Missy got her voice steady and staggered up from under the blow.

"I've been unlucky this summer, as I said, and seem to have managed to give you offense by everything I did."

Now, no woman likes to be told she's not sweet-tempered, even if she knows she is a spitfire, and this nettled Missy sharply, and steadied her voice considerably.

"I am sorry," she said, "that you think me so unamiable, but I don't exactly know why you should think it well to tell me of it."

"I haven't told you that you were unamiable; I have told you that I hadn't been able to do the thing that pleased you, though Heaven knows I've tried hard enough."

"It's a pity that I'm such a dragon. Poor little Jay, even, is afraid of me by this time, isn't he?"

"I don't know about Jay. I'm rather stupid about things, I'm afraid. Women perplex me very much."

Missy drew the scarf that she had picked up in the hall as she came out, about her shoulders, and beat her foot upon the gravel as if she were cold and a trifle tired of Mr. Andrews' sources of perplexity.

"What I wanted to say," he went on, "is, that I thank you always for what you've been to the children."

"Ah, please," she cried, with a gesture of impatience.

"And that I shall always regret the misstep that I took in bringing my cousins here. I did it in the hope that it would make it possible for you to come familiarly to my house and remove all the annoyances from which you had suffered. I made a mistake, it has all gone wrong. As I said before, I don't understand your sex, and it is best, I suppose, that I should give up trying to. Only there are some things that I should think you might express to a woman as you would to a man. I desire to say I am sorry to have given pain and annoyance to you all the time, as I and mine seem to have been the means of doing. I have great cause to feel grateful to you, and nothing can ever change the high esteem in which I hold you."

"Thank you very much," said Missy; "not even the opinion of the ladies of your household?"

Mr. Andrews turned his head away, with a stolid look towards the lead-colored bay.

"I don't suppose anything will be gained by discussing them," he said.

"No, Mr. Andrews, for I don't like them, and you know when women don't like each other they are apt to be unreasonable."

Mr. Andrews was silent, and his silence roused a fire of jealousy in his companion's mind. Why did he not say to her that he despised them, that he saw through them, that he did not think her prejudice against them in the least unreasonable?

"We shall get cold if we stay here any longer I'm afraid," she said, moving slowly forward up the path.

Mr. Andrews walked beside her for a moment without speaking, then he said very deliberately:

"You have given me much pain, at various times, Miss Rothermel, and a heavy disappointment, but nothing can ever alter my regard for you. A man, I suppose, has no right to blame a woman for disliking him; he can only blame her for misleading him—"

The path from the beach-gate to the house was too short—too short, ah, by how much! they were already at the steps. Missy glanced up and saw more than one eager and curious pair of eyes gazing down upon the tête-à-tête. It was over, it was ended, and Missy, as in a dream, walked up the steps and into the chattering groups that stood about the summer parlor. She knew all now—what she had thrown away, what her folly of jealousy had cost her. The mists of suspicion and passion rolled away, and she saw all. Many a woman, younger and older, has seen the same, the miserable, inevitable sight—jealousy dead, and hope along with it.

The cold wind had not taken the flush out of her

cheeks ; she walked about the parlors and talked to the guests, and, to her own surprise, knew their names and what they said to her. Since she had gone out upon the lawn to take the shawl to the foolish virgin there, the world had undergone a revolution that made her stagger. Such a strong tide had borne her chance of happiness away from her, already almost out of sight, she wondered that she could stand firm and watch it go. What a babble of voices ! How wiry and shrill and imbecile the clanging of tongues ! It was all like a dream. The woman whom she had dreaded, unmasked and harmless walked before her, a trifler among triflers, a poor rival indeed. The man whom she had lost stood there silent in a group of flippant talkers, more worthy and more manly now that he was beyond her reach. What was the use of regretting ? No use. What was the use of anything ? No use.

Miss Rothermel looked uncommonly well, they said to each other driving home, almost pretty, really, and so young. What could that tête-à-tête have signified between her and Mr. Andrews ? He was evidently out of spirits. What an odd thing it would be after all if he had really liked her. There was something queer about it all. Going abroad with his cousins, however, didn't much look like it. It was a puzzle, and they gave it up.

CHAPTER XXIII.

P. P. C.

VERY day of that week Missy walked about as in a dream, and with a single thought in her mind. When and how should she meet Mr. Andrews, and was there any possible hope to be built upon the meeting? A hundred times, to be more accurate, a thousand times, she went over the scene; she made her confession, she entreated his pardon, she felt the joy of perfect understanding and confidence. She met him by the sea—on the cliffs —in the garden—in the library—at church—by the roadside—sometimes it was alone—sometimes there were others in the way. Ah! who does not know what ingenuity fancy has to multiply those interviews? How between troubled moments of sleep one goes through scene after scene of the ensnaring drama; underscored, obliterated, blotted, incessantly altering time and place—but through all walking and speaking the two, beside whom all other created souls are shadows? Who does not know the eloquence, the passion, the transport? Who has not burned with shame at the poor reality; the blundering words, if they ever come to be spoken; the miserable contradiction of Fate, if the interview ever comes about?

There were but six days and nights for Missy to dream and hope about her reprieve, and she employed them well. She was white and languid-looking in the morning, but from the first sound of the knocker, the

first step heard upon the walk outside, a spot of color
burned in her cheeks, and a strange glow shone from her
light eyes. She was absent-minded, imperious, impatient. She was living upon a chance, the throw of a
dice, and she couldn't say her prayers. She wanted
to be let alone, and she hated even her mother when
she interfered with this desire.

The six days had worn themselves away to one,
uneventful, save for the blotted score of Missy's dreams.
This day must bring some event, some occurrence,
good or bad. It was impossible that Mr. Andrews
would go away and offer such a disrespect to, at all
events, her mother, as not to come and say good-bye.
It was a fixed fact in her mind that he would come.
She dressed for it, she waited for it, she counted off
the moments, one by one. Not a motion of wind in
the trees missed her ears, not a carriage rolled along the
road, nor a step crossed the lawn that she did not hear.

At last, in the afternoon, there came some steps up
from the gate. A group under the trees; for a moment
she could not discern them, but presently she saw he
was not with them. There came the two ladies, with
Jay and Gabrielle, Flora and the latter laughing and
romping, and apparently trying to get themselves
quieted down before entering the house of their stiff-
necked neighbors. Missy came down stairs to find
them talking with her mother in the parlor. Flora
was in brilliant spirits, the prospect of " dear Europe "
again, she said, had quite upset her. Mrs. Eustace was
rather overbearing, and less suave and conciliatory
than usual. She found herself so near " dear Europe "
and a settlement for Flora, that she could afford to be
natural for once. She fastened herself upon Mrs. Va-

rian, and was sufficiently disagreeable to cause even
that languid lady to wish the visit over. Flora, sweet
young thing, stood to her guns manfully till the very
last minute, and made Missy's cheeks burn and her
eyes glow. Though she knew she had given her whatever success she would ever have, and had played into
her hand, and thrown up her own game in a pet, she
could not bear her calmly.

" We are all so eager to get off," she said. " I was
telling the Olors they mustn't think it uncomplimentary
to Yellowcoats, though it does sound so ! I have had
a *lovely* time. I never shall forget it ! A beatific
summer ! And mamma has enjoyed it, too, though
she has had a great deal of care and worry getting
things into shape after those dreadful servants that we
found there. But poor Mr. Andrews has had such a
horrid time ever since he took the place that I think he
fairly longs to get away, and never see it again.
' Thank heaven, it's the last day of it !' he said this
morning, poor dear man, with such an emphasis."

" Papa meant the hall stove," said Gabrielle, in an
insinuating little voice. " Because it smoked so dreadfully."

This took Flora aback for a moment ; she choked as
if somebody had hold of her throat, then, with a sweet
smile to Gabrielle, " Very likely he said it about the
hall stove too, dear," she said, and putting her arms
around the engaging child's waist, went on to ask Miss
Rothermel if they meant to spend the winter in the
country.

Miss Rothermel thought it probable, though it was
not quite determined.

" How dreary !" exclaimed Miss Eustace. " It

passes me to understand how you can exist. I suppose, though, one doesn't mind it so much as one gets—I mean—that is—as mamma says—at my age—" And she stopped with a pretty naïve embarrassment, which was surprisingly well done. She recovered from it to say :

"And Mr. Andrews tells us you are *so* domestic. He thinks he didn't see you once all winter long."

"No," said Missy. " I don't remember seeing him at all, all winter. But the children came, and Jay was a great pleasure to me."

" Fancy," cried Flora, "being amused by a child to that extent. I dote on children, but oh, I dote on other things too. Mr. Andrews thinks he will settle us at Florence, and if he finds a satisfactory governess, we shall be free to leave the children, and he will take us to Rome, and Naples, and there is a talk of Spain. Oh, we spend all our leisure hours in mapping out excursions. I tell mamma it is like the Arabian Nights. I have only to wish a thing, and it comes. Mr. Andrews has such a way of ordering and carrying out what you want, and putting things through. Don't you think so ?"

" I don't know," said Missy. "I never traveled with him and I can't judge."

" Well, I never did either, except on paper, and we've been around the world that way. But I mean in excursions, picnics, and sailing parties, and all that. You see he has kept us busy this summer, always planning something for us. I don't think there ever was anybody so good as Gabrielle's good papa !" cried the young lady, giving Gabrielle a little hug and a kiss.

Gabrielle received this attention in silence, shooting a penetrating glance across towards Missy. It is probable that this gifted child fully understood the position of affairs.

"But it seems dreadful to think of you here all winter," pursued Miss Eustace. "Nobody is going to stay, as far as I can hear. And I should think you'd be afraid, only you three ladies, and yours the only house open anywhere about. It was a sort of protection, last winter, when Mr. Andrews was here, even if you didn't see him."

"Yes, it was pleasant to feel the next house was inhabited. But I don't think there is anything to be afraid of."

"Suppose you had another fire. What a fright you must have had, Miss Rothermel! It must have been quite an experience. And so droll. I suppose there is always a droll side to things, if one has the ability to see it. Mr. Andrews has told me all about it. Don't you think he has a strong sense of humor, Miss Rothermel?"

Miss Flora's face expressed great amusement at the recollection of something connected with the fire. She repeated her question, which Missy had not answered.

"He is so very quiet, one wouldn't suspect him of it, but don't you think he has a keen sense of the ridiculous?"

"I have never thought of it," said Missy. "I should rather have said not. But of course you know him best."

"I've always threatened to ask you some questions about the fire," she continued, with merriment in her eyes. "But he made me promise not."

"Then I don't see that I can help you," Miss Rothermel said.

"I shall be anxious to know how you get out of the next fire, without Mr. Andrews here to see to it."

"I hope we sha'n't have another fire ; but if we do, we shall miss Mr. Andrews, I am sure, for he was most kind in every way. But it is possible that we may not be alone ; my brother may spend the winter with us ; he is coming home this autumn."

"Your brother ? Is it possible ? That is the young —the young—monk, that I've heard them talking of."

"Yes."

"Oh, then I am almost sorry that we're going away. I had such a curiosity to see him. Probably you don't know, but I take the greatest interest in the Catholic movement."

"I certainly had not suspected it."

"Oh, dear Miss Rothermel, how sarcastically you said that. I find Mr. Andrews was right about that

> "keen, sarcastic levity of tongue,
> The stinging of a heart the world hath stung."

"Papa said that about old Mr. Vanderveer ; it wasn't about Missy," put in Gabrielle again, and this time she didn't get a kiss for it.

"You are a very pert little girl," said Flora, withdrawing her arm, "and would be the better for a year or two of boarding-school."

Gabrielle gave a frightened look at Missy, and dropped her eyes. At this moment Jay, on the other side of the room, pulled over a stand of flowers, and in consequence of the noise and alarm, began to cry.

Missy ran to him, and putting her arms around him, whispered that he needn't care about the flowers, that if he'd give her a dear kiss and be her own little boy again, she'd like it better than all the flowers in America. This comforted him, and he consented to dry his eyes, and accompany her to the dining-room, to look for cake on a shelf which he knew of old. Missy did not hurry to take him back, and they had an old-time talk, and a great many kisses and promises. He was quite like himself when he was away from his cousins.

"You'll be a big boy when I see you again, Jay," she said, "and you'll have forgotten all about me when you come back from over the water."

"Why don't you go 'long with me, then," he said, with a voice rendered husky by cake.

"Oh, you've got your cousin Flora. I should think she was enough for any little boy."

"She can go to boarding-school with Gabby," said Jay, settling himself closer into Missy's lap, and taking another piece of cake. Missy laughed at this disposition of the triumphant young lady in the other room.

"I don't know what she'd say to that, nor papa either," she added, in a lower tone.

"Papa wouldn't mind. Papa's a man, and he can do anything he wants to. You can come with us, and you can ride my pony that I'm going to have, and papa can drive you with his horses, like he did that day."

"Ah, Jay, that would be nice indeed, only I'm afraid Gabby and the two cousins wouldn't agree to it."

"I'd make 'em," said Jay. "Papa's going to buy me a little pistol, and I'd shoot 'em if they didn't."

In such happy confidences the minutes slipped away. Presently the voice of Flora called Jay from the hall, and, recalled to civility, Missy took him by the hand and went back. She found them all standing up, preparing to take leave.

"I am sorry to hurry you, Jay, but we must go."

"Won't you please leave Jay to spend the afternoon with me?" asked Missy. "I will send him safely back at whatever hour you say."

"That would be very pleasant," said Mrs. Eustace, "but Mr. Andrews is going to take us for a drive, and charged us to be back at four o'clock, to go with him. He has been hurrying all the morning to get through with everything, so that he might be at liberty to take this drive, which is a sort of farewell to Yellowcoats. He seemed to want to have the children go, though I am afraid we shall be rather late getting back for them. We take the early train in the morning, but I believe everything is in readiness for the start. You may imagine I have had my hands full, Mrs. Varian."

Mrs. Varian expressed her sympathy, the good-byes were said, Missy held Jay tight in her arms, and kissed his little hands when she loosened them from her own, and watched the group from the piazza as they walked away.

Then he was not coming this afternoon. He preferred a drive with these ladies, to coming here. No, she did not believe it was any pleasure to him to go with them. He had his own reasons. She would rest upon the belief that he would come in the evening.

The afternoon was fine and clear, with a touch of

autumn in the air. She longed to be alone and to be free—so, telling no one of her intention, she wandered away along the beach and was gone till after six o'clock. The short day was ended and dusk had already fallen. She was little tired by her long walk, but soothed by the solitude, and braced by the thought of what evening would surely bring her.

The lamp was newly lighted at one end of the hall, and was burning dimly. As she passed up the stairs, her eye fell on some small cards on the dark table near the door. With a sudden misgiving, she went back, and picking them up, went over to the lamp to read them. They were three cards of "Mr. James Andrews," with p.p.c. in the corner.

I don't know exactly what Missy thought or felt when she read them. She stood a few minutes in a stupid sort of state. Then, the drive had been a fable, and the hand of fate was against her. The precious opportunity was lost, while she was wandering aimlessly along the beach, saying over and over to herself, the words that now never would be spoken. She had tossed away from her her one chance, as she had tossed pebbles into the water while she walked that afternoon. She had felt so secure, she had been so calm. Now all was over, and the days and nights that had been given to this meeting were days and nights that mocked her when she thought of them. How she had been cheated! She realized fully that the chance was gone. She knew that months of separation, just as they were situated, would have been enough to make a renewal of friendship impossible, and here were years coming in between them. No, the only moment that she could have spoken would have been while the recollection of what he had said to her the other day upon the lawn, was fresh in both their minds. Perhaps, already, it was too late to revive any feeling for her; but at least, she could have tried. She hadn't any pride left. At least, she thought she hadn't, till, in her own room, she found herself writing to him. Then, when she saw the thing in black and white, she found she had still a little pride, or perhaps, only a sense of decency. Here was a man who hadn't talked to her about love, who hadn't said anything that anybody mightn't have said about an ordinary friendship. She knew quite well that he meant more, but he hadn't said more, and by that she must abide. So she tore her letter up; ah, the misery of it all. She bathed her eyes and smoothed her hair, and went stonily down to tea when the bell rang. When the tea bell rings, if the death-knell of your happiness hasn't done tolling, you hear it, more's the marvel.

The monotonies of Mrs. Smatter and the asperities of Miss Varian for once roused little opposition. Missy had a fevered sense of oppression from their presence, but she was too full of other thoughts to heed them. After tea there was something to be done for her mother, who was ill from the strain of the afternoon's visitors, and two or three persons on business had to be attended to. She felt as if she had begun a dreadful round of heartless work that would last all her life.

When at last she was free from these occupations she threw a cloak around her shoulders and went out on the piazza. The night was dark and still, an as she listened she could hear voices and sounds from the other house—a door close, a window put down, a call to a dog, the rattle of his chain. Then she heard the shrill whistle, which she knew was the summons for the man from the stable, and after a few moments she heard Mr. Andrews' voice on the piazza.

With an impulse that she made no attempt to resist, she went down the steps and ran quickly across the lawn, and, standing behind the gate, under the heavy shadow of the trees, strained her eyes through the darkness, and gazed over toward the next house. Mr. Andrews was talking with the man, who presently went away, and then he walked up and down on the piazza slowly; it was easy to hear his regular tread upon the boards, and to see a dark figure cross the lighted windows. That was as near as he would ever be to her again, perhaps.

After a few moments he came down the steps, walked slowly along the path, and stood leaning against the gate. She could see the spark of his cigar. They were not two hundred feet apart. If she had spoken in her ordinary tone, he could have heard her ; the stillness of the night was unusual. There was no breeze, no rustle of the leaves overhead ; no one was moving, apparently, at either house—no one passing along the road. Her heart beat so violently she put both hands over it to smother the sound. Why should she not speak ? It was her last chance, her very last. If the night had not been so dark, she might have spoken. If the stars had been shining, or moonlight had made it possible for them to see each other, if the hour had been earlier, if there had been any issue but one, from the speaking—if, in fact, it were not what it was, to speak, she might have spoken.

The minutes passed—how long, and yet how swift,

they were in passing. She had made no decision in her own mind what to do ; she meant to speak, and yet something in her held her back from speaking. There are some things we do without thought, they do themselves without any help from us, and so this thing was done, and a great moment in two lives was lost— or gained perhaps, who knows? She stood spell-bound as she saw the tiny spark of light waver, then, tossed away, drop down and go out in the damp grass. Then she heard him turn and go slowly towards the house— always slowly, she could have spoken a hundred times before he reached the piazza steps. Then he took a turn or two up and down the piazza, and then, opening the front door, went in, shutting it behind him.

It was not till that door shut, that Missy realized what had come to pass in her life, and what she had done, or left undone. A great blankness and dreariness settled down upon her with an instant pall. She did not blame herself—she could not have spoken, no woman of her make could have spoken. She did not blame herself, but she blamed her fate, that put her where she stood, that made her as she was. An angry re- bellion slowly awoke within her. It is safer to blame yourself than to blame fate. Poor Missy took the un- safest way, and went into the house, hardening her heart, and resisting the destiny that lay before her.

———— ••• ————

CHAPTER XXIV.

SHUT AND BARRED.

HE destiny that lay before her was a litttle harder than even she knew, when she went into the hall that night, throwing off the damp cloak that she had worn, and mechanically walking to the fire in the library to warm herself, after her half-hour in the chilly night air. She thought she knew how dull and hateful her life was to be, how lonely, how uneventful. She was still young—twenty-seven is young when you are twenty-seven, not, of course, when you are seventeen. She had just found out what it is, to have life full and intense in emotion and interest, and now she was turned back into the old path that had seemed good enough before, when she did not know any better one. But still, with resolute courage, she said to herself, her mother, and duty, and study, and health, and money, might do something for her yet, and, after a year or two of bitterness, restore her to content and usefulness.

These things she said to herself, not on that first night of pain, but the next day, when she walked past the shut-up house, and wondered, under the cold gray sky, at the strength of the emotion that had filled her as she had watched, through the darkness, the glimmer of the cigar spark by the gate. Thank heaven, she hadn't spoken ! She knew just as well now what she had lost, as then, but daylight, and east wind, level values inevitably. It was all worth less—

living and dying, love and loneliness. She could bear what she had chosen, she hadn't any doubt.

How gloomy the day was ! Raw and chill, and yet not cold enough to brace the nerves. The gate stood ajar. Missy pushed through it, and walked down the path. Some straw littered the piazza steps ; an empty paper box lay on the grass. The windows were all closed. Only the dog, still chained to his kennel, howled her a dismal welcome. He was to go, probably, to some new home that day. Well, Missy thought bitterly, he will at least have novelty to divert him.

She didn't go on the piazza ; she remembered, with a sense of shame, the last time she had crossed that threshold, saying it should be the last time. What a tempest of jealousy and anger had been in her heart ! Oh, the folly of it (not to say the sin of it). How she had been conquered by those two women (not to say the enemy of souls). She could see it all so clearly now. Every word and look and gesture of Mr. Andrews took a different meaning, now she was in her senses. That dinner had been his last hope, his last attempt to conciliate her. She had repulsed him more sharply than ever that night, stung as she was by the insults of her two rivals. After that, he had made his plans to go away and end the matter. Miss Flora might thank her for " dear Europe," this time.

But poor little Jay, what had he to thank her for ? Ah ! that gave her heart a pinch to think of. Poor little Jay might set down as the sum of his gratitude to her, a miserable youth, a mercenary rule at home, deceit and worldliness, low aims, and selfishness, that would drive him shelterless into the world to find his pleasure there. For Missy never doubted that Flora would gain her end. She knew Mr. Andrews was not clever enough to stand out very long. "He's just the sort of man," she said to herself, "to be married by somebody who is persistent. He doesn't know women well enough to stand out against them. He will give in for the children's sake, he won't care for his own. And he will spend a life of homeless wretchedness, silent and stolid, protecting the woman who is cheating him, laboring for the children who will disappoint him. Ah! my little Jay, forgive me," she cried, stooping and picking up a broken whip of his that lay in the grass beside the path.

Everybody makes mistakes, but it isn't often given to any one to make such a wholesale one as this. We must be charitable to Missy if she was bitter and gloomy that dark morning. She wandered about the paths for a little while longer, then, picking a few artemesias that grew close up by the house, she turned to go away. At the gate she met a boy with a yellow envelope in his hand. He was just going to her house, he explained, presenting the envelope. It was a telegram, and Missy opened it hastily.

"It is all right," she said, giving him the money, and putting the paper in her pocket. We are apt to be very selfish when we are miserable, and Missy's first thought on reading the message was a selfish one. The message was from her brother. He had just landed, and would be at home that evening. She did not think of the joy it would be to her mother, of the joy it might have been to her; she only thought, "Thank Heaven, this will give me something else to think of for a little while." She was quite bent upon curing herself, even at this early date ; but with the supreme selfishness of great disappointment, she thought of nothing but as it influenced her trouble.

CHAPTER XXV.

AMICE ASCENDE SUPERIUS.

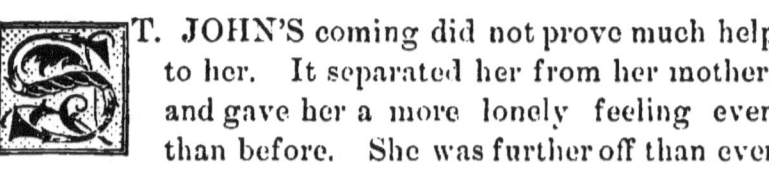T. JOHN'S coming did not prove much help to her. It separated her from her mother, and gave her a more lonely feeling even than before. She was further off than ever from sympathy with them. She was smarting over the loss of what they were giving up. Their lives looked heavenward, hers, she did not disguise it from herself, looked, earthward, and earthward only. Their exalted faith had upon her simply the effect of depressing her own. She had a supreme estimate of common sense. She quite made it her rule of life just now. Whatever was opposed to it, she was ready to condemn ; and, it must be admitted, there was a good deal in the lives of St. John and his mother that did not bear its stamp. Tried by its standard alone, in fact, it would have been difficult to find two people who were wasting their time more utterly. This Missy was not backward in saying to herself, and in suggesting to them, as far as she dared. That was not very far, for there was something about St. John that prevented people from taking liberties with him. His reality, sincerity, and simplicity of aim commanded the respect that his humility never claimed. No one felt it possible to remonstrate with

him, however much inclined to blame. Dignity would
have been his last aspiration, rather his abhorrence ;
but his self-less-ness answered pretty much the same
purpose. The thing we are most apt to resent in
others is personal claim to—anything. When a man
claims nothing, and has given himself away, we can't
quarrel with him, however poor a bargain we may consider he has made. Neither was it possible to pity St.
John, or to feel contempt for him. The natural force
of his character forbade that, and (those who sympa-
thized with him would say) the grandeur of his purpose.

So it was that his aunt fretted and scolded about
him to his mother, and made her life a burden to her,
but in his presence was quite silent about the matter of
his vocation, and much more agreeable and well behaved than in anybody else's presence. And Mrs.
Hazard Smatter was quite unable to ask him questions
or to gain information from him. Very soon after
his arrival, oppressed no doubt by the mediæval murk-
iness of the atmosphere, and the unfamiliarity of the
situation, she quietly gathered up her notes and
queries and prepared to wing her way to more speculative regions and a freer air. Even Goneril's tongue
was tame when he was by, though she beat and
brushed and shook his black habit as if it were the
Pope, and harangued about the Inquisition to her fellow-servants by the hour together.

This same black habit was a great snare to Missy.
She always spoke of it to her mother as " his costume,"
as if it had come from Worth's ; and it was a good
many days before she could be resigned to his walking

through the village. She even importuned her mother
to beg him to give it up during his visit home.

"In the name of common sense, mamma," she exclaimed, "why need he disedify these country people,
over whom he has some influence, by this puerile affec-
tation? What virtue is there in that extra yard or two
of cloth? He could save souls in a pea-jacket, I should
think, if he were in earnest in the matter."

It was rather hard on Mrs. Varian to have to bear
all these criticisms. That she had to bear them came
of her natural sweetness and softness, which led every
one, beginning with Missy, to dictate to her. But
there was something even harder than this, that fell to
her share of the oblation. She had to tell Missy of
something very bitter, and to endeavor to reconcile
her to it. She had prepared herself for it, in many
silent hours, but it is hard, always, to give pain, harder,
to some natures, than to bear it.

It was one evening, when Missy came to her room
for her good-night kiss, that she chose. St. John had
gone away to be gone two or three days, and it is
probable that the hour had been settled upon for a
long while. But prepared as she was, there was a
tremble in her voice when she said :

"Come and sit down by me for a little while. I
have something to say to you," that made Missy feel,
with a sharp tightening across her heart, that there
was something painful coming.

She sat down where the light of the lamp did not
fall upon her and said, with a forced calmness, as she
bent forward to do something to the fire,

"Well, mamma, what is it? If you have anything
to say to me, of course it must be nice."

"You don't always think so, I'm afraid, my child," said her mother, with a sigh. "I wish that I might never have anything to tell you that did not give you pleasure."

"Which is equivalent to telling me you have something to tell me that will give me pain. Pray don't mind it. I ought to be used to hearing things I don't like by this time, don't you think I ought?"

"Most of us have to hear things that are painful, more or less often in our lives—and change is almost always painful to natures like yours, Missy."

"Oh, as to that, sometimes I have felt, lately, that change would be more acceptable than anything. So don't be afraid. Perhaps you will find it will be good news, after all."

"I earnestly wish so. Of this I am confident, one day you will feel it was what was best, whether it gave you pain or not at first."

"Proceed, mamma, proceed! If there is anything that rasps my nerves it is to see the knife gleaming about in the folds of your dress, while I see you are trying to hide it, and I am doubtful which part of me is doomed to the stroke. Anything but suspense. What is it, who is it this time? We don't slay the slain, so it can't be St. John. You are not going to ask me to mourn him again?"

"No, Missy, and I am not going to ask you to mourn at all."

"Oh, excuse me. But you know I will mourn, being so blinded and carnal. Mamma, let me have it in plain English. What sacrifice am I to be called upon to make now? Is it you, or my home, or what?"

" Both, my child, if you will put it so—I cannot make it easy."

Missy started to her feet, and stood very pale beside her mother's sofa.

"You have shown so little sympathy with St. John's plans, that I have been unable to ask you to share in their discussion, as day after day they have matured. You know the house belongs to him, he has given up all—you can see what it involves."

" I see, and his mother is to be turned out of house and home, to satisfy his ultra piety."

" Missy, let me speak quickly, and have done. I cannot bear this any better than you. It is impossible for me to give myself up as St. John has given himself. I have no longer youth and health to offer. But there is one thing I can do, and that is not to stand in his way—and another. Hear me patiently, Missy ; I know it will be pain to you; I am going to identify myself with his work in a certain way."

"You ! What am I hearing ? Are you going to India, to Africa ?—I am prepared for anything."

"No, Missy. Your brother's India is very near at hand. His order are establishing a house in one of the worst parts of the city. Next to the church which they have bought—"

" With his money," interpolated Missy.

" With his money, if you choose ; next to the church which they have bought—there is a house which I am going to buy. It may be the starting point for the work of a sisterhood, it may be a refuge, a shelter for whoever needs refuge or shelter. It is given—its uses will be shown if God accepts it."

"And you?" said Missy, in a smothered voice, standing still and white-faced before her.

"And I—am going to live there, Missy, and do the work that God appoints me, or bear the inaction that He deems to be my part. It is a poor offering and no sacrifice, for it is the life I crave. Only as to the suffering I lay on you, I shrink from. God knows, if you could only sympathise with me and go too—what a weight would be lifted off my heart;—but I feel I cannot hope for that. It is always open to you, and I shall always pray that it may come to pass, and we shall not really be separated so very much. I shall not, perhaps, be bound by any rule, and if my health suffers or if you need me ever, I shall always be free to come to you—"

"Let me understand," said Missy, in an unnatural voice, sitting down upon the nearest chair. "You go too fast for me. Where am I to be, when you are to feel free to come to me? This house is no longer to be our home, you say. What is to be my home? What plans, if any, have you made for me? Don't go any further, please, till I comprehend the situation of things a little better. This staggers me, and I—don't know exactly what it all means."

She put her hands before her face for a moment, but then quickly withdrew them and folding them in her lap, sat silent till her mother spoke.

"The house was inevitable, of course I always knew that—and St. John is now of age. I do not know whether you had thought of it, I supposed you had."

"It never had occurred to me. I had forgotten that the house was left to him."

"And our united income, Missy, yours and mine,

would have been seriously crippled if we had attempted to buy it from him, and to keep it up. This
is an expensive place, and it would make you unhappy
to see it less well kept than formerly. Even if—if I
had not resolved upon this step for myself, it would
scarcely have been possible to have remained here, at
least, as we have been. This has been a great care
and anxiety to me for many months. It would have
been a great relief to me to have spoken to you, but
your want of sympathy in St. John's work, made it impossible for me to talk to you about it. It has seemed so
to St. John and me—we have given it much anxious
thought—that the income from your father's property
which I have settled all on you, is ample for your
maintenance any where you choose to live. But—to
me it has seemed a good plan, that you should take the
old Roncevalle house across the way, with Aunt Harriet, and live there. It is vacant now you know, it is
comfortable, the rent is low—"

Missy's eyes gave forth a sudden glow of light;
she started to her feet, but then sank back upon her
chair again.

"Mamma, that is too much—that is more than I
can stand. The home is to be broken up—my whole
life is to be laid waste. I am no longer set in a
family—I am adrift—I am motherless and homeless—
but that is not what I complain of. I only ask, why
am I to take up the unpleasantest duty of your life?
Why am I to be burdened with a blind, infirm and
hateful woman who is in no way related to me by ties
of blood or of affection? A beautiful home you have
mapped out for me! An enchanting future! It
seems to me you must think better of me than I have

ever been led to believe you did, if you think me
capable of such self-sacrifice."

"It is for you to take it up or lay it down as suits
you, Missy. If Harriet will come with me, you know
she will have a home and all the care that I can give
her. But you can see that it is of no use to make
such a proposition now. When she is older and more
broken, she may be glad of the refuge we can give
her, but now it would be in vain to think of it. And
you, oh my child, do not be unkind when you think
of what I have done. Reflect that I have given to
you my life, for twenty-seven years. All that I have
had has been yours, all that I have would still be
yours, if you would share it in the consecrated retire-
ment to which I now feel called. It would be the
dearest wish of my heart fulfilled, if I could have you
with me there. There would be scope for your
energy, for all your talents, in the work that lies before us. But, I know I must not dream of this till
you see things differently."

"No," said Missy, in a cold, hard tone. "You
have one child, with whom your sympathy is perfect.
He must suffice. Live for him now; I have had my
share, no doubt."

"Missy! do not break my heart ; I am not going to
live for St. John. I am not going away from you for
any human companionship. How can I talk to you?
How explain what I feel, when you will not, cannot
understand ?"

"No, I cannot understand," cried Missy, with a
sudden burst of tears. "Oh mother, mother, how can
you go away from me ? How can you leave me in this

frightful loneliness? I am not to you what you are to me or you would never do it."

"Missy, you could have done it. I have not read your face in vain for these last few weeks. You could have done it, and you would. I cannot make a comparison between the affection that would have satisfied you to leave me—and the—the feeling of my heart that draws me out of the world into stillness, retreat, consecration. I cannot explain, cannot talk of it. If you do not understand, you cannot. It is no sacrifice, except the being separated from you—that will be the pain hidden in my joy, as it would have been the pain hidden in your joy if you had married. The pain would not have killed the joy, nor made you give it up. This is not the enthusiasm of a moment, Missy. It is what has come of long, long years of silence and of thought. A way has opened, beyond my hopes— possibilities of acceptance—of advance. There is a great work to be done : I must not hold it back from humility, from timidity. It seems so unspeakable a bliss that I—stranded—useless—wrecked—should be made a part of anything given to the glory of God. I daily fear it may be presumption to dream of such a thing, and that I shall be rebuked and checked. But even if I am, my offering is made—all—for Him to take or leave. All ! ah, poor and miserable all, 'the dregs of a polluted life !' Would that from the first moment that I drew my breath my soul had reached up to Him with its every affection—with its every aspiration ! Oh 'that I might love Him as well as ever any creature loved Him !' That patience and penitence might win Him to forget the wasted past, and restore the blighted years that are gone from me ! "

She hid her face in her hands, and Missy, sinking down on the floor beside her, cried out, with tears :

" Why cannot you serve Him and love Him here as you have always done, all your good and holy life ! Why can't you worship Him in the old way, and be satisfied with doing your duty in your own home, and staying with those who need you, and whom He has given you to love and care for ! Oh, mamma, this is some great and terrible mistake. Think before it is too late !"

" Listen, Missy," she said, after a few moments ; her brief emotion passed. " Listen, and these are words of truth and soberness. I am useless here. There is a possibility *there* I might be of some humble service. You are more capable of managing and directing in every day matters than I ever was. You are no longer a young girl. I leave you with conventional propriety, for your Aunt Harriet is all that is requisite before the world. If you make it a question of family duty, St. John is many years younger than you, and may need me more. The home here is expensive, luxurious. The money is wanted for the saving of the souls and bodies of Christ's poor. To me there seems no question. I wish there might not be to you. If it were a matter of the cloister, I might waver, it is possible. I am not permitted to go that length in my oblation. I am now only separating myself from you by the length of time that you choose to stay away from me. In a house such as this is designed to be, you could always have your place, your share of work and interest. We shall win you to it, dear child ; when you see what it is, your prejudice will wear away."

"Prejudice!" cried Missy, passionately. "What is not prejudice? Yours and St. John's have cost me dear. Oh, mamma, how could you have had such an alien child? Why must we see everything in such a different light? You and St. John are always of one mind. I am shut out from you by such a wall. I am so lonely, so wretched, and perhaps you can't understand enough to pity me. Oh, mamma, you are all I have in the world! Don't go away and leave me! Don't break up this home, which must be dear to you; don't turn away from what your heart says always. It can't be wrong to love your home, it can't be wrong to be sorry for your child. Oh, what misery is come upon me! Mamma, mamma, you will kill me if you go away! You must not, cannot, shall not go!"

From such scenes as this, it is better, perhaps, to turn away. When men are not of one mind in a house, how sore the strife it brings—how long and bitter the struggle when love is wrestling with love, but when self is mixed up in the war. It was a longer and crueller struggle than she had foreseen. Missy could see no light in the future, and grew no nearer being reconciled. Day after day passed, scene after scene of wretchedness, alternate pleading and reproaching, reasoning and rebellion. From St. John, Missy could not bear a word. She refused to treat with him, but threw herself upon her mother. Those were dark and troubled days. St. John looked a little paler than usual; the mother was worn and tortured, but gave no sign of relenting. A gentle, pliant nature seems sometimes more firm for such an assault as this. At last, all discussion of it was given up; Missy, hardening herself, went about the house cold-eyed, imperious,

impatient. St. John was absent much of the time—
Miss Varian had not yet been informed what was in
store for her; all tacitly put off that very evil day.

Meanwhile the preparations for the change went
quietly on. The old Roncevalle house was one that belonged to the Varians; having been bought by Mr. Varian in those lordly days, when laying field to field, and
house to house, seems the natural outlet of egotism and
youth. Felix Varian, young and used to success, had the
aspirations of most young and wealthy men. He proposed in the first flush of satisfaction in his home, to
make it a fine estate, worthy of his name and of the
yellow-haired baby, who had now grown up to wear
a black habit and a girdle round his waist. He bought
right and left, and made some rather unprofitable
purchases. His early death left matters somewhat involved, but yet, when all was settled up, the Varians
were still a wealthy family, and the young heir had a
good deal to take with him to his work in that dirty
down-town street, of which Missy thought with such
loathing and contempt, and he with such fervor of
hope. Missy's father had had a comfortable little
property, which had been thriftily managed, and this
was now to be hers exclusively. It was by no means
a princely settlement, but it was quite as much as an
unmarried woman needed to live comfortably upon,
and she felt that her mother had done quite right in
not offering her a cent of the Varian money, which she
never would have touched. She had hated her stepfather fervently as a child; now she felt strangely
drawn to him, and as if they had a common injury.
How he would have scorned this infatuation, and re-

sented this appropriation of his gorgeous and luxurious
gold.

The Roucevalle house had always been kept in
order, and rented furnished. It was a comfortable
looking house, standing close to the street, with a
broad piazza, and having a pretty view of the bay.
It was very well—but oh! as a home, coming after
the one she had grown up in! Poor Missy loathed it.
She had made it part of her capable management of
things to keep this house furnished from the over-
flow of their own. It was a family joke that this was
the hospital for disabled and repaired furniture, the
retreat to which things out of style and undesirable
were committed. If a new carpet were coveted at
home, it was so good an excuse to say the Roucevalle
carpets needed renovating, and it was best to put the
new ones on the floors at home. When Missy's dainty
taste tired of a lamp or a piece of china, it was ordered over to the Roucevalle. It may be imagined
with what feelings she contemplated living over those
discarded carpets, eating her dinner off that condemned china, being mistress of that third-rate house.

But to do her justice, this formed a very small part
of her trial. She was of a nature averse to change,
firm in its attachments. To give up her home would
have been heart-breaking, even though she should still
have had the companionship of her mother. But when
that was broken, and the whole face of her life
changed, it seemed to her, indeed, a bitter fate. She
could see no righteousness in it, no excuse, no pallia-
tion. She felt sure that it was but the beginning of
the end, and that her mother could but a short time
survive the fanatical sacrifice she had made. She

imagined her in the reeking, filthy streets of mid-summer, surrounded by detestable noises and sights, without the comforts to which she was accustomed.

"Nothing prevents my coming to you, if I am ill," said her mother. "And, Missy, if I can live through *this*, I can endure anything, I think."

CHAPTER XXVI.

THE BROOK IN THE WAY.

IT was, indeed, the hardest part, that first step, to all, but it was accomplished, somehow. The early spring found Mrs. Varian in her new home, St. John established in his work, Missy and Miss Varian settled in the Roncevalle house, and the dear home shut up. It was in the market, to be sold if any one would buy, to be rented if nobody would. They had gone out of it, taking little, and it was in perfect order.

About this time Missy broke down, and had the first illness of her life. St. John came up to her, and brought one of the newly-imported Sisters to nurse her. She would have rebelled against this, if she had been in condition to rebel. She was not, however, and could only submit.

What is the use of going through her illness? We have most of us been ill, and know the dark rooms we are led through, and the hopelessness, and helplessness, and weariness; the foreign land we seem to be in,

with well people stealing on tip-toe out of our sight to
eat their comfortable dinners, with kind attendants
reading the morning paper behind the window curtains, with faithful affection smothering yawns through
our tossing, sleepless nights. Yes, everybody is well,
and we are sick.   Everybody is in life, and we are in
some strange, half-way place, that is not life nor death.
We may be so near eternity, and yet we cannot think
of it ; so wretched, so wretched, the fretted body cannot turn its thoughts away from itself.   We are alone
as far as earth goes, and alone, as far as any nearness
to Heaven feels.   What is the good of it all ? What
have we gained (if we ever get back) by this journey
into a strange land, that didn't seem to be joyous but
grievous ?   Well, a great many things, perhaps, but
one thing almost certainly : Detachment. It is scarcely
possible to love life and see good days with the same
zest after this sorrowful journey.   It abates one's relish
for enjoyment, it tempers one's thirst for present pleasures ; it loosens one's hold upon things mundane.
That is the certain good it does, and the uncertain,
how infinite !

Poor Missy felt like a penitent child, after that illness of hers.   She did not feel any better, nor any
surer that she should be any stronger or wiser ; but
she felt the certainty that she had put a very wrong
value upon things, and that life was a very different
matter from what she had been considering it.   She
felt so ashamed of her self-will, so humbled about her
own judgment.   She still did not like long black dresses
on men or women, but she felt very much obliged to
St. John and the good Sister for all the weeks they had
spent in taking care of her.   And although stained

glass windows, and swinging lamps, and church embroidery did not appeal to her in the least ; she began to understand how they might appeal to people of a different temperament. Let it not be imagined that Missy came out of this a lamb of meekness. On the contrary, she was very exacting about her broth, and once cried because the nurse would not keep Miss Varian out of the room. But then she was more sorry for it than she had been in the habit of being, and made Miss Varian a handsome apology the first time she was well enough to see her.

She looked out of the window, across the road, upon the trees just budding into loveliness on the lawn of her dearest home, and wondered that she should have thought it mattered so very much whether she lived in this house or in that, considering it was not going to be forever, either here or there.

St. John came and sat down by her one afternoon, as she lay in a great easy chair, looking out at the spring verdure and the soft declining sunshine. She had never got to talking of very deep things to St. John, since her unhappy controversy with him, but she felt so sure that he would not talk of anything that she objected to, that she was at her ease with him. They talked about the great tulip tree on the lawn, that they could just see from the window, and the aspens by the gate, just large-leaved enough to shiver in the softly-moving breeze. Then Missy forced herself to ask if a tenant had been found for the house, and he answered her, yes, and also, that he had heard that the Andrews' place was rented too.

"I'm sorry," he said, "that Mr. Andrews has gone away from here. I felt as if it were the sort of place

he might have been happy in, and much respected.
Did you ever get to know him well? I remember
that you took a fancy to the children."

"I saw a good deal of them last summer," said
Missy, wearily. How far off last summer seemed!

"What a terrible life!" said St. John, musingly.
"Not one man in a thousand could have borne what he
did; it was almost heroic, and yet I think my first impression was that he was common-place."

"I don't understand," said Missy, " tell me."

"It isn't possible you don't know about his wife?"

So St. John told her something that she certainly
hadn't known before about his wife. St. John had
learned it from others; the story had been pretty well
known in an English town where he had been the
year before, and had come to him in ways that put it
beyond any doubt. Mr. Andrews had married a young
woman, of French extraction, of whom nobody seemed
to know anything, but that she was distractingly
pretty. After three or four years she had proved to be
the very worst woman that could be imagined. She
had a lover, who was the father of Gabrielle; she had
married just in time to conceal her shame from the
world and from her husband. They went to Europe
after the little girl's birth, and in about two years Jay
was born. When he was a few months old, the suspicions of the husband were aroused by some accidental
circumstance. The lover had followed them, and had
renewed his correspondence with her. Some violent
scenes occurred. She professed penitence and promised amendment. Her next move was a bungling con-
spiracy with her lover to poison her husband. A horrid
exposé of the whole thing threatened. It was with

difficulty suppressed, the man fled, leaving her to bear all. In her rage and despair she took poison, and barely escaped dying. It was managed that the thing never came to trial. Mr. Andrews, out of pity for the miserable creature, whose health was permanently destroyed by her mad act, resolved not to abandon her to destruction. His love for his little son, and his compassion for the poor little bastard girl, induced him still to shelter her, and to keep up the fiction of a home for their sakes.

"I don't think," said St. John, "one could fancy a finer action. Protecting the woman who had attempted his life, adopting the child who had been palmed off upon him, establishing a home which must have been full of bitterness all the time. There are not many men who could have done this. It seems to me utter self-renunciation. Doesn't it seem so to you?"

"How long have you known this?" cried Missy, bursting into tears. "Oh! St. John, if you had only told me! You might have saved me from being—so unjust."

CHAPTER XXVII.

SANCTUARY.

 FEW weeks later, when St. John had come up again to see after her, Missy asked him to take her to her mother, and so, in the summer, when the country was at its loveliest, and the city at its worst, he came for her, and took her, still too weak to travel alone, to the new house

of religion in the old haunts of sin. It was not a favorable season certainly, but the weather fortunately was rather cool for July, and Missy's longing to see her mother was so great, her distaste for city streets was overshadowed.

The church which the Order had bought was not a model of architecture, but it was large and capable of receiving improvement. The house adjoining it, which was to be the nucleus of a Sisters' house, was roomy and shabby. It had rather had pretensions to elegance in days very long past, but it had gone through varied and not improving experiences, and was a pretty forlorn place when St. John took it in hand. It seemed to him so renovated and advanced, in comparison, that he could not understand his sister's slight shudder and look of repugnance as they entered the bare hall. Of course there were no carpets, as became a Sisters' house, and the rooms that Missy saw as she passed them were very plain indeed as to furniture, and very uncheerful as to outlook. Naturally, you cannot have a house in the midst of the lowest population of a large city, whose windows would have a pleasing or cheerful outlook.

But when Missy came to her mother's room, it was different to her from the others, and not repugnant. It was a large room, of course plainly furnished ; but the color of the walls, the few ornaments, the book-shelves, all proclaimed that St. John had not been as severe in arranging his mother's room, as in the treatment of his own. This house "joined hard to the synagogue," and a door had been cut through on this second story, and a little gallery built, and there, at all the hours, Mrs. Varian could go. It was never necessary for her to leave her room. What a center that room became of helpful sympathy, of tender counsel, of rest for tired workers! What a sanctuary of peaceful contemplation, of satisfied longing, of exalted faith! It was the dream of her life fulfilled; the prayer alike of her innocence and penitence answered.

From the little gallery that overhung the church, she heard her son's voice in the grey dawn, as he celebrated the earliest Eucharist, and from that hour, perhaps, she did not hear it again till, at eight o'clock in the evening, he came to her room for a half-hour's refreshment after the hard work of his day. The clergy house was on the other side of the church, about half a block away. It was as yet a very miserable affair, only advanced by an application of soap and water from its recent office of mechanics' boarding-house. But St. John seemed to think that half-hour in his mother's peaceful room made up for all. It was very self-indulgent, but he always took a cup of tea from her hands, which she made him out of a little silver tea-pot that she had used since he was a baby a week old. And the cup out of which he drank it, was of Sèvres china, a part of the cadeau brought to the pretty young mother's bedside in that happy week of solicitude. This little service was almost the only souvenir they had brought of the past life now laid away by both of them, but it was very sacred and very sweet, and probably not very sinful. It was a fact, however, that St. John reproached himself sometimes for the eagerness with which he looked forward to this little *soulagement*, during the toils of the day. If he had not felt that it was perhaps as dear and necessary to his mother, I am afraid he would have given it up.

17

Missy saw all this, and much more, of their life, and wondered, as she lay on the lounge that had been brought for her into her mother's room. She saw and wondered, at the interested happy lives of the women in long black dresses, who came and went, in their gliding, silent way, in and out of her mother's room. She could not help seeing, that in the offices, to which the inevitable bell was always calling them, there was no monotony, not so much weariness as in the one-day-in-seven service in a country parish. Their poor, their housekeeping, the interests of their order, seemed to supply all beside that they needed. There was no denying it, their faces were satisfied and happy—except one sister who had dyspepsia, and nobody can look entirely satisfied and happy who has dyspepsia, in the world, or out of it.

As to her mother, there was no visible failure in health, but a most visible increase of mental power and energy, and the inexpressible look that comes from doing work your heart is in, from walking in the path for which your feet were formed. Patient doing of duty against the grain may be better than not doing duty at all, but it always writes a weary mark across the face. That mark which her mother's face had borne, ever since Missy could remember it, was gone.

Weary no doubt she often was, for her hand and brain were rarely idle now; but it was the healthy weariness that brings the sleep of the just, and wipes out toil with rest. Neither did Missy understand—how could she?—the bliss of those hours spent in the little gallery that overlooked the empty and silent church. She could have understood the thrill that it might have given her, to see the crowd that sometimes filled the church, hanging upon the words of the preacher, if that preacher had been her son. But, alas for Missy! St. John did only humble out-of-sight work. He rarely preached, and then only to supply some one's place, who had been called away or hindered by illness. There were two or three priests, older than he, who did the work that appeared to the world, and who were above him in everything, and who were praised, and who had influence. What was St. John, who had given all his money, and all his time, and all his heart, to this work? The lowest one of all, of less authority or influence or consideration than any. Well, if he was satisfied, no one need complain, and he evidently was.

CHAPTER XXVIII.

VESPERS.

ATE one afternoon, during this visit of hers, Missy stole into the little gallery by herself, and closed the door. The plaintive and persistent bell had shaken out its summons in the house. Her mother slept through it, overcome by the heat and by some unusual exertion in the morning. Missy did not consider herself bound to assist at all the offices, but she rather liked it, and crept in very often when no one was noticing, and when she happened to feel well enough. A few poor people came in this afternoon, and two or three Sisters.

St. John said the prayers. When the prayers were over, and he had gone into the sacristy, Missy still lingered, leaning her head on the rail, and gazing down into the church. St. John came out, after a moment, and the poor people came up, two or three of them, and preferred petitions for pecuniary or spiritual aid, principally pecuniary.

After their audiences were ended, they shambled away; the Sisters had disappeared, and the church was empty but for one figure, standing near the door. St. John gave an inquiring look, and made a step forward. The lady, for it was a lady, seemed to hesitate, and her attitude and movements betrayed great agitation. Some late rays of the afternoon sun came piercing down through a high-up, colored window. Missy looked down with keen interest upon the two; it was another scene in her brother's life.

"You are too young for the care of penitents like that, my dear St. John," she said to herself, sententiously. For the lady was pretty, more than pretty, and young and graceful.

She came forward rapidly, her resolution once made, and stood before St. John, half way down the aisle. He did not look very young, thanks to its being "always fast and vigil, always watch and prayer," with him; his peculiar dress made him seem taller than he really was, almost gaunt. His face had a sobered, worn look, but an expression of great sweetness. He carried his head a little forward, and his eyes, which were almost always on the ground, he raised with a sort of gentle inquiry, an appealing, wondering interest, to the face before him. Because, to St. John, people were "souls," and he was always thinking of their eter-

nal state. As to a lawyer, those he meets are possible
clients, and to a doctor, patients, so to this other professional mind all were included in his hopes of penitence
or progress. He raised his eyes to the new-comer's face,
and Missy saw the start he gave, and the great change
that took place in his expression. It was as if he were,
for a moment, sharply assaulted with some strong pain.
He put out his hand, and laid hold of the wooden rail-
ing of a prayer desk near him, as if to steady himself.

The lady, meanwhile, had not been too agitated to
notice his emotion. She eagerly scanned his face,
stretched out her hand to him timidly, then drew it
back and clasped it in the other, and said something
pleadingly to him, looking up to him with tears.
Seeing she did not make him look at her again, and
that he was rapidly gaining self-control, she flushed,
drew back, with a manner almost angry. But in a
moment, some humiliating recollection seemed to
sweep over her mind and blot out her involuntary
pride. Her face darkened, and her mouth quivered as
she said, quite loud enough for Missy, in her loft, to
hear :

" The only right I have to come to you, is that the
wretched man whom you have befriended, and whom
you are preparing for the gallows, is the man—to whom
I am married."

St. John started again, and said—? The name
Missy did not catch. The stranger assented, and
went on speaking bitterly, and with a voice broken by
agitation. " He tells me he has confessed to you. I
do not believe it—I do not believe he would tell the
truth, even upon the gallows. His perfidy to my poor
sister, ruining her, breaking her heart, destroying her

chance of being happy in a good marriage—to me,
enticing me away from you—and then dragging me
through shame and suffering that I cannot even bear to
think of—his l w vices—his heartless frauds—has he
told you all these?—You used to be young. I should
think you would soon be old enough if you have to
hear many such stories. I should think you would be
tired of living in a world that had such things done in
it."

St. John did not answer. His eyes never now left
the ground. .

"I am tired of it," she cried, with tears. "I am
tired and sick of life. I want to die, and only I don't
dare. Sometimes I come here to the church and the
music and the preaching seem to make me ashamed of
my wicked thoughts ; but it doesn't stay, and I go
back to all my miseries and I am no better. I don't
know what has kept me from the worst kind of a life.
I don't know what keeps me from the worst kind of a
death. I have sometimes wondered if it wasn't that
you pray for me—among your enemies, I suppose, if
you do."

There was a pause, and then she went on : "Last
Sunday night I heard you preach ; I had only heard
your voice reading the prayers before that. Ever
since, I have wanted to speak to you to ask you about
something that you said."

Then St. John lifted his head and said, in a voice
that was notably calm, "I hope you will come here
often, and, if you will let me, I will ask Father Ellis
to talk with you and to give you counsel. He has had
great experience, and he will help you."

Missy listened breathless for the words that came

at last, after a succession of emotions had passed over her face. "You have not forgiven me!" she said. "Is that being good and holy, as you teach? You will not talk to me and help me yourself, but send me to some one I don't know and who won't understand. Why won't you forgive me? Heaven knows I have been sorry enough and repented enough!"

A lovely smile passed over St. John's face, one would almost have said there was a shade of amusement in it, but it was all gone in a moment, and the habitual seriousness returned.

"I had never thought of any question of forgiveness," he said. "Be assured of it in any case."

"Then why," she hurried on, keenly searching his face, "why will you not let me speak to you? Why will you not teach me, and help me, as you say Father Ellis would do?"

"Because it is not my part of the work. He has more experience."

"But you teach Armand. You spend hours in the prison. You have the direction of souls there."

"That is a different work," he said, simply.

"Then," she exclaimed, passionately, "since you refuse me I will go away. I have been hoping all this time for help from you. If you won't give it, God knows, that is the end. I will not speak to strangers and lay open my miserable past. I shall not listen to my conscience any more. I will get out of my wretchedness any way I can. I might have known that churches and priests would not do me any good."

"I should be sorry," he said, calmly, "to think you had come to such a resolution. No one person is likely to do you more good than another. If the intention of your heart is right, God can help you through one person as well as through another."

"You distrust me," she said. "I suppose I ought not to wonder at it, but I did not think men as good as you could be so hard. Why do you doubt that the intention of my heart is right?"

"I have not said that I doubted it. I have only thought that if it were, you would be glad to accept any means laid before you, of getting the assistance that you feel you need."

The girl, for she looked only that, buried her face in her hands, and a faint sob echoed through the empty church. "It would be so much easier to speak to you; it's so hard," she murmured, "to tell a stranger all you've done wrong, and all the miserable things that have happened to you."

"You don't have to tell him all that has happened to you," he said. "You have only to tell him of your sins. Let me add, that the priest to whom I advise you to go, has great sympathy with suffering, and is very gentle."

Missy hardly breathed, such was her interest in the scene before her. She took in all the complication, the shock that seeing the woman for whom he had had such strong feeling, had given St. John, the sorrow of finding her bound to the miserable criminal, whose last hours he was trying to purify, the fear of repulsing her, and the danger of ministering to her. At first she had been overwhelmed with alarm for him, the grace and beauty of the young creature was so unusual, her desire to re-establish relations of intimacy so unmistakable. But something, she did not know what, re-assured her. Perhaps it was the faint gleam of a smile

on his face, when she asked him to forgive her; as if
he had said, "You ask me to forgive you for doing me
the greatest favor you could possibly have done." Perhaps it was that she felt intuitively the inferiority of
the woman's nature, that she knew St. John had been
growing away from her, leaving her behind with such
strides that she could not touch him. He was beyond
danger from silken hair or peach-bloom cheeks. If danger came to him, it would be in a subtler form. She
wondered at herself, feeling so confident; she felt very
sorry for the girl, not afraid of her. She looked back
at the past, and said to herself, "This pink-faced, long-
lashed young thing has held a great deal in her hands,
but she holds it no more." Her sin and folly turned
more than one life into a new channel. St. John's, his
mother's, Missy's own, what marks they bore of her
flippant treachery! She tried to picture to herself how
they would have been living, if, on that October night,
so long ago, St. John had brought her home, instead
of coming alone, with his ashy, dreadful face. If he
had married her, and come to live at Yellowcoats, perhaps, or near them. Ah! perhaps they would all have
been in the dear home. Would it have been better?
Looking at St. John, and looking at her, with the ap-
preciation that she had of her character from those few
moments—would it have been better? No, it would
not have been better. Bitter as this change had been
to her, Missy knew in her heart it would not have been
better. She knew St. John might well smile at the
idea of forgiving her, and she herself, though she did
not smile, could thank her, as she had said she thanked
her, when she stood by the mother's sleepless bed that
night and heard the story.

17*

There are some things that we cannot find words for, even in our thoughts. She could not tell why, but she knew as well as if she had spelled it out of Worcester and Webster that it was better for them all to be living this life and not the old. She would have fain not thought so, but she was convicted. The scene passing in the aisle below her, a year ago, would have filled her with alarm, and have given her assurance that her predictions were to be fulfilled. Now, in these bare walls, in this dim house, "this life of pleasure's death," she felt how powerless were such temptations, how different the plane on which they stood. It was all to be felt, not explained. The young creature below her, turning with a late devotion to the man who had outgrown her, still "blindly with her blessedness at strife," could not see or feel it. Missy could pity her, even as she watched her alternate art and artlessness, in trying to arouse in him some of the old feeling. It was all in vain.

When the interview ended, and she went away, Missy watched her brother, as he stood for a while, with his eyes fastened on the ground. Then, with a long sigh, he walked through the church, adjusting a bench here, picking up a prayer book there, and then went and kneeled down before the altar. Missy felt he was not praying for himself, and for power to resist a temptation, but for the soul of the poor undisciplined girl, and the sinful man to whom she was bound.

The end of the story she did not hear at once. Her visit ended about this time, and she only learned later from her mother, that St. John had moved Heaven and earth to get the man pardoned. During the time of suspense, the poor girl had been in a destitute and deplorable state, but with enough good in her to listen to the teaching of Father Ellis and the Sisters. In their house she had found shelter; and during several weeks, Mrs. Varian had had her constantly with her. She never saw St. John again, except in church. The pardon was despaired of, the sickening days that were now growing fewer and fewer, were spent by St. John, mainly with this man, and in the cells of the prison where he lay. The wretched criminal was a coward, and broken down and abject, at the approach of death. His late compunction softened his wife towards him; with one of the Sisters she came often to the prison.

It was hailed with joy, in the still house, when word came, that at the last hour he was pardoned, and that his wife was to meet him on board the vessel that was to take them both to the new life, to which they had pledged themselves. Poor Gabrielle was half reluctant, but she was trying to be good, and was in earnest, in a childish sort of way. St. John looked rather pale and worn after that, and came to Yellowcoats to recruit for a day or two, or perhaps to see after Missy. His work had lain principally among "wicked people," as he had proposed to himself in early days. For some reason he made himself acceptable to prisoners and outcasts. It is possible his great humility had as much to do with it, as his sympathetic nature. At all events, he had had plenty to do, and was quite familiar in prison cells, and at work-house deathbeds. When this man (Armand) had come under his care, he was under sentence of death, and was probably the wickedest of all his wicked people.

He was a foreigner, with a hideous past—how hideous, it was likely none but St. John knew. He was condemned to suffer the penalty of the law, for a murder committed in a bar-room fray, possibly one of the lightest of the sins of his life. It was he who had ruined the life of poor little Jay's mother, and plotted the death of her husband. He was a desperado, a dramatic villain, the sort of man respectable people rarely meet, except on the stage or in police courts.

St. John had not suspected the identity of his penitent with the man to whom he owed it, that he wore a girdle round his waist, till the day that Gabrielle came into the church. Poor Gabrielle! It was hard lines for her to be sent off with the cowardly villain, but there seemed no other way to settle the fate of both of them, considering that they were married to each other. A lingering pity filled St. John's heart when he thought of her, and of the terrible fate to which she had bound herself. All this sort of thing is exhausting to the nerves, and no one could begrudge St. John his day and a half of rest by Yellowcoats bay. He and his fellow-workers took very few such days. Their hands were quite full of work, not of a sentimental kind. It takes money to send criminals and their families away to lead new lives in new lands, and money does not always come for the wishing. It takes time and the expenditure of thought to prepare men for the gallows, to get their pardons for them if may be, to smoothe their paths, whichever way they lead ; it is good hard work to do these things, and many like them, and takes the flesh off men's bones, and wears out nerves and brains almost as effectually as stocks and speculations.

But there are men who choose to work in obscurity in a service for which the world offers them no wages—only a very stiff contempt.

CHAPTER XXIX.

SURRENDER.

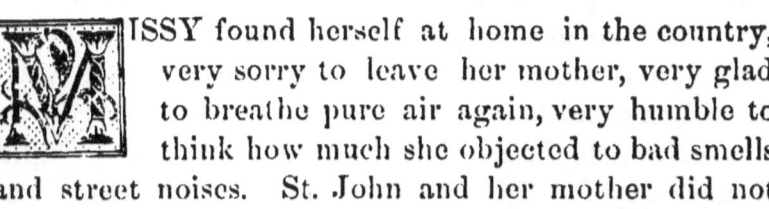ISSY found herself at home in the country, very sorry to leave her mother, very glad to breathe pure air again, very humble to think how much she objected to bad smells and street noises. St. John and her mother did not seem to take them into account at all, and the Sisters she was sure enjoyed them. Her housekeeping and Aunt Harriet took up a good deal of her time, but it was pretty dull work, and her heart was heavy. It was something of a strain to have to see people and to answer their curious questions ; but to tell the truth, Missy was much less ashamed of her brother and her mother since she came back, and chiefly felt the impossibility of making anybody understand the matter. She understood comparatively little herself, but the comfortable rector, " with fat capon lined," the small-souled doctor, the young brood of Olors, the strait-laced Sombreros, the evangelical Eves, how much less could they comprehend. She knew that the keenest interest existed in the whole community regarding their family matters, and that much indignation was felt at the breaking up of the home. There were a

great many people who were inclined to look upon her as a martyr to the fanaticism of her mother and brother, and she would have been overwhelmed with civilities if she had consented to receive them. As it was, she considered every unusual demonstration of regard, as a disapprobation of her mother, and resented it in her heart, and possibly showed much coldness of manner. So she gradually isolated herself, and became daily less a part of the Yellowcoats community.

How odd it was to be so unimportant! Her small housekeeping required so few dependents, contrasted with their former ways. Now that they did not entertain, and that she was neither young nor old, and that illness had kept her from even the ordinary duties of visiting, she had fallen almost entirely out of sight. A very gay family had taken their house, which was now quite a centre of amusement. The Andrews cottage had been occupied by people whose delight it was to be considered swell. They drove all sorts of carts, and sailed all manner of boats, and owned all varieties of dogs. The village gazed at them, and the residents who were entitled to be considered on a visiting equality, called on them, and all united to gratify their ambition to be talked about. At these two houses, poor Missy felt she would be excused from calling. Indeed, no one seemed to notice the omission ; it is so easy to sink down into obscurity, and to become nobody. She sometimes felt as if she had died, and had been permitted to come back and see how small a place she had filled, and how little she was missed, to perfect her in humility. After all, St. John and his mother—were they so very wrong? What was it all worth ?

Miss Harriet Varian, about these days, was much easier to get along with than in more prosperous ones. Perhaps she was touched by Missy's changed manner and illness; perhaps the insignificance into which they had fallen, had had for her, too, its lesson. And perhaps the spectacle of her sister's faith, had, against her will, shocked her into a study of her own selfish and unlovely life. She had many silent hours now, in which she did not call for Balzac and diversion; she submitted to hear books which she had always refused to listen to. She was less querulous with those around her, less sharp-tongued about her neighbors. She said nothing about St. John and his mother, only listened silently to the news that came of them weekly to Missy. Missy and she understood each other pretty well now; their trouble had drawn them together. In talking, they knew what to avoid, and each considered the other's feelings as never before. Two lonely women in one house, with the same grief to bear, it would have been strange if they had not come together a little, to carry the load.

Goneril had so much more to do nowadays, she was much improved. She had had her choice of going away, or staying to do three times the work she had had to do in the other house. It is difficult to say why she stayed, whether from a sort of attachment to Missy, and pity for Miss Varian, or from a dislike of rupture and change. She had had enough of it herself to know real trouble when she saw it, and she certainly saw it in the two women whom she elected to serve. Her wrath had boiled over vehemently at first. She had been anything but respectful to her employer's form of faith. But that was completely

settled, once for all, and she now made no allusion to
the matter, at least above stairs. It is quite possible
that below she may have had her fling, occasionally,
at "popish 'pression." The Sister who nursed Missy
during her illness, she had, with difficulty, brought
herself to be respectful to, but there was so much of
the real nurse in the peppery Goneril, that during
long watches they had come to be almost friends.

The summer passed slowly away ; the autumn came,
and with it, the flight of the summer birds whose
strange gay plumage had made her old home so unnatural to Missy. The dog-carts and the beach-carts
and the T-carts had all been trundled away; the boat-
houses were locked up, the stables emptied ; the six
months' leases of the two houses were at an end, and
quiet came back to the place.

It was in November, a sunny Indian summer day.
After their early dinner, Missy went out to roam, as
she loved now to do, over the grounds and along the
beach from which for so many months she had been
shut out. The evergreens made still a greenness with
their faithful foliage, the lawn looked like summer. It
was an unusual season. There was a chill in the shut-
up rooms, and it made her heart too sore to go often
in the house, but outside she could wander for hours,
and feel only a gentle pang, a soft patient sorrow for
what was gone from her never to return. She had
been walking by the narrow path that led through the
cedars, wondering, now at the highness of the tide
which was washing up against the bank, now at the
mildness of the air that made it almost impossible to
believe it was November, when the woman who took
care of the house came running after her. Out of

breath, she told her some one had just come up by the
cars, to look at the house ; would she give her the
bunch of keys which she had put in her pocket instead
of giving them back to her, a few minutes before?

Missy felt a thrill of anger as she thought of some
one to look at the house. This was indeed her natural
enemy, for this time it must be a purchaser, for it was
not yet in the market for rent. She gave the woman
the keys, and then walked on, a storm of envy and
discord in her heart. Yes, the one that should buy this
house, she should hate. It was endurable while people
only had it on lease, and came and went and left it as
they found it. But when it should be bought and
paid for, when trees could be cut down and new paths
cut and changes made at the will of strangers, it would
be more than she could bear. So few had come to
look at it with a view to buying, she had unconsciously
got into a way of thinking it would not be sold, and
that this temporary misery of letting would go on, and
she could yet feel her hold safe upon the trees and the
shrubs and the familiar rooms and closets. Just as
they were now, perhaps, they would remain for years,
and she would have the care of them still, and grow
old along with them ; and some day the dark dream of
alienation would dissolve and she would come back
and die in her own room.

She had not known how this plan and this hope
had taken possession of her, till the woman's out-of-
breath story, of a stranger from the train, revealed it
to her. Some one coming up from town at this season, meant business. Yes, the place was as good as
sold : or, if this man didn't buy it, others would be
coming to look at it ; some one would buy it. At any

rate her peace was gone. She had not known how insensibly she had depended upon escaping what she had declared to herself she was prepared for. People said they were asking more for the place than they would ever get. Perhaps St. John had gone to the agents and put it at a lower figure ; perhaps the Order needed the money and couldn't wait. A bitterer feeling than she had known for a long time, came with these reflections. She walked on fast, away from all sight and hearing of the unwelcome intruders. She fancied how they were poking about the plumbing, and throwing open the blinds to see the condition of the paint and plaster, and standing on the lawn, with their backs to the bay, and gazing up at the house, and saying that chimney must come down, and a new window could be thrown out there, and the summer parlor must have something better by way of an entrance. She hated them ; she would not put herself in the way of meeting them. She walked on and on, along the bank, till she was tired, and then sat down on an uprooted cedar, and pulled the cape of her coat over her head to keep warm, and waited till she should be sure they had gone back to the train. She sat with her watch in her hand, not able to think of the beauty of the smooth, blue bay, spread below her, nor the calm of the still autumn atmosphere. Nothing was calm to her now ; she found she had been quite self-deceived, and was not half as resigned and good as she had thought herself.

"I wish it were all over and done," she said to herself, keeping back bitter tears. "I wish the deed were signed, and the place gone. It is this suspense that I can't bear. Every time the train comes in, I shall think some one has come up to look at it. Every time I walk across the grounds, I shall dread that woman running after me, to ask me for the keys. Oh, the talking, and the lawyers, and the agents, and St. John coming up ; one day it will be sold, and the next day there will be some hitch, and there will be backing and filling, and worrying, and fretting, that wears my life out to look ahead to."

Poor Missy, she certainly had had some discipline, and not the least painful part was that she did not find herself as good as she had thought she was.

At last she heard the whistle of the cars, faint and far off, to be sure, but distinct through the still autumn air, and she got up, and walked back. She went quickly, feeling a little chilled from sitting still so long, and, full of her painful thoughts, did not look much about her, till, having emerged from the cedars, and standing upon the lawn, she looked up, and suddenly became aware that the intruders had not gone away. A horse and wagon stood before the side entrance, the horse was blanketed and tied. She looked anxiously around, and saw at the beach gate, a gentleman standing, his hands in the pockets of his ulster, and his face towards the bay. He was not at all in the attitude of criticism that she had fancied, but seemed quite unconscious of the chimneys and the entrances. His face she could not see, and she hoped to escape his notice, by hurrying across the lawn before he turned around. But even her light step on the dry leaves broke his revery, which could not have been very deep, and he turned quickly about, and came towards her, as if he had been waiting for her. She uttered a quick cry as she recognized him, and when he stood

beside her and offered her his hand, she was so agitated
that she could not speak. She struggled hard to overcome this, and managed to say at last:

"I did not know—I wasn't prepared for seeing
anybody but a stranger. I thought it was somebody
to look at the house—"

"The woman told me you would soon be back—"

"And I—I can't help feeling," stammered poor
Missy, feeling her agitation must be accounted for in
some way, "that people that come to look at the house
are my enemies. I'm—I'm very glad to see you."

"Even if I have come to look at the house?"

"O yes, that wouldn't make any difference in my
being glad."

"Well, I have come a great many thousands of
miles to look at it. If I hadn't heard it was for sale,
I suppose I should be somewhere about the second
cataract of the Nile to-day."

"How did you hear about it?" said Missy, not
knowing exactly what she said; but there are a great
many times when it doesn't make much difference
what you say, and this was one of those times. Mr.
Andrews would have been a dull man if he hadn't felt
pretty confident just then.

"I saw it in a newspaper, Miss Rothermel, and I
felt that that announcement must mean some trouble
to your family. I hoped it was money trouble, and
that I might be able—might be permitted to do something to put things right."

"No," said Missy, with a sudden rush of tears to
her eyes, "no, it isn't money trouble. Nobody can
help us.'

"I know absolutely nothing," said Mr. Andrews,

hesitatingly. "I only landed last night from the steamer. I have seen no one to-day. I have only heard from the woman here that everybody was well— that there had been no death to break your home up, and I couldn't understand. Don't tell me if you don't want to. I hadn't any right to ask."

Missy was crying now, in earnest, as they walked up the path, and Mr. Andrews looked dreadfully distressed.

"O no," she said, through her tears, "it's a comfort to find anybody that doesn't know. Everybody here knows so horridly well! I never talk to anybody. I haven't said a word about it to anyone for months and months. It's a comfort to talk to you about it—if I ever can—only I've got crying and I can't stop."

She sat down on the steps of the summer parlor, where it was sheltered and where the afternoon sun was still shining. Mr. Andrews sat down silently beside her, and after a few more struggles with her tears he took her hands away from her face and began to tell him the story of the past year. Her eyes were a trifle red, and her skin mottled with her strong emotion ; but I don't think Mr. Andrews minded.

"Mamma has gone away from me," she said, "to be with St. John and help him in his work. She has founded a sort of religious house, of which she isn't to be all the head, or anything like that, I believe ; but a Sisterhood are there, of which she is an associate, and she sees St. John every day, and the room in which she lives opens into the church that St. John gave the money to buy—and they do a great and beautiful work among poor people and they are very happy.

" It didn't kill mamma as I thought it would, she is better than she was at home. Everybody here blames her, and that is why I can't talk to any of them. But you mustn't blame her. Hard as it has been to me, I begin to see it was not wrong for her to do it. If I had been good I should have done it too ; but I wasn't, and I had to suffer for it. O, if I could only be like her and like St. John ! I don't see how I came to be so different. At first I hated St. John, and I blamed her, but now I know in my heart they are all right, and I am all wrong. I can't understand it or explain it. I only know the truth—that people that can do what they've done are—are God's own. If I lived a hundred years, I couldn't be like them, nor be satisfied with what satisfies them. I couldn't ever be anything but very poor and very common-place, but oh, I mean to be better than I used to be—a year ago. O, I can't bear to think of it. But there is no use in talking of what's past. It was right that I should have to go through what I've gone through, but oh, it was very hard. And I have been so ill, and everything is so changed in my life. You can't think how like a dream it all seems to me, when I look back. This place has been let all summer to strangers, and your place too, and we are living in the old Roncevalle house, Aunt Harriet and I. And somehow or another I have got further and further off from all our friends here. I know they blame mamma and they pity me, and I don't like either one or the other thing, and I haven't any friend or any one to talk to, and it has been loneliness such as you can't understand. But I had got used to things in a certain sort as they are, and I had been promising myself that nobody would buy the house, and that I could still have it to myself for a part of the year, and could still think of it as our own, and was quiet and almost contented, when the woman came running after me this afternoon and told me some one had come to look at it, and I was almost as unhappy as at first. I have been crying down on the bank there by myself all the afternoon. So you must excuse me for being so upset. I have gone through so much for the last year, being ill and all—a little thing unnerves me.'"

For Missy was beginning to feel a little frightened at her own emotion, and at the silence of her companion.

"It wasn't a little thing," he said at last, "seeing me and knowing what had brought me back. I don't think you need be ashamed to be showing agitation. For you ought never to have let me go away, Miss Rothermel, don't you see it now? My being here might have saved you, I don't say everything, but a great deal. I cannot understand why you sent me away. For I thought then, and I think now, that you relied on me in a certain way—that you had a certain feeling for me. I should think you would not have repulsed me."

"Those horrid women," said Missy faintly, turning very red.

"I am sure I am very sorry about them. I couldn't help it. I was stupid, I suppose."

"I hope they didn't come back with you?" said Missy, with sudden uneasiness.

"O no, they are safe in Florence."

"And you haven't married them?" she asked, with a look of relief. It made her jealous even to think of their existence.

Mr. Andrews looked at her as if he were beginning

to understand her, and, half amused and half sad, he
said : " No, neither one nor both. And there is no danger and never was of my wanting to, because for a year
and a half, and may be more, I have wanted very
much to marry some one else."

" Oh, that reminds me," said Missy, turning rather
pale, as if what she was about to say cost her an effort. " That reminds me of something I ought to say
to you. I heard, last spring, of a thing about you that
I didn't know before. If I had known it I should have
felt very differently about—about you generally—Oh !
—why *do* you make it so hard to say things to you—I
won't say it."

For Mr. Andrews was quietly, attentively, and perhaps, critically, listening. He certainly did make it
hard to say things. He naturally showed so little emotion, and said such tremendous things himself, in such
a calm way, Missy found it very difficult to believe
them, and very hard to make statements of an agitating
nature to him.

" I don't know why you won't say it," he said.
" Do you think you shall be sorry ? "

" I don't know. I generally am, whatever I do,"
she cried, with some more tears. " But no matter. I
suppose you *do* feel things, though you have such a
cold-blooded way of looking. Well, I didn't know till
a few months ago about—about your wife. And I can
only say, I had liked you so much in spite of believing
you were not kind and generous to her—and—and—if
I had known you had been nobler and better than any
other man in the world has ever been—"

Mr. Andrews got up and walked a few times up and
down the path before the steps, which was the only in-

dication that he gave of not being cold-blooded when
that deep wound was touched.

"I trusted to your being just to me when you
knew the truth," he said, at last.

"I wonder you didn't hate me," she exclaimed.

"Well, I didn't," he said.

"You have so little egotism," she went on. "I
suppose it's that makes you able to bear injustice.
You were so patient and overlooked so much, and I
was—so horrid."

"I had been deceived so before," he said, "perhaps I was more pleased with your honesty than
offended by it. I was conscious of not deserving
your contempt, and I felt so certain of your truth. I
was a little pleased, too, with your liking me in spite
of yourself. You see I knew you liked me, 'horrid'
as you were to me."

"Then why did you go away, if you knew I liked
you?" cried Missy, looking up at him with fire.

"Because, at last, I got tired of being snubbed," he
said. "I believe I had got to the end of that patience
you are pleased to give me credit for. I thought
I'd go away awhile and let you see how you liked it."

"And you went away and meant to come back?"
exclaimed Missy, beginning to cry again, "and left me
to this dreadful year of misery. I never will forgive
you—I might have died. I only wonder that I didn't."

"I didn't suppose you cared enough to die about
it, but I thought you'd see you did care when you
thought it was too late. I don't know much about
women, but I know that sort of thing occurs. And I
didn't mean to come back as soon as this, either. It
was only seeing the place advertised frightened me a

18

little and made me think you might be going through
some trouble. Do you know, I didn't believe, up to
the very last day, that you would let me go? I have
never been angry with you, but I own I was very sore
and disappointed when I found you had gone out that
afternoon, when I sent word by Jay, that I was coming
in to say good-bye. And yet it looked so like pique,
I half thought you would send me some sort of message in the evening.

Missy hung her head as she remembered that half
hour in the darkness at the gate, but she did not tell
him, either then or after, how nearly right he was
about it.

"Jay did not tell me. Of course you might have
known that. And—those horrid women—said you
were going to take them for a drive at half past three
o'clock."

"They did? Well, I think you're right about
them—they are very 'horrid.' There is one thing I
don't quite understand ; what has possessed the younger
one, at least, to entertain this sort of plan. She has
had more than one offer since we've been abroad, that
I know about. But I believe she has set her heart on
being Jay's mamma."

"It seems to me," said Missy, firing up, "that you
have gained in self-esteem since you have been away.
So many young women want to marry you !"

"Only two, that I can feel absolutely certain of,"
he said, sitting down beside her again, and giving her
a most confident, unembarrassed look.

"I don't like you when you talk that way," she
said, flushing, and pulling her cloak around her as if
she were going away.

"Why, haven't I eaten humble pie long enough? Sit still, Missy, don't go away yet. I have a great deal more to say to you."

"I don't like to be called Missy; it isn't my name, to begin with, only a disrespectful soubriquet, and I haven't given you any right to speak to me in the way you do," said Missy, palpitating, as she tried to rise.

"Yes, you have, you have said two things that committed you, besides all the emotion you showed when you saw me. You can't require me to misunderstand all that."

"I don't require you to do anything but let me go away. I—the sun is setting. It is chilly. I want to go."

"How do I know that you will let me go with you? It suits me well enough here. I want to talk to you. It is more than a year since I have had that pleasure. You haven't even told me if I can have the house. You used to be a very clever business woman, I remember. Are you going to make a sharp bargain with me?"

"I don't care about the house; but I've told you this doesn't please me in the least."

Then Mr. Andrews laughed a little. "Well, if you push me to it, I shall have to buy the house, and bring Flora here as mistress of it. I know you wouldn't like her as a neighbor, but I can't keep house alone—that was demonstrated long ago.

"Mr. Andrews, I—I wish you would let me go. I am tired and I don't understand why you talk to me in this familiar and uncomfortable way."

"I won't let you go from these steps, where the sun is still shining and where you won't get cold, till you surrender unconditionally; till you tell me that you love me, love,—remember, like is not the word at all,—and that you have loved me for a year or more ; and that you will marry me, and make me happy, and pay me for the misery you have made me suffer."

Surrender was not easy to a young woman who had had her own way so long—but once accomplished, she was very well contented with her conqueror, and forgot to resent his confidence in her affection. She forgot that the sun was going down so fast, and that there was danger of getting cold by staying out so late. It was twilight when they went up the steps of the Roncevalle house.

"What shall I say to Aunt Harriet?" she asked, rather uneasily, feeling it was odd that this one of the family should be the first one told of her mighty secret.

"I should say you'd better tell her, and get the credit of it," he returned, "for she certainly will guess."

"Why ? I could tell her you had come to buy the house."

"But you look so happy. What would you tell her to explain that ?"

It is in this way that some long-suffering men avenge their wrongs of years.

THE END.

www.ingramcontent.com/pod-product-compliance
Lightning Source LLC
Chambersburg PA
CBHW020240110726
47898CB00004B/1329